Jill Mansell

Two's Company

headline
review

First published in 1996 by Bantam Books,
a division of Transworld Publishers Ltd

First published in paperback in 2003
by HEADLINE PUBLISHING GROUP

This edition published in paperback in 2014
by HEADLINE REVIEW
An imprint of HEADLINE PUBLISHING GROUP

1

Cataloguing in Publication Data is available from the British Library

ISBN 978 0 7553 3263 2

Printed and bound by Clays Ltd, St Ives plc

Headline's policy is to use papers that are natural, renewable and
recyclable products and made from wood grown in sustainable forests.
The logging and manufacturing processes are expected to conform
to the environmental regulations of the country of origin.

HEADLINE PUBLISHING GROUP
An Hachette UK Company
338 Euston Road
London NW1 3BH

www.headline.co.uk
www.hachette.co.uk

To Cory
with all my love.

Chapter 1

Cass Mandeville, gradually stirring from sleep, stretched out an arm and encountered warm bare flesh. She gave it a light tap. When the warm bare flesh in turn shifted and its owner mumbled, 'OK, OK,' Cass raised herself up on one elbow and dropped a playful, nuzzling kiss on the back of her husband's neck.

'Forty-one today,' she sang quietly, 'forty-one today . . .'

Jack, rolling over onto his back, prodded her in the ribs.

'I'm forty.'

'I know, but it doesn't rhyme.' Cass prodded him back. 'And forty's quite shameful enough. Should an old man like you be lying in bed naked anyway? Are you sure you wouldn't be more comfortable wearing stripy pyjamas and a string vest?'

Jack pinched the tender flesh at the top of her thigh.

'Great idea. And you can parcel yourself up in one of those frilly flannel nighties with a draw-string round the hem, to stop dirty old men like me taking advantage of tender spring chickens like you. Cass, it's my birthday,' he wheedled. 'I don't ask for much, just a kiss from my lovely wife and a cup of tea in bed.'

Cass giggled as he began trailing kisses up her arm.

'Is that all?'

'Well, toast and marmalade would be nice.' The kisses reached her elbow. 'Then maybe a bacon-and-mushroom

1

sandwich or two, and a few newspapers to keep me company.'

'I could keep you company.'

The kisses, having reached her shoulder, abruptly stopped. Jack gave her a sorrowful look.

'You'll be too busy making the bacon-and-mushroom sandwiches. Besides, what would I want with a thirty-nine-year-old woman? We older men prefer nubile young beauties, not a day over twenty-three, to tell us how wonderful we are.'

'How grey, you mean.' Gleefully, Cass ran her fingers along his temples, where the first flecks of silver mingled with the unruly, swept-back black hair that always seemed to need cutting.

'Cass, my angel.' Jack was reduced to begging now. 'I'm starving. It's still my birthday. Cup of tea, bacon sandwich . . . ?'

'Aaargh!' In answer, she reached across and seized the alarm clock, giving it a frenzied shake. 'Shit, it's stopped! Jack, what's the time?'

'Don't tell me we've slept through my whole birthday,' he grumbled, seeing no reason to panic. His own watch, an unglamorous but infinitely reliable Sekonda, rested on the table next to his side of the bed. 'Nine forty-five. Is that so desperate?'

It was, actually. With a flash of guilt Cass remembered that she hadn't quite been able to bring herself to tell him about this morning's interview with the people from *Hi!* magazine. Having been forced to put them off last week at embarrassingly short notice because she'd forgotten she was supposed to be present-ing the prizes at Sophie's school sports day, she hadn't had the heart to say no when *Hi!* had suggested rescheduling the visit for this morning.

Hi! was one of the numerous magazines cashing in on the phenomenally successful formula initiated by *Hello!*, a formula mocked by many but devoured by millions. Cass, who read them herself, enjoyed seeing how other people lived. Appearing in them – she had been 'done' by *Hello!* years ago – was both lucrative and painless because you knew there was no way in the world the saccharine-penned journalist would write a single unflattering comment about you, your family or your choice in pink-and-green tartan wallpaper.

The drawback was Jack, who thought all such magazines were nauseating beyond belief, an insult to journalism and completely crappy to boot. Jack had been away working for a month in Australia when the *Hello!* people had interviewed Cass. On his return, she had eased the pain of presenting him with the *fait accompli* with a new conservatory already in situ and paid for with the magazine's ludicrously generous fee.

They had made Cass an offer she couldn't refuse. The trouble was, as Jack so acidly pointed out, she never could refuse anyone anything anyway. She would have said yes if they'd offered her fifty pence to swim the Channel.

Oh dear, thought Cass, her heart racing slightly at the prospect of having to tell him now, and this time I've said yes for even less than that.

'What?' Watching her, Jack frowned. 'You're twitching. You look guilty. What is it?'

'Ah . . .'

'Mum, Dad. Someone downstairs to see you,' bawled Sophie, on the other side of the bedroom door. She sounded as if she was yelling through a mouthful of cornflakes, which was entirely likely.

Jack raised his eyebrows. He turned his gaze back to Cass. 'A strippagram? I'm so old and in need of humiliation you've got me a *strippagram*?'

Cass hesitated, still wondering how best to word it.

'Sophie!' shouted Jack. 'This someone. Is she by any chance wearing stockings and suspenders?'

'I don't know, I haven't looked.' Even through the closed door they could hear their fourteen-year-old daughter's prosaic sigh. 'It's possible, I suppose. D'you want me to ask him?'

It was no good. Cass, as incapable of keeping guests waiting as she was of saying no in the first place, grabbed a pink-and-white striped satin robe with yellow butterflies on it and threw it on.

'I'll make the tea. He's a journalist, come to do a piece on us. I got kind of bamboozled into it,' she went on hurriedly, as with a loud groan Jack began to slide down under the duvet. 'We had a phone-in on the show about the best ways to fund-raise and this sweet girl rang in to say she's never seen us interviewed in a magazine so why didn't we do it and donate the fee to charity?'

'My God . . .' Jack had by this time disappeared from view.

'So I said what a good idea, because what else *could* I say on live radio?' Cass protested. 'And within minutes this Editor-in-Chief from *Hi!* was on the phone pledging ten grand to the charity of my choice if I took her up on it.'

The groans increased in volume. 'And who was the sweet girl, her secretary?'

'Oh, now that isn't *fair* . . .'

Jack raised his eyebrows in disbelief at his trusting wife's gullibility. Cass was about as streetwise as Bambi.

'Maybe not, but I'll bet it's true.'

'You're so cynical,' Cass protested.

'That's because I'm so old.' He smiled slightly as he hauled himself back into a sitting position. 'You go ahead, sweetheart. This is your problem, you deal with it. All the more reason for me to stay in bed.'

'Hi, hello, so sorry to have kept you waiting like this!'

Gushing and breathless, Cass arrived downstairs to find her visitor waiting in the kitchen. Sophie had been joking, it wasn't a male visitor with transvestite leanings but a friendly looking girl in her mid-twenties wearing a dark green fitted jacket and a short red skirt that clashed wonderfully with her streaky orange hair.

To make matters even worse than they already were, she was sitting at the kitchen table which was strewn with the debris of Sophie's haphazard breakfast together with last night's supper dishes. Belatedly as usual, Cass remembered that Mrs Bedford wouldn't be in until midday because her husband needed her with him to make sure he didn't pass out at the dentist's.

'Really, it's no problem.' The girl rose to her feet, smiled and shook Cass's hand. 'It's my fault anyway. I'm early. It's a failing of mine.'

'And I'm always hopelessly disorganized,' Cass admitted with a sigh. 'I forgot to set the alarm last night, so I'm afraid we overslept. Oh dear, this is terrible . . . What must you think of us? Did Sophie even offer you a cup of tea?'

She was getting into a flap. As she frantically attempted to clear the worst of the mess on the table, the loose sleeve of her dressing gown caught on the handle of the milk jug shaped like a cow, a ghastly monstrosity given to them for Christmas by Mrs Bedford. Before Cass knew what was happening, a tidal wave of milk shot up her sleeve and down her front. The cow skidded with its feet in the air across the table.

Like lightning, the girl in the smart outfit put out an elegant hand and caught it before it hurtled over the edge.

'Oh I say, well held,' Cass gasped. Then she gazed down in dismay at the milk dripping down her front. 'Yuk, just like breastfeeding.'

'Look, why don't you sit down?' To her amazement the girl was taking control of the situation, piling up dirty plates and transferring them briskly to the sink. The kettle was switched on, the milk jug refilled. At this rate Jack was in danger of having his breakfast cooked for him by someone far more efficient than his own wife.

'Sorry, it looks as if it's going to be one of those days.' All Cass could do was sit and watch and look suitably appreciative. It seemed safer somehow.

'You've only just woken up. I'm exactly the same.' The girl gave her a reassuring grin.

'But you've come here to do an interview, and look at the state of this place . . .'

'Let me tell you, it makes a nice change.' The girl laughed. 'All I usually ever get to see are glittering showhouses where you're scared to step on the carpet. It's so much more reassuring to know the people you're interviewing are human. Now, milk and sugar for you? Is this strong enough?'

Cass, accepting the cup of tea, was almost pathetically grateful.

'You're being so kind. I still can't believe Sophie didn't offer to make you one earlier,' she fretted. 'She's usually quite good.'

The girl sat down opposite her.

'Well, she did ask me if I was wearing stockings and suspenders.'

Cass groaned and clutched her head. 'Oh God . . .'

Over the course of the next fifteen minutes the girl from *Hi!*, whose name was Imogen Trent, made more tea, helped Cass stack the dishwasher and regaled her with discreetly scurrilous stories of other celebrities she had interviewed over the past year. Cass, enchanted by her friendliness and unaffected, down-to-earth manner, forgot all about Jack lording it upstairs waiting for his breakfast to be brought to him in bed. Only when they had polished off five croissants between them – somehow the flaky crumbs didn't plaster themselves around Imogen's mouth as they did hers – was Cass jolted into remembering by the clunk of more mail than usual being shovelled through the letter box.

'Hell . . . instant divorce.' Hurriedly she drained her own teacup, refilled it from the pot and began heaping in the sugar. Jack drank his black and hideously sweet.

Imogen grinned. 'Can I quote you on that?'

'It's Jack's birthday. I was supposed to take this up twenty minutes ago.' Even as she spoke, Cass heard the sound of bad-tempered footsteps on the stairs.

'Ah,' said Imogen, when the kitchen door opened. She didn't

seem at all intimidated by the look of irritation Jack shot her. 'Mr Mandeville. Many happy returns of the day.'

In one hand Jack was clutching an assortment of post. Some were cards, others were evidently bills. With his free hand he took the cup Cass held towards him and swallowed the lukewarm contents in one go.

'Sorry, darling. This is Imogen Trent.' Cass silently willed him to smile. 'She's been wonderfully understanding about all the mess. Now what was it you wanted, bacon and mushrooms . . . ?'

Jack, who was wearing a pale pink sweatshirt and grey tracksuit bottoms, took his car keys down from the hook on the dresser.

'I'm going to the club for a swim. Maybe a game of squash.'

There wasn't any point protesting; he had clearly made up his mind.

'OK. See you later.' Cass signalled apology with her eyes.

'You will be here tomorrow afternoon for the photographer, won't you?' Imogen swivelled round in her chair to look at him.

Jack, in return, glanced at her skirt. He didn't smile.

'No.'

When he had gone and Cass had quickly changed into a white T-shirt and jeans, Imogen said, 'Right,' and prepared to get down to business. She took a small tape recorder from her bag and placed it on the table between them.

'Promise you won't say anything about Jack being stroppy,' Cass begged her. 'He really isn't like that as a rule. I don't want you to think we're one of those nightmarish couples who only pretend to be crazy about each other.'

'Please,' Imogen protested. 'This is *Hi!*, remember? You and your husband could be flinging grenades across the sitting room at each other and we'd still say you had the happiest marriage in London. Apart from anything else,' she added with a widening smile, 'you *do* have one of the happiest marriages in London. You're famous for it . . . wonderful husband, terrific kids, brilliant career . . . Let's face it, all-round bliss.'

'Well, it's nice of you to say so.' Cass hesitated, embarrassed by such an accolade. 'I suppose I've been very lucky . . .'

'Come on, don't be modest,' chided Imogen. 'It's a fairy-tale thing, isn't it? How many women really and truly have it all? And what's so great, *I* think, is the fact that people don't resent you for it. They're pleased for you because everyone likes you.' She paused, then said, 'You give them hope.'

Cass looked amazed. 'Hope?'

'Yes! Think of all your fans: the housewives, stuck at home with the kids, listening to your show,' said Imogen eagerly. 'The thing is, that's how you were, once upon a time. And now you're here, but you haven't let it go to your head, you're still wonderfully natural . . . So they can listen to you and dream of making a success of their lives, just as you did.' She shrugged and concluded brightly, 'Well, that's my theory.'

Laughing, Cass said, 'Is that what you're going to put in the magazine?'

'That kind of thing.' Imogen beamed at her. 'The works, really. I mean, I know most of it but if you could just run through the early days for me, how you got involved with

9

radio in the first place and how it escalated from there. That's what the punters love most of all, isn't it? The humble beginnings.'

Chapter 2

Cass's beginnings hadn't been that humble but she knew her break into radio had a fairy-tale tinge to it. Her first meeting with Jack Mandeville, many years earlier, had been equally romantic. Well, as romantic as it was possible for a meeting on the dodgems between teenagers to be . . .

It was Cass's fifteenth birthday and her protective mother had reluctantly allowed her to go to the fair on Wandsworth Common with her friend Annie Murray provided she didn't speak to any boys. The moment they were out of sight of the house, both girls shortened their skirts by about a foot by rolling the waistbands over and over like Swiss rolls, and plastered each other with strictly forbidden make-up filched from Annie's older sister. Not surprisingly, upon reaching the common where the Saturday-afternoon fair was in full swing, they found themselves attracting all kinds of attention, in particular the unsubtle interest of a couple of leather-jacketed biker-boys from Walthamstow. Spotty, unwashed and sorely lacking in the social graces, they weren't at all what Cass and Annie had in mind. Neither did they take rejection well.

'Stuck-up little bitches,' snarled the taller of the two, who had set his sights on Cass. Her long blond hair, shining eyes and heavenly legs were right up his street.

'Yuk, just ignore them,' shrieked Annie, pushing Cass in the direction of the dodgems. 'Oooh, look at that boy collecting the money! He looks just like Elvis . . . quick, you jump into that blue one and I'll have the red. See if you can get him talking . . . he's dreamy.'

The bikers in their fringed leather jackets had other ideas. Unhappy at being ignored and deciding that the stuck-up bitches needed putting in their place, they leapt into two more dodgems and proceeded to batter the living daylights out of Cass's and Annie's cars. With each successive shunt they jeered and cat-called. Cass, not finding this at all funny, began to feel afraid but the Elvis lookalike was forty feet away chatting up two brunettes. In the meantime she found herself being hammered slowly but surely into a corner. The bikers, by this time having decided to concentrate their joint attentions on her, were making increasingly nasty threats.

Help was at hand. The moment the ride finished, even as Cass was wondering if her trembling legs would hold her up, she found herself being lifted out of the car in one smooth movement. A strong hand, clasping hers, left her with no alternative other than to follow her rescuer down the steps, away from the dodgems and in a fast zigzag through the crowds until they were safely out of sight.

'Oh thank you,' Cass gasped, panting for breath as she leaned against the chugging side of a hot dog stand. 'I was so scared . . . You don't think they'll come after us, do you?'

'Shouldn't think so.' The boy, whom she had never seen before, glanced over her shoulder. His dark eyelashes flickered. 'Well, maybe to be on the safe side . . .'

Cass, her heart racing, didn't argue when he led her swiftly up the steps of the ghost train. As he searched in his jeans pocket for the money to pay for two tickets she covertly studied her rescuer, whom she guessed to be a year or two older than herself.

His hair, so dark it was almost black, was quite long and swept back. He had very clear dark brown eyes, a lightly freckled nose and a humorous mouth, the kind that looked as if it was smiling even when it wasn't. He was tall and thin, which Cass also liked. Her last boyfriend had been an inch shorter than she was and the effort of endlessly trying to make herself look smaller had been exhausting.

With a start, she realized how presumptuous she was being. Talk about jumping the gun! Her imagination was running riot and so far she didn't even know his name.

It was Jack, she learned, once they were safely installed on the train.

'Cass,' said Cass, wondering if she could also discover his surname. Annie was sure to ask, since surnames were vital. Was there, after all, any point in even bothering to get to know someone called Winkle or Shufflebottom? Too embarrassing to go out with, Annie bossily maintained, let alone marry. Cass blushed under the cover of darkness and cleared her throat. 'Cass Ashton.'

'Oh well, if we're being formal,' said Jack lightly, 'John Marius Frederick Rothschild the third.'

The train chugged along the rickety track and juddered round the first bend. They were enveloped in total blackness and something that felt like a giant spider's web slid across Cass's face.

'Rothschild?' she gasped. 'You're kidding!'

'Please don't make a big thing of it.' As Jack sighed, an eerie howl echoed in the darkness above their heads. 'If you're scared,' he said matter-of-factly, 'you can hang on to me.'

* * *

'Thanks a bunch,' said Annie when they finally emerged, blinking, into the sunlight. She was leaning against the white wicket fence surrounding the ride and looked very cross indeed.

'Sorry.' Cass experienced a belated paroxysm of guilt. 'I thought they were only pestering me. Are you OK?'

'Well, alive.' Annie wasn't only cross, she was deeply jealous. Trust Cass to get herself rescued, if not by a knight on a white charger then by an unfairly good-looking boy in a Led Zeppelin T-shirt.

'Rothschild!' Annie screeched, when Cass had proudly introduced him. 'Oh come on! We aren't all as gullible as Cass.'

'You aren't as pretty, either.' Jack was smiling but the glint in his dark eyes showed he meant it. 'Why do you suppose I rescued her and not you?'

That had been the end of Annie's friendship with Cass.

'Just as well,' Jack airily declared. 'With friends like that you'd only end up getting a name for yourself. Besides, you don't need her any more. You've got me.'

It had been a typically intense teenage romance. The only untypical aspect was the fact that it hadn't ended. Cass adored Jack, even if his name wasn't really Rothschild, and they spent all their time together. Her mother fretted at first, complaining that Cass should be out having fun instead of tying herself down at such a ridiculously young age. Then, hearing what her daughter's untied school friends were getting up to on wild nights out at the local disco, she shut up. Jack Mandeville was bright, charming and well-mannered, great fun to have around and highly motivated. How could she complain when he helped naturally lazy Cass through her O levels? As she watched the two of them studying together out on the newly mowed lawn, revising for the last few exams, Geraldine Ashton realized she had a lot to be grateful for. It was just a shame Jack was only sixteen. As son-in-law material, in ten years' time he would be perfect.

She didn't have to wait that long. Continuing to defy the odds, Jack and Cass remained together through the next two years. A levels came and went, Cass grew blonder, more beautiful and ever more devoted and Jack – handsomer than ever – won a coveted place to study economics at Cambridge.

Cass, less ambitious and without the faintest idea of what she wanted to do in terms of a career, ended up half-heartedly studying English at the somewhat less prestigious Bristol Polytechnic. She shared a house with five other students in Clifton, hated her course and suffered appallingly from home-sickness. Or, to be more accurate, Jack-sickness.

Every night, instead of working on essays, Cass wrote long desolate letters to Jack. Each time he phoned her, she cried so much she could barely speak. At every available opportunity she either caught the National Express coach to Cambridge or met him halfway, in London.

'This is hopeless,' said Jack, hugging her to him as she spent the evening of her nineteenth birthday in tears because it would be at least a month before they could see each other again. He missed Cass just as much as she missed him. The two hundred miles separating them were doing neither of them any good at all.

Cass wiped her face on the sleeve of his dark blue sweater and sniffed loudly. 'I hate Bristol. I hate everyone on my course.' She hiccuped miserably. 'I'm never going to pass my exams, Jack. I hate it all so much I can't think.' With an air of defiance she added, 'And I miss you so much I don't care.'

'In that case,' said Jack, 'you'd better tell them you're jacking it in.'

'Really?' Cass's eyes shone. Her knees sagged with relief. She had spent the last six months begging to be allowed to leave but Jack had always said no, things would get better in time.

'I know what I said.' Jack's smile was rueful. 'But it didn't work, did it? I think we'd better get married. God, your mother's going to go wild.'

Cass had never been so happy. Her all-time favourite film was *Love Story*, where Ali McGraw fell in love with Ryan O'Neal. Now she and Jack were living it for real. They were happier than the two film characters, they were even more in love and best of all she had no intention of dying heartbreakingly of leukaemia at the end.

Chapter 3

'So did she?' Imogen, who adored love stories, couldn't wait to hear the rest. 'Your mother, I mean. Did she go wild?'

Cass grinned. 'Oh, completely. Although it was more for show than anything . . . you know, she felt she had to do the "you're too young and inexperienced" bit. Poor Mum, she kept saying, "But what about the sexual revolution? This is the nineteen seventies, for heaven's sake!" She adored Jack, but even at the wedding reception she kept pointing out gorgeous men and hissing in my ear: "See what you're missing." '

'But no regrets, obviously.'

'None.' Cass shook her head, her expression dreamy. Then she smiled. 'Jack's the only man I've ever slept with, or wanted to sleep with. I suppose we're a bit of a rare breed nowadays.'

'Particularly when you consider the kind of circles you move in.' Imogen nodded, impressed. 'Anyway, I'm interrupting. Carry on.'

Cass shrugged. 'What can I say? We were poor but nauseatingly happy. I took a waitressing job to help out with the rent and loved it far more than I'd ever loved college. Not that it lasted very long – a couple of weeks after the wedding, we discovered I was pregnant with Sean. Once he arrived we were poorer than ever, but it didn't seem to matter. Then, hot on his heels, Cleo turned up and that was it. I was twenty-one years old, a housewife, mother of two . . . not at all the kind of glittering career my mother had set her heart on for her only daughter!'

'And in the meantime Jack was working for his degree, building the basis of his own glittering career,' Imogen observed drily. She tilted her head to one side. 'Did you never feel even the tiniest bit of resentment that you were the one who'd had to give everything up?'

'No.' Cass spoke with simple honesty. 'It was what I'd wanted. Jack and I were together. And we had our babies. It didn't even occur to me then that I *had* given anything up . . . anything that I might regret, at least.'

'Some people are just natural homemakers.' Smiling, Imogen ejected the tiny tape, flipped it over and started recording the second side. 'It must be lovely. I'm not sure I could do it myself.'

'Ah, you'd be surprised.' Cass spoke with enthusiasm. 'People talk about being trapped at home with the kids but there are so many things you can do, even without heaps of money . . . well, like getting on to local radio when they have their phone-ins.'

Imogen, along with the rest of the country, already knew about this. It was how Cass had achieved her initial break into radio, when, as a supposedly typical young housewife and mum, her sense of humour, irresistible giggle and unerring ability to say what everyone else wished they could have said, captured the attention of all who heard her on air. Cass was down-to-earth. She was fluent, funny and never *ever* said, 'Um . . . y'know.' The presenter of the show, fed up to the back teeth with his usual depressing roster of calls from weirdos, bores and people who peppered their every sentence with 'Um . . .

y'know', was enchanted by Cass's delicious, unpretentious, easy manner. Taking the highly unusual step of calling her back after the show, Terry Brannigan urged her to become a 'regular'. Before long he was contacting Cass to ask her what the next day's topic of discussion should be. When Sean, at nearly three, was admitted to hospital with measles and Cass missed a whole week of the show, the radio station was inundated with complaints. Terry, realizing he had a potential star on his hands – not to mention a ratings booster – spoke first to his producer, secondly to Jack and Cass, and hammered out a deal. Cass became his co-presenter.

Their double act flourished. Together, Terry and Cass were a winning formula. Ratings soared. Terry, a merciless tease, poked fun at Cass and told their listening audience she was a frump in hair rollers and a flowered apron who made Hilda Ogden look chic. Cass, unfazed by his dreadful insults, giggled and gave as good as she got. With her husky, beautifully modulated voice, nobody believed for a moment she was as raddled and ghastly as Terry made out. Besides, there was that indefinable chemistry between the two of them to give the game away, the particularly tantalizing chemistry that only ever exists between a man who fancies a woman like mad and the woman who in return treats him like a best friend.

When the time had come to leave Cambridge – Jack had got his honours degree and been offered work as a political journalist with one of the better quality nationals – Cass simply handed in her notice. Terry went on a bender of Titanic proportions and a week later came to the conclusion that he must leave too. He was Wise without Morecambe, Torvill without Dean. He had also, without Cass ever becoming aware of it, fallen hopelessly and irretrievably in love.

Terry took his broken heart off to New York where he landed a job on one of the larger stations presenting the suitably melancholy midnight-to-five slot. Each December he held his breath, praying that this might be the year Cass's Christmas card didn't say, 'With love from us *all* – Cass, Jack, Sean, Cleo and Sophie.' And each year he was disappointed. Everyone else in the damn world got divorced, it seemed, except Cass and Jack who went on for bloody ever.

Cass, meanwhile, had gone from strength to strength. Snapped up by one of the capital's most listened-to commercial stations, she was given her own mid-morning show. Over the years she had become an institution, a part of her devoted listeners' own families. Jack, progressing rather more steadily up through the ranks of political journalism and not yet having made his own break into television, became used to being introduced as 'You know, Cass Mandeville's husband.'

'And he was never resentful of your success?'

Imogen shook her head in admiration. Cass really did have it all. She was thirty-nine, yet sitting there opposite her, in her T-shirt and Levis and with the bright sunlight streaming through the windows turning her long fair hair almost white-blond, she looked more like twenty-five.

'Are you kidding?' Cass laughed. 'He was thrilled. When you've been as poor as we were, you don't care who's earning the money! No, that's never been a problem for Jack.'

Behind Cass, propped up against the pine dresser, was an

unframed, curling-at-the-edges snapshot of an alfresco lunch party. Since Sophie wasn't in it, she was presumably the one who had taken the photograph. But there, sitting around the wrought-iron table out on the sun-bleached terrace, were the glamorous Mandevilles. Jack's arm rested across the back of Cass's chair. To the left of them lounged Sean in his Ray-Bans, blowing a kiss to the camera. To the right was Cleo, currently Britain's fastest-rising star on the modelling circuit, her famously sinuous body almost doubled in two as she roared with laughter at something her father had just said.

'You are *so* lucky.' Imogen gestured loosely around her at the sunny, cluttered yellow-and-white kitchen and the sloping gardens beyond. 'I know it sounds corny, but I have to say this: I've interviewed some celebs in my time but you really are by far the nicest. I don't suppose you'd be interested in fostering a twenty-eight-year-old redhead?' She grinned. 'Fairly house-trained . . .'

Cass, in turn, had taken an instinctive liking to the girl who had come to interview her. Now, touched by her openness, she reached impulsively across the scrubbed pine table.

'I know what you must do. We're having a small party here tonight, to celebrate Jack's birthday. Nothing too elaborate, just drinks and a few friends, but it'll be fun. Will you come along?'

'Really? I'd love to!' Imogen was delighted.

'And do bring a partner.' Cass hesitated, glancing at Imogen's left hand. 'Boyfriend, husband . . . whatever.'

'No, I'm not married.' Imogen, having intercepted the glance, pulled a wry face. 'I haven't been lucky enough to find the right man yet.' Then, with a hint of mischief, she added, 'At

21

least, not one to match up to my expectations. I need someone like your Jack.'

'Oh for God's sake!' Jack groaned when Cass told him that afternoon what she had done. '*Why?*'

'I like her.' Cass was lying in the bath watching his reflection in the mirror as he shaved. 'You've invited that chap you met at the Groucho last week, haven't you? "He's a good bloke," you said, so you invited him along. Well, that's exactly what I've done. If you meet new people and you like them, you keep in touch,' she explained pointedly. 'It's called making friends.'

He shot her a suspicious look over his shoulder. 'You rehearsed that.'

'I needed to,' Cass protested. 'You know what you're like when you start arguing; you make Jeremy Paxman sound like a wimp. Besides . . .'

'Besides what?'

'Well, I half-invited her so she could see how nice you *can* be.' Cass bit her lip, hiding her smile. 'You were so vile this morning. I wanted her to know you had a good side, too.'

Chapter 4

It was a warm, still night. As the sky darkened from violet to indigo, the stars multiplied. Imogen, pausing for a moment at the foot of the drive as her cab reversed and pulled away, admired the picture before her of a large, comfortably sprawling Victorian house with Gothic features and all its windows lit up like an Advent calendar. She could hear music and laughter too, emanating from the back of the house where the party had evidently spilled out into the garden.

Cass Mandeville had said eight for eight thirty and it was now almost ten but as far as Imogen was concerned it was always the best way for a girl arriving at a party on her own. By the time she turned up all the ice-breaking would have already been done and everyone would be well enough into their third or fourth drinks to think nothing of introducing themselves to a complete stranger.

Imogen briefly checked herself over before setting off up the drive. Her hair, which she had put up into a chignon, felt OK. Bra straps hidden. The black, above-the-knee summer dress wasn't tucked into her knickers at the back. And since her legs were bare she didn't have to worry about laddered stockings. As far as she could tell, everything was fine.

Just to make doubly sure, and because it was what she always did before making an entrance, Imogen slid a bottle of what she thought of as her confidence-booster out of her bag.

She had barely got the top off before a screech of car tyres sounded behind her. A dark car, being driven at ridiculous speed, zoomed up the drive and with a blast on the horn squealed to a sliding halt less than three inches from the backs of her knees.

'What the—' Shaken, Imogen wheeled around. It had all happened so suddenly. She could have been killed.

'Well, I'm sorry,' came an aggrieved male voice through the driver's window as it slid noiselessly open, 'but have your reflexes always been that slow? Didn't you *hear* me coming up the drive?'

Imogen stared at the boy making such fun of her. As he spoke he was using mock sign language, as if she really were deaf. He was smiling, too; something he undoubtedly wouldn't have been doing had she been a complete stranger encountered in the street. But she wasn't, she was clearly an invited guest, and it didn't do to lose one's temper with a guest.

Likewise, if he had been a stranger, Imogen would have called him every name under the sun. But he wasn't, so she held her tongue. He was Sean Mandeville, featured in the papers these days almost as often as his famous parents, and ripping the aerial off his stupid car to teach him a lesson wouldn't be the done thing at all.

Instead, her fingers still resting against the dusty, midnight-blue bonnet of the BMW, Imogen took a steadying breath and said untruthfully, 'I'm sorry, my fault.'

Sean wasn't stupid. He grinned. 'And I was in a hurry. We're both pretty late. I don't think we've met before.'

'If we'd met before,' Imogen replied smoothly, 'you would have remembered.'

'I should certainly have remembered the smell.' He gave her a dark look. 'Don't take this personally, but is that really you?'

It was Imogen's confidence-booster, her almost full and jolly expensive bottle of Lancôme's Trésor. The shock of almost being run over had catapulted it from her hand and the bottle had hit one of the rocks bordering the gravelled drive. The fumes, wafting heftily up through the still night air, surrounded the car like cyanide.

'Quick, get in.' As the passenger door opened, the driver's window slid shut. 'If we hurry, it can't follow us. Who are you, anyway? Tell me your name.'

Imogen wasn't at all sure she liked him but at least he was someone to walk in with. Sean Mandeville, with his flashing dark eyes and extraordinary good looks, was currently making quite a name for himself on the comedy circuit and if his name and natural talent were contributing factors then so were those looks, for the simple reason that seriously attractive stand-up comedians – men capable of making a girl simultaneously drool *and* laugh – were as rare as hens' teeth. And if Sean was no funnier than at least a dozen of his contemporaries at Comedy Inc., the Soho club which had given him his first regular spot, he was infinitely more bankable because all the girls and most of the gays were so besotted with him. His gigs were always packed out.

'We bumped into each other outside,' Sean told his mother as Cass greeted Imogen with a delighted kiss on the cheek.

'I'm so glad you were able to come! Sean, darling, fetch Imogen a drink. Now, where's Jack disappeared to? Ah … Jack, come and say hello and try to do it nicely this time.

Imogen, this is my ancient husband Jack. Jack, Imogen Trent.'

'Hello.'

No friendly kiss on the cheek from ancient Jack, thought Imogen. Reaching into her bag she withdrew a dark green envelope and a flat parcel gift-wrapped and beribboned in dark green and gold.

'Happy birthday,' she said, handing them to him and wondering if maybe now he would have the grace to be embarrassed.

Jack's dark eyes, however, betrayed no hint of apology.

'What's this?' He glanced at her. 'Some kind of bribe? If you're expecting me to change my mind and turn up for this photo session tomorrow, you're out of luck. The answer's still no.'

'Darling!' Cass visibly cringed. Jack was supposed to be making up for this morning's rudeness, not compounding it.

'It's OK.' Imogen shrugged. Then she added quietly, 'And it wasn't a bribe. *Hi!* didn't pay for it. I bought the gift myself.'

She watched him unwrap the unadorned, solid silver photograph frame.

'I thought the lovely snap on your kitchen dresser deserved it.'

'Oh Imogen, you shouldn't have,' Cass exclaimed. 'It's beautiful! Jack, isn't it beautiful? Just perfect for that photo.'

'Perfect,' said Jack.

Imogen jumped as Sean materialized beside her.

'My father,' he stage-whispered, 'has no shame.'

'Your father is beyond the pale.' Cass was beginning to despair. Imogen smiled to let her know it wasn't her fault.

'Don't flap.' Jack smiled too, but only just. 'You think I'm in danger of hurting our guest's feelings. She's a journalist, Cass. Of sorts. Journalists don't have feelings.'

'Some of them certainly don't have manners,' Cass responded tartly. She wondered why Jack couldn't let the matter rest. He was in danger of spoiling his own party.

'Come along.' Sean touched Imogen's bare arm. 'Let me take you away from all this. If you're hungry, there's food in the dining room.'

Cass had hired a well-known firm of caterers to supply the food but Sophie was the one busily piling shepherd's pie and chilli onto plates.

'Everyone else here is old,' she complained, giving Sean a messy extra helping of chilli. 'I'm bored. And I heard Dad being mean to you just now.' The wide grey eyes behind wire-rimmed specs turned their attention to Imogen. 'Honestly, he can be such a grump. You should have heard the go he had at Mum this afternoon, all about nosy bloody strangers invading *his* birthday party. To be fair, I have to say he isn't usually this premenstrual.'

She was a funny-looking little thing, Imogen decided. The out-and-out glamour of the Mandevilles made Sophie's averageness even more startling by comparison. With her small, pale face, short mid-brown hair and light eyes magnified by those unflattering spectacles she bore no immediate resemblance to any of them. The fact that she had probably cut her own hair and was so casually dressed in a beige sweatshirt and khaki shorts signified that she didn't give a hoot. Yet her complexion was flawless, the figure beneath the baggy clothes perfectly proportioned. It would be interesting, Imogen thought, to see how she turned out in three or four years' time. There

27

was a definite hint of promise. Sophie had the kind of looks that could tweak themselves into place and suddenly click . . .

'I don't mind about your dad,' Imogen told her. 'Will you be here tomorrow afternoon when the photographer from *Hi!* comes round?'

Sophie continued to ladle out shepherd's pie. She cringed. 'No fear. Cleo's the one around here for all that draping herself in front of a camera. Not me.'

'Our little Sofe?' Grinning, Sean pinched her white cheek. 'Having her photo taken is a bit too frivolous, a bit too much like show business for Sophie's liking. Unless she's being arrested at some save-a-tree rally, that is.'

An hour later Imogen excused herself from the group she had been talking to out on the terrace and made her way upstairs. One of the disadvantages of being a redhead was having to wear instant tan in order to prevent her skin glowing fluorescent-white in the dark like those plastic skeletons in cereal packets. On hot nights such as this, instant tan had a horrible habit of going streaky. It was always advisable to keep an eye on it. Ever prepared to carry out a quick repair job before other people could spot the mess and recoil in horror, Imogen kept a spare tube with her at all times.

A glance at her reflection in the full-length mirror which dominated the glitzy blue-and-gold bathroom told her she was right to do so. Turning this way and that, Imogen used a wad of white loo roll to mop up the melted bits at the backs of her knees, in the elbow creases and – most noticeably of all – in her cleavage. She cursed beneath her breath as someone outside the bathroom turned the door handle. Hurrying always made it worse and there was no way she was going to leave until her white patches were safely covered up.

The door handle rattled again, just as she unscrewed the top. Imogen whimpered, aghast, as a gleaming dollop of conker-brown tanning cream fountained out of the tube, landing with an almost audible splat on the glorious lapis lazuli bathroom carpet.

First the perfume, now the tanning cream, she thought despairingly. If Jack Mandeville should find out about this, no doubt the next thing to be spilled would be her own blood.

The next two minutes were spent on her knees, frantically scrubbing at the stain on the carpet with yet more handfuls of loo roll and someone's yellow flannel. Imogen's heart nearly stopped when a thunderous hammering at the bathroom door was followed by the instantly recognizable voice of Jack Mandeville.

'Come on now, time's up. If someone's passed out in there I'll have to break the door down.'

'Just coming,' squeaked Imogen, stuffing the shredded, incriminating loo roll down the toilet and pulling the flush. With shaking hands she rubbed just enough cream into her cleavage and behind her knees to camouflage the white bits. Now her face was all pink, shining with perspiration and guilt. Behind every effortlessly chic career girl, Imogen thought ruefully, was a fraud, a hopeless mess struggling to get out. At least she hoped there was. She couldn't bear it if she was the only one around.

'You.' Jack Mandeville gave her one of those despairing, told-you-so looks when she unlocked and finally opened the bathroom door, as if he might have known it would be her.

Oh, but goodness, he was attractive. Imogen hung on to the door handle and held his gaze.

'Look, I'm not sure what I've done to deserve this.' She spoke quietly, though there was no one else in sight. 'You don't approve of me, that much is screamingly obvious . . . but I'm sorry, I still don't understand why.'

'Maybe I don't approve of what you do,' Jack retaliated. 'I mean, this magazine of yours, this form of so-called journalism,' his tone was cutting, 'it's hardly Pulitzer prize-winning stuff, is it? Doesn't it bother you, turning out such endless pap?'

'Yes.' Imogen shook back her fringe and stared him out. 'Of course I'd rather be doing something more intellectually stimulating, but this was the job I was offered and I needed to pay the rent. It isn't that terrible, anyway,' she added with a flicker of anger. 'We're hardly talking hard-core porn here. Our magazine is harmless.'

'Not to mention pointless.'

This was bizarre. Imogen took a deep breath.

'Look, your wife is donating her fee to charity. She's asked us to send it to Great Ormond Street. Is it still pointless if that money helps to save a child's life?'

Since there was really no answer to that, Jack glared at her and used the politician's tactic of changing the subject.

'I don't much care for the way you angled an invitation to this party either. My wife might fall for the professional flattery, Miss Trent, but it cuts no ice with me.' He paused for a second, his mouth narrow. 'And if you so much as consider selling little snippets of gossip about tonight to *any* publication, I shall sue.'

There was no doubt he meant it. For a second, in the face of such venom, Imogen felt her throat tighten. She wasn't that awful, other people usually liked her as much as she liked them . . . and she had certainly liked the idea of meeting Jack Mandeville. He was deeply attractive, he had intelligence and charisma, he was even wearing the most delicious mulberry and dark green striped shirt she had ever seen in her life. Who wouldn't be attracted to a man with such a catalogue of assets? And why, when she had undeniable assets of her own, wasn't he in turn attracted to her?

Then, quite suddenly, it clicked. Imogen felt almost light-headed as realization dawned. Of course . . . this whole barrage of abuse had come down on her precisely because he *did* find her attractive!

I'm right, Imogen acknowledged with a surge of triumph. That's *it*!

She could see it now, in his dark eyes and in the way he leaned against the bathroom door, apparently casually but in reality not casual at all.

The sense of power it gave her was thrilling.

Well, well, she thought with a smile, now here was a turn-up for the books. Even Jack Mandeville, that most famously faithful of husbands, had his moments of weakness.

Imogen tingled all over, revelling in the discovery.

He was, he really was, as attracted to her as she was to him.

And he didn't like it one bit.

Chapter 5

Comedy Inc., situated halfway along Jelahay Street in Soho, didn't look terrific from the outside. Squashed between a strip joint and a burger bar, with blue paint peeling from its ancient door and the brass Comedy Inc. nameplate devoid of polish, it boasted an unprepossessing grey stucco exterior, less than twelve feet wide and splattered with graffiti.

Inside, it was a Tardis. It was also Sean Mandeville's second home, a place where he felt loved and secure and to which he gravitated at every opportunity. Who needed a villa in Barbados, he privately felt, when you had Comedy Inc. right here on your doorstep? As far as he was concerned it was perfect, from the tobacco-stained ceiling right down to the tacky – in every sense of the word – carpet. The thirty-four round tables at which the customers sat in order to drink, laugh and heckle were crammed so close together it took half an hour just to squeeze your way across the room. The stage wasn't brilliantly lit, the sound system could be temperamental and the barmaids – who had heard every joke in the world at least fifty times over – never smiled at anyone, but Sean loved them all anyway. If the place could only have air-conditioning, as he told Barney the manager at least once a week, it would be perfect.

But Barney was a notorious tightwad, hence the twenty-year-old swirly red-and-green carpet so sticky with spilt beer it glued your feet to the floor. The stage wasn't much better either; the boards were probably saturated with the sweat of a thousand nervous comics. At least, Sean hoped it was only sweat . . .

Half his mind began to wander off on this new tangent, considering the possibilities of fitting it into the act even as he carried on chatting to the audience, addressing an imaginary nun at table thirteen about the perils of drinking rum and black in half-pint mugs.

This was how Sean worked; his stream-of-consciousness monologues concerned everyday people and issues. Jokes with punch lines weren't his style. He preferred to strike chords, making people rock with laughter because what he said was so *right* and leaving them wondering why they couldn't have thought of it themselves.

His act was never the same two nights running.

A compulsive ad-libber, he was always careering wildly off in new and hitherto unexplored directions as fresh ideas came to him. Mostly it worked, sometimes it didn't. Sean never let that bother him. As long as he was on stage, performing, he was happy. And because laughter was an aphrodisiac, he had more than his share of offers. There were always plenty of girls ready and willing to show him their idea of a good time . . . like that stupendous blonde on table seven, in for the third night running. Neither she nor her incredible shrinking skirts had escaped Sean's notice. Maybe tonight, he decided, after the show, he would make a move. Introduce himself.

'. . . come on, I'm not making this up,' he protested, as the audience rocked in their seats. He was on to the latest Californian fad: plastic surgery for dogs so they could resemble their owners' favourite film stars. 'There's the

Streisand works especially well on Afghans . . .' Turning half away, he covered his mouth as if stifling a cough. This was a new idea of Donny's, a try-out. When the blood capsule was lodged safely between his back teeth he turned his attention back to the audience once more, his expression one of injured innocence. 'So I thought of having my own dog done – she's a bitch, forever on heat – but the surgeon's already been sued by Madonna. No, please, I know you think I'm having you on, but trust me. May the dentist from hell rip out all my teeth if I'm lying to you . . .'

As he said it, he bit down on the capsule. The idea was that as he carried on speaking, apparently unaware of what was going on, blood would gush from his mouth.

But the capsule had other ideas. The odd-tasting fake blood spilled out, hitting the back of his throat. Without warning, Sean began to choke. As he attempted to fit the mike back onto the stand, he coughed. Fake blood shot out of his mouth. Table three, closest to the stage, was occupied by a group of girls. Sean could only watch, horrified, as a great spray of blood – in apparent slow motion – splattered itself over the front of one of them.

It was sod's law, of course, that she had to be wearing a short white dress.

Hell, thought Sean as the rest of the audience, assuming this was all part of the act, erupted with laughter once more. If it had been a bloke on the receiving end he might have played along, pretending he had meant to do it. But he couldn't do it to a girl.

She wasn't laughing, either.

'OK, you lot, that's enough.' He spoke rapidly into the mike before stepping forward and jumping down from the stage. One of the girl's companions was trying to scrub at the front of the bloodstained dress with a handful of tissues.

The girl met Sean's gaze.

'I'm so sorry.' Mortified by the expression in her luminous dark eyes, he took her hand and raised it to his mouth, pressing a kiss onto her knuckles. 'It was a horrible accident and you must let me make this up to you. Please, come to my dressing room after the show.'

'Won't be doing that again in a hurry.' Donny, poking his head round the dressing-room door twenty minutes later, was evidently highly amused. Public humiliation was his stock-in-trade. 'Did you see the expression on that bird's face when you did it? What a state! Mind you, she wasn't a bad looker . . . don't suppose you got her phone number?'

It was all right for Donny Mulligan, Sean thought irritably. He had inherited his Jamaican mother's good looks and his Irish father's charm. If it had happened to Donny he wouldn't have been racked with guilt – it probably wouldn't even have occurred to him to apologize. With his shoulder-length dread-locks and broad Dublin Bay accent, Donny could get away with just about anything he liked.

Sean changed into a fresh shirt – the girl in the white dress wasn't the only one who'd been splattered – and ran a comb through his dark hair. It was fifteen minutes now since he'd come off stage but there was still no sign of her. Puzzled and slightly put out, he tucked his wallet into the back pocket of his jeans and followed Donny out into the corridor. He would have bought her a drink to show her he really was sorry. Maybe she had felt too embarrassed to stay on in a ruined dress. Maybe she had stormed off to phone the press. Sean could just imagine the story in tomorrow's *Evening Standard*.

He was relieved to spot her standing over at the bar with her friends. So she hadn't left. Instead, despite the warmth of the evening, she had chosen to cover the damage with a long, cinched-at-the-waist beige trench coat.

'Hi, it's me.'

'Hello, you.' She tilted her head to one side and gave him a brief smile of acknowledgement. Donny had been right; she was a looker, though in a quiet, unflashy way. Not Sean's usual type at all.

'You didn't come backstage.' The rebuke was gentle. He couldn't afford to offend her more than he already had.

'And what would I have looked like, a groupie?'

Now it was Sean's turn to be offended. 'Of course you wouldn't! Thanks a lot.'

'Well, I might have felt like one.' The girl shrugged, unconcerned. 'Doesn't matter, anyway. You found me. What do you do now, smile a lot, buy me a large gin and tonic and bung me a fiver to cover the dry-cleaning?'

It was exactly what Sean had planned on doing. Positively affronted by the accuracy of her guess, he said, 'Charming. As a matter of fact I was going to invite you out to dinner. Or would that make you look even more of a groupie?'

For a second she said nothing. Terrific. She was probably one of those fanatical, fire-breathing feminists out on an undercover mission to expose chauvinist bastards who dared to ask them out. Out of the corner of his eye Sean glimpsed the blonde with the legs making her way towards the exit. Thanks,

Donny. What a totally brilliant idea the blood capsule had been. He wouldn't forget tonight in a hurry.

'OK.' The girl nodded. Quite suddenly she broke into the most ravishing smile, revealing perfect teeth like pearls.

'OK?' Sean, hearing himself idiotically echoing her reply, could have kicked himself. Now he sounded like some gauche schoolkid. He'd been so certain she would say no.

'I'm hungry.' Sliding down from her stool, she drained her glass and placed it on the bar. 'You did mean tonight, didn't you?'

'Fine, fine.' Sean, who hadn't even meant to ask her out in the first place, gave up. The blonde had by this time disappeared; he may as well get it over and done with. 'I don't know your name.'

'It's Pandora,' the girl replied gravely. 'And if you make one joke about it, you're dead.'

Chapter 6

Pandora had never been to The Blue Goose before, though it was clearly one of Sean Mandeville's regular haunts. At least it was now he was becoming successful and making enough money to be able to afford it, she guessed as the waiter greeted them with enthusiasm and tried to part her from her trench coat.

'It's OK, she'd like to keep it on,' Sean told him. When they had been seated and handed the menu he took his wallet out of his jeans pocket, rifled through it beneath the table then slid a twenty-pound note into her hand.

'Before I forget,' he murmured. 'For the dry-cleaning. I don't really know . . . um, will that cover it, d'you think?'

'Cover it?' Pandora smiled at the look of concern on his face. Away from the club and the company of all those wisecracking friends of his, he was altogether less confident than he liked to make out. 'It's enough to buy me two new dresses.' She pushed the money back across the table. 'Don't worry. Fake blood's bound to wash out.'

Sean was touched by her honesty. 'You could always turn it into a fashion statement.' He broke into a grin. 'The Psycho, just-stepped-out-of-the-shower look. Or did Vivienne Westwood use that idea last year?'

Her full name was Pandora Jacintha Grant, Sean discovered over dinner. She was twenty-four and shared a tiny, rented, end-of-terrace house in Kilburn with her elder brother Joel. She worked long hours as a waitress at a bistro, also in Kilburn, called The Moon and Sixpence. The pay was lousy but it was a friendly place with a great atmosphere and when the last customer had been booted out the staff sat down each night to a terrific meal. The bistro was closed on Mondays, which was why she and the other girls who worked there had come for an evening out to Comedy Inc. instead.

So far, so very ordinary. It was hardly the most riveting life story he had ever heard, yet there was something about her that intrigued Sean.

He didn't even know why, since Pandora Grant was just about the opposite of every kind of girl who normally interested him. He went for blondes and long-haired blondes at that. He liked tall, thin, long-haired blondes with blue eyes and plenty of make-up. His ideal women were Cameron Diaz, Gwyneth Paltrow and the girl in the short skirt whom he'd planned on chatting up tonight, until fate in the form of a blood capsule had buggered up his innocent plan.

His ideal woman certainly wasn't coffee-coloured, with shrewd brown eyes, no make-up at all and black hair less than an inch long all over. She wasn't wrapped from head to foot like Inspector Clouseau in a beige trench coat either.

So what the bloody hell *was* it about her, Sean thought with a touch of despair, that so intrigued him?

When Pandora excused herself between courses and disappeared to the loo, she didn't take her shoulder-bag with her. Sean, not even realizing she'd left it on her chair, stretched out his legs and managed to hook the trailing leather strap round the toe of his shoe. When he straightened up in his seat, the bag crashed to the ground. The clip sprang open and the contents spilled out.

Sean winced as a couple of Lil-lets rolled merrily across the wooden floor, coming to rest against the highly polished shoe of the bank-managerish type at the next table. A pot of Body Shop kiwi fruit lip-balm had skittered off in the opposite direction. Keys, a diary, an *A-Z* and an Afro comb – with hair *that* short? – were easier to retrieve.

It was as he was stuffing everything back into the bag that Sean spotted something which hadn't fallen out. The discovery both jolted and enthralled him; the unexpectedness of it acted like an adrenalin rush. Now he knew why he had been so subconsciously attracted to her. There was more to Pandora Grant than met the eye.

All of a sudden Sean found himself consumed with desire, as surely as if she had emptied some mystical aphrodisiac into his drink. He realized he had never wanted anyone so badly in his life.

'Thanks.' Those big, innocent eyes turned to him. For a fraction of a second her fingers hovered above his arm, then moved away again. 'That was really kind of you. I've had a lovely time.'

'You could always invite me in for a coffee,' Sean suggested lightly. The body language was promising. The thought of what was in her shoulder-bag was even more of a turn-on now they were back at her place. Best of all, she had already told him her brother was out of town.

But Pandora shook her head.

'Sorry, I can't. I have to be up horribly early tomorrow . . . but thanks again for dinner and the lift home.'

Sean could hardly believe his ears. He'd spent the last two and a half hours being charming and generally irresistible to the kind of girl he wouldn't normally look twice at, and now she had the nerve to turn him down! What was the matter with her? What, he wondered wildly, was the matter with him?

He hadn't been turned down by anyone since he was twelve.

Pride had prevented him asking for her phone number or whether he could see her again but over the course of the next week Sean found himself unable to put Pandora Grant out of his mind.

It was hopeless, not to mention mystifying. Was he *only* this interested in her because she had shown herself to be a girl who could say no? Whatever the reason, Sean found himself – for heaven's sake – dreaming about her. He spent hours poring over the phone book, finally ringing directory enquiries to discover the number was ex-directory. Every night on stage he scanned the audience, hoping against hope she might turn up.

By Sunday Sean had had enough. Pandora – or rather, the non-appearance of Pandora – was seriously getting to him. The audience had just applauded Donny's act more loudly than his own. At the bar after the show Donny had protested, 'What's up, man? You're losing your edge. Come on, look, there's that blonde you had your eye on last week.'

He couldn't even be bothered to chat up the blonde when she sauntered over, gave Sean a broad knowing smile and leaned so close to him that the soft pink leather of her skirt brushed against his thigh.

41

She reeked of Obsession. Close-up, too, he could see the way her honey-coloured foundation clogged the skin around her nose. Her face was melting in the heat.

'Don.' Sickened by the sight, he tapped his friend's arm. 'I'm off.'

As he left, he heard the blonde murmur frustratedly, 'Ohhh . . .'

The Moon and Sixpence was situated in a narrow side-street just off the Kilburn High Road. By the time Sean reached it the last few customers appeared to be leaving. Not having the nerve to simply march in, grab Pandora and whisk her into his arms like Richard Gere in *An Officer and a Gentleman* – she was, he sensed, only too likely to stand her ground and say no again – he parked the BMW ten yards away from the entrance to the bistro and settled down to wait. If she was going to humiliate him, at least she wouldn't be doing it in front of all her smirking friends. It was eleven fifteen. Surely he wouldn't have to wait too long.

But in his hurry to see her again, Sean had forgotten the meal shared by the staff at the end of each evening. The lights in the bistro continued to blaze. Through the open car window he could hear the buzz of animated conversation interspersed with shrieks of laughter. Bored and hungry, he rummaged through the glove compartment and found half a packet of fruit pastilles. Even they were a letdown: two greens and three yellows.

Sean finished the last boring fruit pastille and heaved a sigh. Midnight. This was ridiculous. What was he, completely out of his mind?

As if in answer to his prayers, the door of the bistro opened. Two girls spilled out, neither of them Pandora, but at least it must mean he wouldn't have long to wait. Sean sat up, switched off Radiohead and realized he had butterflies in his stomach. This was *definitely* ridiculous.

The door swung open again. This time he saw with a leap of excitement that it was Pandora. For a second all he could do was sit there and gaze at her, the object of his helpless fantasies for the past week – a week that had seemed to stretch on without end. Now, as she stood silhouetted in the narrow doorway, he saw the miraculous shape of her head, the graceful neck, the slender but still curvy figure. She was wearing neat gold earrings, a black T-shirt and combats. The large black leather shoulder-bag hung from one shoulder to rest against her hip. She looked even more desirable than Sean remembered. He took a deep breath before opening the driver's door. All he had to do was act cool . . .

Just as his fingers reached the car door handle, the silence of the darkened street was broken by a piercing whistle. Sean's head swivelled to identify it. A couple of hundred yards up the road, in the shadows between street lamps, he saw a tall figure break into a run.

For a moment he wondered if Pandora was about to be mugged; then he saw her raise her arm in greeting. Without even so much as a glance in the direction of the parked cars she ran out into the empty road, waving with both arms now. Sean, feeling sick, slid down in the seat so she wouldn't spot him. Not that she appeared to have eyes for anyone other than the tall, blond, athletic-looking bloke pounding his way down the road towards her.

43

It was pure bloody Hollywood. When he finally reached Pandora, the athlete picked her up as if she weighed nothing at all and swung her round three times. Pandora, her arms curled around his neck, let out a squeal of delight and buried her head against his chest as he lowered her gently back to the ground.

Lacerated with jealousy, Sean waited until they had reached the end of the road, disappearing arm in arm round the left-hand turn which would lead them in less than five minutes to Pandora's end-of-terrace house. He forced himself to wait three more minutes before firing the ignition and setting off along the same route. Having timed it to perfection he drove past just as Pandora and her big blond boyfriend closed the freshly painted blue front door behind them.

Chapter 7

As a successful model, Cleo Mandeville always longed to punch
anyone who suggested she had only got where she was because
of her famous parents. She was amazed how often it happened,
too. Not from those in the business – who chose to work with
her because they *knew* how good she was – but from pig-
ignorant members of the public who invariably thought they
knew best.

Like the amazingly stupid, mouthy, interfering prat of a taxi
driver whose cab she had innocently hailed at Piccadilly
sodding Circus.

'Now there's a coincidence,' he crowed with sweaty delight,
'here I am, tuned in to your dear old mum's show. Never miss
it, y'know. She just about makes my day, 'specially with them
phone-ins of hers.'

'Mmm.' In the back of the cab, Cleo peered into a hand
mirror and redid her lipstick.

'Must be nice, havin' a mother like that,' the driver went on.
'I mean, it's all about contacts, innit? Take my Louise, my
eldest . . . I'm tellin' you, she coulda bin a model. Better lookin'
than any of these skinny, poncey supermodel types, she is, but
she went round all them agencies an' got turned down flat by
every last one.' He paused for breath and to honk at a Renault
with the temerity to try and pull out in front. 'An' d'you know
why they didn't want to know? Because *she* didn't know the

right people! I'm tellin' you, if I'd bin famous with me own radio show they'd 'ave said: "Oh, so you're Tom 'arris's daughter, *the* Tom 'arris? Course you can be a model, darlin', just sign 'ere . . ." '

Yawn, yawn. His Louise was probably cross-eyed, buck-toothed and walrus-shaped to boot. Furthermore, if she smelled anything like her father it was hardly surprising she'd been turned down. Cleo pulled a fearsome face at the taxi driver's damp, mountainous back and chucked the lipstick back into her bag. She was meeting Linda for lunch and Linda was in dire need of cheering up. Mind you, Cleo mused, if she'd been six weeks away from marrying Linda's pain-in-the-bum fiancé, she'd have needed cheering up too.

Linda and Cleo were both with the same agency. They had been friends for years. Since Linda's idea of lunch was three radishes and a nectarine for dessert they had arranged to meet at the café on the first floor of Emporio Armani. She was already there, sipping iced mineral water, when Cleo, late as usual, panted up the stairs.

'Look, I've bought five shirts.' Linda held open the brown carrier to show them off, but there was an air of desperation about her. Cleo looked. All the shirts were white. Linda wasn't even a shirty person. She'd been panic buying again.

'I know, I know.' Linda sounded defensive. 'It's just that Colin says I'm going to have to pull myself together and stop acting like a selfish child . . . and I know he's right,' she added hurriedly, 'what with the massive mortgage and all the expense of getting the house right. But every time he gives me a lecture on not frittering my money away I just come over all *desperate*

. . . and now Colin's saying I should hand everything over to him as soon as I get paid. That way, he can make sure I don't do anything silly with it. Oh Cleo, he wants to give me an allowance. He says a hundred pounds a week for "sundries" is more than enough for anyone.'

One of the hardest things in life to bear, as far as Cleo was concerned, was having to watch your girlfriends either moving in with or marrying completely unsuitable men. You could know with absolute certainty that it wouldn't work out, that it would all end in tears, that it was the most disastrous relationship since Tom and Jerry . . . but could you do anything to stop it happening? Could you heck.

'But it's your money,' she protested. 'You earn ten times as much as Colin. He's bullying you and he has *no* right to do that! Oh Linda,' her voice softened, 'are you sure he's the one for you? Do you really want to marry someone who shanghais all your earnings and doles out pocket money?'

She already knew the answer to that. Linda, plucking nervously at the sleeve of her navy T-shirt, was looking more twitchy by the minute. Despite the outward glamour, she was convinced she had all the personality of Looby Loo. Such chronically low self-esteem kept her superglued to Colin's side. His bossiness where money was concerned might be a bit of a drawback but she trusted him implicitly. She believed him when he told her he would never be unfaithful to her. She loved him because he made her feel safe.

He made Cleo feel sick.

I can do something about this, Cleo decided suddenly. It was no good, she simply couldn't sit back and allow it to happen. And she had an idea how to go about it, too. Last

47

week's trip to the States, where she had appeared in a promotional video for the new Donna Karan collection, had introduced her to a new and interesting concept. One of the other models there had told her about it, a company called Checkamate. The idea was both outrageous and perfect.

'OK, don't say anything, just listen.' Cleo spoke rapidly, before she could have sensible second thoughts. Then she told an open-mouthed Linda how the scheme worked in New York.

'You're not serious!' Linda looked appalled. So engrossed that she picked a brown sugar lump out of the bowl on the table and popped it into her mouth, she mumbled, 'Go on.'

'Well, say a woman wants to know if she really can trust the man in her life. She contacts this Checkamate agency and tells them where he can be found. One of the girls from the agency then turns up on cue – say, at a bar he regularly drinks in after work – and falls into conversation with him. She has a hidden tape recorder going, to play back to the girlfriend later. Anyway, they have a friendly chat and a drink and if the guy leaves it at that, fine. He's passed. In the clear.' Cleo's eyes sparkled. She thought the whole idea was brilliant. 'If, on the other hand, he flirts like crazy and ends up asking her out to dinner, he's proved what a cheating bastard he is. And he can't even try and wriggle out of it later when his girlfriend confronts him with the evidence, because it's all there on tape.'

Linda looked worried. 'Seems a bit mean.'

'Mean? *Mean?*' Cleo howled. 'You should hear what some of these apologies for men come out with! Daisy, this girl who told me about it, did some part-time work for the agency. Her very first assignment was with a bloke who'd only been married for six months. He spun her this long tragic story that he was a

widower and ended up inviting her to spend the weekend with
him skiing in Aspen.'

Linda winced. 'It still sounds like entrapment to me.'

Cleo, who was on a crusade, replied blithely, 'Only the men
who get caught call it entrapment. Look, it's quick and it's
cheap – much less expensive than hiring a private detective –
and it tells the women all they need to know. You have to admit,
it's ingenious.'

'And you think I should have Colin checked out.' Abruptly,
Linda's enormous violet eyes filled with tears. She picked up
another sugar lump. Her lower lip wobbled like a toddler on a
bike.

'Please don't cry,' Cleo begged, squeezing her thin hand.
'I'm just saying, isn't it better to find out now rather than later?
And who knows, anyway? He might pass with flying colours!
Then you'll *really* know you can trust him . . .'

'I hate you, Cleo Mandeville.' Wiping away the tears, Linda
managed a weak smile. 'How did you ever get to be so damn
cynical anyway? Your mum and dad are the happiest married
couple in London, according to *Hi!* magazine.'

'That's what's so depressing,' said Cleo. 'Theirs is the only
happy marriage I *do* know. Otherwise it's wall-to-wall divorces.'

'I was talking to Cherry Chandler yesterday. I didn't realize
she'd been married four times.' Linda hesitated. 'Look, I'll
think about it. Give me a few days. Will you arrange everything
if I decide to give it a go?'

'Just leave it to me.' Hiding her triumph, Cleo gave her a
reassuring smile.

'Thanks.' Linda bit her lip. 'I'm feeling a bit panicky. Do
you think another hour of shopping might help?'

'Best therapy in town. Harvey Nicks?' suggested Cleo.
'Oh, yes *please*.'

Chapter 8

The Cameron was a private sports club in Hampstead, owned by Rory Cameron and boasting six squash courts, four outdoor tennis courts, an indoor swimming-pool, gym, aerobics studio and solarium. The bar, situated on the first floor, was separated from the aerobics studio by a glass wall, enabling the drinkers to watch the exercisers being put through their paces. Consequently the exercisers were always very done-up in designer leotards and matching nail polish. Visibly sweating was frowned upon. Full make-up was *de rigueur*.

Jack Mandeville found the dress-to-impress attitude of the majority of the club's female members laughable, but he and Rory Cameron had been friends for years and the club was both conveniently close to home and extremely well equipped. It was also somewhere he could relax and not be gawped at by over-excited celebrity spotters. Members of The Cameron weren't the gawping kind, unless sitting at the bar watching the aerobics classes counted.

Jack preferred to take his drink out onto the sunny terrace overlooking the immaculately maintained grass tennis courts. Here he could either sit and chat to Benny, his regular squash partner, wrestle desultorily with the *Telegraph* crossword or simply relax and enjoy the view.

He had the crossword with him today, Benny having driven off reluctantly to a board meeting in the City. Jack, thankful that he didn't need to drive anywhere on such a sweltering day, meandered out to his favourite table overlooking court one, stuck his sunglasses on and folded the paper to the appropriate page.

'Have a cough on a horse,' said a voice close behind him some minutes later. 'Fifteen across. It's hack.'

It was certainly appropriate. Jack watched his fingers tighten around the ballpoint pen as it hovered over the page. When he looked up, he saw Imogen Trent grinning down at him as if their last furious exchange had never taken place.

She looked as if she'd just finished an aerobics class and had actually been putting some effort into it. Her long red hair was held back from her face with a green ribbon, though damp tendrils of it clung to her forehead. Pink-cheeked and still slightly out of breath, she looked younger than she had at the party with all her evening make-up intact. A pale grey hooded top was hanging open over a yellow-and-white polka-dotted leotard and dark blue shorts. The fact that she wasn't decked out in the obligatory ultra-coordinated sportswear went in her favour. Jack still wished, though, that she hadn't turned up.

'I saw you at the bar just now.' Imogen puffed a strand of hair out of her eyes and leaned her elbows along the back of the empty chair opposite his. 'While I was busting a gut in the torture chamber across the way. I thought I'd better come and warn you I was here. Save you getting a nasty shock.' Not looking at all repentant, she observed the expression on his face and said, 'Oh dear, have I ruined your day?'

Jack's mouth narrowed. 'This is a coincidence, I take it?'

'You mean, did I break into Rory Cameron's office at dead of night, sneak a look at the membership list, spot your name and *then* decide to shell out a huge amount of money to join this particular club?' It had actually been far simpler; she had overheard Benny at the party, talking about his last squash game with Jack. Still, no need to mention that now. Imogen's eyebrows lifted in mock horror. 'Please, Mr Mandeville. If I wanted to really irritate you I could do it a lot more cheaply than that. Is something the matter?' Her attention was diverted by the direction of his gaze. 'What are you staring at? Oh God, is it a wasp?'

Jack was looking at her legs, light brown and slender beneath the dark blue shorts. He knew he shouldn't do it but the compulsion was overwhelming. Leaning across the table, licking his thumb as he did so, he reached out and ran it several inches down her shin. So amazed she didn't even move away, Imogen watched the fake tan slide off. A bright white track remained in its place.

'Funny', Jack remarked, 'how it comes off skin but not carpet.'

Imogen flushed scarlet. Damn. Abruptly she pulled out the chair and sat down.

'Look, I'm really sorry about that. I can't tell you how awful I felt. I wanted to say something but you were so dreadfully angry with me already . . .' She wriggled, looking more uncomfortable by the second. 'Well, I was just too scared.'

The stain, thanks to Mrs Bedford, had come out the following morning after much frenzied scrubbing with Vanish. Jack decided to let Imogen Trent feel guilty for a few minutes more. Removing his dark glasses, he rose to his feet.

'You look as if you could do with a drink. What'll it be?'

'You know what you're like? The flush had drained away. Gazing up at him, Imogen shook her head in frustration. 'One of those police interrogators who go from being horrible one minute to nice the next. Are you doing this deliberately to confuse me?'

Jack smiled. 'Maybe I'm just interested in finding out whether you have anything else to confess.'

Up on the stage Sean was doing his condom routine. 'Take my old mate Rupert, for instance,' he said with an admiring shake of the head. 'Now Rupert has charm. He can get away with anything. Last week at a party he managed to persuade his girlfriend to lend him her last condom . . .'

The next moment he almost lost his thread completely. At the back of the club, a door had opened. A group of late arrivals slid in. Straining to see through the smoke haze that hung over the audience bringing visibility down to practically nil, Sean experienced a sudden leap of hope. His heart began to pound like a tom-tom. Surely the figure on the far left of the group was Pandora. Better still, none of the others with her – if it *was* her – was tall enough to be the big blond boyfriend.

If it was her. Other than yelling at the stage manager to put the house lights up, Sean had no way of knowing for sure. All he could do was get through the rest of this bloody set. Thank goodness he only had a few more minutes to go.

Thank goodness, too, she didn't know how long he'd spent waiting in his car to talk to her the other week, Sean realized with a shudder of relief. If she'd spotted him lurking like a prat outside The Moon and Sixpence, his street cred would have gone crashing straight through the pavement.

But none of that mattered now, because Pandora was here. It had been her, arriving with the same group of friends halfway through his act. All he had to do now was make his way over, casually greet her and carry on where he had left off.

Oh, and this time not splatter her from head to toe with blood.

Downstairs a clock chimed three. Sean lay on his back in bed, tucked one hand beneath his head and gazed out through the semi-drawn white curtains at an almost full moon. The sky was black and dotted with stars. Somewhere, outside, a cat yowled. Sean, who had never felt more wide awake in his life, wondered if he could slide out of bed without disturbing Pandora.

The evening had gone like a dream; he could still hardly believe it had happened. When Pandora had seemed so pleased to see him after the show he had got quite carried away and whisked her off for a ludicrously expensive dinner at Caviar Kaspiar. In a soft, jade green silk shirt and a wonderfully demure black bias-cut skirt she had looked both classy and infinitely desirable. It was all Sean could do to keep his hands off her in the restaurant. No mention had been made of a boyfriend, past or present, but he didn't care about that either. At least she was here with him now.

'You're different tonight,' Pandora said finally, over coffee. 'I don't get it. How can you be so different?'

'What can I say?' Sean grinned. 'Absence made the heart grow fonder.'

For a second she pressed the back of her boiling-hot coffee spoon against his wrist. 'Come on, I'm interested.'

Sean hadn't been able to resist telling her.

'You'd taken your dress off,' he said simply. 'You sat there in The Blue Goose, wrapped up in that damn raincoat, and all the time your dress was in your handbag.'

Pandora looked amazed. Then she smiled. 'So?'

'You were naked under that coat,' Sean explained. 'And you didn't even tell me.' He shook his head, lost in admiration all over again. 'I thought that was just so . . . *cool* . . .'

'Not completely naked.' Pandora's tone was matter-of-fact.

'Well, you know—'

'I was wearing my Aertex vest tucked into big woolly knickers.'

'Careful.' Sean found himself grinning uncontrollably. He touched her fingers, outstretched on the snowy tablecloth. 'I think I could be falling in love with you. Do you believe in love at second sight?'

'Better wait', Pandora warned him, 'until you've seen me in my knickers and Aertex vest.'

It was no good; he wasn't going to be able to get back to sleep, at least not until he'd had a glass of water. Peeling back the duvet in slow motion, he slithered out of bed. A blue towelling robe of Pandora's hung from a hook on the door. Sean, who didn't fancy wandering round a strange house naked, put it on.

He didn't mean to pry. In coming downstairs, it certainly hadn't been his intention to snoop around. It was only natural, however, that once he'd helped himself to a glass of ice-cold water he should wander around the sitting room admiring Pandora's taste in paintings, running his fingers idly across her CD collection and checking out the books in her bookcase. It wasn't nosiness, merely healthy curiosity, Sean reasoned. When you'd just been to bed for the first time with a girl you liked a lot, you *wanted* to discover more about her. All he was doing was picking up a few clues, learning that she was a fan of Tom Sharpe, Aretha Franklin, Impressionist art and Scrabble.

The photographs were tucked casually behind a pink porcelain candlestick on the crowded mantelpiece. Taking care not to disturb the fragile-looking stem vase to the left of it and a saucer of iridescent marbles on the right, Sean scissored two fingers together and slid the photos away from the wall.

There were only three, together with a hastily scribbled note:

Pandora, just had to send you these. What a great day – we must do it again soon! Love, Wendy.

Sean gazed intently down at the photographs, two of which featured Pandora and the blond boyfriend horsing around together at the side of an azure swimming-pool. In the first she was tipping a bucket of water over him. In the second he was about to tip her head-first into the pool.

The third picture, presumably taken by Tarzan himself, showed Pandora sitting with her legs dangling in the water, flanked on either side by a freckled, ginger-haired girl and a man who looked like Richard Whiteley. They were all laughing up at the camera, evidently enjoying the sunshine and each other's company. Pandora, in particular, wearing the smallest bronze bikini Sean had ever seen, looked as if she were having the time of her life. Flipping back almost obsessively to the other two photos, he studied the handsome, tanned face of the blond hulk with the all-American physique and gleaming teeth.

Anger welled up in him; anger and a sense of rivalry. Shocked, Sean realized he was jealous. When he heard the creak of an upstairs floorboard moments later he jumped a mile, almost dropping the photographs into the empty grate.

He only just had time to stuff them back behind the porcelain candlestick before the sitting-room door opened.

'Here you are.' Pandora smiled slightly. 'I thought you'd done a moonlight flit.'

She looked relieved to see him, which Sean felt to be a good sign. Normally an effortless liar, he stood with his back to the fireplace and watched his hand shaking as he raised his half-empty glass to her.

'I was thirsty; couldn't sleep. Um, I see you like Tom Sharpe. I've read all his books too.'

'Tom Sharpe makes me laugh out loud on the tube,' said Pandora. 'Deeply embarrassing. If you can't sleep, how about a cup of tea?'

Sean wasn't in the mood for tea. A fresh wave of jealousy swept over him as he wondered whether the big blond guy in the photos was better in bed than he was. Putting down his water glass, he crossed the room and kissed Pandora very slowly on the mouth. When her arms slid around his neck and he felt her warm, scented body begin to respond, he murmured, 'I've got a much better idea.'

But Pandora was smothering giggles against his shoulder. She was shaking all over, so helpless with laughter he practically had to hold her up.

'What?' Sean demanded, his suspicions instantly aroused. He only liked people to laugh when he'd said something funny. What if she was actually making fun of him?

Pandora wiped her streaming eyes, hiccuped twice and tried valiantly to control herself.

'I'm sorry, I'm sorry. You're being so macho and seductive.' She gazed apologetically up at him, but her lip was trembling. Laughter threatened to spill out once more. 'I just can't cope with being seduced by a man in a blue towelling dressing gown with daisies all over it and a hard-on.'

Chapter 9

Ten days after their first meeting at the Cameron Club, Jack spotted Imogen again. For some time he surreptitiously watched her pant her way through the last stretch of a strenuous aerobics routine. Imogen, on the other side of the glass, pretended she hadn't spotted him.

When the class was over she emerged, pink and glistening in a black leotard and rainbow-striped leg-warmers, with a russet towel slung around her shoulders. Jack found himself acknowledging her with a brief nod and a smile. The next moment he heard himself say, 'This time you definitely look as if you could use a drink. What'll it be?'

Yes, *yes*, thought Imogen triumphantly. She had been wondering how long it would take him to make the first vital move. These happily married types, as she knew only too well, could drive you wild with impatience. Sometimes it took them weeks just to pluck up enough courage to *think* adulterous thoughts . . .

And what a wicked waste of time that was.

Smiling, Imogen mentally congratulated Jack Mandeville. Ten days was neither too keen nor too slow. As far as she was concerned, ten days was just about perfect.

Jack knew what he was doing but was powerless to stop. The magnetic attraction sparking between Imogen and himself was so intense he hadn't the will to resist. It went, too, against

60

all his long and vigorously held principles – but then, nothing like this had ever happened to him before.

The only way Jack had been able to justify the effect this could have on his marriage was by telling himself that for the past ten days he had been far nicer than usual to live with. Whether it was out of sheer guilt or because just thinking about Imogen Trent made him feel better, he didn't know. It just worked. Cass had even remarked on the fact herself.

'I hate to say this, but people are beginning to raise their eyebrows in our direction.'

As she spoke, Imogen drained her glass of orange juice and glanced up at the clock. It was nearly one and she was ravenous. If she didn't eat soon she would pass out.

Jack read her mind. He also had a deadline to meet on the weekly column he wrote for the *Daily Herald*. Missing the deadline somehow seemed less important than missing out on another hour with Imogen.

'There's a little Italian place on Cardew Street,' he said rapidly. 'No one goes there – it's practically empty at lunchtime. Why don't I go on ahead and order while you shower and change?'

That way they could be seen leaving the club separately. For a novice in the field, Jack felt he wasn't doing too badly at all.

Imogen, who knew better, didn't have the heart to tell him the double-bluff was far and away the more effective ploy. Lunch at a crowded restaurant where you were bound to bump into heaps of people you knew was so much more sensible than running the risk of being caught hiding out in an empty one.

Still, she was touched by this demonstration of Jack's lack of experience in such matters. She was further amused, upon reaching La Traviata forty minutes later, to see that he had chosen to ignore the half-dozen or so free parking spaces directly outside the restaurant. Instead, his car was on a meter round the corner next to a tatty-looking bookshop.

Jack was pretending to study the menu when she pushed the door open. Imogen's heart contracted with lust at the sight of him. He was forty and so ridiculously good-looking it almost took her breath away. In that pale pink polo shirt and those faded jeans, with his tanned, finely muscled arms resting on the table before him, the idea that he could be the father of grown-up children seemed ludicrous.

By mutual agreement they stuck to mineral water. Imogen ordered tagliatelle with artichokes, Jack chose spaghetti carbonara and found he couldn't eat it. His appetite had gone, possibly for ever. He watched and drank the iced Pellegrino as Imogen, now changed into a purple shirt and short white skirt, did enough eating for the two of them.

'Sorry,' Imogen said at last, not sorry at all. 'I always eat when I'm nervous.'

'I never can.' Jack, his dark eyes intent, touched her hand. They were the only customers in the pretty, blue and white dining room. There was no longer any point maintaining the pretence. 'And there's no need to be nervous anyway. One should only be nervous about things one doesn't want to happen.'

Imogen, hopelessly excited, tried to look demure.

'What about the things that shouldn't happen?'

As far as Jack was concerned, it was already too late. Fate had taken over. He shrugged.

'Sometimes they just do.'

This was seriously erotic stuff. Imogen wondered if this was how people felt when they matched six numbers on the lottery. It was the silliest situation, too, she realized: here they both were, acknowledging that they were on the brink of an affair – and nothing physical had even happened yet. They hadn't even kissed.

'I want to kiss you.' Goodness, she was getting quite emotional. Her voice caught in her throat. Nodding to show how much she meant it, Imogen tried again. 'I do.'

'So do I.' A smile flickered across Jack's face. His eyes darted in the direction of the chef and the waiter hunched over espressos and glasses of Strega at the far end of the restaurant. But his was a television face and there were some risks only a madman would take. He couldn't afford to kiss Imogen here.

She knew he was right, but that didn't stop it being frustrating. Had courting couples in the old days really endured years of desperate waiting until they were decently married? Too much anticipation, Imogen thought, surely couldn't be good for you. She barely knew how she was going to survive the afternoon.

'It's two thirty.' Jack looked at his watch and tried to care about his fast-approaching deadline. All he really wanted Imogen to do was suggest going back to her place.

More disappointment was in store.

'We haven't organized ourselves very well, have we?' She gave him a rueful smile. 'I'm interviewing some Arab princess in Belgravia at three. If I'd known this was going to happen today, I could have unfixed it. Oh, Jack . . .' She clutched his hand and concentrated on not looking too gleeful. 'I still can't believe this *is* happening. I keep thinking about Cass.'

Showing a bit of concern for the wronged wife was always a good move. Nobody liked an out-and-out bitch.

'And you think I haven't? What Cass doesn't know can't hurt her.' Jack shook his head. Unoriginal maybe, but it was what he kept telling himself. 'She mustn't find out, that's all.'

Plenty of men led full and happy lives, successfully maintaining both marriage and mistress. Jack knew of several who did just that, men whose wives remained blissfully unaware of the situation for years on end. Why shouldn't that happen to him?

Some men, on the other hand, got found out in no time at all.

It was as much as Jack could do, as they left the restaurant, not to slide his fingers beneath the red-gold tumble of Imogen's hair and caress the vulnerable nape of her neck. The urge to touch her was almost irresistible. So deep in thought was he, trying to work out when they could see each other again, that he didn't even register the gaggle of schoolgirls spilling out of the bookshop onto the dusty pavement ahead.

Those spindly little legs were oddly familiar, Imogen realized. With her journalist's eye, she noticed such details. Now who was it she knew with spindly legs and a funny DIY haircut?

Chapter 10

'Um . . . isn't that your daughter?'

Jack barely had time to groan before Sophie, with almost telepathic timing, spun round.

'Dad!'

'Sophie . . .'

Heavens. Imogen reminded herself that this wasn't funny. Oh, but please . . . how could such a smart man look so *amazingly* guilty?

Sophie, meanwhile, was struggling to recall where she had seen the woman at her father's side before.

'Imogen Trent, *Hi!* magazine,' Imogen prompted. 'Remember me, the one not wearing stockings and suspenders?'

'Of course.' Sophie's face cleared. 'The one Dad was incredibly rude to at his party.'

'Not incredibly rude.' Jack was still looking shell-shocked.

'Yes you were.' Imogen turned back to Sophie. 'He was a pig, wasn't he? I can still hardly believe he's speaking to me now.'

'Don't tell me he's agreed to do an interview.' This time Sophie's tone was one of frank disbelief. 'Not for *Hi!*'

'He might be a pig,' said Imogen cheerfully, 'but he hasn't sprouted wings. Nothing that dramatic, I'm afraid. We just bumped into each other at the Cameron Club. He apologized for being awful the other week, I nearly passed out with the shock . . . and we decided to seal the truce with a quick spaghetti at La Traviata.'

Beside her, Jack stiffened. It clearly hadn't occurred to him that they must both reek of garlic. He's such a novice, Imogen thought fondly.

But Sophie was in too much of a hurry to catch up with the rest of her friends to be that interested. Shifting her bookshop bargain – *Teach Yourself Swahili* – from one hand to the other, she merely gave her father an approving nod.

'Good. Mum'll be pleased, anyway.'

Mum wouldn't if she knew what was really going on, thought Imogen.

She tried to feel ashamed of herself, and failed.

Cass was sunbathing out on the terrace when Jack arrived home. As he had watched Imogen from a distance earlier, so he now stood in the cool sanctuary of the living room, studying his wife and wondering just what it was that created sexual attraction.

He also wondered why, after so many years of almost indecently happy marriage, the attraction to Imogen should have struck him like this out of the blue. It wasn't something he'd gone looking for, nor something he had particularly wanted to happen – except that now, since it *had* happened, he wanted it furiously, more than anything else in the world.

It wasn't even as if he had one of those wives who had let herself go. With some men – some women too, of course – you saw the appalling state of their respective spouses and felt they positively deserved a bit on the side to cheer themselves up.

But Cass never had let herself go. Who, in all fairness, could ask for more? At thirty-nine, she possessed the kind of body many twenty-year-olds would envy. No stretch marks, no cellulite. Her stomach didn't sag, she waxed her legs regularly and always smelled gorgeous. She had an innate sense of style, too; whatever she wore looked good. Now, with her blond hair glinting in the sunlight as it spilled over the back of the dark-blue sun-lounger, and with her golden breasts spilling out of a green bikini, she looked utterly delectable.

On a scale of one to ten Cass rated a nine, because the heavenly Audrey Hepburn had been Jack's one and only ten. But even as he now found himself in the grip of this new and overwhelming infatuation, he had to admit Imogen Trent was no nine. The red hair was gorgeous, the fake tan less so. She was undoubtedly good-looking and her figure was fine, but stand her next to Cass and ask an impartial audience who was the more attractive and – no question about it – Cass would win.

Jack hated himself for even thinking anything so crass. He remembered the words of that famously faithful actor, Paul Newman: why go out for a hamburger when you have steak at home? The trouble was, after twenty-three years of non-stop steak, wouldn't *anyone* find themselves yearning to try a burger, just for a change?

Ugh, that was crass too. He watched Cass wriggle into a sitting position, adjust her sunglasses and pick up a buff folder of the notes and letters she needed to go through for tomorrow morning's programme. Reminded – as if he needed reminding – of his own fast-approaching deadline, Jack stepped out of the shadowy sitting room onto the sun-drenched terrace.

'Darling.' Cass lifted her face for a kiss. 'I thought I heard the car just now. It's so hot out here . . . you couldn't do my back and shoulders?'

Glad of the excuse to stand behind her, Jack began slowly massaging Ambre Solaire into her smooth, sun-warmed skin.

'You'll never guess who I took out to lunch today.'

'Tom Cruise, Paddington Bear, Madonna, Bill Clinton . . . ?'

'Your friend Imogen Trent.'

Cass's mouth dropped open in astonishment. Expecting him to say 'Joke', she swivelled half round on the lounger.

'Really?'

'Really really.' Jack carried on massaging the oil into her shoulders with slow, deliberate strokes.

'My God, I think I'm going to faint.'

'That's what Imogen said. She sends her love, by the way.'

'But how—'

'She's just joined the Cameron Club. We bumped into each other at the bar and I remembered how angry you were with me after the party, so I thought I'd better apologize. That's when she nearly passed out with the shock,' Jack continued drily. 'Anyway, we chatted for a bit. When she mentioned how hungry she was, I did the decent thing and took her out for some pasta. So that's it, we've made up.' Screwing the top back onto the Ambre Solaire bottle, he wiped his hands on a nearby towel. 'She's not so bad, I suppose. We got on fairly well. Oh, and Imogen says if you ever fancy a spot of torture, she'd love the company. She does the advanced aerobics class, run by Susie the Sadist. I said there was no way in the world you'd go to that.'

'I might.' Cass, amazed and delighted by the news of Jack and Imogen's reconciliation, took off her dark glasses to make sure it really was true.

'But you hate aerobics.' It was Jack's turn to be taken aback.

'I know, but these things are always more fun if you're with a friend. I wouldn't mind if I knew Imogen was going to be there. Besides,' Cass prodded her brown midriff, 'I should start doing something before it's too late. All the girls in the office go to keep-fit classes and Cleo keeps nagging me too. I am pushing forty, after all.' She frowned. 'Although I'm not sure I could handle an advanced class. Is Imogen amazingly fit? I wouldn't want to show myself up.'

'You wouldn't show yourself up.' Jack's tone was curt. His guilty imagination, working overtime, had conjured up once more the mental image of Cass and Imogen standing next to each other, being judged by an audience of club regulars through the glass partition that separated the aerobics studio from the bar.

'Really?' Cass looked pleased. 'In that case, I might give it a go.'

Chapter 11

Setting up and checking out Colin Matheson had proved ridiculously easy. All Cleo had needed to do was enlist the help of a friend, Miranda, who had wandered into the bar where Colin was drinking and had promptly found herself being chatted up.

He hadn't so much taken the bait as guzzled it whole. And he had clearly had plenty of practice, Miranda had reported back. Meeting other girls and being unfaithful to Linda was all in a day's work for him. He probably regarded it as no more than a harmless pastime, like cricket. Miranda had taken enormous pleasure in turning his offer down.

Delighted with the success of her plan, Cleo nevertheless felt her courage begin to slip away at the prospect of having to actually break the news to poor Linda. Colin might be pond-life and a creep of the first order but Linda's life had revolved around him for the last three and a half years.

In the event, when they met up again in a little wine bar just off Berkeley Square, Linda did the dirty work for her.

'He went for it, didn't he?' She took a deep, despairing drag of her cigarette. Her huge violet eyes drooped at the corners. 'It's OK, you can say it. I'm not going to slit my wrists.'

Cleo had to remind herself she was doing Linda the favour of her life.

'I'm so sorry.' The words came tumbling out. 'You said he always stopped off for a couple of drinks at Vampires when he finished work. I sent Miranda along, because you said he liked brunettes; all she had to do was stand next to him at the bar and drop her purse. Colin helped her pick up the money, started chatting, introduced himself . . . and that was it. Two drinks later he was inviting her to dinner at San Lorenzo. When Miranda asked if he was involved with anyone, he told her he'd just broken up with a girlfriend and was enjoying being single again.' Cleo shook her head in disgust. 'God, why *are* men such devious shits?'

The famous violet eyes now filled with shimmering tears. 'I'll have to cancel the wedding. Oh, this is horrid. What if I never meet anyone nice again? I'll end up a dried-up, miserable old spinster. *Nobody* will want me.'

'Look, if he chatted up Miranda in three seconds flat, it means he's done it before and he'll do it again, for ever and ever amen. But it's up to you,' said Cleo more gently. 'If you really want to marry him, go ahead.'

'No. I know you're right. Better to get out now.'

Tears were dripping steadily down Linda's long, elegant nose. The young Australian barman tried hard to look as if he hadn't noticed.

'And you won't end up a spinster anyway,' Cleo reassured her. 'You'll find someone heaps nicer in no time at all. Look at you, who *wouldn't* want to snap you up and give you the kind of future you deserve?'

Linda sniffed and rummaged in her bag for more tissues, dumping the ball of soggy used ones in the already overflowing ashtray.

71

'I saw your brother on some Channel 4 programme the other night.' She dabbed her eyes, sniffed again and sat back with a sigh. 'He's awfully good-looking, isn't he?'

Cleo beamed. 'Takes after his gorgeous sister.'

'And he seems so nice, too.' A flicker of hope showed in Linda's red-rimmed but still spectacular eyes. 'I mean, I don't mean just yet of course,' she said shyly, 'but I wouldn't mind being introduced to him in a couple of months' time.'

Poor Linda, that was all she needed. Cleo realized with alarm she had to act fast.

'No. You're my friend and I couldn't do it to you.' This time she spoke as firmly as she knew how. 'Sean might be fun to have as a brother but he gets through more women than you've had cold salads. He's a tart, darling. Where bastards are concerned he's the biggest one of all.'

Sean wasn't having the best evening of his life. He didn't know what was wrong and, having looked forward to this evening for over a fortnight now, the sense of disappointment was crushing. It was pissing him off no end too.

The last couple of weeks had been crazy. No sooner had he finally got together with Pandora than his agent had come up with a five-day trip to Scotland where he was booked to appear on three different TV shows. Immediately after this, he had been booked to fly down to the Channel Islands for a couple of live gigs. Back in London, between shows at Comedy Inc. and interviews for the national press, he barely had time to do more than change his shirt. When he *had* finally managed to wangle a free thirty-six hours, repeatedly punching out Pandora's number had got him nothing more rewarding than the endless, infuriating purr of an unanswered phone.

'I swapped shifts with one of the girls and took a couple of days off,' Pandora had told him last night when he'd finally managed to get hold of her. 'I went to stay with friends in Bath.'

'Brilliant.'

'Sorry.' She had sounded amused. 'Isn't that allowed?'

'I wanted to see you.' Sean heaved a sigh, trying without much success not to sound irritable. 'You don't realize how hard I had to work to make that free time.'

'Well, how was I to know you'd *be* free? No need to get stroppy,' said Pandora.

There had been a slight but definite edge to her voice. Impressed despite his annoyance that she wasn't another simpering yes-girl – he had known as much already, but it made a refreshing change from the groupies who flocked to Comedy Inc. – Sean broke into a smile.

'OK. I've missed you, that's all. So how about tonight?'

'I'm working.'

'After work. I'll pick you up.' He decided to be magnanimous. 'Which would you prefer, dinner or a club?'

Pandora hesitated for a moment. Finally she said, 'Could we just go back to my place? Um . . . I'll cook.'

Something was definitely going on. As soon as he had picked her up from The Moon and Sixpence Sean sensed a difference in Pandora, yet he was unable to put his finger on what it might be. It wasn't quite nervousness, but she was undoubtedly less relaxed than before. Then, back at her house, she had handed him a bottle of Cabernet and a glass the size of a grapefruit.

'We can eat in ten minutes. Why don't you wait in the living room while I get everything onto plates?'

The photographs had disappeared from the mantelpiece. Sean wondered if it meant she didn't want him to see them, or that the relationship was now over. He still wanted to know why Pandora was so on edge. Surely she wasn't about to tell him their own relationship was over, almost before it had begun?

But that made no sense either; she could have told him as much over the phone. And why, Sean reminded himself, would she not want to see him again anyway?

'This is stupid.' Pushing open the kitchen door, he announced the fact to Pandora's back as she stood at the stove stirring prawns and chunks of pineapple into a pan of bubbling Creole sauce. 'Why don't you turn that off? Let's forget dinner and just go upstairs to bed.'

Pandora was wearing a slim-fitting, scarlet cotton dress, high-heeled red and gold leather sandals and nail polish to match. Sean, deciding she really did have the most irresistible shoulders he'd ever seen, moved up behind her and slid his arms around her waist. Kissing each perfect collar-bone in turn, he murmured, 'Maybe that's what we need to relax us. Get us used to each other again. You know something? You smell absolutely gorgeous . . .'

'I'd like to do that.' Pandora switched off the gas burners and put a lid over the saucepan of almost-cooked rice. She twisted round to face him, her big eyes serious. 'But we have to talk.' She took a deep breath. 'I'm really sorry about this, but I'm afraid I'm pregnant.'

Damn. Sean's gaze slid automatically downwards. She didn't

look pregnant. So that was that, he thought. The party was over. Great.

'Oh. I see.' No wonder she hadn't seemed her usual relaxed self. He smiled, to show he was sympathetic to the problem. 'Shame.'

Pandora's mouth was slightly open. Finally, after staring up at him for several seconds, she said, 'What?'

'Classic case of bad timing, I suppose.' Sean shrugged. 'Just when we were getting on so well, too.'

'*What?*'

Confused by this reaction, Sean took a step back.

'Look, obviously I'm disappointed.' He spoke in ultra-reasonable tones. 'But what on earth else *can* I say? Just how excited do you seriously expect me to get about the fact that you're having some other bloke's baby?'

Another ominously prolonged silence, then: 'It isn't some other bloke's baby.' Pandora glanced up at the kitchen clock, whose ticking seemed to have grown inexplicably louder. 'It's yours.'

'Oh come on.' For a bizarre moment, Sean wanted to laugh. This was crazy, more than crazy . . .

'I'm sorry. It is.'

'But we only . . . did it . . . a fortnight ago! You can't possibly pin this on me!'

Pandora's expression changed. Her eyes seemed to darken.

'I'm not pinning this on you,' she replied evenly. 'I'm stating a fact. Two days ago my period didn't happen. I'm always pretty regular. I did the test this morning and it was positive. It's come as a shock to me too, you know. I'm sorry, but it's definitely you.'

Sean was by this time feeling sick. He didn't believe her for a second, and the idea that she was doing her damnedest to make sure he took the rap only fuelled his anger. Did she take him for a complete mug? Had she decided that because he was becoming well known and earning cash to match, he could be relied on to fork out huge sums in hush money, maybe even child support?

For God's sake, did he *look* stupid?

'Oh dear,' said Pandora drily when he didn't reply. 'This *is* going well.'

'This is one bloody lousy trick.' Sean's eyes narrowed. For all he knew she could be a professional blackmailer. 'I used condoms, in case you'd forgotten.'

'I know. And one of them obviously failed the medical.'

Pandora was doing a good job of looking outraged. At least she hadn't attempted the floods-of-tears routine, Sean thought. If there was one thing he couldn't stand it was that.

'How can you be so sure it's mine?'

'Because you're the only man I've slept with in the last year.' Anger was beginning to creep into her voice. 'Look, I know this isn't the kind of evening you had in mind, but why on earth would I tell you this if it wasn't true? Are you always so trusting?'

Sean couldn't believe this was happening to him. He wished he could be back at the club, drinking with Danny and chatting up blondes – safe, giggly blondes, who were on the pill and who wanted nothing more from him than the opportunity to boast to their friends about who they'd spent an evening with.

'Why should I trust you? This all seems amazingly conveni-ent to me.' Sean lowered his voice to add extra emphasis. 'A great opportunity to make the best of a bad job. You could be lying,' he went on, privately convinced of it. 'You could have been seeing someone else and recently have broken up with him. Now you find out you're pregnant, you know damn well *he* won't want anything to do with it so you decide to bestow the honour on me instead because at least you know I can afford to do something about it.'

'But—'

'Right, let me put it this way,' Sean continued smoothly. 'I *know* you've been seeing someone else. I've seen the two of you together . . . I've seen photographs of the two of you together . . . bloody great blond chap, ring any bells? So as far as I'm concerned you can leave me out of this. Run back to that Incredible Hulk of yours and see if he won't marry you or—'

THWANNNGG went the frying pan against the side of Sean's head. Bloody hell, that really hurt.

'Get out,' Pandora yelled as he staggered sideways against the fridge, knocking a mesh bag of oranges with his elbow. One by one the oranges rolled off the fridge and bowled along the black-and-white tiled floor. 'Get out now before I hit you again. You're disgusting and I hate you,' she hissed, visibly shaking with rage. 'You told me you loved me and now you're calling *me* a liar! How *dare* you say that to me?'

Chapter 12

It was lovely to see Imogen again and lovelier still, Cass decided, that Jack had managed to overcome his initial mistrust of her. Not that they were ever likely to become bosom pals – on the couple of occasions all three of them had met up at the Cameron Club Jack had adopted the kind of polite-but-distant manner more usually encountered between off-duty doctor and hypochondriac patient – but at least Jack was no longer downright, blush-makingly rude.

Cass thought how nice it would be if only Imogen had a boyfriend, then she could invite them to dinner. It was the kind of entertaining she liked best.

'There was someone,' Imogen finally admitted as they relaxed out on the terrace one afternoon after a particularly muscle-wrenching aerobics class. She stirred her Pimm's with a lazy forefinger. 'We were together for almost two years, until last autumn when he was offered a terrific job in Los Angeles. I didn't want to leave *Hi!* so that was it.' She shrugged. 'There hasn't really been anyone else since.'

'You put your career first.' Cass, who never had, still found it an admirable quality in a woman, a sign of true inner strength.

'I'm not that driven.' Imogen's face softened. 'If I'd really loved James, I would have gone with him like a shot. I was scared, I suppose, of jacking everything in here, moving out to

California and realizing too late we didn't have a future together anyway.'

Even the most apparently sophisticated career woman, Cass realized, could feel insecure. And Imogen was so nice; here she was, at the peak of attractiveness and without a man in her life when she would clearly like one. What a dreadful waste. Cass, eager to help, racked her brains, running through all the available men of her acquaintance, thinking that a spot of gentle matchmaking wouldn't go amiss.

Imogen stretched and yawned. 'Where's Jack today?'

'Do you know, I can't remember.' Cass thought for a moment and shook her head. 'Nope, it's gone. Nothing enthralling, anyway; either the TV studios or Fleet Street. I'll find out when he gets home tonight.' She smiled. 'I know I've said this before, but I'm so glad you two are friends now. It makes *such* a difference.'

'His bark's worse than his bite,' Imogen said easily. She smiled. 'Once you get to know him, Jack's all right.'

Imogen's mews flat, with its sugar-almond pink exterior, white window-boxes and picturesque wooden shutters, was surprisingly sparse inside.

'Not what you're used to,' she said, instinctively on the defensive even though Jack hadn't uttered a word. She liked her flat but it wasn't the be-all and end-all of her existence. Simple, efficient lines, modern furniture and good quality abstract prints suited Imogen; they were easy to live with and no trouble to keep clean. Compared with what Jack was used to, however – the vast, sunny, cluttered-but-glamorous Hampstead family home he shared with Cass – it suddenly seemed cool, impersonal and oddly masculine.

Although what her choice in wallpaper had to do with anything was scarcely the issue. Imogen dropped her blue jacket over the back of a polished beechwood chair.

'There's wine in the fridge, if you'd like some.'

There was a well-chilled bottle of Bollinger as well, but she didn't say so. It sounded too corny for words.

He was here, which was all that really mattered. It was happening. At last.

'Better not,' said Jack. 'If I have one glass I may not be able to stop, and Cass thinks I'm at the office. I don't want to roll home legless.'

Imogen didn't want him to roll home at all. Weeks of planning and breathless anticipation had led up to this, they had three heavenly hours alone together and already Jack was talking about getting back to Cass.

Turning to face him, Imogen slid her slender, freckled arms around his waist.

'I think we've wasted enough time admiring my flat. I'd much rather admire your body.'

Up until this afternoon, their relationship had classified only as a flirtation. Scarily aware that he was about to take that final, irrevocable step, realizing that the strength of his feelings meant he couldn't *not* take it, Jack cupped Imogen's pale, quivering face in his hands and slowly kissed her mouth. His arousal was almost instantaneous. It was going to be so strange, making love for the first time in over twenty years to someone who felt and smelled and reacted differently from Cass. He only prayed he wouldn't disgrace himself, leaving Imogen to wail, 'Was that it?'

As if reading his mind, she murmured, 'I'm scared too, you know.'

'I think you'd better take me to your bedroom.' Jack half smiled. 'I'm too old to do this kind of thing on the floor.'

He didn't want to run the risk of going home with carpet burns, either.

'That', Imogen sighed much later, 'was seriously, *seriously* good.'

Maybe she would open the Bollinger now anyway, to celebrate. She couldn't help wondering whether Jack took as much trouble with Cass, or if all those years of familiarity had taken their toll. Maybe the longer the marriage, the shorter the act until you were both too ancient to do it anyway.

Jack, lying beside her, risked a surreptitious glance at his watch. It wasn't yet time to leave, he knew that; there was just that overwhelming compulsion to keep double-checking. How, he wondered, was it possible to feel so happy and so racked with guilt at the same time?

'Don't get up.' He put out his arm to stop Imogen sliding out of bed. 'Speaking of serious. This is, isn't it?'

'I bloody hope so!' She raised her eyebrows in mock outrage. 'I'd hate to find out you're only here because you had a bet with your friends at the club.'

Jack pinched her wrist. 'You could have been doing that. I'm not completely naive, you know. I may not have done anything about it before, but I have been approached by the bed-a-celeb brigade before now.'

'I've never wanted to go to bed with anyone more,' said Imogen. 'But I wish you weren't a celeb. As far as I'm concerned, all it does is make things a million times more difficult.'

She had indirectly answered his question, although he'd known the reply already. What had happened this afternoon wasn't simply a matter of satisfying mutual curiosity. This was no casual, short-term affair. The prospect of being found out – of hurting and maybe even losing Cass – was too horrible to contemplate, but at the same time Jack knew he was powerless to stop what had begun.

They would just have to be ultra-careful, he decided, that was all. Fate was already lending a hand, having supplied a door which led from the back of Imogen's drive-in garage up to the flat above. This meant he would be able to enter and leave the flat without being spied on by nosy neighbours. They might not be able to go out and about much but at least they had a safe house. Other people in his situation managed it anyway; look how often you heard about some respectable married media personality or politician suddenly announcing that he had been involved with another woman for the past six or seven years.

If they can do it, Jack decided, comforted by the thought, so can I.

The Tuesday-morning problems phone-in on the Cass Mandeville show was a big ratings-puller, one of the highlights of the week. Cass, discovered all those years ago by Terry Brannigan, had made an equally happy discovery of her own. Hauling big, bosomy Jenny Duran out of the radio station's dingy post room and into the studio had been one of the most inspired moves of her life.

Jenny, a natural problem-solver, was never stuck for an answer. Her brash, no-nonsense, go-for-it attitude contrasted perfectly with Cass's gentle, more laid-back style. Their differing senses of humour complemented each other. Jewish, in her late twenties and an inveterate collector of boyfriends – most of them wildly unsuitable – Jenny knew everything there was to know about the singles scene. When listeners rang in with more family-orientated complaints concerning interfering in-laws, boring husbands and nerve-racking kids, they turned instinctively to Cass. Between them, no problem ever went unanswered. Together they were a resounding hit.

'It's my best friend, you see.' Marianne from Coventry was on the line sounding agitated. 'She thinks she's married to the most wonderful man in the world. The thing is, I found out last week he's been seeing another woman and I don't know what to do about it.'

'Nothing,' Jenny replied promptly. 'You may be mistaken. Forget it. Put it out of your mind.'

'Oh please, how can you say that?' Cass protested. 'I can't *believe* you said that! What about her poor friend if it's true?'

This was how they operated, as a double act arguing the pros and cons of each situation as it presented itself. Cass wasn't putting it on, either. She had automatically assumed Jenny would belong to the string-the-bastard-up-by-his-gonads brigade.

'Ah, but I'm speaking from personal experience.' Jenny wiggled her expressive eyebrows at Cass. '*Bitter* personal experience, too! I was in exactly the same situation as Marianne . . . and since my friend had once said she'd want to know if it happened to her, I told her. Well, it turned out she didn't want to know after all. She called me a spiteful bitch and said she never wanted to speak to me again. And that was it, the end of a beautiful friendship. She stayed with her lying rat of a husband and never forgave me. Take it from me, Marianne,' Jenny firmly concluded, 'keep this one to yourself. If you tell her, she won't thank you for it. As you said just now, as far as your friend's concerned, she's married to Mr Wonderful. If her illusions end up being shattered . . . well, then you can offer endless comfort. In the meantime, don't breathe a word.'

Cass, still astonished, said, 'Yes, but not all women are like that! I imagine most of them would *want* to be told by a sympathetic friend if they were being cheated on. I know I certainly would.'

'Well, aren't we the helpful ones?' Jenny put in cheerily. They were only forty seconds away from the news at midday; it was time to wrap up the call.

'Maybe some others of you out there have opinions about this.' Cass prepared to slot in a jingle. 'Please, ring in and tell us what you think Marianne should do. We'll be back after the news and weather, so get dialling. We want your views . . .' Grinning across at Jenny, she added, '. . . especially if you agree with me.'

'She's only being this brave', Jenny countered, 'because she knows she'd never have to deal with this kind of bombshell herself. Vote for me, everyone out there, because this time I'm definitely right!'

Chapter 13

Almost a fortnight had passed since Sean had been hit by his own personal bombshell, in which time he had neither seen nor heard from Pandora. Like an ominous-looking envelope from the Inland Revenue, however, not opening it because it probably contained an outrageous tax demand wasn't going to make the problem go away.

Once again Pandora was occupying virtually his every waking thought, only this time he wasn't enjoying it one bit. She had lied to him, denying the existence of anyone else in her life, but he was still uncomfortably aware that his behaviour had been atrocious. If what she'd told him about the baby was true, he would feel terrible . . . almost as terrible as Pandora was probably feeling now.

And there was, of course, still that sliver of a chance that it might actually be true. Sean, never having given the matter much thought before now, had sidled into Boots the Chemist, bought a pregnancy testing kit and discovered upon reading the instructions that it was indeed possible to get a positive result as quickly as Pandora had claimed.

Each time it occurred to Sean that he might really be responsible for the mishap he was seized with shame. One night he even dreamt he was holding his own baby. Finally, unable to live with the guilt any longer, he rang Pandora at home.

'Hi, it's me.' His heart began to race when she picked up the phone. 'Um . . . how are you?'

Pandora, as he supposed she had every right to be, sounded cautious in the extreme.

'Fine, thanks.'

'Still . . . ?'

'Pregnant? Oh yes, still that.'

Sean's palms were sweating. He wiped his free hand on the side of his jeans. At least she hadn't slammed down the receiver.

'Look, maybe we should talk.' He spoke hesitantly. The sound of Pandora's cool voice still had an unnerving effect on him . . . he just wished this crazy baby thing hadn't happened. Under different circumstances they could have had such a great time together.

'Go ahead,' said Pandora, 'I'm listening.'

'Not on the phone. Can I come round?' Sean consulted his watch. 'I can be there by five.'

'OK.' She didn't sound exactly thrilled. 'It won't take long, will it? I have to be at work by six.'

All Sean wanted to do was get matters straightened out, as much for his own peace of mind as anything else. When he arrived on Pandora's doorstep forty minutes later he certainly wasn't expecting the door to be opened by the big blond boyfriend who had been the cause of all the trouble in the first place.

He was big, too, even taller and wider close up than Sean remembered. For a hideous second he wondered if Pandora had set him up for this. Was he about to be pounded to a pulp? Were all his teeth going to end up clattering down his throat? Would he ever live to tell a joke again?

But his erstwhile rival, much to Sean's confusion, was grinning broadly at him.

'Hi, you must be Sean. Come on in. Pandora's upstairs, but she'll be down any second. I'm Joel, her brother.' He glanced at his watch and grabbed a tennis racquet from the hall table behind Sean. 'And I'm late. Sorry, have to go. Nice to meet you, anyway – maybe see you again some time . . .'

Next moment the door had slammed shut behind him. Sean, who had instinctively winced as the tennis racket whistled within inches of his left ear, took several seconds to make sense of what he had just heard.

Pandora appeared at the top of the stairs, wearing a pale grey T-shirt and combats.

'That expression on your face,' she observed. 'Interesting. I take it the penny has just dropped?'

'He's your brother,' Sean replied stupidly. He felt quite numb. 'Really? I mean, he really is your *brother*?'

'Well, half-brother. Mum married twice. She's white,' Pandora explained. 'So was Joel's father. My dad was black.'

'Terrific.' Sean stared at her in exasperation. 'Thanks a lot. You could have mentioned this, you know. When I said I'd seen you with some big blond guy you could have *told* me . . .'

Slowly, one step at a time, Pandora came down the stairs.

'Oh? Would it have made a difference?'

'Of course it makes a fucking difference!' Sean shouted back at her. What was she doing, being deliberately obtuse?

'Well, I'm afraid I don't see it that way. Look at it from my point of view,' Pandora said calmly. 'You spied on me *and* you rummaged through my personal possessions. You refused to believe for one second that you could be the father of this baby, you called me a liar and a cheat and you made it perfectly plain that all I'd been to you was a bit of a challenge, an amusing diversion . . . a . . . a . . .'

As Sean watched, her complexion turned greeny-brown. With a groan of resignation Pandora spun round and bolted back upstairs. Concerned that she was on the verge of passing out, he raced up after her.

'Go away,' Pandora moaned between retches, her head over the toilet bowl and her right hand blindly casting around for the loo roll. 'Don't *stare*. If you want to do something useful, go down and make a cup of tea.'

Appalled by the sight of her vulnerable neck and heaving shoulders, Sean leaned across, unravelled the roll of Andrex and pressed a great wodge into her hand.

'What is it?'

'Ooohh,' wailed Pandora. 'Morning sickness, you moron—'

'But . . . but it's twenty past five.'

'Tell that to the baby. Sean, I mean it. Get *out* of here.'

He was hopelessly confused. His whole life was in the process of being turned upside down. Pandora was still trying to argue with him and all he wanted to do was hug her. He didn't even care that she was being sick.

But since it clearly bothered Pandora, he retreated. When she staggered downstairs ten minutes later, pale and subdued and reeking of toothpaste, Sean handed her a cup of hot sweet tea and a McVitie's digestive.

For the first time that afternoon, having sipped the tea, Pandora smiled.

'I don't take sugar.'

He knew so little about her.

'Here, have mine.' Sean did a swap. 'And eat your biscuit.'

'What are you all of a sudden, Dr Kildare?'

'Just do it. Shall I phone work and tell them you won't be in tonight?'

'If I don't work, I don't get paid.' Pandora shook her head. 'It's OK, I'll be fine.'

'Look, I came here today because there were things we needed to sort out.' Sean's eyes softened. The urge to reach out and touch her was overwhelming but he still didn't quite dare. 'So far we've got more sorted out than I'd bargained for, but there are still a couple of questions I have to ask.'

'I'm not getting rid of it, if that's what you're dying to know.' Pandora laced her fingers around the teacup. 'I'm sorry, I can't do that.'

'Don't say sorry.' Sean's tone was sharp, covering up the guilt he felt at ever having considered such an option himself. Something else occurred to him. 'You haven't told your brother yet.'

'I'm still getting used to the idea myself.' Pandora looked apologetic. 'He thinks I've gone down with a stomach bug. I have to say, he isn't going to be thrilled when he does find out.'

'Don't worry about it. Between us we'll manage.'

Pandora's eyebrows lifted. He *had* changed his tune.

'You trust me now? You don't still think I'm lying?'

'I trust you.' This time Sean took her hand, gently massaging the slender, ringless fingers. He wanted to say, 'I love you,' but sensed it wouldn't go down too well.

'You don't know me,' said Pandora sadly. 'You don't even know if I take sugar in my tea. And we're having a baby. I never lie, by the way.' Her huge brown eyes fixed on his. 'If you ever do get to know me, you'll find that out for yourself.'

'I think I already have.' Sean smiled, leaned across the kitchen table and kissed her soft, tea-and-toothpaste-scented mouth. 'You never lie. You just don't say the things other people might automatically say.'

'You mean like: Oh no, I think I'm going to be sick again?' Even as she spoke, Pandora was turning green once more. Covering her mouth, she bolted back towards the stairs. 'OK, I'm saying it now . . .'

Chapter 14

Weeks of glorious weather ended with a crash of thunder the following Tuesday. Imogen, who had just spent a tiresome couple of hours interviewing an actor with a brain the size of an acorn, was driving across town to her next appointment. Switching on the radio, she tuned in to the Cass Mandeville show just as the first raindrops pelted like lead against the windscreen. The sky was dark grey, exactly the same shade as the Agnes B silk shirt she was wearing, which Jack had bought her last week.

A Dire Straits album track was currently being played on the radio. Imogen briefly amused herself making the swish of the windscreen wipers fit in with the beat of the music then turned her attention to tomorrow night's dinner party. It had been Cass's idea, of course, and Jack hadn't been able to object. Two of the couples were long-standing friends of theirs, which was fair enough, and the third couple were Imogen and the newly appointed producer of Kingdom Radio's breakfast show. His name was Roly Brent and he was Imogen's blind date for the evening, much to her own amusement and Jack's disgust. Cass, the only one who had so far met him, had high hopes for the outcome. 'He's lovely,' she enthused to Jack. 'Terribly good-looking and the weeniest bit shy. I think he's just what Imogen needs.'

'Don't you dare flirt with him,' Jack had growled only half-jokingly when he and Imogen had met up at her flat yesterday for a lunchtime session.

'I'll have to a bit,' she'd protested, laughing. 'To keep up appearances. And it's what Cass so desperately wants. The least I can do is seem grateful.'

Dire Straits came to an end. Imogen turned up the volume as the rain, drumming on the roof of the car, almost drowned out Cass's voice. Oh good, it was the problems phone-in. Imogen turned the sound up another notch. Other people's problems were always a good laugh.

'. . . and now we have Beryl on the line, calling from Islington. Beryl, I understand you have something to add to last week's debate about what to do if you find out your best friend's husband is having an affair.'

'Or wife,' Jenny chimed in, before a thousand outraged husbands could jam the switchboards complaining that they had been cheated on too.

'Yes, hello.' Beryl from Islington sounded middle-aged and breathless. 'The thing is, Cass, I listened to what you said – that the wife has a right to know if her husband's carrying on – and I've given the matter a lot of thought this past week.'

A juggernaut trundled past Imogen, sending up a wave of scummy water. The driver of the lorry leered down at her, evidently approving of her short red skirt and shapely fake-tanned thighs.

Neanderthal oik, thought Imogen.

'Yes, go on,' prompted Cass.

'Right, well, so I'm ringing to tell you that your husband's been up to no good.' Beryl speeded up. 'And I know I'm not your best friend but I felt you should know about it anyway, because I've watched him, see, sneaking into this girl's house in my road . . . He wears dark glasses and slides down in the passenger seat of her car – it's a bright green MR2 – but it's definitely him, and why would he need to act like that if he isn't doing something he's not supposed to do? Never trust a redhead, that's what I say, Cass. Sly-boots, that's what they are. My husband, he left me for a redhead—'

'Oh dear, we appear to have lost Beryl.' Reaching across a frozen Cass, Jenny cut off the call and pushed another record onto the turntable. Briskly she said, 'Coming up after this from Sting, we have a call about transvestism. Let's hope it's not from my boyfriend, eh?'

As Sting flooded the studio, mournfully singing 'If I Ever Lose My Faith In You', Cass realized she simply couldn't move. No matter how hard she tried, nothing happened. Through the plate-glass wall of the studio she saw interested faces peering in. So this was how it felt to be a monkey on show at the zoo.

'Come on, Cass, you should have cut her off straight away,' Jenny chided. 'That's what the nutter-button's for! Any longer and she'd probably have told you she was the one having an affair with Jack.'

'No she wouldn't.' Clutching the edge of the desk, wondering if she was about to faint, Cass stumbled clumsily to her feet. 'I'm sorry, I've got to get out of here.'

'But, Cass—' The transvestite was still waiting on line three. Alarmed, Jenny signalled through the glass to the producer for help. 'You can't go! What that stupid woman said isn't true. I mean, of all people, what on earth would your Jack want with a redhead?'

'I don't know,' said Cass numbly as her whole world caved in. 'But it seems he does. And I know who she is.'

'Shit, *shit*,' Imogen gasped, so stunned she almost smashed into the car in front. Who the bloody hell was Beryl and whatever had possessed her to blab like that on live radio? What a way to be outed. Moments later, ridiculously, Imogen found herself cringing at a pelican crossing as pedestrians swarmed in both directions in front of the car. How many redheads drove around London in an emerald-green MR2? Were people likely to start pointing her out? Damn, she hadn't wanted this to happen. Jack was going to blow a gasket when he found out.

Cass knew she hadn't helped matters, bolting from the studio like that. If she could have somehow forced herself to remain calm, dismiss Beryl from Islington as a mere nuisance caller, perhaps make a joke or two about it and cheerfully carry on with the show, there was a good chance they would have got away with it.

Doing a lightning bunk, leaving Jenny to cope alone and having to be helped into a taxi because there was no way in the world she could drive, had pretty much given the game away. Word had spread like wildfire. By the time Cass arrived home, the phone was already ringing off the hook. A flustered Mrs Bedford handed her a list of messages telling her the *News of the World*, the *Sun*, the *Mail* and the *People* had already called, sounding most insistent.

'They wanted me to give them a quote,' Mrs Bedford wailed, confused by all the frantic goings-on. 'I didn't know what to say so I just put the phone down. Whatever's happening, Cass? I didn't know nothing about no divorce.'

Cass, functioning on auto-pilot, shook her head and switched the kettle on without putting any water in. 'It's OK, there isn't going to be a divorce. The press have got hold of some silly story from heaven-knows-where. Look, why don't you take the rest of the day off? You go home. I'll deal with everything here.'

'Blow the house to kingdom come, more like.' Unplugging the kettle, Mrs Bedford filled it with water at the sink. Her own panic gave way to pity as she realized how shocked and vulnerable Cass was. 'It's all right, duck. I'll stay.'

But Cass shook her head.

'I'll take the phone off the hook. Jack will be home soon. Really, I'm OK.'

Chapter 15

Jack, who had been at the newspaper offices when the first whispers of the story began to filter through, knew he had to get home right away. Cursing, he drove at top speed past a gaggle of photographers at the gate.

Downstairs, there was no sign of anyone and the phone was off the hook. He found Cass upstairs in bed.

'So that's it,' Cass said quietly, when she saw the expression on his face. It was an absolute giveaway. 'You complete bastard.'

She was shivering, despite the fact that the temperature in the room was near-tropical. The duvet was pulled around her and she was wearing a thick sweater. Jack, dripping wet from the rain which had soaked through his shirt, ran a hand over his face and wondered how on earth to begin. How the hell could he explain to Cass something he didn't even understand himself? And why, he thought wearily, were some men able to carry on discreet affairs for years on end while he was found out in a matter of weeks?

'At least come downstairs.' He didn't mean to sound irritable but it came out that way.

Cass, who had been hoping against hope that maybe it was all some ghastly mistake, felt something inside her die.

'This is the most hideous day of my life,' she snapped. 'If I want to stay in bed I bloody will.'

There had been no time for rehearsals. Gazing through the long window at the storm still raging outside, Jack realized he didn't have a clue what to say.

'Look, I'm sorry.'

Cass couldn't believe this. Sorry was what you said when you forgot to put sugar in someone's coffee, when you accidentally stepped on their toe, when you phoned them in the middle of *Coronation Street*. Needing to lash out, she picked up the nearest flingable object and hurled it at Jack's face. Frustratingly, it was only a box of rose-patterned tissues.

'This isn't going to help.' Catching them, Jack placed the box on the walnut bureau behind him. 'Look, can we at least try and sort this out sensibly?'

'Sensibly? Sensibly! Now I know how it feels to want to shoot someone!' At the top of her voice, Cass yelled, 'Believe me, if I had a gun right now I'd do it! You've been having an affair with Imogen Trent, Jack. Do you seriously *expect* me to be sensible about this?'

Wearily, Jack shook his head. 'OK, but please don't get hysterical. These things happen, Cass. All the time. You've said yourself, everyone seems to be doing it these days—'

'But not us.' Cass stared at him, hollow-eyed. He didn't even sound like the Jack she knew – or thought she knew. And now he was actually justifying his behaviour like any caught-out eight-year-old by saying everyone else did it.

'Not us, Jack. Not me, anyway.' The shivering became more violent; Cass wondered if she would ever feel warm again. Then she wondered if she would ever feel normal again. 'So how long has it been going on? The interview with *Hi!* – was it all your idea? Did the two of you set the whole thing up?'

At least now he could be honest. The endless lying had been a drain on Jack, unused as he was to ever speaking anything but the truth. He sat down on the edge of the bed and saw Cass flinch away.

'Of course not. I wouldn't do that.' He sounded faintly aggrieved that she should think so. 'If you hadn't invited her here to do the interview in the first place, none of this would have happened. I didn't even *want* it to happen—'

'But not hard enough, obviously.' Cass's voice began to rise. 'If you don't want something, Jack, you say no. It's as simple as that.'

Now that he was sitting down, Jack was able to see their joint reflections in the dressing-table mirror: Cass, white-faced and surrounded by duvet, and himself with his hands clasped, his elbows resting on his knees. The mirror effect only served to intensify the feeling that he was watching two actors in a play – and not even a particularly original one at that. The clichés he found himself coming out with were shocking but he felt he had no other choice.

'I tried saying no. Believe me, Cass, I did try.'

'Balls,' Cass said bitterly. For a second she covered her face with trembling hands. 'Go on then, tell me the truth. Who chased who?'

Jack was unable to tell her that Imogen had been the one who'd instigated the relationship. Loving Imogen as he did, he felt the need to protect her.

'Chasing didn't come into it.' He spoke quietly, with a mixture of apology and pride. 'Sometimes these things just happen. The first time we set eyes on each other ... well, I think we both just *knew*—'

'I think I need a bigger sick bag.'

But Cass's eyes, for the first time, had filled with tears. If there was one thing she knew she couldn't compete with, it was this kind of obsessive infatuation. Whether it was love or not only time would truly tell. How, though, after twenty-four years together, could she possibly provide as much novelty and adrenalin-pumping excitement as someone brand new?

'I can hear hammering on the front door,' said Jack.

'Reporters. I disconnected the doorbell.' How bizarre, thought Cass, that we can still discuss something as mundane as a doorbell. The tears having safely subsided, she took a deep breath. 'So what happens next? Are you moving out? Are we getting divorced? I think I have a right to know.'

'Oh my darling, I'm so glad to see you!'

The press had wasted no time uncovering the identity of Jack Mandeville's mystery lover. By nine o'clock that evening Imogen's flat was being staked out too. She, like Jack, had needed to drive like a maniac in order to give the chasing photographers the slip. The otherwise deserted ninth floor of a South Kensington multi-storey car park might lack the glossy allure of the *Orient Express* or the Taj Mahal but at this moment in time it seemed to her the most romantic meeting place in the world. Imogen's fingers stroked the back of Jack's neck as she pressed herself against him.

Her past experience with married men was that they kept their mistresses firmly on the side and never left their wives. It was why she hadn't even dared to hope that Jack would ever leave Cass. Some prospects were simply too unlikely for words.

But this was different. Anything could happen. Their affair was out in the open now and the possibilities were limitless. She had even caught herself earlier this evening doodling Imogen Mandeville – just trying the name on for size – across the phone pad. Jack was, after all, clearly the marrying kind.

'God, what a day.' Jack was clutching her so tightly her breasts almost popped over the top of her blue-and-green patterned dress. His warm breath against her bare shoulder made the little hairs at the top of her spine stand on end.

'You poor thing.' Imogen breathed in the aphrodisiac scent of him. 'Has it been bloody? And Cass, how's she taking it?'

'Pretty much as you'd expect. Asked me if I wanted a divorce.'

The hairs at the top of Imogen's spine rose doubly to attention.

'Oh?' Imogen took care not to sound too thrilled. 'And what did you say?'

Jack sighed. 'It's too soon to say anything. She's in shock. I'm in shock, come to that. Cass hasn't even cried yet, she just . . . shakes.'

'She must hate me.' Imogen tried to feel guilty. She had genuinely liked Cass. The trouble was she liked Jack more.

'Well, you aren't exactly top of her Christmas card list.' Jack gave her an apologetic smile. 'But then you aren't going to be top of quite a few Christmas card lists. This isn't going to be easy for you, sweetheart. Everyone loves Cass. As far as they're concerned, she's Snow White—'

'And I'm going to be cast as the Wicked Witch.' Imogen had already guessed as much. She had seen it done enough times in the papers before now to know the routine. Tomorrow she would have to pose for the photographers. Everyone would compare her with Cass, their beloved golden girl. The entire nation would wonder what she had to offer that Cass didn't. She was going to have to dress with care, making sure she gave no one the opportunity to sneer and ask what the bloody hell Jack Mandeville thought he was up to. She mustn't look like a frump, a bimbo, a hooker or a bitch.

Jack kissed her. 'The next few weeks are going to be tough.'

'I don't care,' whispered Imogen. 'It'll be worth it.' For a moment her eyes feverishly scanned his face. 'It will be, won't it? You aren't going to dump me and pretend we never happened?'

'Don't be silly.' Bending his head, Jack kissed her again, hard. 'How can you even ask? I love you too much for that.'

Sophie, who had been spending the week with a schoolfriend in Hemel Hempstead, had finally got to hear what was happening via another friend from school who had spent the evening phoning everyone she knew in order to spread the delicious news. Horrified, Sophie had begged a lift from her friend's elder brother, arriving home at ten o'clock to find her mother wandering around the kitchen like a zombie in three sweaters, and her father out.

By the time Jack returned it was close to midnight. His heart sank when he saw Sophie, waiting for him, sitting cross-legged in the porch.

'Oh Dad, whatever's the matter with you?' Her tiny, pixieish face beneath the uneven fringe was haunted, the amber porch light only emphasizing its pallor. 'How could you *do* it?'

'I'm so sorry, sweetheart.' Jack knew the words were

inadequate but what else could he say? 'I know this is rotten for you—'

'Not me, *I'm* all right.' Sophie gestured impatiently towards the house. 'I meant how could you do it to Mum?'

'You're fourteen years old.' He tried to put his arm around her narrow shoulders but she shrugged it off. 'Sophie, you can't possibly understand . . .'

She walked past him into the house, her expression one of pure disgust.

'Listen to you. You're the one who's immature. For God's sake, Dad, how can you even think of getting involved with someone like that? Imogen Trent is a two-faced bitch.'

'She is not,' Jack replied icily, 'and if I hear you saying any such thing to *anyone* outside this house you'll be in big trouble. Do you hear me, Sophie?'

As Cass had done earlier, so Sophie now heard the protectiveness in his voice and realized that nothing she could say would sway his opinion of Imogen. He was in too deep to even listen.

'Oh, I hear you all right,' Sophie muttered, 'but you're the one who's wrong.'

Chapter 16

The rest of the week, for Cass, was a complete nightmare. With the heatwave well and truly broken, sheets of rain continued to pelt from an oily grey sky. The only good news, as Sophie pointed out, was the fact that this meant the hordes of photographers still huddled at the gate suffered endless well-deserved soakings.

But they clearly had no intention of leaving until Cass gave them the pictures they wanted. She couldn't hide for ever and Imogen had already done her bit. Hating herself for being so weak-willed, Cass had nevertheless stared for hours on end at the photographs featured in almost every national paper, wondering over and over again how this could have happened, how she could have been such a fool.

For the photo-call, Imogen had chosen a demure but wearer-friendly white shirt and a narrow, just-above-the-knee sunflower-yellow skirt. Her shoes were low-heeled. Her red-gold hair was loosely fastened with combs and the make-up was very girl-next-door. Only the glittering eyes and sexy, knowing smile hinted that she wasn't quite as Doris Day as she might appear. That, and an altogether more voluptuous snap obtained by a press agency from 'an old acquaintance' of Imogen falling out of a too-small bikini as she played an enthusiastic game of volleyball on a Spanish beach.

'You're going in to work?' said Jack on Friday morning

when Cass had come off the phone to her producer. To boost her confidence and go some way towards assuaging his own guilt, he reached across the breakfast table and touched her hand. 'It's OK, we'll face the press together. A couple of minutes and the worst will be over.'

Sophie, glancing up from her Coco-Pops, said nothing.

Cass stared at Jack and jerked her hand away as if he'd just bitten it.

'And tell them what? That my husband's a bastard but I love him so much I'll stand by him anyway? No thanks.' She pushed her plate to one side, leaving the toast untouched. 'If they want me, they can have me as I am. I'm not pretending anything. And sod putting on a brave face.'

Jack, clearly feeling he'd done as much as could be expected, shrugged and disappeared upstairs.

'I'll come out with you,' Sophie offered, 'if you like.'

Cass managed a brief smile. 'I thought you'd never ask.'

Work was as hard to bear as Cass had expected but at least it gave her something to do. Sophie, valiantly forgoing a morning at the Natural History Museum, travelled with her to the studios and said, 'Let me go in first,' while Cass was still looking for somewhere to park.

Cass let her, knowing she would be warning everyone not to mention what was obviously uppermost in all their minds. Brisk, everyday conversation, Cass could handle. Kind words and sympathy reduced her to jelly. Far easier all round to pretend it simply hadn't happened.

But the fear of losing her nerve on-air haunted her like a playful ghost. Twenty minutes into the show Cass saw through the glass partition a vast cellophane-wrapped bouquet of white, glossy-leaved roses being delivered. They were from a darling old gentleman, a retired widower from Rotherhithe, who wrote to her at least twice a week. 'Chin up, my dear, we're all on your side,' urged the accompanying note and Cass had to grit her teeth in order not to cry. Worse was to come an hour later as she took a call from Betty of Essex. The topic of conversation was the latest Kenneth Branagh film, supposedly safe enough, but Betty in Essex took matters into her own hands.

'. . . and I know the girl on the switchboard said I mustn't mention it, but I just had to let you know, Cass, that we think you're coping wonderfully. That silly, undeserving husband of yours must be stark staring mad if he thinks—'

'Dear me, what a shame, we appear to have lost that call.' As Cass pressed the cut-off button she watched her hand begin to shake. Through the glass partition the producer visibly cringed. Cass forced a smile and leaned towards the mike. 'Still, banging on about my private life is just about the last thing we need. We'll cheer ourselves up instead with some music, shall we? How about "That Don't Impress Me Much" by Shania Twain?'

Cass had managed to get through the first day back at work but that didn't mean it had been easy. The early edition of the *Evening Standard* carried one of the photographs taken that morning. Back at home, Cass studied the picture and saw she looked every bit as haunted as she felt, which was only going to make everyone feel sorrier for her than ever. The accompanying feature, entitled, 'Would you *really* want to be told if your husband was fooling around?' just about said it all. An amazing number of women, it appeared, felt it was better not to know.

So many extra-marital affairs ran out of steam of their own accord, they argued, why risk rocking the boat? Too many wives, discovering what had been going on behind their innocent backs, over-reacted. Divorce in haste, repent at leisure, warned some raddled old agony aunt who had evidently seen a thousand marriages ruined and appeared to feel it was all the cheated-on wives' fault for kicking up a fuss in the first place.

'What would that dried-up old cow know about it anyway?' Cleo demanded a few days later.

Stuck in Milan on an assignment when the story had first broken, Cleo had only just arrived home weighed down with duty-free perfume and a vast bottle of Cointreau for Cass. Outraged by her father's behaviour, desperately protective of her mother, she was wading through the mountain of press coverage for the first time, alarming even Cass with the appalling fluidity of her language.

'No point getting your blood pressure up.' Cass attempted to make light of the situation. 'Everyone has their opinion.'

'And my opinion of Nancy Wibberley is that she's a desperate old spinster with about as much sex appeal as a wasp.'

Cleo was furious and with Jack out of the house she had no one else upon whom to vent her anger. Men were bastards, she knew that, but the brutal discovery that even her own father was one too had knocked her for six. It was unthinkable, the ultimate betrayal. And as for that double-crossing tart Imogen Trent . . .

'Come on, let's open the Cointreau.'

It was seven o'clock on Sunday evening and Cass was more than ready for a drink. When she came back into the sitting room carrying two glasses loaded with ice-cubes, Cleo was poring once more over yesterday's *Mail*. So far there had been no let-up in press interest. Everyone wanted to know what would happen next. They aren't the only ones, thought Cass. Jack had disappeared at lunchtime and she had no idea when or if he would be back. Yet when she had asked him this morning if he would be moving out soon he had seemed quite taken aback.

Cleo, who was wearing only a midriff-skimming black T-shirt and pink shorts, shivered.

'I still can't believe this has happened. How can you be so calm?'

'Do I look it?' Cass tried to smile. 'I don't feel calm.'

'You're doing a good job of hiding it then.'

Her mother looked momentarily helpless. 'But what *can* I do? Public punch-ups are hardly my scene. This is as much your father's home as mine. I can hardly boot him out into the street. I could always leave, but why the bloody hell should I, when I haven't done anything wrong?'

'Oh Mum.' Cleo, who had been sprawled across the carpet, knelt up and gave Cass a hug. As newspapers crackled beneath her legs, she saw with satisfaction that one bare knee was grinding into a front-page photograph of Imogen Trent. 'We'll sort this out somehow.' Gesturing towards the Sainsbury's carrier-bag bulging with post which Cass had yet to show her, she added, 'And everyone's on your side. That must help.'

The cards and letters had been pouring in by the bucket-load, to both the house and the radio station. It was, Cass felt, like being publicly bereaved. The outpouring of sympathy, support and sheer goodwill from complete strangers had quite overwhelmed her. Of course it helped, she kept telling herself, to know these people cared so much. But their support was, at the same time, becoming something of a burden. It was all very Disneyland, Cass felt with a surge of irritation, unknowingly echoing Jack's earlier warning to Imogen. She was Cinderella, Jack and Imogen were the Ugly Sisters. She was Snow White, Imogen was the Wicked Witch. She was Bambi's mother, Jack was the big bad hunter with his gun . . .

'I'm fed up with being the goodie,' Cass announced. With a rattle of ice-cubes she finished her Cointreau and nodded at the bottle, holding out her glass for more. Not having eaten anything all day, her stomach was now nicely aglow. 'I don't want everyone to be on my side. Why should I be the doormat, the poor little wife they all feel so bloody sorry for? Why can't I do something about it and get my own back?'

'Take a lover!' Cleo cried. Goodness, what a strange thing to be saying to one's own mother.

But Cass shook her head. 'I couldn't. Not just like that.'

'OK. Take a ravishing man and pretend.'

'Still wouldn't work.' Cass looked despondent. 'Jack knows me too well. He wouldn't be fooled for a second.'

'Is that Dad now?' Cleo's head swivelled round as the front door opened. Ready for confrontation, her pulse began to race. 'Right, I'm going to tell him what I bloody think of him.'

But it wasn't Jack, it was Sophie returning from a geology field trip in Epping Forest. As the front door banged shut behind her, the phone in the hall began to ring.

'That was Dad.' Muddy-booted, she came into the sitting room less than thirty seconds later. 'He won't be home tonight, he needs time to think. He says sorry.' Sophie's face was expressionless as she removed her spectacles, wiped the rain off the lenses with her crumpled shirt-tail and looked across at Cass. 'I did ask if he wanted to speak to you, but he was in a hurry to get off the phone.'

'I bet he couldn't get away quick enough.' Cleo's voice dripped with scorn. 'Time to think, indeed. Bastard.'

'Cleo.'

'It's OK, I have heard the word before.' Sophie slumped down onto the sofa next to Cass and pulled off her filthy boots. 'I've got one for a father, remember? And I'm sorry to have to say this but I am sick to the back teeth of hearing about it. Every single person on my field trip, teachers included, said what a shame it was about the trouble between you and Dad . . . "Your poor mother, it must be dreadful for her." Even batty old Mr Melrose cornered me on the coach on the way back to ask me to pass on his very best wishes. Ugh.' Sophie shuddered at the thought of Edgar Melrose, who had a totally gross perspiration problem and moss-green teeth. 'You're welcome to them. That man makes me feel sick.'

Cass knew she was going to have to do something, the only question was what. Whilst Sophie drank caffeine-free Coke and Cleo wolfed down a packet of chocolate HobNobs, Cass found her glass being refilled again and again with Cointreau.

'I'm going to have a terrible headache in the morning.'

'At least you'll be able to sleep.' Cleo knew her mother would otherwise spend the night tossing and turning alone in the double bed, torturing herself with thoughts of what Jack was getting up to with Imogen.

'Lady Graham-Moon,' Cass suddenly announced. She sat up, excited. 'You remember, the one who cut the sleeves off all her husband's Savile Row suits! What else was it she did?'

Cleo half-remembered. It had happened years ago, but there had been a ton of press coverage at the time. Upon discovering her own husband's infidelity, Lady Moon had wrecked his seriously expensive suits, thrown a couple of gallons of white gloss paint over his smart car and . . .

'Got it!' Cleo exclaimed. 'She raided his wine cellar and left hundreds of bottles of vintage claret on people's doorsteps, like a cross between a milkman and Father Christmas. Brilliant.' She grinned at the perfection of the idea. 'That's what we'll do to Dad.'

'Except we don't have a wine cellar and cutting the arms off Marks & Spencer suits doesn't have quite the same ring,' Sophie pointed out. Keen to do something constructive but ever-practical, she went on, 'And you can't copy someone else's revenge anyway. It lacks impact.'

Five glasses of Cointreau were making their own kind of impact on Cass. She was enjoying this; deciding not to be an object of sympathy any more and planning a suitable punishment for Jack was cheering her up no end, but she was feeling decidedly woozy. She had to blink twice and concentrate hard on her watch to make out that it was, astonishingly, past midnight.

'Think I'm going to have to go to bed.' She enunciated slowly and carefully so as not to make a mistake. 'This is naughty, Cleo, you shouldn't have opened that bottle. Don't either of you dare sell this story to the papers . . .'

'Night, Mum.' Sophie leaned across and kissed Cass's flushed cheek. 'Sleep well.'

'We'll think up more ways to teach your father a lesson

tomorrow,' Cass promised fondly. 'He's quite vain, you know. How about shaving off one of his eyebrows while he's asleep?'

The grandfather clock in the hall was striking three as Sophie and Cleo crept past it, their arms full of bags containing everything they needed in order to carry out the necessary revenge. Not that there was any need to creep; upstairs, helped along by the Cointreau, Cass was out for the count. If she hadn't stirred when Sophie, up in the loft earlier, had tripped and fallen over a crate of china, she was hardly likely to be disturbed by the click of the front door.

With the car loaded up, Cleo drove and Sophie navigated, consulting her battered *A-Z* with a torch as they made their way through the almost entirely deserted city streets.

Chapter 17

It had been Sophie's idea, sparked off by Cass's parting shot, to play on their father's vanity.

'The trouble with the Graham-Moon thing', she had explained to Cleo when Cass had gone up to bed, 'is that it made the woman's husband sound actually quite fanciable. If he wasn't so ancient, of course.'

'As far as you're concerned, seventeen's ancient.'

'Yes, but you know what I mean.' Sophie shrugged. 'He might be ancient but he wears fab suits, drives a swish car and drinks bloody good claret. Sounds like James Bond.'

Cleo had twiddled her fingers. Being talked down to by a fourteen-year-old was amazingly irritating.

'So?'

'So what would seriously wind Dad up is making him look stupid – more Mr Bean than Bond – so that people laugh at him . . .'

They found Imogen's flat without too much trouble, the only one in the silent, narrow street with empty window-boxes and clinical-looking blinds instead of curtains, as Sophie had spotted in one of the photographs in Saturday's *Express*. Parking the car at the far end of the street they unloaded everything from the boot and padded noiselessly back to their target.

'Is he here?' Sophie whispered.

'Of course he's here.' Dumping the bags on the pavement

and propping the stepladder noiselessly up against the garage door, Cleo rolled up the sleeves of her black sweatshirt. At least it wasn't raining.

'What if we get arrested?'

Cleo grinned. She had a particular talent for dazzling policemen which, considering the way she drove, was just as well. One glimpse of her big, conker-brown eyes and apologetic smile was generally enough to soften the heart of the meanest traffic cop. Besides, was what they were doing now so terribly wrong?

'They can't arrest us.' Confidently, she began to climb the ladder. 'We're playing a harmless prank on Daddy, that's all. Big deal.'

'*She* won't like it.' Sophie gazed up at the darkened windows of Imogen's flat.

'So let her sue.' Cleo really couldn't care less. 'Good luck to her. Come on, don't stand there like a prune . . . pass me up one end of that rope.'

Jack woke with a start at six thirty. Imogen, having thrown back the yellow duvet, was out of bed and heading for the window.

'What's the matter?'

'Noises outside.' She approached the window with caution, ducking down to avoid being seen in all her naked glory. 'I can hear people laughing.'

'Surely not at this time of the morning.'

It was meant to be a joke but even as he said it Jack realized with a pang of guilt that someone who definitely wouldn't be laughing this morning was Cass. He hadn't even had the guts to speak to her on the phone last night. But he'd been desperate; all he knew was he couldn't carry on much longer like this. He loved Imogen. He loved Cass too, but the two kinds of love were poles apart. It was like being asked to choose between two exquisite dishes on a Michelin-starred menu. Jack wanted both, but that wasn't allowed. And this wasn't a menu. He had to decide in which direction his whole future lay . . .

'Shit!' Imogen dropped from her semi-crouched position onto all fours. Yanking the blinds shut, she scuttled like a crab away from the window. 'I don't know what the hell's going on but there have to be fifty photographers outside. Bloody Cass must have blabbed that you were staying the night.'

Jack felt sick. 'No. Why would she say that? What good would it do her?'

'Well, someone told them.' Imogen knew scorned women didn't always need a good reason. Scorned women had a habit of behaving irrationally. Her mouth narrowed in annoyance as she tugged an oversized orange T-shirt over her head. Her stuffy bosses at *Hi!* weren't thrilled with her anyway for having waltzed off with the husband of one of her recent interviewees, feeling that it reflected badly on the image of the magazine and could deter future candidates. The prospect of losing her extremely well-paid job wasn't funny, and it was a possibility that was strengthening by the minute. Why, Imogen wondered, should there be this many photographers outside her flat at such a God-awful hour? More to the point, why the hell *were* they all laughing like drains?

The doorbell started shrilling less than ten minutes later.

'Come on, Jack, we know you're in there,' a gravelly voice

shouted through the letter box. 'We aren't leaving so you may as well come out now.' The voice cackled with helpless laughter. 'Get dressed and come and see what's been going on out here while you've been . . . otherwise occupied.'

'You go.' How he wished now that he hadn't come here. If there was one thing Jack hated more than being laughed at it was not knowing why.

But Imogen, who didn't have to go to work today, put her foot down.

'No. It's you they want.' Defensively, she began rummaging through the wardrobe. 'You go.'

The moment Jack opened the front door he was dazzled by a firework display of flashbulbs going off. Some of the photographers even cheered; that haughty, irritable expression was perfect. He really was making their day.

When Jack turned, he saw why.

He guessed at once that Cleo must have been behind it; this wasn't Cass's style. No, it was definitely Cleo who had raided the loft, unearthing just about everything an intellectual, image-conscious forty-year-old wouldn't want to be seen.

Two washing-lines had been rigged up along the front of the flat. Pegged to them were all Jack's old Showaddywaddy, Rubettes and Osmonds LPs, along with a pair of flared, raspberry-pink loons, several flowered shirts with pointy, eight-inch collars, a pair of yellow three-inch platform shoes, a lime green *Partridge Family* T-shirt and a Bay City Rollers scarf. There was also a creased old photograph, taken at a party during his university days, of him absolutely plastered, waving a pair of red frilly knickers in one hand and pretending to kiss a bulldog.

A huge banner, slung across the garage, bore the hand-painted message: *Sometimes I have no taste* . . .

They were all Jack's things, parcelled up and bunged in the attic because Cass could never bear to throw anything away. Completely unfairly, he saw that Cleo had also hung up a bottle of fake tanning cream, a huge medallion and a nylon toupee left over from last year's Christmas party, none of which he had ever worn in his life. The press, however, didn't know that. They were still busy using up roll after roll of film and cracking jokes about the pegged-up banana-yellow platform shoes. Jack wondered if he would ever be allowed to live this down.

'Come on then, Jack, how about a statement?' bawled one of the reporters at the back. 'You're not denying this stuff's yours, then?' He grinned at his companions. 'Not even the Donny Osmond LP? How about giving us a quick blast of "Puppy Love", eh? Just to remind us how it goes.'

Cass, at home later that afternoon, knew she should be working through the script for tomorrow's show. Instead she found herself on her hands and knees in the kitchen, manically emptying out and scrubbing clean all the cupboards. Staring into space and endlessly going over and over in her mind the events of the past week was doing no good at all; far better to wear herself out physically and have something to show at the end of it – even if it was only surgically sterile cupboards.

The phone rang just as she finished emptying the contents of the larder out onto the kitchen floor. Cass had to tread a careful path through the bags of sugar, rice and pasta in order to answer it.

'Hello, it's me. Imogen.'

'Oh.' Cass wished she hadn't picked the phone up now.

'Look, are you alone?'

'Why?'

Imogen sighed. 'Come on, things are getting out of hand. We need to talk.'

Cass wondered if the break-up, after over twenty years, of a perfectly good marriage counted as one of the things getting out of hand. She had had imaginary conversations in her head with Imogen over the past few days but she couldn't even begin to imagine how it would feel actually to see her again. Imogen certainly had plenty of nerve, but then she already knew that.

'OK.' Cass gazed at the piles of food on the floor. However had they managed to accumulate seventeen tins of pineapple chunks?

'If you're alone, I'll come round now.'

'OK.'

'I'm in a cab at the end of the road,' said Imogen. 'I've just checked there's no one at the bottom of your drive, so it's safe.'

Extraordinary, thought Cass. Twenty-two tins of chopped tomatoes. She nodded into the phone.

'OK.'

True to her word, Imogen arrived at the back door less than a minute later. As she let her into the kitchen Cass wondered if Imogen had done it on purpose, not even giving her time to run a brush through her hair or wash the Ajax off her hands. Still, at least Imogen was used to seeing the kitchen in a mess.

'I may as well say this.' Pulling out a chair, Imogen sat down and carefully smoothed her blue skirt over black-stockinged thighs. 'I am sorry you had to find out. You weren't meant to. I was perfectly happy for the affair to remain a secret.' She paused, her fingers brushing against a thin gold chain around her neck. 'I certainly didn't plan any of this, in case you were wondering. It wasn't supposed to happen.'

'Oh,' said Cass with just a trace of irony, 'that's all right then.'

'I know, I know.' Imogen sounded impatient. 'But it *has* happened, so we do need to sort things out. For your sake as much as ours.'

'Ours,' Cass repeated, marvelling at her easy use of the word. 'You mean you and Jack?'

Imogen's eyes flickered. 'For all our sakes. This morning's pantomime, for example. Did your daughter even stop to think of the effect it could have on Jack's career?'

'Daughters. They did it together. And no,' Cass's voice was like chipped ice, 'probably not. How about screwing some young bimbo journalist? Do you think that'll do his career the world of good?'

Imogen flushed, the jibe catching her off guard.

'I'm not a bimbo. And I didn't come here to fight.'

No, just gloat, Cass thought bitterly, sitting back down amongst the tins of Scottish raspberries and Ambrosia creamed rice so beloved of Sophie. She glanced up at Imogen, sleek and businesslike with her hair swept up in a bronze barrette.

'So why did you come here?'

'It's Jack. This isn't easy for him.'

Cass blinked. 'Is this some kind of a joke?'

'He's torn,' Imogen said bluntly. 'He's afraid to leave you because he thinks you won't be able to cope, but I'm the one he wants to be with. This isn't one of those silly flings, Cass. Neither of us wanted it to happen . . . it just did. Jack loved you, but now he loves me more.' Pale now, she leaned forward, her eyes alight with passion. 'And if you love Jack you'll let him go. Torture him by clinging on, Cass, and you'll only end up making him ill.'

This was outrageous. More humiliating still, it was coming from a girl Cass had taken such an instinctive liking to from the start. She had even nagged Jack to make an effort to be nice to Imogen when he had objected to her being invited to his party.

Maybe Jack was right, what was happening now *was* all her own fault.

Pop, pop, went the plastic on a bag of Basmati rice as Cass's roughened fingernails sank through. She wanted to hurl something at Imogen's head but if she threw the rice it would seem like a wedding and if she whacked her with a tin of tomatoes Imogen would only bleed everywhere, keel over unconscious and probably die out of spite.

'OK, you've said what you wanted to say.' Cass wiped her perspiring palms on the sides of her old Levis. 'You can leave now.'

Imogen stood up.

'I really am sorry,' she said, 'but if your marriage had been as good as you thought it was, this could never have happened in the first place. You can't only blame me, Cass. I didn't kidnap Jack. He wanted me as much as I wanted him. But I'm still sorry. I'm really not as horrible as you think.'

'Oh yes you are,' whispered Cass.

Chapter 18

It had been a nightmare of a day for Jack and the evening was turning out even worse. The press were back baying at the gate, the phone didn't stop ringing and the *Standard* had him on the front page. By tomorrow when the rest of the papers followed suit he would be a national laughing-stock.

Cleo and Sophie, meanwhile, were being hailed as heroines and Sean was finding the whole thing too funny for words.

'That was a researcher for GMTV wanting to know if you two could do Wednesday,' he announced, grinning his head off as he came back to the dining table. 'I told them you were already doing *Richard and Judy*.' As he passed Sophie, he rumpled her short hair. 'Who'd have thought it, eh? Our little Sofe, a celebrity in her own right! She'll be getting herself a minder next.'

'Ruffle my hair once more,' said Sophie equably, 'and I'll punch you.'

'Tell whoever it is to go away,' Jack ordered as the phone began ringing again, 'and for God's sake, leave it off the hook. What are you doing?' he demanded as Cleo, rising to her feet, took her dinner plate with her.

'Answering the phone.' Cleo, who was still barely speaking to her father, was brusque. 'It's what you wanted, isn't it?'

'Put your plate down.'

'If I leave it here, Sean will pinch all my king prawns.'

Exasperated, Jack said, 'Don't be so bloody childish.'

'Excuse me,' jeered Cleo, 'you think *I'm* the one acting like a child?'

'Please don't.' Wearily, Cass tried to stop another fight blowing up. Even attempting a normal family dinner was hopeless just now.

Sean, next to her, had spilled red wine on the tablecloth. Mopping it up with the nearest thing to hand, the *Evening Standard*, he pulled out a couple of centre pages and started to laugh.

'Oh brilliant, they've got a cartoon here of Dad interviewing Prince Charles. Dad's wearing six medallions and bloody great platform boots and he's saying to Prince Charles: "But don't you worry that people might not take you seriously?" '

'Very funny.' Jack glared at Cleo, who was back smirking in the doorway. 'You've forgotten your precious plate.'

'Too much excitement.' Cleo's expression was jubilant. 'That was a friend of mine who works for Channel 4. She was just ringing to say if we want a really good laugh to tune into Rory Bremner next week.'

During the course of the evening Cass had developed a thumping headache. Unable to cope with the friction downstairs she made herself a cup of tea, forced down two aspirins and went up to bed.

Jack followed her.

'It's only nine o'clock.'

'I'm tired.' Cass shook her head, barely able to meet his gaze. 'I'm so tired of it all.'

'What?' Jack looked alarmed.

Cass, who had been in the process of undressing, realized she didn't want him to see her naked. Suddenly, her almost middle-aged body had become something to be ashamed of. At the same time she hated Jack for making her feel that way.

'Oh, not that kind of tired.' She forced herself to take her jeans off but climbed into bed still wearing the white T-shirt. Mockingly she said, 'I'm not going to kill myself, if that's what's bothering you. If you want to leave, Jack, it's fine by me. I'm not keeping you here . . . and we're perfectly capable of managing without you.'

The pain showed in Jack's dark eyes. 'But you are keeping me here, just by being here yourself. I don't want to leave, Cass. I still love you.'

'So what are you saying? That you'll tell Imogen it's over, it's all been a terrible mistake, you're going to stay with me and never have anything to do with her again?'

A shadow fell across his face.

'I can't . . .'

'Oh well then,' Cass said evenly, 'that's easy. Off you go.'

'But—'

'And don't forget your toothbrush.'

Cass turned away to hide the tears pouring down her face. She hadn't even known they were there, they'd just suddenly started gushing out. And the oddest thoughts were going through her mind: if this really was it, the absolute end, she would never see Jack cleaning his teeth again. She would never hear him sing in the shower again. They would never *ever* make love together again . . .

It was this last thought, the realization that they had made love for the very last time and she hadn't even known it, that upset Cass most of all. If only she'd known, she would have paid more attention, concentrated properly and made sure she remembered every moment, no matter how insignificant it may have seemed at the time. Damn, Cass thought as the tears continued to spill down her cheeks, it's not fair, he should have *warned* me . . .

Jack couldn't bear it. For all her softness Cass wasn't a crier. These were the first tears he had seen her shed all week.

When he pulled her into his arms she let out a low moan of grief, hiding her wet face against the front of his blue-and-white striped shirt.

But Jack lifted her chin, forcing her to look up at him. This was the woman he had loved unwaveringly for twenty-four years. Behind her on the bedside table were framed photographs of their three children as babies, children they had created between them and whom he also loved beyond all imagination.

Having to bear the brunt during the past few days of Cleo's fury and Sophie's quiet disgust had been seriously getting to Jack. The fact that as a family they had always got on so well together only made the current situation that much harder to bear. He had hurt them just as much as he had hurt Cass and they weren't afraid to let him know it. If I leave, thought Jack, could I ever forgive myself, let alone expect them to forgive me?

'What are you doing?' Cass gasped, though as her white T-shirt was pulled off over her head it became pretty obvious.

'I love you.' Jack pushed her gently back against the massed pillows. Having removed his own shirt and flung it behind him, he kissed Cass as he hadn't kissed her for years.

Their love-making was only heightened by the strength of their emotions. Helplessly, Cass raked his back with her fingernails. As Jack's climax approached she had to smother his groans against her shoulder so the whole street wouldn't hear. All the pent-up hurt and anger of the past week was spilled out as passion took over, blotting out the unimaginable pain.

'Oh my God,' Cass sighed, her ribcage still heaving, when it was finally over. 'That was . . . I don't know what that was . . . I can't think of the word . . . incredible.'

Jack, beside her, grinned. 'Now I see why people break up to make up. Cass, now we really need to talk.' He ran his tongue over dry lips. 'Are you as thirsty as I am? If I don't get a drink . . .'

Lazily, Cass nodded. 'Please. Orange juice, splash of tonic, loads of ice.'

'Two minutes.' Sliding out of bed, Jack reached for his dark-blue towelling robe. He couldn't resist leaning across the bed and kissing Cass's warm, flushed cheek. Then, more lingeringly, he found her mouth.

'Orange juice,' ordered Cass, smiling. 'Before I dehydrate.'

Downstairs, because one meal was never enough, Sophie was making one of her beloved peanut-butter-and-honey sandwiches. Glancing up as Jack came into the kitchen, taking in the expression on his face, the towelling robe and tousled dark hair, she said hopefully, 'Is this good news?'

Jack smiled. Kids today.

'Could be, sweetheart. Your mother wants a glass of orange juice.'

Sophie winced. 'I've just finished it.'

But all her father did was open the fridge and take out a bottle of Bollinger instead. Reaching up to the cupboard for two glasses he said, 'Maybe this is more appropriate anyway.'

'Oh Dad, I'm so glad.' It was Sophie's turn to spout helpless tears. Abandoning the sandwich – which was as thick as a dictionary – she flung her arms around Jack's neck and breathed dreadful peanut-butter fumes all over him. 'This is the best news *ever*.'

Jack kissed the top of her head and patted her bony spine before gently disentangling himself. 'I know, I know. Come on now, don't want to keep your mother waiting. You could probably do with an early night yourself,' he added mildly. 'To make up for yesterday.'

'Orange juice,' Cass protested when she saw the dark-green bottle, beaded with condensation, in his hand. 'Jack, what on earth do you want to open that for? I said I was *thirsty*.'

'We can celebrate, can't we?' Dropping the glasses into her lap, feeling as if a great weight had fallen from his shoulders, Jack began to ease the cork out with his thumbs. He couldn't stop grinning. 'Cass, it's all over. Behind us. I won't see Imogen again. You're my wife and I love you. We belong together . . .'

Cass stared at him, unable to believe what she was hearing.

'You mean I've *won*?'

The cork shot out of the bottle with a whoosh, ricocheting off two walls and a light-fitting before landing in one of Cass's strappy high-heeled evening shoes.

'Glasses, glasses,' shouted Jack as foam cascaded over his hands, but who really cared if the champagne spilled out? He was back and that was all that mattered. God knows how

Imogen would take it; he couldn't think about that now. He would simply have to make her understand.

'Well,' said Cass, 'thanks, as they say, but no thanks.'

The contents of the bottle, where he must have shaken it running up the stairs, were still overflowing onto the duvet. Jack stopped smiling.

'What?'

'You heard.' Cass spoke clearly, all trace of tears gone. 'You wanted to leave, Jack. You know you wanted to, you just couldn't bring yourself to make the decision. So I'm doing it for you. There you are, see? I'm making it easy for you. All you have to do is pack your things and go.'

It was blissful, watching the expression on his face. Such a handsome face, thought Cass, steeling herself to see it through. He was only forty, still young, still toe-curlingly attractive.

Jack stared at her. 'I've just said, I don't want to go.'

'Too late.' The duvet was safely tucked up over her breasts. Cass folded her arms as if insulating herself from attack. 'I want you to.'

'But why?' Jack was stunned, clearly unable to believe this was happening. 'I've just told Sophie—'

'Better go and un-tell her, then.' Furious that he should have so pointlessly raised Sophie's hopes, Cass felt the heat begin to rise in her cheeks. 'How bloody *dare* you, Jack? Without even bothering to ask me first! How bloody patronizing can you get?'

'Cass, please—'

'No,' she shouted. 'No way. Forget it! Why should I forgive you for screwing that little tart? Why should I be the one to have to spend the next fifty years listening to you blaming *me*

126

for ruining *your* life? Jack, you want her, you can have her. You're forty years old. Divorce me, marry Imogen and when you're ninety you can celebrate your golden wedding anniversary with her. Don't you see? You can start a whole *new* life—'

'Stop this,' Jack hissed, his eyes very dark against the sudden pallor of his face. 'You're hysterical.'

'Hysterical ha-ha or hysterical scream-scream?' Bitterly, Cass glared back at him, her whole body rigid with fury. 'You're the one who's hysterical ha-ha, Jack. You're the one everyone's laughing at.'

'What about just now?' he shouted. 'We made love . . . didn't that *mean* anything to you?'

'Of course.' Cass was mocking him now. It was so easy to be cruel. 'Just what I wanted, to go out with a bang. I thought it finished things off nicely.'

Chapter 19

Cleo knew she had done the right thing, letting Linda discover for herself just how eager Colin was to be unfaithful to her, but it had still been a depressing experience. Were all men, she wondered, as untrustworthy as that? Were they physically incapable of remaining faithful to one woman?

When Maisie, her booker at the agency, began asking tentative questions about the way she had gone about catching Colin out, Cleo backed away in despair.

'Oh Maisie, no. Not Tom, I can't bear it.'

'Not Tom.' Maisie smothered a giggle. At forty she was about as far removed from lithe blond Cass as it was possible for a forty-year-old to be, but Tom adored every shapeless grey inch of his beloved wife. 'No, it's my mother's new boyfriend. I'm sure he's up to no good but she's smitten. If you ask me, he's after her money.'

'Hmm. So it's in a good cause.' Cleo, perched on the edge of Maisie's desk, drummed her heels thoughtfully against the waste-paper basket and began to cheer up. 'What is he, ancient?' She'd met Maisie's mother, a vivacious sixty-something widow, a couple of times and liked her a lot. 'Some kind of Terry-Thomas bounder with a leer and a waxed moustache?'

'Guess again,' said Maisie wryly. 'His name's Damien and he's younger than me.'

* * *

Damien Maxwell-Horne, with his expensively highlighted hair, overpowering aftershave and boyish crinkle-at-the-corner eyes was, as far as Cleo was concerned, guilty from the word go. Such suspiciously blue eyes must be the result of tinted contact lenses.

Apart from anything else, anyone who wore bright red socks had to be all bad.

Damien, lounging against one of the black marble pillars of the Kellaway wine bar in Fulham, exactly where Maisie had said he would be, was pitifully easy to pick up. All Cleo needed to do was saunter up to the bar, order herself a lemonade and choose an empty table for two by the window.

He was over faster than you could say slimeball.

'You're Cleo Mandeville.'

Cleo widened her eyes and smiled up at him. Of all the dumb statements in all the world, he'd had to come out with this one.

'So I am.'

'Damien Maxwell-Horne. I must say, you are even more beautiful than your photographs.' Having taken Cleo's hand, he showed no sign of giving it back. 'I'm a huge fan of yours, by the way.' The crinkly-eyed grin widened. 'I'm also allergic to the sight of gorgeous girls buying their own drinks. You can't possibly drink that stuff anyway ... please, let me get you something decent.'

Cleo hesitated. 'Well . . .'

'Come on.' Damien gave her a complicit smile. 'How about a glass of chilled Chardonnay?'

'Chardonnay would be great. Thank you, Mr Maxwell-Horne. You're very kind. I'm supposed to be meeting a girlfriend but I was half an hour late getting here myself.' Cleo glanced at her watch and gave a shrug of resignation. 'Looks as if I've been stood up.'

'Her loss,' Damien smugly announced. 'My gain. Let me tell you, Cleo, anyone who stands you up, male or female, must be off their heads. One Chardonnay coming up. And,' he added with mock severity, 'call me Damien, please.'

Annoyingly, Damien was having far too good a time greeting everyone he knew who came into the wine bar, and making sure they noticed who he was with, to say anything wholly incriminating. Cleo, stuck with him until he did, forced herself not to yawn. Maisie's mother, Harriet, must really be smitten if she could put up with hearing the same jokes almost every fifteen minutes. OK, so Damien was good-looking enough in a *Baywatch* kind of way, but if Harriet thought a man like him could love her for the maturity of her mind she had to be kidding. Harriet's last facelift, thought Cleo, had evidently gone to her head.

'So you've been divorced for two years.' Valiantly she soldiered on, covering her glass with her hand as Damien tried to top it up for the fourth time. 'Any plans to try again or was once enough?'

'Twice,' smirked Damien, 'and that's more than enough. Won't catch me getting trapped again. Play the field and have some fun, that's my motto. Unless you're volunteering for the job . . .'

Cleo smiled and managed not to kick his legs from under him. Last week Damien had suggested to Harriet that they might get married. The fact that he was having trouble finding financial backing for some new business project in Baltic

Wharf and Harriet had inherited squillions from her own beloved late husband had, of course, nothing whatsoever to do with it.

But the doors had swung open, giving Damien yet another heaven-sent opportunity to show her off.

'Hey, it's the lads.' Swivelling round in delight, squeezing Cleo's hand as he waved to attract their attention, he almost knocked a brimming ashtray into her lap. 'Sorry, sorry. Great crew, the lads from the rugby club! Hey boys, my shout . . . c'mon, what'll it be? Sweetheart, how about you? Another Chardonnay?'

Cleo was really beginning to wish she hadn't come here. Doing Harriet a major favour was one thing, but this was horrible. Her own integrity was being put on the line. What if people were secretly laughing at her?

Only the mental image of Maisie, sad-eyed and helpless to do anything herself, kept her there. Maisie was a darling who had done her endless small favours in the three years they had known each other. Having come this far, Cleo knew she couldn't let her down now.

Enjoying the momentary breather while Damien was ostentatiously waving tenners across the bar, Cleo wasn't overjoyed to see one of his rugby-playing 'lads' looking towards her. With that sunbleached blond hair and impressive body he might look OK but Cleo had no illusions. Any friend of Damien's was bound to be as awful as he was. Men like that always went around in packs.

'Hi. My name's Joel Grant.' Introducing himself in a low voice barely audible above the yells and whoops coming from the bar, he smiled briefly at Cleo as he took Damien's seat. 'I was introduced to your brother a few weeks ago, coincidentally. He's been out a few times with my sister.'

So that was his big claim to fame. Since Sean must have been out with half the girls in England in his time, as a boast it lacked novelty value. Cleo only prayed he wasn't about to start regaling her with Sean-style jokes.

Warily, because this was what Sean's fans had a boring tendency to do, she said, 'I see.'

But all Joel Grant did was move closer and lower his voice further still.

'Look, I know we don't know each other and it probably isn't my place to say this, but I'm not sure getting involved with Damien is such a wise move. Take it from me,' he went on, 'you could do a hell of a lot better.'

Like you, you mean, Cleo thought. It was obvious what he was trying to do. She'd been right: Damien's friends were every bit as charmless as she had imagined.

Disgusted by this one's ability to badmouth someone who was at this very moment buying him a drink, she gave him her coldest stare.

'Are you always this loyal to your friends?'

He sighed. 'Look, I'm not—'

'Please don't,' drawled Cleo. She stood up. 'You were right the first time; what I do with Damien is none of your business. And I'd far rather make my own decisions than be told what to do by someone like you.'

'Hey up, what's going on here then?' Smirking and trailing rugby players in his wake, Damien returned to the table. 'Hands off, if you don't mind! I saw her first.'

'Don't worry, she's all yours.' With a derisive smile, the

blond giant vacated his chair. 'If you ask me, you make a perfect match.'

Damien preened. 'I think so too. Sweetheart?' Observing the expression on Cleo's face, he touched her arm. 'Hey babe, you OK?'

He had called her babe. Ugh, *ugh*.

'Just hungry. My fault, I missed lunch.'

Cleo knew she was breaking one of her own rules, but if she didn't get out of here soon she would explode.

'Hungry? No sweat, we'll finish this drink and leave. I know a terrific little Mexican—'

Cleo gritted her teeth. 'I'm hungry now.'

Terrified of losing her, Damien pushed his untouched drink to one side.

'Hey, no problem, we'll eat now. Sorry, chaps, gotta love you and leave you! Come on, sweetheart, let's go.'

The man was supposed to ask the woman to dinner. That was the whole point of the exercise; he was meant to make all the running. Cleo, unable to even summon up much of an appetite, realized she'd blown the whole thing. She was haunted, too, by the memory of the look on the blond giant's face as he had watched her go, a look of unremitting disdain. Furious with herself for not being able to put it out of her mind, Cleo gave up on the meal and heaved a sigh.

'I know what you need.' Not realizing he had spilled guacamole down his already hideous pink-and-yellow patterned tie, Damien crinkled his eyes at her and decided to take the plunge. 'You need cheering up. Look, a great mate of mine has a villa in Portugal. I can use the place whenever I like. How about getting away from it all for a few days?'

Cleo looked up, her pulse quickening.

'Getting away? Who with?'

'Me, of course!' He roared with laughter. 'Sweetheart, I mean it, you look as if you could do with the break. How about next week? Seriously, this chap wouldn't mind. I know he's busy here for the next fortnight,' Damien added in confiding tones, 'so it'd just be the two of us. How does that sound to you, hmm?'

Almost too good to be true, thought Cleo joyfully. Aloud she said, 'Whereabouts in Portugal?'

'The Algarve. A pretty little place near Albufeira.' Eagerly Damien leaned across the table. 'Private gardens, own pool, maid service . . . hang on, what are you doing?'

'It's called money.' Cleo was pulling tenners out of her purse. 'My very own.'

'You don't have to pay!' Smiling but confused, Damien tried to push the notes back in. 'I told you, the villa belongs to a pal . . . it won't cost us a penny.'

'This is to pay for my dinner,' said Cleo, relieved that at last she could go home. 'And the villa doesn't belong to any pal, it belongs to a very nice lady called Harriet Coburn who deserves an awful lot better than a two-faced, lying little turd like you.'

Chapter 20

God, men really were the pits. Finding herself the following lunch-time with an afternoon free, Cleo planned a cheering-up session of serious spending in South Molton Street. Then Sean had the nerve to disrupt even that, phoning her mid-morning and practically begging her to meet him for lunch.

'I'm doing a charity thing at midday at the club. Meet me there,' he said, sounding more subdued than Cleo had heard him sound for years. 'Please.'

If he was saying please, it had to be serious. Consoling herself with the thought that at least she would be saving thousands of pounds, Cleo arrived at Comedy Inc. at one o'clock, just as Sean was winding up his act.

'. . . and for everyone who is thinking of giving up fags,' he told the audience, there to raise money for a new hospital body scanner, 'I'd just like to say it's fucking hell with Nicotinell. But try anyway, it's worth it. Thank you very much, ladies and gentlemen. You've been great.'

'What's this?' Cleo mocked when he joined her at the bar five minutes later. 'Moral lectures on smoking from sinful Sean Mandeville? We don't have to leave yet, I've just ordered drinks.'

'Never mind the drinks, let's just get out of here.' Sean, who had her by the arm, was dragging her towards the door. 'I need a cigarette.'

He took her to The Blue Goose because Cleo had already warned him that giving up South Molton Street for the sake of lunch with a lousy brother meant making it seriously worth her while. By the time their first course arrived, Sean was stubbing out his fourth Marlboro.

'Let's hope you manage to raise the money for that scanner,' Cleo observed. Then, glimpsing the troubled look in his dark eyes, she softened. 'OK, so something's wrong. What is it?'

'I've been seeing this girl . . . well, kind of.' Finding himself unable to eat, Sean buried the quail breasts beneath a mound of glistening rocket. 'The thing is, I was really crazy about her to begin with. I thought she was amazing. Couldn't stop thinking about her. Dammit,' he admitted crossly, 'I used to drive past her house in the middle of the night just because it made me feel better.'

'Bloody hell, sounds like love.' Cleo was genuinely amazed. 'So you are human after all. Why haven't we met her? Oh . . .' Her eyebrows rose another inch as the unthinkable occurred to her. 'Don't say she's dumped you!'

If it was sympathy he'd been after, Sean realized he'd picked the wrong person to tell. Cleo was about as sympathetic as Jaws.

'No,' he snapped back, irritated by her obvious amusement. 'If anything, the other way round. She's dumped *on* me.'

'She, she. Does she have a name or do we just know her as mystery woman?' Cleo, her own appetite undimmed, tucked greedily into her langoustines. She licked garlic mayonnaise from her fingers. 'And what's the big problem anyway? I suppose she's married.'

'No. Pregnant.'

Cleo stopped licking her fingers.

'Oops.'

'And her name's Pandora,' said Sean. 'No box jokes.'

'So what's going to . . . happen?' To illustrate her meaning, Cleo nodded in the general direction of Sean's stomach.

'Bit late for a vasectomy, if that's what you're hinting at.' But he managed a wan smile. 'She wants to have the baby.'

Cleo thought things through while Sean lit up another cigarette.

'So you're absolutely crazy about this amazing girl, maybe even in love with her, and now she's pregnant. Is that really so terrible? If she was some hideous old dog maybe you should be worried, but—'

'But she isn't so why don't I do something drastic like marry her?' Sean had thought of nothing else for the last two weeks. 'Cleo, I'm twenty years old. I'm too young to settle down and play happy families. OK, so I was crazy about her at first, but you know what I'm like . . . by next week I could have met someone else. I mean, can you seriously see me doing the goo-goo bit and pushing a pram?'

Cleo's eyes glittered. As if she needed it, here she was being faced with yet another shining example of how completely and utterly shitty the male sex could be.

'Don't be so bloody selfish. And I'm still eating.' Reaching across the table, she tweaked the smouldering cigarette from his fingers and brutally stubbed it out. 'Has it even occurred to you that Pandora might not be able to see herself pushing a pram either? The thing is, Sean, when you sleep with someone you take a risk and if you get caught out you face the consequences. And don't make out she dumped on you,' Cleo went on bitterly. 'Why do men always blame the women when things go wrong? You should have used a condom.'

'I did,' Sean hissed back. He prayed the couple at the next table weren't able to hear every word. 'I bloody did, OK? So this isn't my fault.'

Cleo trawled the last langoustine through a sea of mayonnaise.

'Should have worn two.'

It was hard to tell who was the more surprised when Pandora opened the front door. The last person in the world she had expected to see there was Cleo Mandeville, more glamorous in the flesh than in any of her photos and sick-makingly thin in an off-the-shoulder black top and pink flares.

Cleo in turn gazed down in amazement at the girl who had answered the doorbell, plump in a long loose-fitting yellow T-shirt, bare-legged and definitely pregnant.

'*You're* Pandora?'

The baby in Pandora's stomach squirmed.

'Yes. And I know who you are.'

'Good Lord,' said Cleo, frank as ever. 'Sean's told me about you but he didn't mention you were—'

'Black?' Pandora smiled. 'It's OK, you can say it. I already know.' Then, warily, she added, 'Does it . . . um, make a huge difference?'

'Don't be daft.' Cleo followed her through to the living room, heaved her shoulder-bag onto the floor and flopped down. 'It's just typical of Sean, not saying it. Like forgetting to mention someone's bald, or only has one leg. He's useless like that. He doesn't know I'm here, either. We had lunch earlier and he told me about the baby.' She beamed. 'I said I wanted your address to send a congratulations card.'

Cleo had made herself quite comfortable on the green-and-white striped sofa. Stupidly Pandora hoped she wouldn't dislodge the cushions piled up at each corner and catch sight of the frayed bits underneath.

'I don't think Sean feels congratulations are much in order.' Pandora tried to sound matter-of-fact about it, to disguise the pain she couldn't help feeling. 'He isn't thrilled about this. As I suppose you've already heard,' she added ruefully. 'A baby doesn't quite fit in with his image. Neither, of course, do I.'

'Oh, but . . .'

Smiling at the appalled expression on Cleo's exquisite face, Pandora said, 'It's OK, I don't mean black. If I were Halle Berry I dare say I'd be fine. But I'm not, I'm four years older than Sean and a waitress to boot. Hardly glamorous.'

'If I loved somebody,' Cleo declared with passion, 'I wouldn't care what they did for a living. Look, when Sean started telling me about you he said you were amazing. He was so besotted he used to drive past this house just to feel close to you . . .'

'And now he's scared silly.' Pandora nodded, to show she understood and accepted the situation. 'I wasn't part of his plan. Girlfriend and screaming baby not included.'

'He *is* scared, dammit,' Cleo admitted with a gusty sigh. 'At least you know. I'm sorry, he's my brother but he can be hopeless. That's why I had to come here today, to warn you in case you didn't realize it already. Just don't get your hopes up too much.'

'I won't.'

'Honestly, men are such weasels.' Shaking her head in despair, Cleo absent-mindedly helped herself to an apricot from the fruit bowl. 'Even the ones you think are all right to begin with.'

'You seem to know how to deal with them, anyway.'

Pandora was smiling. For a second Cleo thought she'd somehow heard about her recent adventures, checking out the unfaithfulness of men. Wondering how she could possibly know – and praying Pandora wasn't about to request trying it out on Sean, who would undoubtedly fail – she looked blank.

'Your father,' Pandora prompted. 'Stringing all that stuff up outside Imogen Trent's flat. I thought it was completely brilliant.'

'Didn't help, though.' Gloomily, Cleo started popping seedless grapes into her mouth. 'He still moved in with her. Poor Mum's trying to put on such a brave face but she's crumbling inside.'

Pandora nodded. 'Sean told me. That's why he hasn't mentioned the baby to her. He felt she had enough to cope with just now.'

'Still, he can't expect to keep you hidden away for ever.' Cleo looked cross. She was sure Sean's motives weren't that pure; he just didn't have the guts to go public. 'Oh hell, now I've eaten all your fruit. Look, you're really nice. I've only known you this long and already I can tell how nice you are. Just as I know you sure as hell deserve better than my useless brother.'

It was odd, hearing one of the nation's most lusted-after celebrities being dismissed as useless. As his sister, Pandora supposed, Cleo was immune to the charms which so effectively floored everyone else.

'I do love him you know.' Pandora spoke simply, from the heart. 'I realize this isn't going to be easy but I love him anyway. I haven't even told him that.'

A lump came to Cleo's throat; she could so plainly foresee that Pandora and Sean were a disaster waiting to happen. And Pandora would be the one who ended up getting hurt.

'That's why I had to come and see you.' Determined to help, Cleo leaned closer. 'Look, I really hope everything works out. But if it doesn't . . . well, you might not always have Sean's support, but you'll definitely have mine.'

Chapter 21

Pandora had been so dreading breaking the news of her predicament to Joel that she had found herself putting it off and off for weeks. This was only possible because he had been away more often than he was home, thus missing out on the worst of the appalling morning sickness which, in the first couple of months, actually had her losing weight instead of putting it on.

But that, mercifully, was behind her now. Instead, Pandora found herself shovelling down mountains of buttery, peppery mashed potato and at least five packets of crisps a day. The crisps had to be dipped in Hellmann's mayonnaise which she kept in a jar in her handbag – the craving for them was so all-consuming it would even wake her up in the night – and the bathroom scales were barely able to keep up. Horrified but helpless to prevent it happening – there simply wasn't a moment in the day when she wasn't ravenous – Pandora watched herself balloon and wondered how on earth Joel could have failed to notice what was going on practically under his nose.

But that was men for you. And the time, Pandora decided, had finally come. If Sean could confide in his sister, she could tell Joel. It was either that or go out, buy a cot and let him guess.

They were sitting out in the tiny back garden enjoying the early-evening sun. Pandora was trying to enjoy it, anyway. Cleo had left two hours earlier and Joel was just home from work. Pandora braced herself against the white wrought-iron chair, waiting for the inevitable storm of outrage. Joel might be only three years older than she was but he could be as protective when he wanted as any father.

But this really wasn't the end of the world. She hadn't murdered anyone, hadn't even run over next door's cat. If she made light of the situation maybe Joel would relax a bit too.

'Pregnant?' He stared at Pandora. 'What the hell do you mean, pregnant?'

'You know, the kind of pregnant where you end up having a baby.' She had made a lamb casserole, Joel's favourite, specially to help her through. With lots of mashed potato.

'But you don't—'

'I do, actually.' He looked so stunned she had to smile. 'Every now and again.'

'—have a boyfriend,' spluttered Joel. 'You don't have a *boyfriend*. What's going on? Is this some kind of a joke? If it's a joke, Pandora, please tell me now.'

'No joke.' Oddly, having finally said it, she felt quite calm. 'And I have been seeing someone, just not very often. He's been working a lot, so have you. And you have met him,' she added with a touch of pride because not everyone, after all, could boast a relationship with one of the ten most desirable men in Britain. According to a poll in last Thursday's *Express*, anyway. 'It's—'

'Jesus,' shouted Joel, sitting bolt upright in his chair and going three shades redder. 'You're going to tell me it's Sean Mandeville! Oh Pandora, are you out of your mind? You can't get mixed up with someone like him . . . you certainly can't get pregnant by him!'

'Well I have.' Pandora's eyes flashed in defiance. 'Too late, it's already happened. So there.'

Joel closed his eyes. As far as he was aware, Pandora had done nothing more intimate than share a couple of meals with Sean Mandeville. Two brief outings and that had been the end of it. She hadn't so much as mentioned him since. And now this . . .

'Does *he* know?'

'Of course he knows.'

'And?' said Joel heavily.

'And he hasn't run off screaming into the sunset,' Pandora snapped back. Well, he hadn't. Not quite.

'Oh, so I'm invited to the wedding?'

'Don't be so bloody patronizing,' shouted Pandora. When he wanted to, Joel could be infuriatingly old-fashioned. 'Who says I want to get married?'

'You mean if he went down on one knee and asked you, you'd refuse? Don't make me laugh,' Joel retorted. 'You'll be asking me to believe in fairies next.' More gently he went on, 'Pan, don't get upset. I'm thinking of you. These kind of people live their own lives . . . they aren't *like* us.'

'You don't know. You met Sean for all of three seconds,' Pandora accused him. 'You can't only judge people by what you read in the papers. His sister came round to see me this afternoon and she couldn't have been nicer.'

Joel gazed at her in total disbelief.

'You mean Cleo Mandeville? Now you really are having me on! I met her last night. She's having a thing with Damien

Maxwell-Horne of all people. Talk about pond-life,' he went on bitterly. 'The man's nothing but a gigolo. I even tried to warn her off him, more fool me, but she soon put me in my place.'

'You're joking.' Pandora stared at him, dumbfounded.

'The silly bitch thought I was only doing it because I wanted to chat her up myself.' Joel shook his head in disgust. 'Wrapped herself round Maxwell-Horne and flounced off in a huff. I mean, please! She may have the looks and the body but there *has* to be more to life ... Imagine trying to hold a real conversation with someone like that! Imagine', he went on with a shudder, 'having a relationship with the kind of girl whose idea of current affairs is whether *Vogue* says fur coats are in or out this year.'

Big, easy-going Joel seldom lost his temper but he was certainly cross now. Pandora, who couldn't remember the last time he'd got so overheated, was both amazed at Cleo's abysmal taste in men and grateful to her for having so brilliantly diverted Joel's attention from her own sorry state of affairs.

Sadly though, not for long.

'But that', he said, 'is only one more reason why you'd have to be out of your mind to get involved with Sean Mandeville. Don't you see? People like them just aren't—'

'This is silly.' He wasn't helping. Pandora had had enough. 'I've heard of racial prejudice, but celebrity prejudice? Come on, Joel. Besides,' she added flatly, 'it's not as if I'm asking you whether or not I should get involved with Sean. I already *am* involved. I'm having his child, for heaven's sake! How much more involved can I get?'

145

Chapter 22

Of all the stupid songs to get stuck in your head, thought Cass, I have to get 'Jingle Bells'.

Even more annoyingly, it wasn't going to go away. Kingdom Radio had adapted and adopted it as this year's Christmas jingle. Cass, who had heard it a thousand times over the past couple of weeks, wondered if she was ever going to get it out of her brain. Jingle bells, jingle bloody bells ... She hoped every Kingdom listener in the country was as plagued by it as she was. Why should she suffer in silence and alone?

Still, only two days to go before Christmas and it would all be over. As she reached home, driving through the gates at the bottom of the drive, Cass couldn't help remembering those terrible weeks when the pavement outside had been awash with photographers scrabbling for position every time anyone either came or went, in order to get the best shots. Jack moving his things out, Cleo losing her temper one morning and yelling at them all to piss off, Sophie looking pale and upset following the departure of her father ... the press had got it all.

At least that was over now, Cass mused. As summer had drawn to an end so public interest had gradually waned, the photographers had sloped off and things had got back to normal.

Except it hadn't been normal at all, because Jack was no longer there. He had gone. Shacked up with his carrot-headed floozy. They had even, amongst themselves, taken to calling her Flooze. Cass pretended it helped but it didn't really. She was still completely unable to envisage Christmas Day itself without Jack.

When she unlocked and pushed open the front door, the first thing she smelled was his aftershave.

She breathed in the achingly familiar scent, mingled with pine from the eight-foot tree shimmering in the hallway, and wondered if she was hallucinating. There had been no sign of Jack's car anywhere outside. According to Sophie, he and Flooze were spending Christmas in Paris. He couldn't possibly be here.

Jack was there. He hadn't been able to stay away. Never a great drinker, several glasses of Chablis at the office Christmas party earlier that afternoon had weakened his resolve, exerting an almost mystical pull in the direction of Hampstead. The taxi driver who had brought him here, recognizing him at once, had been characteristically up-front.

'Season of goodwill, eh mate? Gonna make it up wiv the missis? Wanna watch out; good-lookers like Cass don't 'ang around for ever, reckon you oughta snap 'er back up quick before someone else does.'

It wasn't a question of snapping Cass back up; Jack had just needed to see her again. He had needed to see his family, to make sure all the decorations had been put up properly and the tree was standing in its usual place.

Everything, to his relief, was as it should be, from the eclectic assortment of baubles they had collected together over the years to the battered papier mâché bells made by Cleo in her last year of primary school, festooned with scarlet-and-silver ribbons and hung – along with a football-sized bunch of mistletoe – above the kitchen door.

And although Sean was out, Sophie had been touchingly pleased to see him. Even Cleo, just back from a week-long assignment in the Seychelles, and in a more forgiving mood than usual, had teased him for not being as brown as she was and offered him a microwaved mince pie.

Jack, who missed his family desperately, had been more than happy to just sit there in the kitchen, catching up on his daughters' news, watching Cleo paint her nails red and sign her way through a pile of Christmas cards destined – if he knew Cleo – never to be posted. Sophie, who had sent all hers off three weeks ago, was simultaneously wrapping presents, updating him on the amount of conversational Swahili she was now able to speak and making tremendous headway through a family-sized jar of Quality Street.

The kitchen was warm, the atmosphere friendly, the chatter non-stop. One of Mrs Bedford's specialities, steak-and-kidney casserole, was baking in the oven. Cleo was singing along intermittently with the Phil Spector Christmas tape playing in the background. When Jack heard Cass's car draw up outside he felt his pulse break into a gallop.

And here she was at last. As his wife appeared in the kitchen doorway, her blond hair glittering with rain, Jack stood up. She was wearing a white angora dress he hadn't seen before. She looked beautiful, even with slightly smudged grey eye shadow and all her lipstick – after a hard day in the studio – worn off.

'No need to stand.' Cass dumped her coat over the back of a

chair and nodded gratefully at Sophie who was putting the kettle on. 'This isn't a job interview.' She glanced across at him. 'I thought you were in France, anyway.'

'Flying tonight.' Jack watched her ease her leather boots off and thought of all the hundreds of times he had massaged Cass's tired feet for her. 'Not until eleven. I thought I'd just drop by and see how you all are.'

'Pretty much the same as we were four days ago.'

That was when he had called round to deliver the Christmas presents. Leaning forward in her chair, Cass gently massaged her own feet. 'And you?'

She didn't mean to sound stilted, it just came out that way. Jack's unexpected arrival had unsettled Cass, who was spending far more time than was sensible imagining him celebrating Christmas in a fabulous Paris hotel with Imogen. She hadn't asked, but they would undoubtedly be staying somewhere swish, either the Georges Cinq or the Paris Ritz. When Sean and Cleo had been tiny and she and Jack had still been terrifyingly poor, they had left the children with her mother and escaped to Paris together for a much-needed weekend break. Their hotel, in the foggy back streets of Montmartre, had been a Gauloise-infused fleapit with damp crawling up the walls and a manager permanently out of his mind on Pernod, but it had been one of the most romantic, magical, idyllic weekends of her life.

So much for romance, Cass thought. She carried on rubbing the soles of her feet.

'I'll make it.' The kettle had boiled. Jack rose to his feet once more. 'Tea or coffee?'

'Coffee. Better make yours black.' Realizing he'd had one

or two lunchtime drinks too many, she couldn't resist making the dig. 'You wouldn't want to miss your plane.'

'Cards, Mum.' Sophie pushed this morning's arrivals across the table before the bickering could escalate into an argument.

The third one Cass opened was from Terry Brannigan in New York: 'To Cass, Jack and kids,' he had scrawled across the inside in his hectic handwriting. 'Here's to the best Christmas and happiest New Year yet! Much love to you all, Terry.'

'Our cards must have crossed somewhere over the Atlantic.' Cass had to smile at the cartoon on the front of a depressed radio presenter playing 'Lonely This Christmas'. She passed it over to Jack. 'I sent his off last week, telling him you'd moved out.'

The phone rang. Cleo answered it.

'Mum? The *Daily Mail* wants to know what you'd most like for Christmas.'

Jack, who had been studying Terry's cartoon, glanced up at Cass. For an instant their eyes met. Hope flared in Jack's heart.

'That's easy,' said Cass without a flicker of emotion. 'A divorce.'

Arriving back at the flat an hour later, Jack was met at the top of the stairs by Imogen.

'You're late. I phoned the office and they said you'd left ages ago. For heaven's sake,' she said crossly, 'we have to leave for the airport at eight.'

'I had to see the kids.' Jack was sober now. Compared with the glittering house in Hampstead, the flat seemed dreadfully bleak. Imogen, not one of life's Christmas decoration putter-uppers, was unable to see the point of doing anything at all if they were going to be in Paris anyway. Her one concession had been to buy a small, severely elegant fake tree from Harrods, hung with seven matte, dark-blue glass icicles and nine olive-green ones.

Imogen was packed, ready and sipping a gin and tonic.

'What for? You saw them the other day.'

'It's Christmas.' With a weary gesture, Jack pushed his fingers through his hair. 'I wanted to see them again.'

'And they're hardly kids.' Imogen didn't ask whether or not Cass had been there too. She knew these feelings of jealousy were futile but they wouldn't go away.

'Sophie's only just fifteen.'

'And more of a grown-up than I am,' Imogen said tightly. She glanced at her watch. 'Look, I hate to sound like a nagging wife but are you planning to pack a case or not?'

When Jack didn't move, she was gripped with fear. In an instant her composure dissolved.

'What is it?' Fearfully, she searched his face. 'You don't want to come to Paris, do you? You'd rather spend Christmas with them.'

Jack watched the tears slide slowly down her cheeks. He felt terrible. Torn. How honest did Imogen seriously expect him to be?

'Look, I'm sorry. They're my children . . . they *are* Christmas.'

'And you want to be with them.' Imogen fished desperately in her jacket pocket for a handkerchief.

Of course I do, thought Jack. But it wasn't even that simple. He wanted to spend Christmas with his family and Cass wanted a divorce.

'Don't cry. We're going to Paris.' He put his arms round

Imogen's heaving shoulders and kissed her wet, freckled face. 'I love you. We'll have a wonderful time. Come on,' tenderly he took her hand, 'come and help me pack.'

Chapter 23

The doorbell rang at eleven thirty p.m. on Christmas Eve. Cleo and Sean were both out and Sophie was in bed. Cass, in her dressing gown with her hair tied back and her face shiny with moisturizer, was up to her eyes in Sellotape and curly ribbon frantically wrapping the last of the presents for Sophie's stocking.

She almost passed out with shock when, having peered through the spy-hole, she saw who was standing on the doorstep.

'Terry!' Utter amazement turned her fingers to Playdoh. Finally, after fumbling for several seconds with the lock, she managed to open the door. 'I don't believe this . . . !'

'The ghost of Christmas very much past.' Terry Brannigan threw his arms around her. Cass found herself being lifted into the air and spun round like a top. It seemed an age before he put her down.

'Oops, my dressing gown's coming undone.' Laughing, Cass retied it before hugging Terry again. Then she slipped her arm through his and led him through to the sitting room where a fire still burned in the grate. 'You're freezing. Sorry about the mess, I'm doing a stocking for Sophie . . . Goodness, I still can't believe you're actually here . . . do I look as dazed as I feel?'

'You look like heaven on legs,' Terry assured her. He meant

153

it too. As far as he was concerned, Cass always had been the most beautiful girl on the planet. Now, at thirty-nine, she was an even more beautiful woman. Her dressing gown, in Terry's opinion, could come undone as often as it liked.

'I got your card three days ago,' he explained when Cass, having poured him a spectacular measure of Jack Daniel's, had curled up beside him on the sofa in front of the fire. 'I couldn't believe it. You and Jack, of all people . . . after all this time. What happened, did you boot him out?'

Sixteen years had passed since they had last seen each other, yet the old magic, that instantaneous rapport, was still there.

Cass nodded.

'But only because he'd got himself a bimbo.'

'He didn't!' Terry was genuinely appalled. 'Is the man mad? A *real* bimbo?'

They had always been able to tell each other everything. 'Well, no,' Cass reluctantly admitted. Then she told him all about Imogen.

'. . . but I'm still alive,' she concluded some time later with a shrug and a ghost of a smile. 'I thought the world had come to an end but it hasn't. We keep going. The kids have been brilliant, *everyone's* been brilliant. Even the show's ratings shot up and stayed up, God knows why.'

'Maybe because the kids and "everyone" aren't the only ones who are brilliant,' Terry mock-scolded, because Cass's modesty had always been one of her most endearing features. It would never occur to her that her ratings might have risen because she was good at her job.

'It's Christmas Day!' At twenty past midnight, Cass had only just noticed the time. Reaching across, she cupped Terry's stubbly chin in both hands and planted a kiss on his travel-weary cheek. 'There, merry Christmas. I don't even know why you're here but I don't care. It's just so great to see you again,' she said simply. 'You've cheered me up more than you'll ever know.'

'You've cheered me up,' Terry told her. He pointed to the card he had sent, which hung in pride of place above the mantelpiece. 'See that miserable sod of a DJ? That's been me for the last five years, that has. Yesterday I decided I'd had enough and told them to stick their lousy job.' He squeezed Cass's hand. 'It was time to come home, I realized, and look up a few old friends.'

'Happy Christmas, Mum.' Sophie, already washed and dressed at eight o'clock the next morning, woke Cass with a kiss and a cup of tea. 'By the way, do we have a burglar or do you know something about the complete stranger I've just bumped into outside the bathroom?'

Cass stretched and rubbed her eyes before hauling herself into a sitting position.

'You mean Terry? That's Terry Brannigan, sweetheart. He turned up last night after you'd gone to bed. He'll be staying for a few days. You'll like him.'

'I do like him,' Sophie murmured to Cleo later that morning as between them they inexpertly basted the roast potatoes for lunch, 'but not a millionth as much as he likes Mum. You don't think she fancies him, do you?' Sophie looked worried. 'He's ancient.'

'Not to mention obvious.' Cleo glanced through the kitchen window. The temperature outside had dropped several degrees and a heavy frost had formed overnight. Cass was wandering arm in arm with Terry at the bottom of the garden, showing him round and chattering non-stop as they caught up on the events of the past sixteen years.

'I asked Mum how old he was,' Sophie went on. 'She said fifty-two, but he looks miles older than that. What if they get married?'

'Calm down.' Cleo grinned. It was unlike Sophie to get so twitchy. 'He only arrived last night.'

'Out of the blue.' Gloomily Sophie slid the roasting-tin back into the oven and gave the turkey a tentative prod. 'I don't think Mum even realizes what's going on. He's been living in New York for umpteen years. Then, three days ago, he gets Mum's Christmas card telling him Dad's buggered off. By an amazing coincidence, the very next day Terry jacks in his perfectly good job and flies over here, turning up on Mum's doorstep at midnight.'

'What you're saying', Cleo replied solemnly, 'is that we need to sit her down and give her a good talking-to about getting involved with the wrong kind of man.'

'Don't make fun. Well ... yes.' Sophie's spectacles had misted up in the heat from the oven. She cleaned them on the sleeve of her new blue shirt, a present from Cleo. 'And you know what I mean,' she persisted stubbornly. 'Mum's so nice she wouldn't want to hurt Terry's feelings. She wouldn't be able to say no.'

Sean, who had been on the phone in the study for the last twenty minutes, came into the kitchen grinning from ear to ear.

'What's this? Can't say no? Are you calling our mother a trollop?'

'I'm calling you a lazy bum,' said Cleo. 'We've been slaving away all morning and you've done sod all.'

Sophie's eyebrows rose. She hadn't noticed Cleo doing any slaving unless you counted snipping the corner off the orange juice carton at breakfast.

'I have been doing something, as a matter of fact.' Sean's dark eyes glittered. He was looking pleased with himself. 'You'd better lay an extra place at the table. Pandora's coming to lunch.'

'About bloody time too,' Cleo declared.

Sophie was gazing out of the window. Terry had grey hair, a million wrinkles and the look of a drinker about him. She just hoped he didn't also have anything as bizarre as an engagement ring in his pocket.

'So are you going to warn Mum first,' Cleo sounded interested, 'or let it be another surprise?'

'Who', demanded Sophie, 'is Pandora?'

'You have no idea how scary this is.' Pandora clung to her seat as Sean took a sharp corner. Her teeth were chattering despite the fact that the heating in the car was turned right up.

'My driving's brilliant,' Sean protested.

'I'm not talking about that. Meeting your mother is what's scary.' Still loaded with misgivings, she said for the fifth time, 'Are you sure this is a good idea? I mean, on Christmas Day of all days . . .'

They were nearly there. Sean flashed her a sideways grin. 'I'd have thought it was entirely appropriate. Like Joseph and Mary turning up at the inn.'

'And they were turned away,' Pandora ruefully reminded him. She pulled a face. 'Besides, I'm only five months pregnant. I wasn't actually planning to give birth during the Queen's speech.'

Inside the house, Cleo was putting Cass in the picture. It was, she felt, horribly unfair of Sean to expect to spring this kind of surprise without warning. As far as Cass was concerned, all he was doing was bringing a new girlfriend round to lunch.

'OK, Mum, this girl of Sean's. I've met her and she's lovely, but there's something else you should know before she gets here.'

Cass cast a worried glance in the direction of the glistening golden turkey surrounded by bacon-wrapped chipolatas. 'She's not vegetarian?'

'No. Pregnant.'

'Good heavens.'

Cleo stifled a smile.

'And black.'

Chapter 24

Pandora could have wept with relief when Cass, emerging from the house, ran across the gravelled drive and flung her arms around her.

'Spoilsport,' Sean said to Cleo.

'This is the very best present I could have had,' Cass assured Pandora, hugging her tighter still. 'You have no idea how much I was dreading this day, after everything that has . . . you know, happened. And it's turning out so much better than I'd dared hope. First a dear friend from the past turns up out of the blue . . . and now this. I'm going to be a grandmother! It's just the most amazing news!'

'Come on, Granny. Indoors.' Cleo winked at Pandora, who was looking quite overcome.

'Hang on, something I have to do before I forget.' Turning, Cass cuffed Sean around the ear.

'Ouch.'

'That's for not telling me sooner. We should have met Pandora months ago,' she scolded.

'I thought you had enough on your plate.' Sean was the picture of wounded innocence.

'But this is wonderful news.' Laughing, Cass squeezed Pandora's arm. 'A lovely wedding, I can hardly wait! Have you set a date yet?'

Pandora looked embarrassed.

'Talking of dates,' said Cleo in conversational tones, 'I'm starving. Let's eat.'

The only other hiccup in an otherwise perfect afternoon occurred after lunch when the phone rang.

'I'll get it.' Sophie leapt up in a hurry, knocking over Terry's half-full tumbler of Scotch. 'Sorry. Dad said he'd phone.'

Cass took a deep breath, preparing to look as if it couldn't matter less. But it wasn't Jack.

'For you.' Sophie held the receiver towards Sean, her grey eyes expressionless. 'I don't know who it is.'

'Oh, hi,' said Sean as a girl he had met at the club a couple of weeks ago huskily sang 'Happy Christmas to you, Happy Christmas to you' down the phone at him. 'Yes, fine thanks. You too? How are Suzy and the kids?'

'When am I going to see you again?' The girl, whose name was either Emily or Amy, he couldn't for the life of him remember which, sounded petulant and slightly drunk. 'I waited for you at the club last night and you didn't show.'

'Busy, I'm afraid.' Sean kept the receiver jammed against his ear. Catching Sophie's disapproving eye, he turned to look out of the window instead. The room behind him had gone horribly quiet.

'Your friend Donny gave me your number,' purred the girl. 'What about tonight then? You wouldn't be disappointed, Sean. I never disappoint.'

'Can't do it. Out of the question.' Sean silently cursed Donny. Reflected in the window he could see his mother and Pandora, both pretending not to listen. 'Look, I'm going to have to go. Give my love to Suzy and the kids, OK?'

'I'd much rather you gave your love to me.' Emily-Amy had a throaty giggle. 'Tell you what, why don't you get rid of whoever's there? I'll ring back in thirty minutes.'

'Bye,' said Sean. Hanging up, he was careful to leave the phone just off the hook.

'That was Max, one of the guys from the club.'

As he spoke to the room at large, it was horribly obvious that not even Pandora believed him.

By seven o'clock Sophie was close to tears.

'Dad said he'd definitely ring,' she whispered when Cleo, wandering into the kitchen, found her crouched shivering on the back doorstep, feeding strips of smoked salmon to next door's Siamese cat. Sophie, outwardly so tough and practical it was easy to forget she was still only fifteen, had found the day far more of an ordeal than she had let on. 'He promised to phone,' she said miserably. 'How could he forget?'

'He wouldn't forget.' Cleo put an arm round her and improvised rapidly. 'He probably couldn't get through. The phones in Paris are hopeless – whenever I'm there it takes me about six hours to dial out. And Christmas Day is especially bad . . .'

'Nice try.' Sophie managed a weak smile. 'If I was six I might even have believed you. Oh come on, let's face it – Dad's with Imogen now. He's got himself a whole new life. We're just too boring for him.'

'That's plain silly. Now you *are* sounding like a six-year-old.'

Sophie said nothing. It had only just occurred to her that if her father was building a whole new life for himself, he might want a whole new family to go with it.

* * *

'So what do you really think?' said Terry, when Sean and Pandora had left. Cleo and Sophie were clearing up in the kitchen, leaving them alone together in the sitting room in front of the fire.

Cass sighed. 'Oh dear, she's a lovely girl. But it's hardly the romance of the century, is it? Poor Pandora.'

Noticing the phone was slightly off the hook, Terry replaced it on his way to the drinks tray, behind the sofa. As he topped up Cass's glass he gazed lovingly down at her gleaming, tousled blond hair and at the way the collar of her white silk shirt fell open to reveal the infinitely desirable nape of her neck. Theirs could be the romance of the century, he thought, given half a chance. Cass was everything he'd ever wanted in a woman. They had the rapport and Cass had – surely, by now – had enough time to get over Jack. All he needed was to be able to persuade her that their kind of friendship could so easily turn to love.

In the meantime, Cass was too hung up about her wayward son to concentrate on her own future happiness.

'Who knows? Sean may settle down.' Personally Terry doubted it, but he knew this was what she wanted to hear. As he sat back down beside Cass he took her left hand in his own, glancing at the still-visible indentation where for so many years her wedding ring had been. 'You can never tell what will happen.'

'Like us.' Cass was thinking of Jack. Idly squeezing Terry's hand, which he took as a huge sign of encouragement, she sighed. 'You wouldn't believe the letters I've had from people. One woman wrote to say he only left me because once, on air, I made fun of his feet. Another said it was my own fault for going out to work. Only last week someone sent me the recipe for a medieval love potion. If I could persuade Jack to drink it, they said, he'd dump Imogen and be back like a shot.'

'So, are you going to try it?'

'I don't think they sell newts' eyes in Sainsbury's.' Cass leaned her head back against the sofa. 'No, Jack's gone and that's that. I've decided to face up to it. Next week I'm seeing a solicitor about getting on with the divorce.'

Better and better, thought Terry, hardly daring to hope that his arrival could have had something to do with her decision. Breathing in, he could smell Cass's perfume, the same one she had worn for over twenty years. And she was still holding his hand.

Emboldened by his own happiness he said, 'I think you're right. Get the divorce, put it all behind you and start again. You never have to worry about being alone, Cass. You do know that, don't you?'

'With my three?' Misunderstanding him completely, Cass broke into a grin. 'I'm never likely to have a minute's peace.'

Terry's heart began to race.

'No, I meant—'

'Mum, quick!' The sitting-room door was flung open and Cleo raced in. 'Switch on the TV, we're missing *Only Fools and Horses*!'

Within seconds she was draped across the other sofa, turning up the volume, tearing open a family-sized bag of Marmite crisps and yelling for Sophie to hurry up, it had started.

'See what I mean?' said Cass contentedly.

'Mm.'

Silently cursing Cleo, Terry poured himself another drink.

Chapter 25

Paris had been perfect. That most romantic of cities, gloriously wreathed in mist, frost and pale milky sunlight, had never looked better.

Imogen had never felt better, either. This break was just what she and Jack had most needed, a chance to escape the pressures of Jack being recognized wherever he went and to revel in each other's company. Their suite at the Crillon was the last word in silk-upholstered luxury, the meals over which they lingered for hours were positive works of art, the après-dinner sex sublime.

Never had Imogen felt more relaxed and desirable. The tetchy exchange which could so easily have spiralled out of control at the flat was forgotten. They were together, reaffirming their love, and apart from an irritable couple of hours on Christmas Day itself when Jack had repeatedly tried and failed to get through on the phone to Sophie, concluding finally that the phone had been left off the hook on purpose, he hadn't so much as mentioned his family once.

Good, thought Imogen, pleased to see he was getting that particular guilt-trip under control. She didn't feel she was being unreasonable. She wasn't an ogre. If his children were still small then fair enough, that would be different, but they weren't. So why on earth the fuss?

* * *

London, grey and slushy by the time they returned, was looking very down-at-heel in comparison, not romantic at all. Imogen didn't care; she had more important things on her mind. And London had its advantages, she thought with a secret smile the next morning as Jack set off for Fleet Street and a post-Christmas meeting with his editor. At least here, instructions were printed in English.

'Guess what, guess what?'

'You learned how to do joined-up writing.'

Sophie was trying to finish her muesli and gulp down a glass of chocolate milkshake before rushing off to the library. The new book she'd ordered, *Living with the Masai*, had just come in and the last thing she needed was Jennifer Smith-Elliott twittering down the phone, telling her in awful detail how she'd been French-kissed over Christmas by some gross boy. Jennifer, who was in her class at school, was famous for spending her whole life on the telephone instilling terminal boredom in her victims. Like Samaritans in reverse, thought Sophie, tilting her head back to get the last chocolatey dregs from the bottom of the glass.

'Jen, the library shuts at lunchtime. I really mustn't miss it—'

'Hold your horses,' Jennifer giggled, 'this is good. I was out shopping with my mother this morning. We had to pick up a prescription for Granny Elliott, her legs have been terrible over Christmas. She can hardly walk.'

Wish you could hardly talk, thought Sophie. Tucking the phone between ear and shoulder, she carried on spooning muesli into her mouth.

'Anyway, so there we were, queueing up in this little chemist's shop in Islington and guess who I recognized ahead of me?'

'No.' Sophie began to lose patience; it was twenty to one. 'Why don't you just tell me?'

'Spoilsport,' chanted Jennifer. 'OK then, but you're no fun. It was that woman your dad's living with. Imogen what's-her-name,' she said proudly. 'Mum and I both recognized her, even with a coat on and her hair hidden under a hat.'

Big deal, thought Sophie, hopping from one foot to the other. 'So?' she demanded, suppressing a sigh. 'What was she doing, buying condoms?'

'Not quite.' Jennifer sniggered down the phone. 'One pink Max Factor lipstick, one tube of Colgate toothpaste. And', she added smugly, 'a pregnancy testing kit.'

'Just in time!'

At the sound of Jack's key turning in the lock, Imogen flew downstairs to greet him. It was no good, some secrets were just impossible to keep. If she didn't tell him now she would burst.

'What?' Jack good-humouredly allowed himself to be dragged up the stairs. Through the open kitchen door he glimpsed an icy-looking bottle of Taittinger and two glasses lined up on top of the fridge. 'What?' he said again, marvelling at her energy as she propelled him instead into the sitting room. Looking ridiculously young in a peach cashmere sweater and faded jeans and with her red-gold hair flying, Imogen was practically aglow with whatever form of surprise she was about to spring. Her enthusiasm, as she made a great show of checking the time by Jack's watch, was infectious.

'Don't tell me, Michael Aspel's on his way up,' said Jack. 'I'm about to be This is your Lifed.' He grinned. 'I hope they don't forget to bring on my old French teacher, Mademoiselle Dupont. She looked like Bardot, she really did. That woman must have launched a thousand schoolboy fantasies—'

'Better than that.' Imogen's eyes were shining. For the second time she consulted first his watch, then her own. 'Oh Jack, I can hardly bear it. One more minute. Brace yourself, darling . . .'

In a flash, Jack knew what it was. That look of hers was one he'd seen before, one he now clearly recognized. The trouble was, it was a look he was used to seeing in Cass's blue eyes, not Imogen's brown ones.

'You're pregnant. My God, you're pregnant.'

Letting out a squeal of delight, Imogen flung her arms around him.

'You can tell? You mean it shows? You really can tell?' She showered his face with ecstatic kisses. 'Oh Jack, I still can't believe this is happening! I've always been so regular I knew at once something was up. I've just done the test, it's in the bathroom . . . You have no idea how complicated it all is, you practically need a chemistry degree to figure it out and my hands wouldn't stop shaking.'

She was babbling with excitement, scarcely recognizable as the cool, in-control Imogen he knew. Beyond words, Jack let himself be hauled off to the pristine black-and-white bathroom, where a test tube stood in solitary splendour on the black marble shelf.

Home-testing kits weren't something with which he was

familiar. In his day, Cass had left the necessary specimens with their doctor and phoned up a week later for the results.

'I knew it anyway, as soon as I was a day late,' Imogen beamed, 'but this proves it. Oh Jack, I can't believe how different I feel already!'

'How does it tell you?' He was peering at the white stick semi-submerged in the test tube. 'What happens?'

'The end bit goes pink. Hang on, you have to take it out and run it under a tap.'

'It isn't pink.'

'It must be.' Imogen frowned, holding the stick under the cold tap. 'I saw it start to change colour as soon as I put it in the test tube. Jack, get the instructions out of the bin, they've made some kind of mistake. It *must* be pink . . .'

But the stick stayed obstinately white. The result of the test was negative. And Imogen, who until three days before had never even thought she wanted a baby, was inconsolable. When at nine o'clock that evening her period started, Jack seriously considered phoning for the doctor. Her grief was all-consuming. When the flow of tears finally dried up, grim determination took its place.

'OK, so it'll happen next month.' Emerging from the shower, pale and red-eyed, Imogen spent several minutes poring over her diary. 'This is no good, the best time to conceive is here.' Having already checked out fertile periods in the Miriam Stoppard baby book she'd bought at lunchtime, she ticked off five consecutive days in red felt pen. 'I'm in Budapest from Tuesday to Thursday and you're off to the Eurosummit on the Friday. I'll cancel Budapest.' She looked up at him. 'Can you get out of the Brussels trip?'

'Come on, calm down.' Jack had done his best to comfort her but his patience was beginning to wear thin. He knew women were capable of such desperate yearnings but this was so sudden it was positively bizarre. He took Imogen's hands in his, forcing her to listen.

'Sweetheart, I know you're upset. But we have talked about this before. I've had three kids. I've been through all that. And you said you'd *never* wanted children. You were so certain you didn't want any,' he reminded her, 'you were even willing to be sterilized.'

Fresh tears – where did they keep *coming* from? – slid down Imogen's white face. She knew she was being illogical but it was all way beyond her control. That had been then, this was now. He was right; she never *had* yearned for children. But believing, truly believing, for three whole days that she was carrying Jack's child had, as far as she was concerned, changed everything. The baby would inherit Jack's dark eyes and devastating looks; it would be intelligent, athletic, loving and full of fun. Boy or girl, that didn't matter; in Imogen's daydreams either sex would be perfect.

Except that instead of either, she had neither. The stick hadn't turned pink. There was no baby to devote the rest of her life to, no adorable bundle to set the seal on their love.

Such bitter disappointment was outside Imogen's experience. All her life she had got what she wanted. That she could now be denied something as simple and natural as a baby, when across the world so many thousands of unwanted ones were being born every day, seemed cruel beyond belief.

'I've changed my mind.' Imogen clung to him, drenching the front of Jack's shirt with her tears. 'I want a baby . . . *your*

baby! It's just, I really thought we had one. God, why is life so
unfair?'

Chapter 26

Pandora knew she wasn't going to be able to carry on working for much longer. The tables at The Moon and Sixpence, in true bistro style, were crammed in willy-nilly, the gaps between them growing narrower by the week. With her ever-expanding stomach, squeezing past with plates of cassoulet held high was becoming an increasingly risky procedure. Her back ached too, more than Pandora would have believed possible. She felt like a woman sawn in half.

'I'll be sorry to lose you.' Maurice, her boss, genuinely meant it.

'I'll miss you, too.' Massaging her spine, Pandora gave him a rueful smile. 'But in this state, I definitely won't be sorry to go.'

Tuesday, luckily for her, was a quiet night. A combination of appalling weather and the fact that the coming Thursday was Valentine's Day, so everyone was revving up for that, meant the bistro was almost empty. Pandora was resting behind the bar with her aching feet propped up on an empty wine crate when the door swung open and Cleo came staggering in.

'Stinking bloody weather,' Cleo gasped as half a dozen Harrods carriers slithered to the floor around her. 'Whoever invented winter needs to be shot. Roll on tomorrow.' She broke into an unrepentant grin. 'I'm off to Hawaii.'

Pandora, who was delighted to see Cleo, lowered herself carefully down from her bar stool.

'It's a tough life.' She pointed to the green-and-gold bags. 'What's all this? Stocking up on sun cream?'

'My agent sent me a massive royalty cheque this morning.' Cleo looked smug. 'For that yoghurt campaign I did last year, filthy muck. Anyway, I decided if I'm going to be a doting maiden aunt I may as well do it properly, so this is for you. Well,' she amended, 'for the baby.'

Pandora stared at the bags. 'Are you serious?'

'Oh, thanks.' Cleo gratefully accepted a glass of Chablis from Maurice, who was overwhelmed to have such a glamorous celebrity in his humble back-street bistro. Everyone else might be bundled up in winter woollies but Cleo was having none of it. In a fuchsia-pink jacket and violet trousers, she looked every bit as exotic as her namesake. When she flashed her dazzling smile at him he felt almost faint. 'Quite funny, really. All the assistants in the baby department were trying not to stare at my stomach. I had to keep saying, "It's not for me, it's for a friend," and you could tell nobody believed me for a second. I bet the papers will be on to it before the end of the week. Come on,' she urged, when Pandora didn't move, 'open up, have a look.'

'This is far too much . . . oh, you shouldn't have.'

Pandora couldn't believe it; Cleo must have spent an absolute fortune. Hand-embroidered bootees, intricately knitted baby cardigans, lace-trimmed satin pram covers and a perfect Moses basket woven through with white silk ribbons appeared out of the bags like conjurers' rabbits. Next came an ivory cashmere shawl, a set of framed Beatrix Potter prints and the most exquisite musical mobile Pandora had ever seen.

'I mean it.' Pandora was overwhelmed. 'Really, this is far too much. It must have cost . . . hundreds!'

The total bill had run into thousands. Cleo, glad Pandora didn't know, said, 'It isn't for you. It's for my new relative, whom I have every intention of spoiling rotten.' She shrugged happily. 'So there.'

'Well, thanks.' Aware of Maurice hovering behind her and hoping his tongue wasn't actually hanging out, Pandora said, 'At least let me get you another drink.'

Cleo shook her head.

'Sorry, got to dash. That's why I had to drop the stuff in to you here . . . I'm just on my way to the airport now.'

'What a beauty,' Maurice breathed when she had gone. 'Now if she were to come to me asking for a job . . .'

Pandora laughed. 'Cleo doesn't get out of bed for less than ten thousand pounds a day.'

'Fine.' Lost in admiration, Maurice rolled his eyes. 'Who'd want her to?'

The bistro was empty of customers by the time Joel arrived to drive Pandora home. Looking enormously pleased with himself, he strode in waving three white Mothercare bags.

'Wait till you see what I bought today!'

Pandora didn't have to wait; Joel was already spreading the contents across the bar like a hard-sell market trader. Not daring to look at Maurice, whose mouth was twitching beneath his moustache, she said, 'I can't believe you actually went into Mothercare. I can't believe you even knew what Mothercare was.'

As proud as any new father, Joel beamed.

'Chose it all myself. Well, not long to go now. Can't have the poor little sod turning up with nothing to wear, can we?'

Pandora had been too superstitious to buy anything too soon, but he was right. She had reached seven months now; it was definitely time to begin stocking up.

And Joel had definitely stocked up. She counted a dozen serviceable Babygros, six white cot sheets, ten vests, three yellow cellular blankets and a potty shaped like an elephant.

'It plays a tune when you pee in it.' Joel grinned. 'So they tell me, anyway.'

'You are brilliant.' Reaching with difficulty across the bar, Pandora gave him a hug. 'This is great, just what I'm going to need.'

'Come on, you two.' Maurice, having read Pandora's mind, held the front door open. 'Let me lock up.'

Joel was carrying the Mothercare bags and Pandora was halfway through the door when Molly, the Geordie washer-upper, came charging like a rhino out of the kitchen.

'Hang on a second, pet! I don't know, young people these days ... sieves for brains.' Panting, she thrust the glossy Harrods carriers into Pandora's arms. 'Whatever you do, don't forget these!'

'Well,' Joel said stiffly, 'it makes my stuff look pretty poor by comparison.'

He had insisted, as soon as they arrived home, on laying out the rival gifts next to each other on the living-room carpet. The fact that Pandora had tried to leave Cleo's presents behind at the bistro only proved, in his eyes, how hopelessly inferior his own purchases were.

Pandora couldn't believe how much he minded.

'This is silly,' she protested, waving a minuscule pair of hand-smocked, apricot satin dungarees. '*You're* being silly. OK, so it was kind of Cleo to buy all these things but they're hardly practical, are they? Babygros and vests are what I need. They're what the baby's going to be wearing every day.'

'She did it on purpose.' Joel wasn't to be appeased. 'She just has to flash her money about, to show us how much better she is than everyone else. Or thinks she is,' he added darkly.

'Cleo didn't do it on purpose. She isn't like that.'

'Ha.'

'Look,' Pandora's dark eyes widened in despair. 'She doesn't even know who you are, so how *can* she be doing it on purpose? I wish you'd stop all this and meet her properly.'

'I met her quite properly enough, thanks, before Christmas.' Joel began shovelling the Babygros back into their bags. 'Even Maxwell-Horne had the sense to dump her. Said she was a spoilt rich-bitch.' His mouth narrowed. 'And frigid.'

'Nice of him.'

'Yes, well.' Joel, who couldn't abide Damien Maxwell-Horne, concentrated on retrieving the last of the cellophane-wrapped vests. 'He's a git, but for once in his life he's right.'

'Ah.' Pandora smiled. 'You mean he's a right git.'

Chapter 27

Sophie, having decided drastic action was called for, had phoned her father and asked to make a formal appointment to see him. Alone.

So alarmed by her subdued tone of voice and by the fact that for the first time in years she was calling him Daddy, Jack cut short an editorial meeting and arranged to pick Sophie up from school. His heart went out to his younger daughter when he saw her waiting alone on a wall adjoining the school gates, white-faced and swamped by a miles-too-big grey sweatshirt that reached almost to her knees. Rain, to which Sophie seemed oblivious, was running down her owlish glasses. When she climbed into Jack's car they promptly misted up.

'Sweetheart, you sounded so low. What is it? Tell me what's wrong.'

Even as he hugged her, Jack knew it must be something serious. He had never seen Sophie this withdrawn.

'Everything's wrong,' Sophie said quietly. 'I hate it at home, it's just awful. Oh Daddy, can I come and live with you?'

Jack couldn't have been more stunned if Sophie had announced she was joining the Folies-Bergères.

'Awful? How can it be awful? Sophie,' his arm tightened around her shoulders, 'it's your *home*.'

'It's not like home any more. Mum's not like Mum any more.' Sophie paused and drew a deep shuddering breath.

'Sean's never there. Bloody Terry Brannigan's *always* there. Cleo's OK, I suppose, but she's away most of the time . . . it's so horrible, Daddy, I really can't bear it.' Huge grey eyes searched his face. 'Please, *please* say I can come and stay with you.'

Imogen thought she was hallucinating when she arrived home from work that evening to find five suitcases strewn around her pristine sitting room, spilling out awful-looking clothes and a vast number of books. Since she was dying for a pee, she was even more outraged to find the bathroom door firmly locked against her. Inside, some unearthly music blared.

'What's going on?'

Jack was in the kitchen, burning sausages under the grill. When she saw the look on his face as he turned to greet her, Imogen's worst suspicions were confirmed.

'Darling, I'm sorry. I tried ringing you earlier but they said you were out of the office all afternoon.' He kissed Imogen's unresponsive mouth, as if it would help. 'It's Sophie; she was in a dreadful state earlier. I know this is a bit of a bombshell, but basically I was just too worried to leave her. Sweetheart, she was so desperate to come and stay here, what else could I do? You don't mind, do you? Not terribly, at least?'

Imogen minded far more than that. She couldn't believe Jack seriously expected her to smile and shake her head.

Finally she felt able to speak.

'For how long?'

'Not long.' Jack's tone was soothing, like a hypnotist assuring a smoker they no longer want a cigarette. 'Just until we get things sorted out. Honestly, she'll be no trouble at all.'

The sausages were about to ignite. Like an automaton,

Imogen switched off the grill and opened the kitchen window to clear the billowing black smoke.

'This is a one-bedroomed flat.'

'Don't worry.' He gave her a reassuring smile. 'Sophie's more than happy to sleep on the sofa.'

At this, Imogen's temper flared.

'Oh well, as long as Sophie's happy,' she mimicked, 'that must mean everything's fine. Never mind the fact that my bladder is about to *explode*.'

Without looking at her, Jack turned and headed along the landing, rat-tatting efficiently on the locked bathroom door.

'Out of the bath, sweetheart. Now, please.'

The music stopped and the door opened less than a minute later. Clouds of expensively scented steam gushed out. Sophie, wet and pale and with Imogen's favourite pink bath towel around her skinny frame, emerged with a tentative smile.

'Sorry, did you knock earlier?'

The bathroom was like a South American swamp, the ceramic floor-tiles awash and every towel crumpled and damp. Tight-lipped, Imogen replaced the top on her precious bottle of Jo Malone's French Lime Blossom bath creme, although there wasn't much point since Sophie had almost completely used it up. The matching triple-milled soap – at fifteen pounds a bar – was quietly dissolving in the dregs of the bath water. The basin was littered with Jack's razor and strands of straight, mouse-coloured hair where Sophie had hacked at her fringe. There were grubby footprints on the toilet seat and – Imogen shuddered – toenail clippings floating in the loo.

But if what was now happening to her was Imogen's worst nightmare, it was at the same time Jack's dream come true.

Jack's children were his blind spot and Sophie, in particular, the beloved baby of the family, could – as far as he was concerned – do no wrong. To feel needed again after so many months of cold-shouldering more than made up for the minor inconveniences Sophie's arrival was likely to cause. Jack was implacable. Worse still, he couldn't for the life of him understand why Imogen wouldn't want Sophie there as much as he did.

'I'm not trying to be difficult, I'm just saying this flat's too small for three people.'

This was ridiculous; here they were in bed, forced to converse in whispers because Sophie, exhausted after all that mess-making, had settled down for the night on the sofa.

And – in disbelief Imogen rechecked her watch – it was only nine o'clock.

'Cheer up.' Jack, putting the finishing touches to this week's column on his laptop, was only half listening. 'It won't be for ever.'

As far as Imogen was concerned, it was already too long.

'I had no idea one girl could be so untidy.' She looked mutinous.

'Sophie isn't untidy. You should have seen Cleo in action at that age. Anyway,' Jack pointed out, 'children do make a mess. If you're so hell-bent on having a baby, this is just about the best training you could have.'

If I have a baby, thought Imogen, I'll have a nanny to deal with all that.

Aloud she said, 'Babies don't use half a bottle of your best bath essence at a time.'

'No, they chuck the lot down the loo instead.' Jack sighed.

'Look, I'm sorry if this is a pain for you, but Sophie was desperate. How *could* I have turned her down?'

Simple, Imogen thought sulkily. Just say no.

Jack glimpsed the rebellious flicker in her eyes.

'If you had children, you'd understand. Sophie has a mind of her own. If I'd turned her down, who knows where she might have ended up? Imagine how many teenagers living on the streets were rejected by their families when they needed help . . .'

Talk about a losing battle.

'OK, OK.' Imogen smiled as he switched off the laptop, and resolved to give in gracefully. Since they were in bed she may as well make the most of the situation. It was coming up to her fertile period too.

'What are you doing?' said Jack.

Imogen's hand moved further downwards. She grinned.

'Oh, I think you know.'

'Better not.' Gentle but firm, Jack removed her wandering hand. 'We wouldn't want to disturb Sophie.'

'Mum? It's me.'

'Sophie! Darling, is everything all right? Why are you whispering?'

'These walls are like cardboard. And yes, everything's fine.' Sophie giggled. 'I'm having a lovely time. Imogen's gritting her teeth, trying to be nice for Dad's sake, but she really hates me being here. Not that I blame her,' she went on happily, 'considering the mess I made of her bathroom.'

'Oh dear.' Cass sounded worried. 'You aren't doing anything too awful I hope.'

Sophie rolled her eyes in despair. How absolutely typical of her mother; before you knew it, she'd be feeling sorry for Flooze and taking her side.

'You mean compared with Imogen being all best-friendsy with you and at the same time having an affair behind your back with Dad?'

'Yes, but—'

'Mum, don't you dare tell me to behave myself!' Sophie pulled the duvet over her head. Goodness, it was hard work keeping down to a whisper. 'Why should that double-crossing bitch have everything her own way?' she demanded briskly. 'I haven't even started yet. Married men with children have responsibilities and I'm going to make Imogen realize she has to share them. By the time I've finished, she'll wish she'd never even met Dad.'

At the other end of the line, Cass cringed. Sophie sounded so determined, so bitter. Over six months had passed now since Jack had moved out but the pain clearly hadn't diminished.

Cass knew how that felt, only too well. She was beginning to wonder if the wounds would ever heal.

'Well, I can't stop you,' she said quietly, 'but please don't stay away too long. It seems strange already not having you here. I'm going to miss you terribly.'

'I miss you too, Mum. It's just something I have to do.' A lump came to Sophie's throat. She realized she had to hang up fast. 'And don't worry. I'll give it a couple of weeks at the most.'

Chapter 28

Having given up work a week earlier, Pandora announced she was going to stay with friends in Bath for a few days.

'Why?' Sean was instantly suspicious.

'Because they're friends and I'd like to see them.' Pandora was unperturbed. 'They'll feed me up and spoil me rotten. What could be nicer?'

As if she wasn't fed enough already. Sean could barely get his arms around her these days. He wasn't too pleased, either, by the implication that she wasn't being spoiled rotten here.

'Look, you know I've been busy. Once this TV thing has finished filming at the club—'

'I do know,' said Pandora mildly. 'It's OK, you don't have to remind me.'

'But—'

'Please. Any more excuses and I'll start putting it down to a guilty conscience. I'm going to stay with Bill and Wendy, that's all.'

Sean experienced a stab of irrational jealousy.

'Who are they, then?'

Pandora's mouth twitched.

'You saw photographs of them once, when you were spying on me.'

Jealousy changed to relief.

'The Richard Whiteley lookalike, you mean? And the woman with ginger hair?'

'I suppose so.'

'What do they do?'

'Bill's a bank manager. Wendy teaches chemistry.'

'Riveting,' Sean mocked.

'Yes, well.' Pandora hated the way he so effortlessly made fun of ordinary people. 'We can't all have TV programmes made about us. Wendy and Bill are old friends. I'll be back next Sunday, if you're interested.' As she zipped her case shut, she gave him a quick sidelong glance. 'Or maybe you'll be too busy entertaining friends of your own.'

'What's that supposed to mean?' Sean looked wounded.

'It means I saw the photo in yesterday's paper of you and that actress.' Pandora hadn't meant to say it; sounding like a nag would do her no favours at all. She felt her cheeks grow warm, fiddled with the zip on the suitcase and carried on anyway. 'Although I was surprised to see her calling herself an actress. I thought all Mindy Charleson had ever done was get her kit off for page three.'

'They printed it in yesterday's paper? I was going to tell you about that before it came out.'

For once Sean's innocence was genuine. The trouble was, how on earth was he supposed to persuade Pandora to believe him? 'Honestly,' he protested, as she swung the heavy suitcase down from the bed. 'Here, let me do that. I mean it, sweetheart . . . her agent organized it as a publicity push for her career. I wouldn't be interested in Mindy Charleson, for God's sake . . . the girl's a slapper. Credit me with some taste, please.'

The look of dismay on Sean's face was so real Pandora had

to believe him. This time at least, she decided, he had the benefit of the doubt.

'Oh, but was it really any wonder he showed interest in other girls, anyway, when these days even she found looking at herself in a mirror hard to bear? The actress's page-three days might be long gone but at least she still had a figure that went in and out.

Mine, Pandora reminded herself, just goes out.

And Sean was a red-blooded male. In all honesty, Pandora thought with a rueful sigh, how can I blame him for showing interest in anything with a waist?

Arriving back at Paddington Station the following Sunday, Pandora was absurdly flattered to find Sean waiting on the platform for her. Since their relationship hadn't yet become public knowledge, she hung back at a discreet distance while he signed autographs for a group of giggling schoolgirls beneath the arrivals screen. She was almost afraid to be seen with him anyway; with those film-starry good looks and that lean, perfect body he was pretty awe-inspiring even from a distance of twenty feet.

No wonder I can't say no to him, thought Pandora, glancing down at her own pale grey sweatshirt and jogging pants. Not that she could jog, at present, to save her life. Sean, wearing a black cashmere sweater and dark-grey trousers, looked dauntingly glamorous.

She continued to watch him exchange jokes with the schoolgirls, signing their forearms when they ran out of bits of paper. Pandora admired the way his dark glossy hair fell across his forehead, and the knack he had – when he chose to use it –

of making each girl in turn feel special and more important than the rest.

Then, glancing up, Sean spotted Pandora. He broke into a grin, mouthed Hi, and finished signing the arm of a willowy blonde whose pert bottom was barely covered by a red wool miniskirt.

'I say,' gasped Pandora, when she finally managed to come up for air. Flustered, she realized just how many people were now watching them. The girl in the red mini, in particular, was looking on in disbelief. 'Should you be doing this?'

Sean's arms were still wrapped around her. His mouth brushed the tip of her nose.

'Most definitely.'

'I mean, in public?'

'Why not?' He kissed her again. 'I've missed you. More than you deserve to be missed, too. Buggering off to the back of beyond, just to pay me back for that stupid picture in the paper—'

'It was Bath,' Pandora pointed out, 'not the Kalahari desert. And I wasn't trying to pay you back for anything. Help, look at all these people. Do they have to stare like that?'

Sean was used to it.

'Come on, the car's outside. If it hasn't been towed away.'

They both heard the words of the girl in the red mini as she turned away in disappointment.

'She can't really be his girlfriend. It must be some kind of joke.'

Sean, his arm curling protectively around Pandora's shoulders, swung round and fixed the girl with a cold, unamused stare.

'Why should it be a joke?' he demanded. 'Actually, she's my live-in lover.'

Pandora wished the platform could open and swallow her up. She had never felt more humiliated in her life.

'Where are we?' asked Pandora when he pulled up outside a Victorian semi-detached house halfway along a leafy avenue in Putney.

Sean looked across at her.

'I meant it,' he said. 'That bit about the live-in lover.'

'What?' Pandora gazed up at the bedroom windows, framed with ivy and scarlet-curtained, as if expecting to see some female standing there waving down at them. 'Who?'

'Come on,' Sean protested. 'I meant it about missing you too. And I've made up my mind. If we're having this baby we may as well do it properly, the whole bit.'

Pandora turned to him, her eyes like saucers.

'You mean get m—?'

At the sight of the expression on Sean's face, the rest of the word died on her lips. The dreaded M-word clearly wasn't what he'd meant at all.

'Well, nearly the whole bit.' Squirming, Sean pointed to the house, which had cost an exorbitant amount to rent. He even had the grace to go a bit pink. 'Look, sorry, but I'm pretty allergic to the idea of weddings and stuff. Blame it on my parents, if you like . . .'

This was a shameful cop-out and they both knew it.

Hurriedly Pandora said, 'No, I'm sorry. It isn't as if I even want to get married anyway,' which was another big lie. Hanging her head, mortified by her own mistake, she would have kicked herself. If only she could have reached.

All of a sudden Sean's gloriously romantic gesture didn't seen quite so glorious.

'Well, it's up to you.' He hadn't meant it to, but it came out sounding huffy. 'The house is here. If you want to move in, you can.'

Pandora, who hadn't interpreted it as huffiness, assumed the words to be tinged with boredom and began to panic. Goodness, this was a huge step forward! Just because it wasn't the giant step her boringly strait-laced brother felt Sean should be taking ... well, why should she care what Joel thought anyway? Everyone lived together these days.

And now, Pandora thought joyfully, Sean's asking me to live with him.

'Of course I want to.' The words tumbled out before he could change his mind. Undoing her seat belt and wishing her enormous stomach wouldn't keep getting in the way, she leaned clumsily across and hugged him. 'It's what I want more than anything. And this is a beautiful house.'

'I wonder what your brother will have to say.' Sean looked amused. Joel, he knew, wasn't wild about their relationship. 'He should be glad we're going legit.'

Pandora, who wasn't so sure, was too happy to care.

'Never mind about him.'

'Still, he can help you move your stuff.' Fishing in his pocket, Sean pulled out a front-door key. 'I have to work tonight, but I'm sure you could manage between you. How about that?' He grinned and kissed the tip of her nose. 'By the time I get back from the club, you can be all moved in.'

* * *

Pandora had guessed right. For all his outrage over Sean Mandeville's inability to commit himself, Joel didn't take at all well to the news that she was moving out. Without even realizing it, he had been looking forward to the idea of having a baby around the house. He had already warned his partner at Henley-Grant motors that he would be taking a week or two off work when the baby arrived, in order to help Pandora settle into the new routine.

Now, suddenly, his help was no longer needed. She was leaving, moving out just like that.

'It doesn't suit you, you know.' Joel wasn't about to refuse to move her things but that didn't mean he had to approve of what she was about to do.

Pandora sighed as he loaded up the boot of the car with her hastily assembled belongings. How many dark, big-brother-knows-best looks was she supposed to put up with, for heaven's sake?

'What doesn't suit me?'

'You, jumping whenever Sean Mandeville says jump. What did he do, click his fingers at you and say, "Come on, you're moving in with me"? It just isn't *you*,' Joel said crossly. 'Where's your self-esteem? Whatever happened to the independent girl I used to know? The one with a mind of her own?'

She got pregnant, thought Pandora. She glared across the dark-blue roof of the old Bentley at Joel, who couldn't have the least idea how that felt. So maybe he *was* half right, and maybe seven months ago she would have agreed totally with his point of view . . . but the reality of actually finding herself landed in this situation had soon put paid to all that.

Pandora knew she'd changed – and probably not for the

better – but when you were this pregnant and your self-esteem was this fragile, how else were you supposed to act?

Joel, meanwhile, was shovelling clothes haphazardly back into one of the cases where a zip had burst open. Pandora knew how it felt.

'Summer dresses?' He glanced across at her, unable to resist the jibe. 'Do you think you'll last that long?'

'Shut up.' Pandora was uncomfortably aware that much the same thought had crossed her mind when she'd packed them. 'If it doesn't work out, then you can say "I told you so" as often as you want.' She gave him a warning look. 'But not before then, OK?'

'You mean you're going to make me wait?' Joel raised his eyebrows in mock horror. 'What, the full three weeks?'

Chapter 29

He didn't stay, just unloaded the cases, piled them in the spacious panelled hallway of Pandora's new home, showed the minimum of enthusiasm when she gave him a quick guided tour and left shortly afterwards, having planted a perfunctory kiss on her cheek.

When the doorbell rang less than five minutes later Pandora hurried to answer it, certain it was Joel come back to apologize.

But he hadn't. Instead Cass and Cleo stood there, beaming and waving a tissue-wrapped bottle to help celebrate her moving in.

'And another of my babies flies the nest.' Cass heaved a sentimental sigh an hour later, as the third glass of St Emilion began to take effect. 'There I was, thinking they'd all be with me until I was ninety, and look what's happening. First Sophie, now Sean . . .'

'You've still got me,' Cleo lovingly declared. 'I won't run away from home.'

'You could meet someone wonderful and fall madly in love,' said Cass. She smiled across at Pandora. 'Just like Sean.'

'Ugh.' Cleo pulled a face. 'I hate all men, remember? I'm not going to fall in love.' She drained her glass with a flourish. 'And if I did, it definitely wouldn't be with anyone like Sean.'

Cass and Cleo left at ten o'clock. Sean had already warned her not to expect him home from the club before half-past midnight at the earliest. Yawning, Pandora wondered how on earth she was going to stay awake until then.

In the kitchen, waiting for the kettle to boil, she went over in her mind the accusations Joel had levelled at her.

They were only hurtful because they were true. Pandora conceded that much, but she was at a loss to know how she was supposed to go about restoring her own drastically depleted confidence. The Mandevilles were celebrities, each of them famous in their own right, each one breathtakingly glamorous.

And I'm not even a waitress any more, thought Pandora, feeling more diminished by the second. Catching sight of her distorted reflection in the stainless-steel kettle – Michelin man looked positively anorexic by comparison – she felt tears of self-pity spring to her eyes. She was grotesque, she had no job, there was no way in the world she could begin to compete with Sean and his glitzy family.

Unless . . .

Unless maybe there *was* something she could do.

Pandora's heart began to race. Abandoning the kettle she went out into the hall, knelt down and began unzipping cases until she found what she was looking for. Of course it was an awesomely long shot, but imagine the thrill of actually managing to pull it off.

She sat back on her heels, smiling to herself as the plan began to take root. There were two months left before the baby arrived. During these last two months she might not be able to do much – winning Wimbledon was definitely out – but if she put her mind to it she could do this.

At least, thought Pandora with a surge of elation, I can *try*.

* * *

She was woken from a deep sleep by the sound of muffled laughter. Confused, dimly aware that she wasn't in her own bed – or, for that matter, in any bed at all – Pandora kept her eyes closed. The laughter wasn't the least bit familiar, which was disconcerting. And a strange arm was draped across her forehead.

But did burglars really howl with laughter whilst they were actually in the process of ransacking one's home? And why would one of them be resting their arm leadenly on her head?

Pandora opened an experimental eye. The owner of the laugh was a big West Indian male, heavily dreadlocked and clutching a can of Fosters. In the other extremely large hand he held a sheet of foolscap paper. The next moment Sean appeared in the doorway waving another sheet and laughing so hard he couldn't speak.

'That's mine,' Pandora said, struggling to sit up and discovering to her humiliation that the heavy arm draped across her face was her own gone-to-sleep one. Lifting the deadened limb with her good right hand, she placed it gingerly at her side before hauling herself upright. The man with the dreadlocks, she now realized, was Donny Mulligan, one of Sean's great friends from the club.

'You shouldn't be reading that, it's private,' Pandora protested, but only mildly. At least they were laughing. She felt it had to be a good sign.

'How can it be private?' Sean gestured with his own can at the remaining pages strewn across the floor next to the sofa, abandoned there by Pandora when she'd fallen asleep. 'It was there, waving up at us when we came in.'

'Squealing: "Read me, read me." ' Donny Mulligan gave her the benefit of his famous gold-and-white grin. He shrugged. 'I mean, what else could we do?'

'Hmm.' Pandora massaged her arm, now fizzing with pins and needles, and considered raising the subject of the infamous photographs. The fact that they had been tucked out of sight behind a candlestick on her mantelpiece hadn't stopped Sean having a good nose then. If she really wanted to keep something from him, maybe she should consider installing a safe.

But she couldn't be angry with either of them now. They were still reading, still laughing. And they were, Pandora supposed, experts.

Chancing upon a magazine article about TV scriptwriting in the dentist's waiting room last year was what had drawn Pandora to Comedy Inc. in the first place. The idea of creating a comedy script for television had instantly appealed, capturing her imagination and resulting in a torrent of ideas which she had enthusiastically committed to paper.

But that fateful first trip to the club in Jelahay Street had had dramatic consequences of its own and in all the ensuing emotional chaos the impetus to keep going had been lost. It wasn't something she had even mentioned to anyone else, mainly because there hadn't been much to say. But tonight the idea had come back to her, prompted by those daunting feelings of inadequacy. She had realized that writing was something she could perfectly easily do, no matter how pregnant. It was what had prompted her to dig out the folder of ideas, notes and half-written trial scripts. One, in particular, the one Donny and Sean had seized upon, she privately thought might not be bad at all.

Now for the acid test, thought Pandora, crossing her fingers and trying not to look too terrified. She had to find out if the *real* funny men liked her ideas.

'Go on then,' she said bravely. 'You've had a look at it. Tell me honestly what you think.'

'Oh dear.' Sean glanced across at Donny in search of rescue. Donny examined a fraying hole in the knee of his jeans. Briefly at a loss for words, Sean gazed once more at the sheet of foolscap in his hand.

'You can tell me,' said Pandora.

'OK, it's crap.'

Across the room, Donny winced.

'Well, I'm sorry.' Two spots of colour appeared high up on Sean's cheeks, the first time Pandora had ever seen him blush. Defensively he went on, 'But it is. What are you trying to do here, anyway? Compete?'

'No, *no* . . .' Horrified that Sean might think she was trying to jump on the comedy bandwagon on the strength of her relationship with him, and at the same time desperate not to let him see how crushed she was by his verdict, Pandora said, 'It was just something I had a go at, ages ago. It's nothing, really. Rubbish. I'll chuck it in the bin—'

'That's OK then.' Clearly relieved, Sean let the page flutter to the floor. 'For a minute there you had me worried. I mean, I wouldn't want you to think we were laughing just now because it was funny.'

Pandora tried not to feel sick. They'd been laughing at the script because it was so bad. In the pit of her stomach, the baby gave a small, sympathetic kick.

'Never mind,' Donny put in, meaning to be kind, 'you don't

find these things out until you give them a try.'

'No.' She dredged up a smile.

'Let's face it,' his own good humour restored, Sean ruffled Pandora's short hair, 'gorgeous you may be, but Jennifer Saunders you're not.'

Chapter 30

Cass's earlier lament that everyone was leaving home didn't extend to Terry Brannigan. He might, for the sake of propriety, have rented a studio apartment in nearby Kentish Town but all it really did was house his few belongings. Terry spent every spare moment at Cass's house, not because it was a hundred times nicer than his own depressing flat but because it had Cass in it.

Terry's love for her was as unwavering as ever but fear of rejection had so far prevented him doing anything about it. She seemed to adore him but that, Terry kept gloomily reminding himself, was Cass's way. What if she didn't? Dare he take that chance and risk losing everything?

It was a problem that had been tearing Terry apart for weeks. The only thing that seemed to help – cheering him up and dulling the pain of uncertainty – was vast quantities of Johnnie Walker Red Label. Half a bottle every night and he was happy again, reassured that Cass loved him every bit as much as, if not more than, she had once loved Jack.

Tonight, after rather more Johnnie Walker than usual, Terry decided it was high time he did something about it. He had to let Cass know how he felt. If he waited much longer he was going to find himself in the *Guinness Book of Records* under 'Greatest length of unrequited love'.

Terry was waiting by the front porch when Cleo and Cass arrived home after visiting Pandora.

'I don't believe it.' Cleo, who was driving, was tempted for a moment to put her foot down. Even if she couldn't quite bring herself to run him over she could spray him painfully with gravel. 'It's almost eleven o'clock and your fan club's waiting on the doorstep. Can't you just give him your autograph and send him home?'

But Cass was already waving to Terry through the car window.

'He's lonely, that's all.'

'Not to mention boring.' Cleo was suddenly glad she had to be up at five in the morning for a Testino shoot in Edinburgh. She yawned. 'Oh well, if you're going to be nice to the old soak, I'm going to bed.'

'Coffee?' asked Cass, reaching up to take a pair of blue-and-yellow cups down from the glass-fronted wall cabinet.

Terry fingered the quarter bottle of whisky in the pocket of his raincoat. Cass had a distressing habit of running out of drink in the house and forgetting to buy more. Even more alarmingly, sometimes she hadn't run out of drink at all, she just thought he'd had enough and tried to sober him up with coffee instead. It was why Terry had brought along a little something of his own. He'd just have to slosh a good measure into his cup when she wasn't looking. After all, he definitely needed something to spur him on.

Cass thought at first it was a joke. For the past half an hour everything had been perfectly normal. All she'd done was carry their empty coffee cups through to the kitchen, dump them in the sink and kick off her shoes on her way back to the sitting room. When she reached it, the biscuit tin was still perched on the arm of the sofa but Terry, who had been sitting next to it, was no longer there.

The next moment, almost as if he had been deliberately lying in wait behind the sitting-room door, he pushed it firmly shut, took both Cass's hands in his own and said urgently, 'Tell me you love me. Please, Cass. Now.'

'What?'

She smiled, searching his face, waiting for the inevitable punchline.

But Terry was staring at her, his expression intense. The smell of stale alcohol was strong enough to make Cass flinch.

'It's not a joke. I've waited so long for you to say it.' He squeezed her hands so hard Cass felt her knuckles scrape together. 'My darling, you must know how I feel about you. How much longer do you expect me to wait? Just tell me you love me, *please*.'

'Oh, but . . .'

As Cass, horrified, opened her mouth to protest, Terry groaned and pulled her into his arms. His mouth, wet and whisky-sodden, clamped down on hers. She felt his teeth graze her lower lip. It was an inexpert kiss, a desperate one, and fond though she was of Terry she couldn't bear to let it go on.

'Don't . . . mmphhggh . . . *stop* it . . .'

But determination had granted Terry new strength and he wasn't about to give up now. Inflamed by the physical contact he had dreamt of for so very long, he pressed his mouth over Cass's once more and began pulling her towards the sofa. Once Cass realized he meant what he said – that he truly *did* love her – she would stop fighting it, he was sure. All he had to do was convince her.

Cass wasn't scared but she knew she had to deal with the situation before it had a chance to get seriously out of control. As Terry propelled her across the room, the backs of her thighs hit the sofa. So intent was he on kissing her – and persuading her to kiss him back – that he didn't realize what she was reaching for.

The black-and-gold biscuit tin crashed down on the back of his head and Terry saw matching black-and-gold stars.

'What the . . . ?'

Staggering beneath the impact, he overbalanced and fell backwards across the sofa, ending up bum-first in a heap of tasselled cushions. The screw top on the whisky bottle in his jacket pocket had been less than firmly fastened. Even as Cass watched, an amber stain was spreading across the front of his crumpled trousers. She looked down at the tin in her hands and saw it had a fair-sized dent in it.

'Oh dear,' drawled Cleo, who had heard the sound of tussling as she came downstairs for a glass of water. 'I hope those biscuits are all right.'

Terry was distraught. His worst fears had been realized. Not only did Cass not love him but he had made a complete and utter ninny of himself into the bargain.

How he could have got so carried away was beyond him, but he had. Worse still, he had needed to be brained with a biscuit tin in order to be brought back to his senses. Hideously ashamed of what he had done, Terry didn't know which was harder to bear, Cass's sympathetic understanding or Cleo's smirking disdain.

One thing he did know: his enduring friendship with Cass

was over. Even if she could forgive and forget, there was no way he could ever forgive himself.

Tears swam in Terry's eyes as he gazed at Cass for the last time.

'It's all right, you don't have to be polite. Why would you be interested in someone like me anyway? I'm just a decrepit old has-been who drinks too much.'

'Come on now, this is silly.'

Cass was worried about letting him leave but when she put her hand on his arm he flinched like a burns victim. 'There's no need to be upset. It was a simple mistake, that's all. No harm done.'

'No harm done?' Despite everything, Terry almost smiled. 'You really don't understand, do you? You have no idea how it feels to love someone . . .' Unable to go on, he shook his head and opened the front door. 'I'm sorry, sorry about everything. You don't have to worry, either. You won't see me again. And that's a promise.'

When he had gone, Cass sat down on the bottom step of the staircase and buried her head in her hands.

Cleo, who had with uncharacteristic diplomacy retreated to the kitchen during the final emotional farewells, reappeared.

'Look, Mum, maybe it's just as well he's gone. The last thing you need is hassle like that.'

'Oh, but how the poor man must be feeling,' Cass sighed.

'Imagine how you'd be feeling now', Cleo briskly retaliated, 'if he'd raped you.'

'He wouldn't have raped me.'

'You don't know that.'

Wearily Cass shook her head. 'Terry's a good man. A kind

man. To think after all these years, I didn't have the least idea how he felt. And now I've rejected him, made him miserable—'

'That's hardly your fault.' Cleo was unforgiving. 'Anyway, serves him right for being a prat.'

'But this feels almost worse than splitting up with your father,' Cass wailed. 'I don't *want* to hurt someone else that much. I feel so guilty. At least when Jack left I didn't have to feel guilty. Oh God, do you think Terry will be all right?'

'Course he will. As soon as he sobers up.' Cleo, who was hungry, retrieved the biscuit tin from the sitting room. 'Look at that,' she exclaimed in disgust. 'How could you say no harm done? These bourbons are beyond repair.'

Chapter 31

Imogen was at her wits' end. In the ten days since Sophie had moved in, the flat had become scarcely recognizable. It was like being invaded by an army of squatters, except they wouldn't spend as much time hogging the bathroom.

As far as Imogen could make out, Sophie ate fifteen meals a day and used every kitchen implement known to man in order to prepare each one. These she then dumped in the sink along with the plates of half-eaten food which were undoubtedly too disgusting to finish.

Imogen felt sick just having to look at the concoctions Sophie was capable of conjuring up. She cringed at the peanut-butter-and-chocolate-sauce splashes plastered across the wall behind the Magimix. She marvelled at the fact that she was the one expected to do all the washing-up.

'I'll have a word with her,' was Jack's way of fobbing Imogen off, 'but you have to give Sophie a bit of leeway, darling. She *is* studying for her GCSEs.'

Imogen doubted whether Sophie could study anything with bloody Foo Fighters blaring non-stop. Nor did she see why she and Jack should be banished to the bedroom at nine o'clock each evening when Sophie, instead of going to sleep as she was supposed to do, lay in solitary splendour across the sofa watching TV until gone midnight.

As the days wore by, Imogen began to suspect Jack's

precious daughter was doing it on purpose. When Sophie arrived home from school the next day with a box of frogs, she decided the time had come to speak out.

'OK, Sophie, what's the plan? Are you deliberately trying to make my life hell?'

'Oh no, is that what you think?' Sophie looked dumbfounded. 'I'm sorry, Imogen, really I am.'

This was half the trouble; despite the chaos she caused, Sophie was unfailingly polite and apologetic.

'The frogs are part of my biology project. They won't get in your way, I promise. I'm going to take brilliant care of them.'

'Ribbit,' chorused the frogs in their perspex box. 'Ribbit.'

'I'm not just talking about the frogs.' Imogen willed herself to stay calm. 'This morning after you left for school I spent an hour cleaning the bath, wiping marmalade off the television screen and trying to get the smell of pickled onions out of the rug in front of the fire.'

She forbore to mention just how much the rug – cream and white and nineteenth-century Persian – had cost.

Sophie hung her head. 'Sorry again. The jar slipped out of my hand.'

'Yet your father insists you're normally clean, tidy and pretty much house-trained. Which makes me think all this havoc-making is a bit of a put-on.' Imogen gave her a long, cool look. 'And it isn't going to work. So why don't you just give in gracefully, go back home and leave us in peace?'

Sophie's eyes filled with tears.

'I'm not doing anything on purpose, honestly. Of course I'll leave if I have to, but where would I go? Not home . . .' A single tear rolled down the side of her nose. 'You can't make me go home.'

'I don't see why you don't want to.' Imogen's teeth were clenched together so tightly her jaw ached. 'You've been perfectly happy there for the past fifteen years.'

'So was Dad, but you didn't mind when he left.' Sophie looked defiant. 'I don't see why I can't leave too.' Then she heaved a sigh. 'Anyway, I can see I'm not wanted here, so I'll move out tomorrow. Will after school be OK? Say, five o'clock?'

Imogen looked at her. 'Where will you go?'

'Don't worry, I can look after myself.' Sophie wiped the lone tear from her cheek with the back of her skinny white hand. 'That cardboard box your washing machine was delivered in last week, is it still around? And if you could spare a couple of old blankets . . .'

Under the circumstances, Jack did the only thing he could do.

'Right,' he announced, returning home the following day looking extremely pleased with himself. 'That's that sorted.'

'What?' demanded Imogen.

Sophie said nothing, simply looked at her father and blinked.

'Get packing,' Jack declared. 'I've rented a house in Wimbledon. We can move in tonight.'

Imogen glanced across at Sophie.

'What? You mean she's coming too?'

'Of course.' Jack determinedly ignored the tension in the air. 'We're *all* going. The house has five bedrooms, more than enough space for everyone. And,' he announced firmly, 'I've arranged for a cleaning woman to come in five mornings a week. So that's that. All our problems solved. Now maybe we can start to relax and enjoy each other's company. Maybe,' he said, smiling at the two girls in turn, 'the situation in future could be less . . . fraught.'

Oh hell, thought Sophie, appalled by what she had done.

Shit, thought Imogen, her heart sinking as she realized Jack had presented them with a perfect *fait accompli*.

'Ribbit,' cackled the frogs in their perspex box.

Sophie could have kicked herself for getting it so spectacularly wrong.

'Now I've really messed up,' she groaned over a plate of cottage pie in the comforting familiarity of her own home. She looked in anguish at Cass, who sat opposite her at the kitchen table. 'Dad had even hired a van to get all our stuff over there in one go. When he was in Flooze's flat he could leave any time he liked. Now, thanks to me, he's taken a house on a five-year lease. It's made them a proper couple,' she said woefully. 'Five years . . . it sounds so *permanent*. All I've done is made everything worse.'

'It's not your fault.' Cass tried to pretend it couldn't matter less but the news had still come as a body blow. She too had been reassured by the thought that Jack's move into Imogen's mews flat had an air of temporariness about it.

Now, however, Jack appeared to be committing himself and Cass found herself feeling more and more alone. Her family was drifting away from her, for the first time in her life the radio show seemed more of a chore than an adventure, and Terry appeared to have vanished from the face of the earth. Repeated phone calls to his bedsitter having yielded no reply, she had gone round to see him last night only to discover from the girl next door that Terry had moved out.

'I asked him if he wanted to leave a forwarding address but he said there wasn't any point,' the girl had told Cass, impressed to think her ex-next-door neighbour had known someone so famous. She wrinkled her nose and smiled. 'He was a funny old chap, wasn't he? Not that any of us saw much of him but he seemed quite nice. Drank like nobody's business, mind you. Did he really have his own radio show once?'

Blaming herself for Terry's disappearance only made Cass feel even worse than she did already. What if he were to commit suicide or drink himself to death as a result of her rejection of him? What, she thought with a shiver, if he were already dead?

'Don't panic, I'm almost sure you wouldn't get done for manslaughter,' Sophie said soothingly when Cass confided her fears. 'Just so long as we don't say anything to the police about you battering him over the head with a biscuit tin—'

'Very funny,' Cass fretted. 'I don't know how you can joke about it. That poor man. He *could* be dead . . .'

Sophie was eminently practical. 'Come on, he's not that stupid. You've been reading too much *Romeo and Juliet*.' With some relief, she added, 'I think it's definitely time I moved back home.'

'Yes?' Cass's spirits lifted at once. 'What about the big house in Wimbledon?'

'Leave them to it, I suppose.' Sophie shrugged. 'I did my worst and it backfired. Flooze was on to me, anyway. She guessed I was doing all that stuff on purpose.'

'Well, I'm just glad you're coming back.' Getting up from

the table, Cass enveloped her in a hug. 'And even if it didn't work, it was a nice try.'

'Oh, don't worry.' Sophie, who had been spending a lot of time recently on the phone to Cleo, gave her mother a small, controlled smile. 'We haven't given up yet.'

Chapter 32

'So you're planning to spend the summer here in England.' Imogen, checking her notes and double-checking the tape recorder was running smoothly, knew she couldn't afford to make any mistakes. 'But filming *Crackshot* is only going to take up seven or eight weeks at most. So what plans do you have for the rest of your time here?'

Goodness, Dino Carlisle was handsome. Meeting him in the flesh, too, was even more of a revelation. Since the film parts in which he was invariably cast were of the invincible hero variety, Imogen had automatically assumed him to be a keep-fit fanatic, humourless and possibly a bit thick. Instead, upon being shown into his sumptuous fifth-floor suite at the dauntingly swish Lanesborough, she had been quite bowled over by the welcome she had received and by the fact that Dino Carlisle was so very much more charming and approachable than she had imagined.

'What are my plans for the rest of my time here?' He gazed across at her, the spark in his green eyes not humourless at all. 'You mean my *real* plans or the ones we make up for the benefit of your devoted readers?'

Beads of perspiration trickled down between Imogen's breasts. She hoped she didn't look as flustered as she felt.

'Why don't you tell me your plans and I'll decide how much our devoted readers can take.' She gave him a prim smile.

'OK.' Dino Carlisle grinned back. 'Well, I guess I'll be looking up a few old friends. And hopefully making one or two new ones. I'm sorry, do I have the heating turned up too much in here? Is this temperature uncomfortable for you?'

'Well, maybe a touch . . .'

'My fault.' Dino grinned again, revealing Hollywood-white teeth. 'You came here dressed for a misty April morning in London and I'm suffocating you with summer in California.' Mocking his own accent he drawled, 'I'm sorry, I'm just a selfish, pig-ignorant, ill-mannered ac-tor. Here, let me open a couple of windows.'

Imogen began to relax. She removed her grey Jasper Conran jacket and allowed Dino to take it from her. In true California style he was wearing a casual white cotton shirt and well-worn 501s. His toffee-brown tan looked as delicious as the body beneath it. The temptation to reach out and touch that almost too-perfect flesh was overwhelming.

'Right, well, better get on.' Dragging her attention back to the interview, Imogen glanced once more at her notes. 'Your agent granted us thirty minutes and I realize how busy you must be—'

'Take no notice of him.' Dino gave her a disarming smile as he sat back down, stretching out on his side across the yellow sofa. 'He only does that to make the press think I'm more important than I really am. It's the old Garbo thing, see? Treat 'em mean, keep 'em keen.' He winked at Imogen. 'But it's all bullshit. You can stay here as long as you like.'

Imogen was enjoying herself. The interview was going like a dream, Dino Carlisle had kept her thoroughly entertained for almost two hours and room service had supplied them with a fab lunch of asparagus, gingered sea bass and raspberry brûlée. Dino had even refused to let her pick up the tab.

'Hell, why should you? I'm having fun,' he had protested. 'The least you can let me do is buy you lunch.'

He really was a tremendously nice man. Charismatic, too. Basking in the pleasurable glow of such undivided attention, Imogen smiled and nodded when he offered her another glass of white wine. Being flirted with was always an ego-boost. When the man showing such obvious interest was none other than Dino Carlisle it was almost impossible to resist.

It was just about impossible not to flirt back, either. Glancing down at her feet, Imogen saw that without even realizing it she had kicked off her shoes. Her skirt had ridden a couple of inches higher up her thighs and she had swivelled into a relaxed, sideways position in her chair with one foot comfortably tucked beneath the other leg. Talk about body language, thought Imogen. What a dead giveaway.

Leaning forward, inserting a fresh tape into the cassette recorder on the coffee-table between them, she tried to concentrate on the questions she was supposed to be asking. Oh help, next on her list she had written 'sex life'. She took a deep breath.

'OK, girlfriends. I know you like to keep your private life private but *is* there anyone special at the moment?'

Beneath the mane of unruly dark hair, Dino's eyebrows twitched.

'Now there's a question.' His voice softened. 'Well, what can I say? How about possibly?' He hesitated. 'Or should that be hopefully?'

As a journalist, Imogen was unable to resist the dig. 'How about enigmatically?'

'Sorry, I'm not trying to be enigmatic.' Dino was looking at her in such a way that Imogen's throat went suddenly dry. 'The thing is, I'm not too sure myself. I know I've met someone special, I just don't know how she feels about me. It's early days, you see.' He paused, then said, 'Actually, that's not true. More like early hours.'

Heavens. In her chest, Imogen's heart was going nineteen to the dozen. Her palms were damp. She found she couldn't drag her gaze away from those mesmerizing emerald-green eyes. Damn, she must look like a rabbit paralysed by headlights.

'And before you ask, I don't make a habit of propositioning pretty journalists.'

Stalling for time, Imogen said, 'No?'

'No.' Dino's smile was rueful. 'Dangerous hobby. You never know when you might be being taken for a ride. Imagine the blow to the ego if you thought you'd acquitted yourself with honours – then discovered in print that the last time they'd had that lousy a time in bed was when they'd been struck down with flu.'

Imogen managed a shaky laugh, then drew breath.

'How do you know I wouldn't say that?'

'I don't. I just happen to think you're worth the risk.' His gaze flickered for a moment. 'I also hope you wouldn't *need* to say it. I don't know if you realize how attracted I am to you, but—'

'Stop,' Imogen said unhappily. 'Please, don't say any more. I'm sorry, you really are one of the nicest men I've ever met, but you must stop. I'm already involved with someone else, you see. And I love him. I'm tremendously flattered by all this,' her vague gesture around the suite included Dino himself, 'but nothing can come of it. I'm . . . spoken for, I suppose. And I could never be unfaithful to Jack.'

Cleo was utterly disgusted.

'Well,' she grumbled, 'all I can say is you can't have tried very hard.'

'I did.' Dino grinned, unperturbed. 'I gave it my all, as you British so weirdly say. And if I say so myself, I was magnificent. She just turned me down flat. She even apologized but said she loved your old man too much to ever cheat on him. I thought it was kinda cute.' To infuriate Cleo even more, he couldn't resist adding, 'And I know you described her as the hag-from-hell but she really wasn't half as bad as you made out. She's an attractive girl, great body, good company—'

'Fine, let's hope she writes a good obituary.' Cleo seized a blue tasselled cushion and pressed it across his face.

'At least you know she really is in love with your father,' Dino protested when she let him breathe again. 'OK, so maybe it wasn't the result you wanted but isn't that still a reassuring thing to find out?'

'What a completely dumb thing to say,' howled Cleo. 'I don't give a stuff whether or not Imogen Trent loves my father. All I want is for him to stop loving *her*.'

Dino and Cleo had first met two years earlier at a stultifyingly dull celebrity party in New York thrown to publicize the launch of a new perfume. The perfume, named after and supposedly created by a face-lifted, drug-addicted movie star in her fifties was being touted as the explosive new fragrance of the year.

Cleo, walking into the hotel ballroom where the launch was being held and breathing in the scent for the first time, had declared, 'Smells like donkey droppings to me.'

Sadly, she had failed to recognize the drastically relifted face of the middle-aged movie star standing less than three feet away. The star, who favoured toyboys and maintained a pathological fear of having them enticed away by stunning eighteen-year-old girls, had spun round, bagless eyes blazing.

'You. Smart-mouthed English bitch. *Out.*'

'Oh, heavens . . .' Too late, Cleo realized her mistake. Clapping her hands over her mouth, she gazed in abject dismay at the furious female before her. 'I'm so sorry, I didn't mean it . . . your perfume doesn't really smell of donkey droppings—'

'Out,' hissed the star, her capped teeth bared in a snarl. '*Now.*'

'But—'

'Come on.' Dino Carlisle, whom Cleo had never met before in her life, took her arm and swept her towards the exit.

'Dino!' cried the star, who had pinned her hopes on his becoming her next toyboy. 'You can't leave . . .'

The paparazzi, thrilled that something photogenic was at last happening, began frenziedly snapping away.

'Right, let's get out of here,' Dino told a speechless Cleo. Loudly enough for the press to hear, he said, 'And find somewhere that doesn't smell of Eau de Zoo.'

They had been friends ever since that night, the friendship cemented still further by the realization that although they liked each other tremendously, there wasn't so much as an iota of sexual chemistry between them.

'I can't understand it,' Dino had once drawled, amused but at the same time perplexed. 'You're gorgeous and I love you to death . . . so why don't I fancy you?'

'Maybe you're gay.'

He looked appalled. 'I am *not*.'

'Anyway, who cares?' Cleo shrugged and grinned. 'I don't fancy you either. We must have been brother and sister in some past life.'

Now, putting the tasselled cushion with which she had tried to suffocate him back on the sofa, Dino refused to be bullied into submission by Cleo's pig-headed attitude. She had done her best to catch Imogen out and had failed. It was something she was simply going to have to accept.

'You're being unreasonable,' he pointed out. 'The whole point of doing these check-up things of yours was because you wanted people to be happy and faithful. You told me how depressing it was, watching everyone fail their tests. I think you should be pleased someone finally passed.'

'Even if it is my father's tart of a girlfriend?' said Cleo gloomily. 'Oh Dino, I know I wanted my faith in humanity restored. I just didn't want it done for me by Imogen bloody Trent.'

Chapter 33

The sixth and final episode of *Sean Mandeville On Show* was in the can. Each thirty-minute segment was interspersed with behind-the-scenes footage of Sean preparing to go on stage and winding down after each performance. In keeping with his image, there were girls galore to help him wind down. When the Pandora story finally broke only days before the last episode was due to be filmed, the producer was desperate to have her included.

'We need her if we're going to be topical,' he explained to Sean. 'Come on, it's all good human-interest stuff. Get the girl down here.'

But Pandora was still smarting over Sean's accusation that she might be trying to gain attention simply by being associated with him. She steadfastly refused to be involved.

'Just a two-minute piece,' the producer urged over the phone. That Pandora was black, as far as he was concerned, only heightened the intrigue. 'You wouldn't even have to come to the club. We can do it at the house.'

'Sorry,' said Pandora, 'but no. It's Sean's series, not mine.'

'You're Sean's family,' the producer reminded her. 'People are interested. They want to *see* you.'

What, Pandora thought sadly, so they can snigger and wonder what Sean Mandeville ever saw in me?'

'Please . . . ?' wheedled the producer.

'No. Just tell everyone I'm pregnant and the size of a whale,' said Pandora. 'And it's not a pretty sight. They really wouldn't want to see me.'

The end-of-series party was held at Comedy Inc. the following Friday. By ten o'clock the club was straining at its grubby, nicotine-stained seams.

It was, Sean decided, probably just as well Pandora had chosen to stay at home. He hadn't the least idea why she had so stubbornly refused to appear in front of the cameras but steering clear of tonight's party – when it was packed with this many people – was undoubtedly a sensible move.

It also meant he was free to relax and enjoy himself without having to look after Pandora and perpetually wonder if she was all right. Not, he hastily excused himself, that he minded; it was just one of those things. Pandora wouldn't know a soul here, whereas he knew just about everyone.

Sean's attention at that moment was caught by a face in the crowd over at the far end of the room. It was a face belonging to one of the few people there he didn't know but whom he nevertheless instantly recognized . . .

Since breaking off her engagement to Colin, Linda Lazenby had discovered just how painful being single could be. Desperately unprepared for the loneliness which had engulfed her like a tidal wave – for since the age of fourteen she had simply fallen from one relationship into the lap of the next – Linda had taken on more and more work in a panicky attempt to blot out the horror. Only the even more terrifying prospect of having to face the wrath of Cleo Mandeville had kept her from begging Colin's forgiveness and crawling back into his unfaithful arms.

But Cleo hadn't warned her that being young, free and single would be this vile. Nor had spending the last six weeks in New York helped. Male New Yorkers were a decidedly off-putting lot. Now, back in London, she couldn't find anything that could be called an improvement. Help, thought Linda with a renewed pang of fear, won't I ever meet anyone nice again?

And then she saw Sean Mandeville coming towards her and her heart did an odd little skip. Not that his being here was in any way a surprise, seeing as the party was in his honour, but she was jolted by how good-looking he was. It really seemed, too, as if he was heading directly for her.

'Sorry,' said Sean, 'no gate-crashers.'

'Oh . . .' Linda's hands fluttered to her bony chest. Chronic-ally insecure, it didn't occur to her for a moment that he might be joking. 'But I was invited, honestly. I'm here with Margo Hamilton, only I think she's got lost in the loo or something . . .'

'Calm down.' Up close, Sean was able to see the fear in those slanting violet eyes. 'Of course you're invited. I just came over to say hello because I know you're a friend of Cleo's.' He broke into a grin. 'Hello, friend of Cleo's. I'm Sean.'

'Oh.' The fear left Linda's eyes. Hugely relieved that she wasn't about to be turfed out on her ear, and unsure what to do next, she seized Sean's hand and shook it so vigorously the chain belt around her waist rattled like a gaoler's keys. 'Yes, Cleo and I've known each other for years. She's brilliant, isn't she?'

'Hmmm.' Sean looked doubtful. 'Try being her brother.'

'It's so lovely to meet you at last, as well.' Too busy gushing to think, Linda went on, 'I asked Cleo to introduce us ages ago but she wouldn't.'

'Really?' Sean raised an eyebrow. 'Why not?'

'Oh . . . um . . .'

He looked amused. 'Let me guess. I'm the big bad wolf.'

'Well, kind of. Though I'm sure you aren't . . .'

Sean said gravely, 'I'm much misunderstood.'

'Here comes Margo.'

Glancing behind him, Sean saw Margo Hamilton making her way through the crowds. Now there was a model he didn't care for. Margo was a big-boned, big-mouthed Texan. And she was taller than he was.

'She's got her coat on.' Linda sounded unhappy. 'Oh dear, it looks as if we're leaving.'

Rapidly, before bossy Margo could butt in, Sean said, 'You don't have to leave just because she is. Look, how about coming for something to eat with me? To celebrate meeting each other,' he smiled at Linda, 'against all odds and my interfering sister's wishes.'

Thank goodness Cleo was in Milan this week, safely out of the way and unable to stick her oar in.

'Come along, Linda, we've had enough now. Time to go. Oh, hello, Sean.' There was no warmth in the greeting. Sean's dislike of Margo was entirely reciprocated.

Linda glanced nervously from one to the other. Sean's brief nod of encouragement was accompanied by a ghost of a smile.

Margo began to chivvy her towards the door. 'Come *on*.'

'I'm OK here, actually.'

Linda blurted out the words, realizing that Sean wasn't about to intervene. He was leaving it up to her. It was scary but thrilling.

'What are you talking about?' Margo's eyes narrowed. Linda had never answered back in her life.

'You go, I'll stay.' Linda vividly recalled Cleo's urgent pleas that she should learn to stand up for herself. What better time to start, Linda thought with a rush of pride . . . and who better than Cleo's own gorgeous brother to start with?

'Have you been drinking?' Margo demanded crossly.

'Only Diet Coke.'

'Come on now, Linda. I really think—'

'It's all right, I'll take care of her.' Highly amused by the spectacle of the worm turning, Sean slid his arm around Linda's quivering, wafer-thin waist. 'She'll be fine with me.'

It didn't take long for the gossip to filter back to Cleo when she arrived home from Milan three days later. Due to appear at a charity fashion show at the Four Seasons that afternoon, she turned up early. Linda, one of the other celebrity models doing their bit for Children in Need, greeted her with delight.

'You're back! Oh, I'm so glad to see you again. You'll never guess what I did the other night—'

Cleo sincerely hoped she couldn't. Unable to face playing along, she said flatly, 'It's Sean, isn't it? Linda, whatever it was you did, you must never do it again. I can't believe you even *spoke* to him. What did I *tell* you,' Cleo wailed, 'about getting involved with bastards?'

'I know, I know,' Linda gazed at her in earnest, 'but that's just it . . . he *isn't* a bastard. Oh Cleo, he's really nice—'

'Balls,' said Cleo, terrifying one of the show's organizers. The little man backed away in alarm.

'Sean said you'd say that.' Linda shook her head in sorrowful fashion. Her raspberry-pink taffeta frock crackled in sympathy. 'Well, maybe not balls exactly, but he knew you'd get funny.'

'Believe me, I'll get even funnier when I see him.'

'You could at least be a bit pleased for me.' Cut to the quick by Cleo's unsympathetic attitude, Linda's heavily mascaraed eyes swam with tears. 'You know how unhappy I've been since—'

'Since you gave Colin the boot.' Such gratitude, thought Cleo despairingly. 'Yes, yes, I *do* know. But getting involved with my brother isn't the answer. He'll make you unhappier than Colin ever could. You'll end up unhappy beyond your wildest dreams.'

'You're only his sister. How can you possibly understand?' Linda was sticking obstinately to her guns. The other evening with Sean had been one of the most wonderful of her life. 'He made me feel so alive, so special . . .'

'It's a gift he has.' Cleo knew she had to be brutal. 'Some people can play the piano, some can do card tricks. Sean's talent is for making girls feel special.'

'Ahem,' coughed the nervous organizer behind her. 'Miss Mandeville, we're ready for you in the dressing room if you'd like to come with me?'

Linda, who was trying to be assertive, was finding it hard going.

'OK, so maybe lots of girls are mad about him,' she blurted out in desperation, 'but he has to fall in love and settle down some time. Why not with me?'

'Oh for heaven's sake!' Exasperated beyond belief, Cleo

shouted, 'What's he done, brainwashed you or something? What about Pandora?'

'Who?' Linda began to shake. 'Who's Pandora?'

'Oh, come on! The girl Sean lives with.' Cleo glared at the cringeing organizer then returned her attention to Linda. 'The one who's about to have his baby.'

'No,' Linda whimpered, violet eyes wide with disbelief. 'You aren't serious.'

'You mean you don't know? It's been in all the papers!'

Linda, before her, was deflating like an old balloon. The taffeta frock crackled once more as she sank into a chair at the side of the stage.

'I don't read the papers. Only *Vogue* and *Harpers*.'

This was true. Cleo, kicking herself for not having realized that Linda hadn't known about Pandora, put her arms around her.

'I'm sorry I shouted. This is all bloody Sean's fault. This time I'm really going to kill him.'

Linda's mascara was running freely down her face. Cleo hugged her again.

'Cheer up, at least you haven't had time to get properly involved.'

Linda gave her a mournful look.

'Haven't I?'

Cleo sighed. 'Oh dear. Did he seduce you?'

'We went out to dinner, that's all.' Hiccuping, Linda took the handful of tissues thrust at her by the agitated organizer. 'Nothing else happened. Sean didn't seduce me.'

Maybe not physically, thought Cleo, but mentally he had.

'I tried to warn you about him.'

Linda nodded. 'What's she like, this Pandora? Who is she?'

'Pandora's . . . nobody.' Cleo didn't mean to be cruel, she was simply stating a fact. 'She's just very very nice. And she made the mistake of getting involved with my brother.'

Chapter 34

Unable to kill Sean, who was – luckily for him – working in Scotland, Cleo decided to visit Pandora instead. Feeling guilty on her appalling brother's behalf, she popped into Harvey Nichols beforehand and spent an hour choosing a silk dressing gown in glorious sunset shades of Venetian red and saffron yellow for Pandora to wear when she went into hospital. It was a poor substitute for a faithful partner but it might just lift her spirits. And, thought Cleo, it was a damn sight better than that terrible grey-blue towelling thing she had spotted hanging up in the bathroom the last time she'd called round.

'It's beautiful,' sighed Pandora, who wasn't over-fond herself of the blue dressing gown Joel had given her for Christmas two years ago. It had never recovered from being chucked by him into the washing machine on a ferociously hot wash along with four sets of oily mechanics' overalls.

'Those colours really suit you.' Cleo was pleased with her final choice.

'You shouldn't have bought it.' Surreptitiously glancing at the label, Pandora tried not to think how much this new robe must have cost.

Of course I should, thought Cleo, it's to make up for my brother being a shit.

Aloud she said brightly, 'You have to have something decent to wear in hospital. Why are you breathing like that?'

'Like what?'

'Pulling a funny face and kind of holding your breath.'

'Oh hell, is that what I'm doing?' As Pandora spoke, it began to happen again. With a sinking heart she realized why.

Awestruck, Cleo gasped. 'Is this . . . it? Is this . . . *labour*?'

'Looks like it. Typical, just when Sean isn't here. Oh, help—'

'Don't panic, I'm here.' Cleo, who hadn't the faintest idea what giving birth entailed, assumed an expression of importance and guided Pandora into a chair. 'Shall I start boiling saucepans of water?'

'Stick some spaghetti in.' Pandora's breathing eased as the contraction receded.

Cleo looked alarmed. 'In where?'

'The water, silly.' Smiling, Pandora nodded in the direction of the kitchen. 'In my how-to-have-a-baby book it says you're supposed to eat lots of pasta when you go into labour. To give you energy.'

Cleo, who wasn't domesticated, said, 'I could phone our local Italian restaurant and ask Luigi to send something round.' She wrinkled her nose. 'Just think, all that puffing and panting on top of all that garlic. You'll have the doctors dropping like flies.'

Joel hadn't the faintest idea what to expect either, when he arrived at the hospital three hours later. Having jumped red lights, cursed every other driver on the road and abandoned the Bentley on double yellows when he couldn't find a parking space, it came as something of an anticlimax to find Pandora alone, sitting up in bed flipping through a pile of magazines and watching *Blue Peter* on a portable colour television.

'Hi,' said Joel, kissing her anyway and trying to hide his disappointment. 'I thought women having babies clung to the headboards, swore non-stop and bit chunks out of people's hands . . . and here you are looking perfectly normal.' He peered at the copy of *Cosmopolitan* lying open across her lap. The article was headed 'Sixteen New Positions for Sizzling Summer Sex'. 'Should you be reading that?'

Pandora closed the magazine – well, she could dream, couldn't she? – and put it to one side.

'I haven't bitten any hands yet. It only hurts every few minutes. In between contractions,' she said with a look of apology. 'I'm fine.'

'And what's this, some new kind of hospital robe?' Joel rubbed the silk sleeve experimentally between thumb and forefinger. He frowned. 'Why aren't you wearing your own dressing gown?'

Pandora, bracing herself as another contraction began to take hold, didn't have the energy to fib.

'This one was a present from Cleo. She came round to the house at lunchtime.'

'Oh well, fine.' Joel, who had been just about to admire the design, said tightly, 'You may as well throw your old one away then . . . if Cleo's given you something better.'

Beads of perspiration sprang out on Pandora's forehead. Trying to breathe through the swelling wave of pain, she gasped, 'Don't be childish. Cleo was the one who brought me to the hospital. She'll be back in a minute – she's just gone to the canteen for a coffee.'

'I'm here.'

Cleo, standing in the open doorway, gazed across at Joel. Joel stared back.

'Phew,' Pandora sighed as the contraction died away. That had been a strong one. Now all she had to do was introduce Joel and Cleo. Or rather, reintroduce them.

'I know who you are,' Cleo suddenly announced. As if she could forget. It had been one of the most interminable evenings of her life.

'I know who you are, too.'

'But . . . you're Pandora's brother?'

'Such powers of deduction,' Joel murmured beneath his breath. 'Look out, Sherlock.'

He was sitting on the edge of the bed. Pandora kicked him, hard.

'Look, I'm sorry. This is my fault.' She turned to Cleo. 'I didn't quite have the nerve to tell you.'

'I can't believe it,' said Cleo, still looking at Joel. 'You . . .'

'OK, let's get one thing straight.'

Joel stood up. Pandora, watching them both, thought: This is like the gunfight at the OK Corral.

'I wasn't trying to chat you up that night,' Joel said heavily. 'I know you thought I was, but I wasn't. Damien Maxwell-Horne is a liar and a crook. I felt you should be warned off him.'

'I knew what he was.' Cleo's brown eyes glittered. 'He was cheating on the mother of a friend of mine. My job was to prove it, which I did.' With a shudder, she added, 'I was never . . . involved with him. Ugh, credit me with *some* taste.'

227

When she looked again at Joel Grant, Cleo saw the cautious beginnings of a smile hovering around his mouth.

'Honestly?'

'Honestly.'

'He told us he'd had to dump you,' said Joel, 'because you were frigid.'

'He *what*? The lying weasel!'

'Um . . .' said Pandora hesitantly, 'could someone please call a nurse?'

Joel shrugged. 'Well, you can't say I didn't try to warn you.'

'He really said that?' howled Cleo, beside herself with rage. 'And you believed him, I suppose . . .'

'Could someone call a nurse *please*?'

'Damn right I believed him.' Joel was grinning now. 'He said you were an uptight frigid bitch, and—'

'Shut up!' Pandora yelled, realizing that the time had come to start cursing and biting hands. 'Get a nurse in here NOW! Tell them my waters have broken—'

'Yeeuurgh,' Cleo squealed.

'Oh dear.' Joel tried not to laugh. 'All over your new dressing gown too.'

Banished from the delivery suite by both Pandora and the senior midwife – 'Now, now, you two, how on earth is the poor girl supposed to concentrate with all this bickering going on?' – Joel and Cleo retreated to the hospital canteen.

Nurses, doctors and technicians came and went, gossiping over shepherd's pie and mugs of thick Indian tea, snatching a few minutes of much-needed sleep, or guzzling down cans of

Coke and salad sandwiches and poring over textbooks to help them through the next exam.

But if most of the hospital staff noticed and instantly recognized Cleo Mandeville, with her distinctive crop of short, bright blond hair, glittering dark eyes and Slavic cheekbones, Cleo didn't notice them. All she could concentrate on was Joel, Pandora's brother, the man who had so annoyed her all those months ago and whom she had never been able to successfully put out of her mind since.

He had been wearing a faded green rugby shirt last time, and battered jeans. Now, having come to the hospital straight from work, he wore a well-cut dark-blue suit over a blue-and-white striped shirt. Nice tie, thought Cleo, good shoes too. Nice hair, good body . . . *great* body . . .

Discovering that her initial impression of Joel Grant had been so entirely off-beam took some adjusting to.

'I can't get used to this,' Cleo told him when he returned to their table with two cups of coffee. 'I thought you were such a pig that night.' Severely she added, 'Although I still don't approve of the fact that you were happy enough to let Damien buy the drinks. If you hate someone that much you shouldn't accept drinks from them.'

'Happy? I was ecstatic,' Joel retorted. 'That man is forever pushing himself into conversations, getting himself included in big rounds then disappearing before there's any danger of having to buy one back. He'd never been known to open his wallet before. His meanness is legendary. Damn right we were going to let him buy us a drink!'

Cleo sighed. 'I didn't know that. I just despised you. I'm sorry.'

'That's OK.' Grinning, Joel stirred three teaspoons of sugar into his coffee. 'I felt just the same about you. You didn't help much, either, with that fairy godmother act the other week.'

'What fairy godmother act?'

'Buying up most of Harrods.' The time had come, Joel realized, to be frank. 'All those lacy, frilly, hand-embroidered baby things. Way too much stuff – and most of it dry-clean only. I know how much that little spree must have set you back. I decided you'd done it deliberately, to show us just how much we couldn't afford.'

Cleo's eyes blazed with indignation. 'Well, excuse me for being rich! Can *I* help it if I make silly money? And choose to spend it on people I like?'

'No, but—'

'Anyway,' said Cleo, 'think how you'd have reacted if I'd turned up with a couple of lousy Babygros. I can just imagine the kind of names you'd have called me then.'

Of course he would. The coffee was disgusting. Joel pushed it to one side.

'OK, so you aren't as horrible as I thought you were.' He pulled a face. 'Unlike this coffee.'

Cleo sighed. 'I suppose you aren't either.'

For several seconds they gazed at each other in silence. Cleo, never normally at a loss for words, could feel something strange happening in her chest. It was like a giant moth battering frantically against her ribs.

She looked away first, shocked to realize how violently attracted she was to Joel Grant. He wasn't in the least her type; years of modelling meant she was used to chiselled, physically perfect men with bodies like panthers and – far too often – the brains of a six-year-old. None of them had ever made Cleo's insides feel like this.

It was a shock feeling it now. Joel might be good-looking in his own big, blond way but he was never likely to be mistaken for a model. The hair needed a cut, he could probably do with losing a few pounds around the middle and those shoulders were too broad even for someone of his great height.

But none of these minor faults mattered in the least. Cleo liked them because they were part of Joel, just as she liked his broken nose and the way the bags under his eyes were accentuated by that crooked, irreverent smile.

All the attraction she had been unable to summon up for gorgeous, eminently fanciable Dino Carlisle had been saving itself, she now realized, for a different kind of man altogether.

Her mind was wandering so happily in this new and unexpected direction that Cleo had almost forgotten where she was. Bringing her back to earth with a thump, Joel said, 'So what *will* happen, do you suppose, when this baby's born?'

'It'll scream a lot. And look like a fried tomato.'

'I'm talking about Sean. Be honest with me now. Is your brother messing my sister around?'

Cleo sighed. 'Probably. Although he is trying not to. Some people are naturally . . . good, I suppose. And some aren't.'

'If he hurts Pandora,' said Joel, 'I'll kill him.'

'I've already told him that.' Cleo thought unhappily of Linda, who had had the narrowest of escapes. The only truly effective answer seemed to be to put Sean into permanent quarantine.

'Maybe actually having the baby will settle him down.' Joel didn't sound convinced.

'Maybe.' Cleo glanced at her watch. 'Speaking of actually having the baby, perhaps we should go and see how Pandora's getting on.'

Joel looked squeamish. 'How long do these things normally take?'

'How long's a piece of umbilical cord?' said Cleo.

Chapter 35

Not at all sure he wanted to be there for the actual coming-out but feeling morally obliged to pretend he did, Sean had responded to Cleo's phone call earlier by cancelling that evening's show and dutifully catching the Edinburgh-to-London shuttle.

Having rather hoped the whole messy business would be over and done with by the time he reached the hospital, he was horrified to find himself being seized and catapulted through the doors of the delivery suite by Cleo, Joel and an alarmingly burly midwife.

'Just in time,' gasped Cleo, who appeared to have picked up a tremendous amount of jargon in the last few hours. 'She's into the second stage now . . . fully dilated and bearing down nicely . . .'

'Here, you'll need the sponge.' Joel pushed it into Sean's hand.

'What am I supposed to mop up? Blood?' Sean went white. 'And what the hell's the second stage when it's at home?'

'It means the baby's about to arrive.' The midwife, almost as big as Joel and twice as disapproving, marched Sean through a second swing door. 'As you would know, young man, if you'd bothered to attend a single antenatal class. Now get yourself in there and start making yourself useful. Mop that poor girl's brow.'

It was half-past midnight when Sean staggered into the waiting room.

'Well?' Cleo and Joel demanded in unison when he didn't speak.

'It's a girl.' Sean was shell-shocked. 'Seven pounds five ounces. All the bits in the right places . . .'

'A girl!' Beaming like an idiot, Cleo leapt up and hugged him. 'Oh, that's fantastic . . . what's her name?'

'Hell, I forgot to ask,' murmured Sean.

Joel stared at him in disbelief. '*What?*'

But Sean had already fainted into the nearest chair.

'This is so weird,' Cleo sighed. 'Look at us. Whoever would have thought it?'

Joel obligingly looked at her, stretched across the sofa with her bare feet resting in his lap. Her blond hair was slicked back from her unmade-up face, the black cashmere sweater she wore had holes in both elbows and her well-worn jeans were splattered with dried mud, yet she was still the most beautiful creature he had ever seen. Whoever would have thought it indeed? Joel still found the events of the past week hard to believe. It was more than weird as far as he was concerned. It was downright scary.

The fact that Cleo didn't seem to have had so much as a moment's doubt about the situation was the scariest aspect of all.

Could she really feel this way, Joel kept asking himself, about someone like him? OK, maybe it wasn't exactly Beauty and the Beast – he wasn't *that* awful – but it was still the Supermodel and the Used-Car Salesman.

He couldn't help but be wary. Of course it was flattering, but was it realistic? Wasn't he in danger of falling into exactly the same trap as Pandora? It was all very well, thought Joel, for Cleo to talk ecstatically about true love but how did he know she wasn't just amusing herself with a five-minute fling?

'Oh stop it.'

Glimpsing the expression on his face, Cleo guessed at once what was going through his mind. Again.

'Stop what?'

'Don't be such an old pessimist.' She gave his knee an affectionate squeeze. 'How many times do I have to say it before you start believing me? I love you, it's as simple as that. All we have to do now is relax and enjoy it.'

'How can I?' Joel looked exasperated. 'You're Cleo Mandeville. I'm Joel Grant. I'm not rich, I'm not famous and I sell second-hand cars for a living. I mean, what are people going to think?'

'That you must be a fantastically nice person,' Cleo declared with passion. 'Not to mention extraordinary in bed . . .'

The words slipped out before she could help it. As soon as Cleo heard herself utter them she felt her cheeks redden. Now what on earth could have possessed her to come out with a statement like that?

This, of course, was the trouble with getting to know someone in the romantic sense. When you were waiting for . . . IT . . . to happen but it hadn't happened yet – that *delicate* stage – there were certain joky remarks better left unsaid.

Cleo couldn't wait for IT to happen. Normally, she wouldn't have thought twice about instigating proceedings herself. But this time it was different. The situation was a tricky one. Under

---

the circumstances, she felt, the seducing should be done by Joel.

'Of course I'm a nice person,' Joel said drily. It seemed safest to pretend her last statement hadn't been uttered. 'You know that and I know that. I just don't want the rest of the world thinking I'm your bit of rough.'

'Liar.' Cleo grinned. 'You're scared because you think I'm a flighty piece. You think my only real ambition in life is to get laid by Jack Nicholson. How many times do I have to tell you I'm not like that?'

'Hmm. You mean not like Sean.'

She smirked. 'He doesn't want to get laid by Jack Nicholson either.'

'You know what I mean.'

'Oh come on, wasn't I the one who saved Harriet from the dreaded Damien Maxwell-Horne?' demanded Cleo. She didn't make a habit of telling people about the Checkamate system but Joel's refusal to take her seriously was becoming irritating. 'He wasn't the first, either. I don't just talk about fidelity. Believe me, I do something about it.'

'Are you serious?' asked Joel twenty minutes later when she had finished telling him everything. 'You really check these people out? For money?'

'Of course not for money. What do I need with more money?' Cleo looked offended. 'I just did it to try and help a few friends. Maxwell-Horne was the only one I dealt with in person,' she added hastily. 'Other friends helped out with the rest, because it was in a good cause.'

'But you've stopped doing it now?'

Cleo nodded. 'Too depressing.'

'You mean everyone failed the test?'

'Not everyone. But most of them.' She couldn't bring herself to mention Imogen.

'I wouldn't fail the test,' said Joel quietly. He looked down at her for a long, heart-stopping moment. 'If it was tried on me.'

Enough, Cleo decided, was enough. She was dying for Joel to make love to her. It was all very well being noble and telling herself she had to wait and let him make the all-important first move, but how patient could he seriously expect her to be? Much longer and they'd be queueing up together for their damn pensions.

'You mean you're incorruptible?' Cleo glanced teasingly up at him. 'You can resist anything?'

'Anyone,' Joel replied. 'Anything.'

'Hmm.'

'What are you doing?'

'Now there's a silly question.'

Cleo had risen slowly to her feet. Standing before him, in one movement she pulled the black cashmere sweater off over her head. Next, her fingers moved to the zip of her muddy jeans, unfastening it without taking her eyes from Joel's face. He watched the famous body reveal itself, seventy inches of flawlessly sculptured flesh, naked apart from a tiny grey lace bra and matching thong. Cleo's skin gleamed in the firelight, her coral toenails the only spots of colour against the not-quite-all-over tan. There was no getting away from it, she was truly irresistible . . .

'Put your clothes back on,' said Joel in a low voice. 'I'm sorry, I don't want you to be offended but I think you should put them on again now.'

He hadn't moved so much as a muscle. Cleo, smiling slightly, advanced towards him. With her hands on his shoulders she lowered herself onto Joel's lap.

'Stop it,' said Joel.

Cleo kissed him, her warm lips parting as they covered his. Her tongue gently explored the inside of his mouth. Her fingers slid upwards, burying themselves in the blond hair at the back of his head; her hips began to move slowly against him.

'I mean it,' said Joel, when he was able to speak again. His tone was firm. He still hadn't moved. 'Come on now, be a good girl. Pick those clothes up and put them back on.' His voice softened. 'I really am sorry, sweetheart, but it's for the best. Look, why don't I put the kettle on and make us both a nice cup of tea?'

He caught up with Cleo by the front door. Tears streamed down her face as she writhed like an eel to escape.

'Let fucking go of me . . . you bastard . . . get *off*!'

'Don't be silly, of course I'm not going to let go. *Ouch.*' Joel sucked in his breath as Cleo's toe-capped cowboy boot made vicious contact with his shin. Grimly he hung on. 'Calm down. Stop crying. You can't leave anyway, not with your sweater on inside out.'

Cleo didn't care. All she wanted to do was die. Humiliated beyond belief by Joel's brutal rejection – no, not brutal, it had been a kindly rejection, which was a hundred times worse – she couldn't bear to stay in the house a moment longer. She couldn't bear to look at Joel. She couldn't stop crying either.

But escape was impossible. Joel was bigger and much stronger than she was. Lashing out with the other boot, Cleo missed completely and almost toppled over. She covered her wet face with both hands, slumped back against the wall and let out a howl of despair.

'Dear me,' said Joel with a sorrowful shake of his head. 'What a state to get into. And there I was thinking you'd be impressed.'

Cleo, red-eyed, glared at him. 'Impressed by what, your impotence?'

'Impotence?' Joel looked amused. 'You still don't get it, do you? I'm not impotent.'

'Huh.' Cleo spat the word out in disgust. Damn right she hadn't got it. 'Gay, then.'

'Oh come on. You dared me to resist you. No need to have a blue fit,' Joel protested good-naturedly, 'just because I won.'

She shot him a suspicious look. 'Is this a joke?'

'Well, it was supposed to be.' He grinned. 'Not one of my better ones, evidently.'

Cleo still didn't believe him. She had thought it might be a joke at first, but Joel had so adamantly refused to give in he *must* have meant it.

There had been something else, too. Or rather there hadn't.

'I was sitting on top of you,' Cleo whispered, ashamed even to have to say it. 'And nothing . . . happened.'

'Mind over matter.' Joel shrugged, but looked pleased with himself. 'It's not easy, let me tell you. The thing is, you have to concentrate like crazy on dustbins full of maggots . . . shipping forecasts . . . how ugly the students are on *University Challenge* . . .'

'I've never been so humiliated in my life,' said Cleo.

'Well, I'm sorry but I had something to prove.' Joel stopped smiling. 'Like I said, if I had a steady girlfriend I'd be faithful to her. And nobody in the world – *nobody* – could make me be unfaithful. Not even someone as beautiful as you.'

Cleo was on the verge of bursting into tears all over again.

'OK, OK, but you weren't supposed to make me feel *stupid*. You could have kept it going for the first minute, then given in.'

'That,' Joel reminded her, 'would have defeated the object.'

Cleo's knees were trembling. Her eyes swam as she gazed up at him.

'So what happens now?'

'Now?' Joel's mouth twitched. What did she think he was, completely superhuman? 'Now I think I'd better carry you upstairs and start proving a few things to you.'

As he lifted her into his arms a single tear slid down Cleo's cheek. She banished the rest with a noisy sniff.

'What things?'

'That I'm not impotent. That I'm not gay.' Joel kissed the solitary tear away. 'And that I am extraordinary in bed.'

Chapter 36

It had been a good show.

'Come on,' Jenny said to Cass when it was over, 'that one deserves celebrating. I'll treat you to lunch.'

They went to Edwina's, a smartly done-up restaurant less than half a mile from the Kingdom studios.

'I haven't been here before,' said Cass, gazing around.

'They only opened two months ago. Luke told me about it. He said they do amazing pumpkin ravioli.'

Cass said nothing. Jenny tried so hard not to look smug, and so hard not to mention Luke in every sentence – failing abysmally every time – you couldn't help but smile.

Jenny tried to look shamefaced instead.

'I know, I've just done it again. Sorry.'

'Stop apologizing!'

'That's what Luke—' Jenny clapped her hand over her mouth.

'Look,' Cass protested, 'I *like* it that you've met someone wonderful.'

'Now there's a coincidence. I don't like it that you haven't.'

'Please, don't start. Not another lecture.'

'I want you to be happy,' Jenny protested. She meant it. If anyone deserved happiness it was Cass.

'I don't need to be. Cleo's happy enough for both of us just now.' Cass pulled a long-suffering face. 'She's even more besotted than you are. It's quite sweet really, seeing her like this after all these years of being tough and cynical. I was beginning to wonder if she'd ever fall in love.'

The waiter arrived to take their orders. Jenny chose the pumpkin ravioli followed by lemon chicken because Luke had said that was terrific too.

'I'll have the same.' Cass kept a straight face. 'What's good enough for Luke is good enough for me. Ouch, that was my *ankle* . . .'

'So Cleo's keeping it in the family,' Jenny mused when the waiter had left them with a bottle of Barolo, 'with Pandora's big brother.' She nudged Cass's arm. 'Go on then, what's he like?'

'Big. Nice.' Cass had so far only met him twice, and those meetings had been brief, but from what she was able to tell of Joel he was just about perfect for Cleo. 'He's keeping her in order. You know how impetuous Cleo is. She's already jabbering on about wedding dresses and where to hold the reception. But Joel's taking it all with a bucket of salt. The press are dying to get their claws into him but he's not having any of it.'

'Good for him!' Jenny leaned forward and dropped her voice. 'Speaking of the press getting their claws in, how's it going with Jack and the floozy?'

'Oh, couldn't be more wonderful. Love's young dream, according to Jack.'

'Middle-aged dream, more like,' Jenny retorted.

Cass realized she was stirring the wine in her glass with her index finger. It was a long-standing habit that had always driven Jack to distraction. Now she was free to do it as much as she liked. For a moment she was unable to speak.

'He's deluding himself,' Jenny went on, her tone forceful.

'Silly sod. Take it from me. Even if he thinks he's happy now, it'll never last.'

'Not that it's going to affect me either way.' Cass shrugged and tried to look unconcerned. 'It's the decree nisi next week. Not long now to the absolute.'

Jenny's dark eyes widened. 'God, I had no idea. You didn't say.'

Drily, Cass said, 'I was trying not to think about it. The decree absolute's due on the first of July. Our wedding anniversary.'

'Oh Cass—'

'One thing I want you to promise.'

Jenny nodded. 'Anything. What?'

'Just don't get me one of those jolly, joky, congratulations-on-your-divorce cards,' said Cass. 'I couldn't bear it.'

The timely arrival of the translucent pumpkin ravioli diverted Jenny's attention for all of ten minutes. Then she was off again.

'You need to meet someone.'

'And you sound like Sophie.'

'Maybe we're both right.' As the waiter refilled their glasses Jenny dabbed melted butter from the corner of her generously lipsticked mouth with a napkin. 'I mean it, Cass. Honestly, you'd feel so much better! It gives you such a boost, knowing someone really cares about you—'

'Like Terry Brannigan, you mean?' Cass winced. 'He really cared about me . . . and what a tremendous boost to the ego that was.'

'That was his fault, not yours.' Only Cass, Jenny thought, could feel guilty about having inflicted such a well-deserved bash on the head with a biscuit tin.

'I still haven't heard from him.' Cass, who worried endlessly about what might have happened to Terry, still felt her heart skip a beat each time she read in the paper that another unidentified male had thrown himself beneath the wheels of a speeding tube train.

'I'm not going to give up,' Jenny warned. 'I'll ask Luke if he has any eligible friends.'

'Help. You're making me nervous.' Cass shook her head in despair. 'I'm too old for all that.'

'In that case I'll change the subject . . . for now.' Jenny gave her a sweet smile. 'Come on then, *old* lady. Show me those photos you were babbling on about earlier. The ones of your heavenly grandchild.'

Terry Brannigan wiped his wet hands on an already damp apron and watched through the crack in the red-painted swing door as Cass and the plump dark-haired girl made their way out of the restaurant. Cass, wearing a black-and-white jacket, a flatteringly cut above-the-knee black skirt and high heels, looked wonderful. James, the sous-chef, came to peer through the small circular window in the door.

'What's this, celebrity-spotting or just ogling a great pair of legs? That's Cass Mandeville.'

Terry turned away, his face expressionless.

'I know.'

'I'm going to miss you so much,' Cleo murmured. She cradled Joel's face between her hands and covered it with kisses. 'I don't want to go to boring wet old Venice.'

Joel smiled down at her.

'So don't go.'

'I have to.' Cleo smoothed his blond hair away from his forehead, glad he didn't use gel like every male model she had ever known. 'They're paying me squillions.' She brightened. 'But afterwards I'll have a whole week free. We could get away somewhere. Have you ever been to Acapulco?'

It didn't occur to her that he had a car showroom to run. At moments like this Joel realized the immensity of the difference between them.

'I'm working. I can't just take a week off.'

Cleo, opening her mouth to ask why not, closed it again in the nick of time.

'I'm sorry. I'm going to miss you, that's all.' She tried to look penitent, failed miserably and kissed his adorable broken nose instead. 'You'll have to phone me hundreds of times to make up for it.'

Joel could only too easily imagine the scenario; it would take a hundred calls before he managed to get hold of her.

'You'll be in Venice,' he pointed out. 'What are you going to do, lock yourself in your hotel room each night and read the Gideon Bible?'

'I might go out.' Cleo looked offended. 'But it isn't as if I'll be on the pull.'

'It still might be easier if you phone me.'

'We'll phone each other.' She threw her arms around him. 'Morning, noon and night. After all, I have to make sure you stay on the straight and narrow too.'

It was easy for Cleo to say. Joel only wished he could believe her. Just the other night, whilst they had been driving through the West End, he had pointed to a huge hoarding advertising the latest designer aftershave. The male model, brooding down at them from a height of thirty feet, was one of the most successful in the country. He was also rumoured to be amazingly well-endowed, which tied in nicely with the after-shave's advertising slogan: Could you say No to this?

'Well,' Joel had said jokingly, 'could you?'

And Cleo, without batting an eyelid, had replied in casual fashion, 'What, say no to Murphy Mackay? He's a prat. *And* he's doing the Venice shoot next week. Yuk, who says I don't suffer for my art?'

As if, thought Joel, anyone could suffer in Venice. But that had been beside the point; prat or no prat, Murphy Mackay was pretty daunting competition. Particularly if those rumours about the size of his tackle were true.

'If you want me to ring you,' he told Cleo now, 'you'd better tell me where you're staying.'

She scrabbled around in her bag, found her bulging diary and flipped through it.

'Um . . . here we are. The Hotel San Carlo. God, these people are stingy. Why couldn't it be somewhere decent for once like the Cipriani?'

Joel said, 'The San Carlo? Are you sure?'

'Of course I'm sure. Why?' Cleo was instantly suspicious. 'Don't tell me, you've been there and it's a complete fleapit on the verge of disappearing into the lagoon.'

'Don't be silly.' Joel tweaked her nose. 'You can swim, can't you?'

'Hell's bells.' Cleo was looking mutinous. 'Is it really terrible?'

'Just teasing. I've never been there.' He grinned. 'The name just rang a bell. I think a friend of mine stayed there once.

If that's the one, you can stop worrying. He had a brilliant time.'

'Hmm.' Cleo sounded doubtful. 'But he wasn't stuck there for five days with Murphy ding-dong Mackay.'

Chapter 37

In the event, the San Carlo was just about the only bearable aspect of the whole trip. Formerly a fifteenth-century palace, now an elegant cream-cake of an hotel just a few steps from the Piazza San Marco, it was so much better than Cleo had been expecting that for the first couple of hours she was actually deluded into believing she might enjoy herself in Venice after all.

But not even the Cipriani itself could have made up for the awfulness of the rest of the Visa party, the deeply depressing weather and the unexpected, even more depressing arrival of Anton Visa himself.

Visa, the company funding the shoot, were renowned for dependability rather than glitz. Donatella Versace they were not. But their customers, appreciating that, were loyal in return. Visa was hugely successful across both Europe and America, and the biannual advertising campaigns for Visawear were lavish, double-page splashes seen by everyone who had ever picked up a magazine.

If only those people, Cleo thought wearily at the end of their first gruelling day, knew how much misery could be involved in the making of such apparently idyllic ads.

Merry, the stylist, was miserable beyond belief. Her boy-friend had recently left her for another girl and she was taking it out on anyone who came within fifty paces.

248

The photographer's name was Pierre. His boyfriend had also just run off, but with an Australian surf-bum. Pierre was consoling himself with fistfuls of cocaine. He also snarled rather than spoke and had the loudest, most annoyingly persistent sniff Cleo had ever heard.

But Pierre was a positive poppet compared with Jina and Donna, in charge of make-up and hair respectively. They made the Kray twins look sweet and their joint mission in life was to get laid by Murphy Mackay. Whoever got there first, won. Their bitchiness was terrifying. The only consolation, as far as Cleo was concerned, was that nobody deserved them more than Murphy. They were all welcome to each other.

The happy band also included Violette, a reserved French model who seldom spoke at all, preferring to smoke end- lessly instead; Martine the bossy PA who wore her hair in plaits wound Heidi-style round her head, and Anton Visa himself.

Anton Visa was so famously reclusive most people had no idea what he looked like. This, Cleo decided, was a smart move on his part. If she'd looked like Anton Visa she'd be a recluse too. Why he'd chosen to show up in Venice was anybody's guess. Gifted designer he might be, but he made her skin crawl.

'Maybe he *is* the beast from the lagoon,' she'd whispered to Pierre, but all Pierre did was grunt, sniff and shake his light- meter at the filthy grey sky.

Venice was beautiful but the weather wasn't doing it any favours. Cleo, first downstairs for dinner because boredom had only made her hungrier than usual, perched on a stool at one end of the deserted bar and gazed gloomily out at the endless rain, the swirling leaden water of the Grand Canal and the redundant chained-up gondolas bobbing like toy ducks on the far side of the canal.

The gilded double doors to the restaurant swung open and she was joined by Jina and Donna, bickering.

'. . . and why would he be interested in you anyway?' Donna sneered. 'With that spot on your chin the size of a fried egg.'

'Better spots,' Jina said sweetly, 'than herpes.'

'You lying cow! I had a cold sore, that's all—'

Jina's bright green low-cut dress emphasized her round shoulders and pendulous breasts. Donna was wearing a sparkly black top and an almost transparent miniskirt. Both girls reeked of scent. Cleo, trying to look as if she didn't belong to them, smiled at the young barman and ordered an orange juice.

'Come on, Visa's paying.' Jina looked appalled. 'You can't drink that crap. Have a bellissima – the fat bastard can afford it! Three bellissimas, OK?' She snapped her fingers at the barman. 'And make 'em doubles.'

'Bellinis?' The young Irish barman looked almost apologetic. 'Peach juice and champagne, would that be . . . ?'

'That's them.' Unperturbed, Jina pointed to the half-pint glasses. 'Who gives a toss what they're called? So long as they do the job.'

They were soon joined by the rest of their party. Anton Visa, more maggoty than ever, laid a white and clammy hand on Cleo's arm.

'You look sad, my dear.'

And you look like a slug in a dinner jacket, thought Cleo.

She squirmed as his hand inched its way up and began massaging the inside of her elbow. She wished she was back in London with Joel.

'I'm OK. It's just the weather.'

Anton Visa nodded in sympathy.

'One thing, I'm afraid, over which I have no control.'

The first day had been a complete wash-out. As far as Cleo was concerned the sooner they completed this shoot, the better. She managed a brief smile.

'Maybe the rain will have stopped by tomorrow. Let's hope so anyway. Pierre has plans to use us outside the Doge's Palace.'

'Pierre shall bring out your true beauty,' Anton Visa leered, 'wherever he uses you.'

Startled, Cleo wondered if it was usual for recluses to leer. To grope and leer. Behind her she heard Martine the PA scolding Pierre for being late. Merry, the miserable stylist, was droning on to Violette about the number of tranquillizers she was up to. Murphy Mackay, whose obscenely tight black leather trousers were the subject of much admiration amongst Jina and Donna, was stroking Donna's bottom and braying with laughter at one of his own jokes.

Anton Visa was still leering. He showed no sign of moving away. Cleo, who had always prided herself on her professional-ism, felt sick. The temptation to race upstairs, grab her things and do her first-ever bunk was overwhelming. Sod being a professional, she thought, repulsed by the very nearness of the man. This was the ultimate job from hell.

'So sorry,' murmured the young barman, whose tongs had slipped. A cluster of ice-cubes landed in Anton Visa's lap, provoking a torrent of expletives and bringing him rapidly to his feet.

'*Imbecile*,' Anton Visa hissed.

The barman, who spoke with a soft Dublin accent, said, 'Sir, my apologies.'

'It was an accident,' Cleo put in hurriedly.

But when, moments later, the young barman gave her the ghost of a wink and a smile, she began to wonder if it had been an accident after all.

'Madam,' he acknowledged her with a nod when she slipped back into the bar two hours later, 'how may I help you?'

'I think you already have.' Cleo looked at him. 'Those ice-cubes. Did you really drop them on purpose?'

Again that mesmerizing hint of a smile hovering behind the professional façade.

'You mean, to cool his . . . ardour?'

'Did you?'

The young barman's expression was delightfully innocent.

'Well, let's just say I'm not normally such a butter-fingers as all that. And it stopped the old lech groping your arm.' Leaning across the bar for a second, he lowered his voice. 'Although I must say, you don't look the damsel-in-distress type. If it isn't an impertinent question, could you not have dealt with the matter yourself?'

'Of course I could.' Cleo didn't want the barman to think she was a complete wimp. 'I just wasn't expecting it, that's all. He caught me off-guard.' She shuddered. 'Repellent old toad.'

'But you have to be nice to him because he's the boss.'

Was this young Irish lad teasing her?

'I'm not his secretary,' said Cleo, a touch huffily.

He grinned. 'Of course you aren't. You're that famous model who did all those yoghurt ads last year.'

Her good humour restored, Cleo said, 'So famous, you mean, that you can't remember my name.'

The grin broadened. 'Don't take it personally. I have enough trouble remembering my own.'

'Which is?'

'Hang on now, let's see . . . ah, that's it. Declan Mulcahy.'

'Declan. Right. Well, thanks anyway for coming to my rescue earlier.' Cleo, deciding she liked the blue-eyed barman with the fetching smile, stuck out her hand. 'Anton Visa might not be my boss but he's still someone it's better to keep on the right side of. Especially in my business,' she added drily. 'Getting yourself a reputation for being difficult to work with doesn't do your bank balance any favours. It's always better to at least try and get along with the people who count.'

Not that she held out much hope for the rest of this particular week in Venice.

'So where are the rest of them now?' Declan raised a playful eyebrow.

'Gone to visit some nightclub. I told them I had a migraine coming on.'

'Ah, you're not missing much,' said Declan when Cleo had told him the name of the nightclub. 'It's a shame, though, to be here in Venice and not see something of the city at night. I'm off duty myself in another twenty-five minutes . . .' he hesitated, glancing at his watch '. . . if you'd like a bit of a guided tour. I don't know, how's that migraine of yours? Does it feel as if it might clear itself up in the next half-hour or so? Would a quick gin and tonic help, d'you think, to do the trick?'

'Make it a large one,' Cleo beamed, 'and it just might.'

The rain had finally stopped, an almost full moon hung in the inky night sky and Cleo was having more fun than she'd imagined possible.

Declan Mulcahy was great company and the perfect person to show a stranger around a new city. He knew all the best café-bars, most of the owners and a riveting amount of local gossip. Between each café and the next Cleo was regaled with a stream of jokes as unrelenting as the waves lapping against the damp mossy walls of Venice's canals.

At midnight they almost bumped into the rest of the Visa entourage, making their way back to the hotel across the Piazza San Marco.

'Quick.' Declan pushed Cleo into the shelter of a darkened doorway and squeezed her wrist, hard, when her fit of the giggles almost gave the game away. 'Jesus, d'you think I want to be held personally responsible for the decline and fall of Britain's top yoghurt model?'

'I can't help it,' Cleo gasped. 'I feel like a fifteen-year-old on the run from boarding school. Maybe I should've stuffed pillows down my bed, in case they look in my room.'

This time Declan pinched her non-existent waist, the bare brown bit between her crop top and the top of her jeans.

'Napkins, more like. You're hardly the pillowy type.'

This only made Cleo want to laugh more. She covered her mouth as Murphy, Jina and Donna – the eternal triangle –

passed within twenty feet of them. Donna's high heels, clicking through the puddles, were sending splashes of muddy water up over Jina's pale yellow trench coat. Jina retaliated, swinging her imitation Chanel handbag viciously into the small of Donna's back. Murphy, who loved to be fought over, waved his hands in placatory fashion and smirked. 'Girls, girls, take it *easy*. There's enough for everyone . . .'

Behind them Merry gazed longingly in the direction of the nearest deep canal. Pierre, barely able to put one foot in front of the other, sounded like a sniffer dog. Martine, as officious as ever, was barking instructions about the schedule for tomorrow. The toad-like Anton was absent, evidently having decided to go back to being a recluse.

'My hero,' Cleo whispered in Declan's ear when the party had moved out of sight, leaving them alone once more. 'You saved me from the worst night of my life.'

'Ah well, that's to prove I don't bear a grudge.'

He was smiling. She could see his white teeth gleaming in the darkness.

'What grudge? Why should you?'

Declan swung her round to face him. 'Well now, aren't you the very one who persuaded me to buy a six-pack of that inedible yoghurt? I tell you, I couldn't believe how terrible it was. Do you not think we poor consumers deserve some form of compensation for having to eat the stuff?'

'Like what?' Cleo smiled. There were no threatening sexual undertones to the challenge.

'I finish work at eight tomorrow evening,' said Declan. 'And I know some great restaurants. Do you think you could get away with going awol again?'

Delighted, Cleo gave him a hug. Declan really was the answer to a prayer. Thanks to him Venice might not be unbearable after all.

'You are brilliant,' she said happily. 'We'll go somewhere wonderful. My treat.'

Chapter 38

The morning's postbag had, for Cass, been more heartbreaking than usual. Other people's problems made her own seem embarrassingly minor by comparison. One woman had written in a shaky hand to say she was a widow suffering from multiple sclerosis, afraid of what the future might hold for her mentally handicapped young son. Cass had been forced to rush to the loo and sob uncontrollably into handfuls of toilet paper. Jenny, no help at all, had simply groaned and said, 'Pass the sick bag! She's having us on, Cass. It's one of those pathetic begging letters. Bung it in the bin.'

But what if the woman had been genuine? There was so much injustice in the world. Some people, Cass knew, battled against far more than their share of tragedy.

I should be ashamed of myself, Cass thought as she drove home from the studios that afternoon. I'm healthy, my children are healthy, so what do I have to complain about? All I am is nearly divorced.

She pulled in at the garage on the way home. Anything to stop that irritating red fuel light flashing endlessly on and off, distracting her attention from the road.

'Damn—'

Cass leapt away as a wave of petrol shot back out of the tank, splattering her light skirt and pale pink suede shoes. This was always happening to her, she never understood why. It provided endless amusement, too, for other garage users, particularly the men. If there was one thing they enjoyed more than the sight of an incompetent woman driver it was one who couldn't even manage to get petrol into a car.

Sure enough, at that moment the driver of the vehicle behind her blasted his horn, making Cass jump a second time. Colouring up, she risked a quick glance over her shoulder. The car was a denim-blue Mercedes, its windows heavily tinted. It was bound to belong to a smirking bloody man.

When she heard the driver's door being opened, Cass's heart sank. This time she didn't look round. Her fingers tightened around the metal nozzle of the pump and she wondered if she would have the nerve to accidentally spray the maker of the next patronizing remark with as much petrol as she had just splashed over herself.

Patronizing remarks were the least of Cass's worries. Having resolutely refused to look at the other driver when he climbed out of his car, she was unprepared, moments later, for the arm which snaked unexpectedly, and with surprising strength, around her waist. It was a brown arm attached to a solid body. Warm breath fanned Cass's neck. For a fraction of a second she wondered if she should scream for help. Her finger pressed convulsively down on the trigger of the petrol pump. All the pump did was go 'clunk'.

'Of all the filling stations in all the world,' murmured a familiar voice in Cass's ear, 'you had to pull into this one.'

Immensely relieved she hadn't screamed for help – what a fool she would have looked – Cass turned and greeted Rory Cameron with an affectionate kiss on the cheek.

'You idiot. I thought I was being kidnapped.'

'No you didn't.' Rory started to laugh. 'You thought I was some smug chauvinist unable to resist making fun of a damsel in distress.'

'Well . . .'

'Come on, I saw that look you gave me earlier.'

Cass blushed and smiled. 'OK, maybe that is what I thought. I know this is going to sound completely ridiculous but Jack was nearly always the one who put petrol into the cars. And now I just can't get the hang of it,' she concluded lamely. 'These pumps seem to have it in for me.'

'My poor darling.' Taking over, Rory finished the job. 'It's the angle of the nozzle, you see.' He winked. 'Makes all the difference in the world.'

Through the window, the young cashier was watching with interest.

'Now I really look feeble,' said Cass.

'If you ask me, you're looking rather splendid.' Rory stepped back and cast an appraising eye over her. 'And far better than you have any right to look, considering how long it's been since you visited the club.'

'Ah.'

'I know, I know.' He had guessed her reasons for staying away. 'But Jack doesn't come to us any more. Hasn't done for almost a year. Nor does Imogen. So you see, you'd be quite safe.' He smiled. 'And amazingly welcome.'

'Well, maybe.' Cass wasn't sure she had the heart for working-out, let alone the stamina.

'I mean it.' As Rory locked her petrol cap back into place, he was watching the expression on her face. 'We've missed you at the club. I kept meaning to get in touch, but you know how it is. Shona and I were having a few ups and downs of our own.' He grinned. 'I threatened to enter her for suitcase-packer of the year. You have no idea how many front-door keys I've had flung at me in my time. Shona especially. Now she *loved* throwing them.'

Rory Cameron had sensibly got his first two marriages out of the way while he was young. Now nearing fifty, he had spent the last couple of decades getting engaged instead, because it was cheaper, to a series of leggy blondes. Each blonde was more unsuitable than the one before. They were getting progressively younger too. The club regulars organized sweepstakes, betting on how long each doomed relationship was likely to last. Shona, who was twenty-six, had worn a gold ring through her skinny brown navel and a three-carat canary diamond on her engagement finger. She had actually exceeded the club members' expectations, managing a grand total of fourteen months, although Bill Matthews had argued that with all that to-ing and fro-ing she and Rory had only been together for nine. Nine, coincidentally, was the number Bill had drawn in the locker-room sweep.

But Rory remained optimistic. One day, he cheerfully maintained, he would find his perfect love-match and settle down. The club regulars only hoped it happened before he was too old to enjoy it.

'Well,' Cass delved into her bag and took out her purse, 'I suppose I'd better pay for this petrol before it evaporates.'

Rory was still waiting by her car when she got back.

'I've had a terrific idea.'

'Oh.' Cass looked nervous. 'Look, I don't know if I'm really up to aerobics at the moment—'

'We're a sports club,' he gently berated her, 'not Stalag 9.'

Cass smiled. 'Sorry.'

'And this is an invitation. It's not compulsory.'

'Go on.'

'Amanda's getting married the weekend after next. Country wedding down in the Cotswolds, should be fun. The thing is, I don't actually have anyone to go with. I dare say Amanda's glad I won't be turning up with Shona.' Rory looked slightly shamefaced. 'She always said it was embarrassing, her father's girlfriends being younger than she was. But I know she'd be thrilled to have you there. If you think you'd like to come . . . ?'

'I'd love to.' Cass was both touched by the offer and delighted to be asked. She had met Amanda, the product of Rory's first marriage, several times over the years and liked her a lot. More selfishly, the thought of having something to look forward to was more than welcome. In two weeks' time Sophie would be away, grubbing around on some archaeological dig in the Mendips. Cass still found Saturdays and Sundays on her own hard to bear.

'That's great!' Cleo, calling from Venice, had always adored Rory Cameron. He was also, she felt, just what Cass needed right now. 'You'll have a brilliant time. And who knows,' she added in teasing tones, 'this could be the start of something too slushy for words. You and naughty-boy Rory . . .'

'I think you're more his type than I am.' Drily Cass said, 'I'm about twenty years too old for him.'

'Maybe he'll see the error of his ways and throw himself at your feet.'

'It was a friendly invitation.' Cleo, Cass decided, had been watching her *Four Weddings* video again. 'Anyway, enough about my non-existent love life. How are things going with you?'

Cleo snorted down the phone. 'The shoot stinks, I hate everyone on it and the weather's lousy.'

'Oh dear.'

'Anton Visa keeps making slimy passes at me,' Cleo continued, 'the make-up girl smells like she chews garlic for breakfast and every pair of shoes I have to wear is two sizes too small.'

'Heavens . . .'

'The dopey stylist's gone and got a crush on the photographer, who's just broken up with his boyfriend. The hairdresser thinks she's pregnant and yesterday I caught Murphy Mackay stuffing his jockstrap with socks.'

Cass sighed. 'Poor you, it sounds awful.'

'I'm OK.' Cleo certainly seemed chirpy enough. 'I've met up with this great chap, Declan. He's showing me Venice, we're having the most terrific time.'

'Oh.' Cass was taken aback. 'But I thought . . . I mean, what about Joel?'

'Mum! It isn't like that with Declan and me. We just get on brilliantly, that's all.'

'Oh. Well, I'm glad.'

'Just good friends.' Cleo laughed. 'Like you and Rory Cameron, OK?'

Chapter 39

Friday came round at last. The rain, miraculously, was managing to hold off just long enough for the shoot to be completed. A newly emerged sun cast its watery rays across the city. Cleo, in beige satin and yet another pair of too-small shoes, draped herself across the Rialto Bridge while Pierre, still sniffing, shot roll after roll of film from a gondola beneath.

After an irritable lunch, they all moved on to the Canale Della Giudecca. Finally they trooped up the 136 stone steps of Venice's famous clock tower in order to capture the spectacular – if somewhat washed out – Venetian views.

'It's morning sickness,' moaned Donna, clutching her stomach. She dropped her styling brush into Cleo's lap.

'More likely three helpings of cieche.' Cleo, who was cold, was also fast running out of patience. 'How you can eat blind baby eels I don't know.'

Donna, who had been under the impression she was eating some kind of translucent pasta, screamed and promptly threw up into Jina's make-up box.

Jina let out a piercing shriek. 'You *stupid* cow . . . !'

Murphy Mackay, who had persuaded Donna to order cieche in the first place, turned on Cleo.

'It's your fault. Why did you have to tell her it was eels?'

'Maybe for the same reason you shove socks down

263

your pants,' Cleo flashed back. 'To get a reaction.'

Jina honked with laughter. 'He doesn't, does he?'

'Girls, girls.' Martine bristled up, flapping her clipboard and glancing down with revulsion at the mess in the make-up box. 'This is neither the time nor the place. Please can we get on?'

Cleo had had enough. She tapped the Tag Heuer strapped like a grenade around Martine's skinny wrist.

'It's Friday. It's five to five,' she told an uncomprehending Martine, 'and it's *Crackerjack*.'

'*What?*'

'Well, maybe not. But it's definitely time to go home.' Cleo stood up, returned the hairbrush to an open-mouthed Donna and in one brisk movement unzipped the bronze satin dress she had been about to wear for the final shot. It slithered down and fell in a silky pool at her feet.

It was the stylist's turn to let out a squeal of anguish. 'Not on the *ground*—'

'Right.' Cleo, wearing only skimpy knickers, reached for her jeans and black sweatshirt. 'I'm off. I won't say it's been fun, because it hasn't. Bye, all.'

She pronounced it bile.

Back at the hotel, she packed swiftly and went in search of Declan.

'He ees not on duty until eight.' Marco, who was running the bar, looked apologetic.

'Damn.' Cleo didn't want to hang around and face the wrath of Anton Visa. 'You wouldn't happen to know where I could find him?'

Marco shrugged. 'Per'aps ees een 'is room.'

The staff quarters were on the top floor of the hotel. Eagerly Cleo leaned across the bar.

'Oh please, Marco. I have to see him. Be an angel and point me in the right direction . . .'

'Sorry about this, I was asleep.'

Declan, rubbing his eyes, nevertheless summoned a smile. He was naked apart from a pair of crumpled white shorts, and surprisingly well muscled for someone so slim. Cleo, who hated being woken herself, was overcome with remorse.

'I'm the one who should be sorry. Look, you get back into bed. I only popped up to say goodbye.'

'Goodbye?' Declan halted, halfway beneath the green-and-white striped duvet. 'I thought you weren't leaving until first thing tomorrow. I was going to take you to a party tonight at Marconi's.'

Cleo sighed. 'I can't.'

'Why, what's up?'

She told him.

'Oh dear, was that wise?' Declan, properly awake now, looked alarmed. 'Will you still get paid?'

The bed in which he sat took up almost half the available space in the cramped attic room. Since there was nowhere else to sit, Cleo perched on the end and tucked one leg under the other.

'Just about. We'd pretty much finished. Sod it,' she went on with a shake of the head, 'I don't care any more whether I do or not. It's only thanks to you I've stuck it out this far.'

Declan looked crestfallen. 'But you're going to miss the

party, and I was so looking forward to our last night together. Damn, now I'm depressed.'

'You look like a small boy', Cleo teased, 'who's just had his best conker nicked.'

'It's how I feel. There now, did anyone ever compare you with a conker before?'

Cleo looked amused. 'So this is what they call Irish blarney.'

'Only brought out on very special occasions, let me assure you.' His blue eyes skimmed her face with open appreciation. 'Ah, but you're a fine girl. You deserve it. And I have enjoyed myself, you know. Hasn't it been a great week?'

'Terrific. That's why I had to come and say goodbye. And thanks for making it terrific.' He was like a brother, Cleo decided, only much, much nicer than Sean. Knowing how little he earned, too, she had wanted to give Declan money as a gesture of appreciation for all he had done, but now she sensed it would be the wrong thing to do. You tipped porters and chambermaids, not friends.

Instead, she moved up the bed and planted a kiss on Declan's thin cheek, steadying herself with a hand on his shoulder. As unexpected kisses have a habit of doing, this one didn't go according to plan. Cleo's nose bumped clumsily against his left cheekbone.

'Aaargh,' murmured Declan, 'don't you just hate it when that happens?' The corners of his mouth curled with un-disguised amusement as he shifted his own weight. 'All the better to keep my balance, you see. Hang on a sec, that's better . . . right now, let's try again.'

This time, somehow inevitably, his smiling mouth found

Cleo's. It wasn't what she had planned, but she knew it would be churlish to pull away. Besides, where was the harm?

It was only a kiss, after all. And a jolly nice one at that.

Chapter 40

'Oh, I've missed you!' As soon as Joel opened the front door, Cleo threw her arms around him. 'Missed you, missed you, missed you. What a shitty week I've had. Give me a hug. No, better than that. I warn you, I'm going to need some serious cheering up . . .'

When she had finished kissing him senseless Joel said, 'Actually I was just on my way out.'

It was nine thirty on Saturday morning. He was wearing a pale denim shirt and freshly pressed chinos. Aftershave, too. Running a hand through his just-washed blond hair, Cleo drawled with mock-suspicion, 'I see. Anywhere nice? Anyone I know? Come on now, you can tell me.'

'Sainsbury's.'

'A likely story.'

'I know, bizarre, isn't it?' Joel gazed down at her. 'It's where ordinary people go when they run out of food.'

Cleo, who had different ideas, grinned and waggled her car keys. 'Come on, I'll drive. We'll go to Fortnum's instead, stock up on loads of really scrummy things and come back here for the ultimate breakfast in bed. Now how about that for an offer you can't refuse?'

For some reason Joel wasn't smiling much today. All he did was breathe out slowly, much as her old maths teacher had done every time she got everything spectacularly wrong.

'I'd rather go to Sainsbury's.'

Mimicking him, Cleo heaved a Joel-type sigh. 'Oh well, let's go then. If we must.'

'There's no need for you to come. I'm quite capable of carrying my own groceries.'

'Don't be so boring.' Cleo protested. 'We've never done this before. I want to see you shop.'

'Why?'

She beamed. 'To find out if we're compatible.'

'I doubt that,' said Joel. 'Somehow I doubt it very much.'

Cleo screeched to a halt forty minutes later in the middle of rice and pasta. The aisle, crammed with Saturday-morning shoppers, was gridlocked within seconds.

'OK, enough's enough. I think you'd better tell me what's going on.'

Joel's mouth narrowed as he took control of the trolley and moved it to one side.

'I don't know what you're talking about.'

'Oh yes you bloody do.' Cleo glared up at him. 'I've been trying and trying to ignore your rotten mood and it hasn't done a bit of good. So why don't we just get this thing out in the open? Come on, say it. Tell me what's on your mind.'

People were beginning to stare. Joel picked up an economy bag of macaroni.

'Not here.'

'*Yes* here.' Her dark eyes glittered. 'If there's one thing I can't stand it's a moody man. If there's another thing I can't stand it's a moody man who won't say what the damn matter is.

I just don't see why I should have to put up with it. It gets on my *nerves*.'

Even more people were beginning to stare. Cleo was facing him across the half-full trolley as if squaring up for a fight. The sleeves of her cropped, dark-brown leather jacket were pushed up to her elbows. Beneath it she wore a plain white vest and jeans pulled in at the waist with a battered leather belt. The deep brown of the jacket exactly matched Cleo's eyes. The vest very nearly matched her short, white-blond hair. She was so strikingly beautiful, thought Joel, of course people stared. It was only natural that they should.

But it wasn't his fault if Cleo chose to pick a fight in public. This was her decision alone.

'Go on,' Cleo goaded, challenging him now. 'You're mad with me, aren't you? I've obviously done *something* wrong. So tell me what it damn well is.'

She even had the nerve, as she spoke, to pick the bag of macaroni out of the trolley, dump it back on the wrong shelf and choose a packet of tri-coloured conchiglie instead. For Joel, who didn't like poncey pasta shells, even plain white ones, it was the last straw.

'OK,' he said quietly, 'you're right. Except maybe I'm more disappointed than mad. It's over, Cleo. I don't want to see you again. I tell you what, why don't you leave now? I'll get a cab home.'

Now people were really beginning to take notice, nudging each other and jerking their heads in Cleo's direction.

She stared at him in silence for several seconds then lowered her gaze, scanning the contents of the trolley.

'Is all this because I wanted milk chocolate digestives and you wanted plain?'

'I'm not joking.'

Cleo bent down and picked out three multi-packs of *Starburst*. 'Don't tell me, you'd set your heart on fruit pastilles.'

'Now you're being silly.'

'Silly? *I'm* being silly?' Leaning across the front of the trolley, Cleo hissed the words at him through pale lips. 'The fact that you won't tell me what I'm supposed to have done wrong is what's silly. You don't even have the guts to *say* it—'

'No, dear.' A middle-aged woman held back her adolescent daughter. 'I don't think this is quite the moment to ask for an autograph.'

They really shouldn't have come here. Joel wished now he'd dealt with the matter briskly and in private, back at the house.

'OK.' He kept his voice low. 'Let's just say you've been Checkamated.'

'What?'

'I used to have a lad working for me in the showroom at Henley-Grant Motors. Terrific salesman he was too. Name of Declan Mulcahy, if that rings any bells . . .'

Aware of the interest gathering around them, Cleo gritted her teeth and made it out to the car park.

'You bastard,' she hissed when they were finally alone. 'I can't believe you did that. You complete and utter—'

'Bastard. I know.' Joel nodded, his mouth twisting in a grim, unamused smile. 'If it's any consolation it started off as a joke. This wasn't something I planned, believe me. I was just stunned by the coincidence when you told me you were booked into the San Carlo. Declan's always kept in touch, you see, sending us

271

silly postcards from wherever he's working. And you'd been banging on about this wonderful Checkamate system of yours . . . for some reason I thought it would be a laugh to use the opportunity and try it out on you.' He paused, no longer even pretending to smile. 'Stupidly, as it turned out. Or not, I suppose. Because this is the whole point of the exercise, isn't it? Discovering the truth about people. Realizing that what they say and what they do doesn't necessarily match up.'

Cleo was so mad she could barely contain herself. She was doubly mad because not only had Joel been sneaky enough to set the whole Declan-thing up, but now he was claiming victory and she hadn't even done anything wrong. Not *really* wrong . . .

She was too mad to drive as well, which meant they were stuck in this damn car park unable to even put the roof down because all around them people were unloading their groceries with extraordinary slowness, pretending not to watch the furious exchange taking place in the rapidly steaming-up car.

The car wasn't the only one getting steamed up. Cleo tried to wrestle her way out of her leather jacket. Her left arm got stuck. She glared at an elderly couple, watching with undisguised amusement from less than four feet away. She felt like Houdini in a bloody fish tank and all they could do was smirk.

Free of the jacket at last but still seething at the injustice of Joel's accusations, Cleo forced herself to take deep breaths. All she had to do was calm down and explain.

'Look, I told you what the shoot was like. It was a complete nightmare. Declan cheered me up, that's all. He was good company, fun to be with, a *friend* . . . but it's not as if I slept with him, for God's sake! Nothing *happened* between us—'

'Save your breath,' Joel said icily. 'He phoned me last night.'

'But nothing *did* happen,' Cleo yelled, punching the steering wheel in exasperation.

'Don't you mean D.C.O.L.?'

She stared at him.

'Now what are you on about?'

'Come on,' said Joel. 'I may not move in your kind of showbusiness circles but even I've heard of that. Doesn't Count On Location.'

It was hardly relevant just now but still sickening to realize that Declan's apparent friendship had been nothing more than a sham. He'd been acting under orders; prostituting himself, Cleo thought furiously, in order to try and catch her out.

'Try D.H.O.L.' She spat the words through clenched teeth. 'Didn't Happen On Location. Because it bloody didn't and if that lying little shit told you otherwise he'd better watch out. I swear, I'll go back to Venice and *drown* him—'

'I didn't say you'd slept with him.' Joel sounded weary. 'You didn't need to sleep with Damien Maxwell-Horne, did you, to know he was cheating on that friend of yours?'

'No, but—'

'But nothing. He bought you a few drinks, chatted you up a bit, and that was more than enough.' Joel shrugged. 'As far as you were concerned he was guilty.'

This was like being cross-questioned in court. Cleo couldn't bear it.

'Yes, but—'

'And even you have to admit you did more than let Declan buy you a few drinks,' said Joel. 'I mean, maybe rolling around in bed with a naked man isn't your idea of unreasonable behaviour. Call me old-fashioned,' he drawled, 'but I'm afraid it sure as hell is mine.'

The unfairness of it all was overwhelming. Feeling ganged-up on, Cleo said sulkily, 'I wasn't in the bed, I was on it. And he wasn't naked either, he was wearing shorts.'

'I don't care if he was wearing six fluorescent condoms and a suit of fucking armour.' Joel had had enough. 'You can do what the hell you like with whoever you like from now on. It's over between us. I told you from the start we weren't compatible. This just proves I'm right.'

He really meant it. Cleo, unused to losing any kind of argument, felt the first flickerings of fear. This relationship was too important to throw away. She was telling the truth; why couldn't he believe her?

'Please. It sounds much worse than it was. All I did was give a friend a goodbye kiss. Is that so abnormal?'

He didn't speak, just stared directly ahead.

'Joel.' She tried again. 'There's no way in the world I would have slept with him. He was like a *brother*.'

This time Joel turned his head. He looked at Cleo as if she were a stranger, then sighed.

'Don't be stupid. Even Declan Mulcahy doesn't screw around as much as your brother.'

Chapter 41

'I know I've told you this already but I must just say it again.' Rory Cameron shook his head in admiration. 'You do look terrific.'

Cass was relieved. She had been taken shopping by Cleo, who had persuaded her to part with far more money than she would normally have done, on the grounds that now Cass was out on the pull she had to look the part. Cass had closed her eyes whilst writing out the cheque, but now she was glad she'd gone through with it. The Ben de Lisi dress and matching jacket, yellow and white and absurdly flattering, almost made up for the fact that she was forty.

'Sophie calls it my spring-chicken outfit. She said I should wear a feather boa to match.'

Rory pulled a face. 'I hate feather boas. Always covering up the bits you most want to see.'

'Sshh. You're the father of the bride.' Cass gave him a surreptitious nudge. 'Best behaviour.'

The wedding ceremony was over. Everyone had crowded around the entrance to the church for the official photographs. The photographer was struggling to position the smaller page-boys. Rory, tanned and handsome, stood proudly between Amanda and Cass.

'I think I'm behaving impeccably.'

Cass glanced at him. 'Yes, well. For Amanda's sake, make sure you keep it up.'

'If it's for my sake,' said Amanda out of the corner of her mouth, 'I'd rather, for once in his life, he kept it down.'

Shortly after divorcing Rory Cameron, Amanda's mother Alma had married again, moved into her industrialist husband's splendid Jacobean manor house on the outskirts of Cheltenham and set about turning it into one of the most desirable residences in the country. Rory, hugely successful by most people's standards, but unable even to begin to compete with Alma and her dull but obscenely wealthy second husband, had always found their patronizing attitude towards him hard to take.

Giving his beloved daughter away and attending the reception, held in a vast marquee in the immaculate grounds of their home, was one thing, but accepting the pompously worded invitation to spend the night in one of their countless spare bedrooms was too much. No, Rory had decided when the invitation had first been issued, he definitely couldn't stomach that.

Instead, he had booked himself a room at the nearby Old Priory Hotel. When Cass had agreed to come with him to the wedding he had phoned the hotel again and managed to book a second room, the last available at such short notice but every bit as charming, the receptionist had warmly assured him, as his own.

In the end, having made the most of his ex-wife's lavish hospitality at the reception, it was ten thirty before Rory and Cass even reached the Old Priory. Realizing he was over the limit to drive, Rory had retrieved their overnight cases from the car and organized a taxi.

'Do we look like honeymooners?' Cass giggled as her heel

caught in a fringed Persian rug covering the stone floor at the entrance to the hotel. 'Oops, you've got confetti in your hair—'

'Funny honeymooners, booking separate rooms.' As she almost stumbled again Rory put his arm around her waist. It was odd; as Cass herself had pointed out she absolutely wasn't his type, but over the course of the day he had found himself becoming more and more drawn to her. Now, for the first time, he experienced a stab of regret that he should have done the gentlemanly thing and booked two rooms. Cass might not wear leather trousers and a ring through her navel but she was still jolly attractive. For her age.

The receptionist welcomed them with a professional smile.

'We're a bit late, I'm afraid.' Rory watched as a fragment of confetti, dislodged from the arm of his grey morning suit, fluttered down onto the desk. 'The name's Cameron.'

'Ah yes.' The glossy-haired receptionist was pretending not to have recognized Cass. Her pen ran down the list in the ledger before her. 'Room six, on the second floor.' She handed him the key. 'If you'd like to go on up, the porter will follow with your bags in just a moment.'

'And Mrs Mandeville?' prompted Rory.

The receptionist smiled. 'Yes, he'll bring her bag too.'

Cass gave Rory a great nudge. 'You said you'd booked two rooms. You *promised*—'

'I did. I *did*.'

The receptionist's professional smile began to falter. 'Those were the original instructions.' Nodding cautiously, she turned back to Rory. 'But we received a call two days ago from your secretary, altering the booking to one double room only. She faxed the confirmation through yesterday afternoon.'

Cass looked at Rory.

The receptionist looked at Rory.

'But my secretary's been away for the past fortnight,' said Rory. 'On safari in Kenya.'

An uncomfortable silence ensued.

Finally, as all the subtle digs of the past few days clicked into place, Cass said, 'It's Cleo.'

Rory had been about to look round for a lamp and a genie. No sooner had he made his wish than it appeared to have been granted.

Bemused, he said, 'What's Cleo?'

'The phone call, the fax.' Cass shook her head and raised her eyebrows in a you-know-what-daughters-are-like kind of way. 'I'm sorry. It's Cleo, trying her hand at a spot of match-making. I hope this isn't mucking you about too much,' she apologized to the receptionist, 'but we really do need two rooms.'

'Oh dear,' said the receptionist, 'I'm afraid we don't have them. We're full up.'

Rory's room was, as promised, an extremely nice one. Crimson walls and dark-blue bed-hangings conspired to create an almost Gothic atmosphere. The eighteenth-century four-poster was piled with red velvet cushions and the lamps burning on either side of the bed were heavily shaded. It was an outrageously romantic room, designed to enthral visiting tourists. As far as Cass was concerned it was dangerously romantic, the kind of room where things that weren't meant to happen, happened.

Maybe it's just as well, she thought, I'm here with Rory Cameron. Being a decrepit forty, at least she knew she would be safe.

'Right, well, no need for anyone to be embarrassed.'

Rory, rubbing his hands together in hearty fashion, looked so exactly like an embarrassed man hell-bent on not looking embarrassed that Cass had to hide a smile.

'There's a couch,' she said helpfully, pointing to a small chaise longue beneath the curtained window.

'I couldn't sleep on that.' Rory gazed in horror at the narrow steeply curved and ruthlessly upholstered seat. 'Not with my back.'

'And I thought you were a gentleman.' Cass looked resigned. 'I suppose I'll have to be the one to suffer.'

'Oh come on,' Rory protested, 'there's no need for that. We're old friends, aren't we?'

Cass allowed herself a cautious nod. 'Mm . . .'

'So what's the big deal?' Rory's eyebrows went up. He spread his arms like Pavarotti. 'If we were strangers on a long-haul flight to Bali we'd fall asleep next to each other, wouldn't we?'

'Mm . . .'

'And it wouldn't be awkward.'

Doubtfully, Cass said, 'I suppose not.'

'Well then, what's the difference? We'll sleep next to each other tonight. You can keep your clothes on if it makes you feel safer.' The corners of Rory's blue eyes crinkled as he broke into a smile. 'You can even keep your hat on if you like.'

Any more hesitation on her part, Cass realized, and he would only remind her what a prehistoric old fossil she was and how utterly uninterested he was in her wrinkled, worn-out body anyway.

She breathed out. 'OK, fine.'

'Good.' Rory's smile broadened. To prove how innocent his intentions really were, he seized her hand and kissed it. 'Darling Cass. Thank you for today. Have you enjoyed it?'

'Of course I've enjoyed it.'

He stepped back, unloosening his tie.

'I'm glad. You can use the bathroom first.'

It felt weird, thought Cass, lying in bed next to Rory. She hadn't been able to keep her dress on, of course, any more than she could have hung on to her hat, but she was wearing her pink-and-yellow satin robe. And her knickers. Goodness knows what Rory was wearing; she hadn't been able to bring herself to look.

Cass wondered if Rory snored.

'What are you thinking?'

Cass smiled into the darkness. So he hadn't been able to sleep either.

'Just wondering if you snore.'

'Never on a first date.' He barked with laughter. 'OK? What else?'

'I'm trying to pretend I'm on a long-haul flight to Bali.'

This time his laughter was silent. Beside her, she felt the bed shake.

'Poor old thing. Is this really such an ordeal?'

Old. 'Well,' she admitted, 'kind of.'

'You could always close your eyes and go to sleep.'

'I know. I'm not tired.'

'Just scared witless.'

Cass turned her head and saw that he was still laughing.

'Not scared. It feels strange, that's all.' Pushing bits of her fringe out of her eyes, Cass said, 'It's all right for you. You've shared a bed with zillions of girls.'

'Not always the same bed.'

'You know what I mean.' Her tone was reproachful. 'I've only ever slept with Jack.'

'You're kidding!' Rory sat up, genuinely shocked. Such an admission was outside his experience. 'You mean you've . . . never . . . ?'

He switched on the rose-tinted bedside lamp. To her relief Cass saw that he too was wearing a robe, dark-green silk with white piping. She hadn't expected pyjamas; Rory Cameron simply wasn't a pyjama person.

'Well, no, of course not. We met when we were very young.' She shrugged. 'When would I have had the chance?'

Still flummoxed, Rory said, 'But . . . nothing *since* then? Not even a fling?'

Cass blinked and shook her head.

He half smiled. 'I suppose flings aren't your thing.'

'It's not that.' The words came tumbling out before she even had a chance to vet them. Cass listened in astonishment to her own voice. 'They could be. I keep thinking a fling *might* be nice. The thing is, I just haven't met anyone I like enough who likes me back.'

Another silence. Cass felt her heart begin to pound against her ribcage. Had she really said that? Was it true? Was this what she had subconsciously been thinking without even daring to admit it even to herself?

281

'I like you.'

Oh heavens . . .

'Are you listening?' said Rory when she didn't reply.

'You don't like me.' Cass's throat was dry. 'I'm too old for you.'

He looked amused. 'Well, older than I'm used to. That much I'll admit.'

'Compared with what you're used to, I'm pensionable.'

'But do you like me?'

She bit her lip as his fingers brushed her arm. Quite suddenly she wanted Rory Cameron so much it hurt.

What am I, Cass wondered, some kind of wanton, sex-crazed mad woman?

But when he leaned across and kissed her, she stopped caring. It was what she needed, what she *deserved*.

'You are beautiful.' Rory's warm mouth brushed against hers. 'Do you know that? Beautiful.'

Cass's arms, so empty for so long, closed around him.

'Are you sure about this?' She whispered the words. 'You're not just doing it because you pity me?'

In reply, his body pressed against hers. Through their respective dressing gowns Cass could feel how aroused he was.

'Does this seem like pity to you?' Rory smiled as he spoke. 'Darling girl, I've been in this debilitating condition for the past half-hour. Why on earth do you suppose I wasn't able to get to sleep in the first place?'

The glossy-haired receptionist was still on duty when they went down to breakfast the next morning.

'Everything . . . all right?'

The smile this time was less professional, more openly curious. Cass felt her cheeks begin to heat up and mentally kicked herself. Now they really did look like honeymooners. The trouble was, the more insouciant she tried to look, the more it felt as if the words YES, WE DID IT! were flashing, Vegas-style, above her head.

Rory, less easily embarrassed, broke into a broad grin.

'Extremely all right, thanks.'

'Good.' The receptionist looked relieved. 'Breakfast is being served out on the terrace.'

'Come on, darling.' Still grinning, Rory put his arm around Cass. 'No need to go quite so pink. If anyone's over the age of consent, we are.'

Always a poor liar, Cass had even less success pretending to Cleo that nothing had happened. The stupid neon sign simply wouldn't switch off.

'Yeah, yeah,' Cleo crowed, having listened in disbelief to her mother's hopeless protestations of innocence. 'And I'm the queen of the tooth fairies. Mum, it's OK, we're on your side! This is what we *wanted* to happen, remember?'

'Yes, well.' Still flushed, Cass felt she had to make at least a token protest. 'That was very naughty of you.'

'And me,' Sophie piped up. 'It was naughty of me too.'

'It was embarrassing.'

Cleo beamed. 'Nice, though.'

'You took a big risk.' Cass tried to sound severe. 'It could have been a disaster.'

'Ah,' said Cleo, 'but it wasn't, was it?'

Sophie gave her mother a hug. 'We knew it would work out.

And we both like Rory. You have our permission to marry him.'

For a moment Cass was gripped with panic. She was a fortnight away from the decree absolute.

'I'm not even properly divorced yet.'

Chapter 42

There was no answer when Donny rang the front doorbell, but able to hear signs of life coming from the garden, he let himself through the side gate and made his way round to the back of the house.

'Oh my goodness!' Pandora, sitting in the sun, clapped her hand to her chest. 'You gave me a fright. Sorry, I wasn't expecting to see anyone . . .'

'I'm the one who should be sorry.'

Not sorry in the least, Donny flashed his famous white-and-gold grin. Pandora wasn't the only one to be taken by surprise. He certainly hadn't been expecting to see her looking so different from the last time they'd met. Having that baby had done her the world of good.

'Well, come and sit down,' Pandora offered shyly. She patted the blue-and-white checked rug spread out on the lawn beneath a gnarled apple tree whose arthritically twisted branches provided a welcome patch of shade.

Lying on the rug kicking its legs and grasping at shadows was the baby Donny had heard incredibly little about. According to Sean, its sole mission in life was apparently to yell its head off, fill its nappy and throw up.

A less-than-besotted father, Sean had taken to spending more and more time away from the house.

'I'm no good at all that stuff,' he had told Donny, pulling

a face at the mere thought of the nappies he had come across in the swing-bin. God forbid that he should ever have to change one himself. 'It's more Pandora's scene than mine. I mean, women are programmed to like that kind of thing.'

Donny had felt sorry for Pandora, who didn't appear to have much choice in the matter. It was also why he had decided to drop in on her today. Someone had to, after all, and he was fond of his nephews and nieces. He had even been known to change the odd colourful nappy himself.

He gazed down now at the baby squirming on the rug. Her name was Rose, though Sean still called her It.

'Isn't she brilliant?' Pandora was totally besotted with her daughter. 'We had a bit of trouble with colic at first but she's over that now. Look, she's smiling at you. I say, you are honoured. She hardly ever smiles at Sean.'

Probably because he's never here long enough to be smiled at, thought Donny. Entranced by the buttery softness of the baby's skin he eased himself down next to her and stroked her bare brown stomach. Rose gurgled with delight and seized his index finger, grasping it ferociously with both hands.

'What can I get you?' asked Pandora. 'Cup of tea, lemonade or a drink-drink?'

Donny shook his head. 'I'm fine.'

'If you're looking for Sean I'm afraid he isn't here.' Pandora had jumped to her feet anyway, and was heading for the kitchen. Over her shoulder she called, 'He's at the club.'

He wasn't. Donny, who had just come from there, said, 'Maybe I'll have a cup of tea after all.'

She returned minutes later with three vast mugs.

'One for you, two for me.' Pandora looked almost apologetic. 'I'm thirsty.'

'Because of the breastfeeding.' Donny, who had five sisters, gave a knowledgeable nod. 'That's how you've managed to lose so much weight so quickly. Am I allowed to tell you how great you look?'

He wasn't exaggerating. Pandora must weigh less now than she had done a year ago. The pert curves of her bottom and thighs were balanced by new and fetchingly voluptuous breasts. As the extra pounds had melted away, so Pandora's delicate bone structure had reasserted itself. Her eyes looked bigger, her neck longer.

If he tried, Donny thought, he could probably get his hands around her waist.

Pandora looked delighted at the compliment. 'Say it as often as you like.'

Donny obliged. 'You look great.'

Pandora's smile faded. 'Maybe you should tell Sean instead. He doesn't appear to have noticed.'

On the rug, Rose was making strenuous efforts to roll over onto her stomach.

'Of course he has.' Fibbing on Sean's behalf as well as Pandora's, Donny gave Rose the helping hand she needed. 'He's always going on about how brilliantly you're managing and how fantastic you look.' The lie began to expand, like making popcorn. 'And he's crazy about Rose, never stops talking about her . . .'

'Oh dear,' said Pandora regretfully, 'just as I was beginning to believe you too.'

Rose was making futile attempts to swim across the rug.

Donny pressed his palm against the soles of her furiously flailing feet.

'Well, it's what he should be doing.'

'Instead of touring the nightclubs,' Pandora remarked, 'and coming home reeking of other women's perfume. I don't know.' She sighed. It was pointless but she couldn't resist saying it. 'Why *do* they always have to wear such bloody obnoxious perfume? Why can't he ever choose someone who smells normal?'

'He's a mate,' said Donny, 'but I don't always like him.'

'Snap.'

'But you're still here.'

He could have no idea, Pandora thought, how helpless and lacking in confidence she had felt throughout her pregnancy. Coping with a colicky screaming newborn had been no picnic either.

Aloud she said, 'I suppose I feel I owe it to Rose. To do my best, anyway. Whatever happens, Sean's still her father.'

It wasn't until twenty minutes later when Pandora fell asleep almost in mid-sentence, that Donny realized how tired she still was. Waking with a start as a car at the front backfired she apologized profusely.

Donny, who hadn't meant to stay longer than ten minutes, heard himself saying firmly, 'Don't you dare be sorry. Babies are knackering. Look, why don't you go up to bed and have a proper sleep? I'll look after Rose.'

'Oh, that's really kind.' Pandora hesitated, almost as if afraid to say it. 'But what I'd most love is a bath. Rose always yells her head off, you see, the moment I get into the water. If you could just entertain her down here for half an hour, a proper uninterrupted bath would be such bliss . . .'

Bloody Sean, never here. Donny, wandering into the kitchen with Rose tucked frog-like against his shoulder, listened to the taps running upstairs. There had been tears in Pandora's eyes as she had accepted his offer. Exhausted by five-times-a-night feeding and the constant attention Rose demanded during the day, she was ready to drop. Donny looked at the washing-up waiting to be dealt with, then turned away. There was such a thing as going too far.

Making his way through to the sitting room instead, he began to suspect Rose might not be on his side. Having evidently decided to put to the test his proud boast to be able to cope with anything, she had promptly filled her nappy. Donny pulled a face. Rose, thrilled by the contrast between his black face and white-and-gold teeth, let out a squeal of delight and tugged one of his dreadlocks.

But the changing kit was all to hand in a squashy lilac-and-green zip-up bag, recognizable because it was the same as the one his sisters had passed around between them. Feeling profoundly capable, Donny began unloading wet-wipes, cotton-wool balls, baby lotion, changing mat and clean nappy. If he worked really fast, maybe he wouldn't need to draw breath.

He found the diary, quite by chance, at the very bottom of the bag as he was shovelling everything back. Realizing it had been hidden there deliberately, Donny experienced a brief spasm of guilt before opening it. But some things were simply too irresistible to pass up. And a diary belonging to Sean's woefully neglected girlfriend was definitely one of them.

* * *

So this is it, thought Cass, sitting alone at the kitchen table and gazing at the piece of paper in her hands. This is what a decree absolute looks like. This is how one signals the end of twenty-two years of marriage.

Glad to be on her own, gladder still that it had arrived by second post rather than first thing, just as she was leaving for work, she closed her eyes and thought of Jack. All those years, all that shared history, dissolved into nothingness like Aspro Clear.

Cass wondered if he would marry Imogen now. She wondered if she would ever meet anyone and actually want to marry again. She had tried to envisage being married to Rory Cameron and – as ever – failed abysmally. It was an image that stubbornly refused to materialize. Cass shivered. Her whole future, it seemed, was one big scary blank.

Just as her throat began to tighten, the phone rang. Cass's hand trembled as she picked it up.

'Hi, it's me.' Jack, of all people. 'Did you get it?'

The paper was still in Cass's hand. She looked at it once more, then glanced out of the kitchen window. The sun was still shining, the sky was still Mediterranean blue. There wasn't a cloud in sight. It really had been the most glorious day.

'I got it.'

'Me too.' Jack sounded odd, almost hesitant. 'Um . . . are you OK?'

'Fabulous.' Buggered if she was going to let him think otherwise, Cass straightened her shoulders. 'I mean, it's hardly a surprise, is it? We knew it was going to happen.'

But Jack knew her too well. Not fooled for a second by her

show of bravado he said, 'Come on, it still feels strange. *I* feel strange.'

'Get Imogen to give you one of her famous herbal body rubs.'

'Cass, don't.' Her bitchy tone only convinced him how upset she was underneath. 'Are you on your own? Is Sophie there?'

'Yes.' Sophie was spending the night with a friend from school.

'Put her on for a second.'

'She doesn't want to speak to you,' said Cass.

'That means she isn't there.' Jack sighed. 'Look, will you have dinner with me tonight?'

It was the last thing Cass had been expecting him to say. The receiver nearly slid from her hand in shock.

'Dinner? What for?'

Jack, who wasn't sure himself, said, 'Why not? We can be civilized about this, can't we? I'd like to take you to dinner.'

'Ah, but would Imogen like you to take me to dinner?'

'It doesn't matter whether Imogen likes it or not. I'm the one inviting you.' Jack paused. Imogen didn't know yet. 'Unless you have something else on.'

'Let me check my diary.' Cass tried not to sound overjoyed. She had no other plans and the prospect of irritating Imogen was too delicious to pass up. Besides, at least now she would be spending the evening with someone who understood how she felt. 'Ah, I *do* appear to be free . . .'

'Good. I'll pick you up at eight.'

To seem casual Cass said, 'Make it eight thirty.'

Chapter 43

Pandora, making the most of the heaven-sent opportunity, spent almost an hour in the bath. When she finally made her way back downstairs, relaxed, scented and changed into a kingfisher-blue cotton shirt and jogging pants, she found Donny stretched out across the sofa. Rose, her legs tucked beneath her, lay fast asleep on his chest.

'I'm sorry, I know I've been ages.' Pandora tried and failed to sound apologetic. 'That was possibly the best bath of my life.'

'Should have given me a shout.' Donny looked amused. 'I could have come up and scrubbed your back.'

'Shall I take her off you?' Pandora held out her hands as Rose, snuffling contentedly, shifted position in her sleep.

'No need. We're both comfortable.'

'I really didn't mean to take so long. She might need changing.'

Donny shrugged. 'It's OK. She did. I've already dealt with it.'

'Good heavens.' Startled, Pandora sat down in a chair opposite him. Warily she said, 'No . . . problem at all?'

'No problems. We aren't all like Sean, you know.'

'Oh, I know.'

With a jolt, Donny realized he fancied Pandora Grant like mad.

'You seem nervous,' he observed in casual fashion.

'No . . .'

'Almost as if you had something to hide.'

Pandora gave him a searching look and said nothing.

'In the bottom of that nappy-changing bag for example,' he continued remorselessly.

'Oh, you complete bastard!' Pandora wailed. 'I can't believe you did that! Not *again*.'

'It was Rose's fault.' Donny pointed down at the baby asleep on his chest. 'If she hadn't needed to have her nappy changed . . .'

Pandora, still groaning, slumped back in her chair.

'I thought it was a safe place to keep it. God knows, Sean was never likely to find it there.'

'Ah well. As I said—'

'I know, you're not Sean.' Pandora clapped her hands over her eyes as Donny pulled the diary out from behind the cushions wedged between him and the back of the sofa. 'Well, thanks. I hope you realize how embarrassing this is.' Her eyes were bright. 'You do know, don't you, that if you didn't have my daughter plastered to your front I'd kill you?'

'Why do you suppose I didn't hand her over just now?' Donny cupped the baby's padded bottom in the palm of his hand. 'She's my human shield, aren't you, sweetheart?'

'She never stays asleep like that for me.' Pandora looked perplexed. 'I don't understand why she hasn't woken up.'

'It's the timbre of my voice.' Smugly, Donny explained. 'My big, black, male voice. Babies like the way it vibrates against their chest. It's—'

'Comforting. OK, OK,' said Pandora, 'so you're Mary Poppins in dreadlocks. You're still a complete bastard. I wish I'd never had that bath now.'

'Oh cheer up.' Donny's smile broadened. 'How was I to know what it was going to be? I thought it was a diary.'

'So of course you *had* to have a nose.'

He shrugged, unperturbed. 'Wouldn't anyone?'

'I still can't believe you've done this twice,' said Pandora in despair.

Donny realized he'd teased her enough. As if sensing as much the baby began to stir. Tiny starfish fingers flexed and unflexed. Donny stroked the dark, downy, perfectly formed head and for a moment wished Rose could have been his daughter instead.

Then he looked across at Pandora.

'I've read it. All of it. It's brilliant.'

Unable to meet his gaze, she stared at the floor.

'No it isn't.'

Lightly, teasing her, Donny said, 'Oh yes it is.'

'I don't like being patronized.' A fierce pride burned in Pandora's eyes. 'I won't be made fun of. And it was *private* . . .'

The baby, ready for her next feed, began to whimper. Donny pulled himself up into a sitting position and jiggled her against his shoulder. A ribbon of dribble hung between Rose's fretful mouth and the neck of his white T-shirt.

'I'm not patronizing you,' he told Pandora. 'I mean it. If I'd thought it was crap, I wouldn't even have said anything. I'd have read a few pages, shoved it back in the bag and pretended I'd never seen it.'

Pandora didn't look convinced. The last time had been

humiliating enough. Once bitten, Donny realized, twice terminally suspicious. He tried again.

'Look, I'm serious. That last script of yours ... well, it wasn't as bad as we made out. I felt pretty mean afterwards, taking the piss out of it like that. All I can say is we'd had a few drinks at the club and when Sean started making his cutting remarks it was easier to go along with him than start an argument.'

Pandora, slowly beginning to believe him, thought of all the pages of script she had ripped to shreds and hurled into the bin.

'You mean what I'd written was good? Funny?'

'Some of it was good. Not great,' Donny added hastily, 'but not as bad as we made out.'

Pandora looked crestfallen.

'Oh.'

'The thing is, you've learned by your mistakes. This,' Donny tapped the diary, 'is *bloody* good. And I do mean that. It's fast, funny, original. It works.' He paused. 'Do you still think I'm bullshitting you?'

Pandora, seemingly unable to speak, shook her head. Rose, gripped by real hunger pangs now, let out an indignant bellow.

'OK, first things first. Feed this baby.'

Donny passed the bawling infant across to her. Sensing Pandora's hesitation he said, 'Go upstairs if you want to, but it doesn't bother me. I'm not embarrassed if you aren't.'

Pandora smiled slightly, sat back down and undid a couple of buttons of the blue shirt. Within seconds silence reigned once more.

For the second time Donny found himself wishing he was

Rose's father. Sean certainly didn't deserve her. Sean didn't deserve either of them.

'Second things second,' he announced, dragging his attention back to the contents of the diary in his hand. 'Would you like me to help you? See if we can't get this thing off the ground?'

Cautiously, Pandora nodded.

'What about Sean?' said Donny. 'Do you want him to see it?'

'No.' This time she was adamant. 'I'd rather this was between us.'

That suited Donny. He tried to tell himself his motives were pure. Sweat prickled at the base of his neck.

'Right, so we need to get this lot typed up.' He waved the diary at her. Between its mock-leather crimson covers were two hundred or so pages of closely written script, roughly six half-hour episodes, he estimated, of the kind of ground-breaking TV sitcom which might just end up being heralded as the new *Ab-Fab*. That Pandora had even dared to write it following Sean's lacerating verdict on her first attempt said something positive about her character. As far as Donny was concerned, she just went up and up in his estimation. He thought she was an all-round bloody miracle.

'Um,' said Pandora, 'I can't type.'

'Not a problem.' There was no stopping Donny now. 'One of my sisters can do it. And we're going to need a synopsis,' he went on. 'Two or three thousand words should be enough.'

Pandora pulled a face.

'I don't get much spare time. I wrote all that stuff before Rose was born.'

Donny grinned.

'In that case I'll just have to help out. Ring me when the coast is clear and I'll come over. In disguise if you like. This could be fun.'

For an uncomfortable second Pandora wondered whether she should be keeping this kind of secret from Sean. Then she reminded herself how he had reacted last time. He would only start banging on about nepotism again and poking fun at her efforts.

No, Pandora decided, far better to wait until she actually had something to show for it, something concrete to boast about. That is, if it ever actually happened.

Sean, arriving home minutes later, wasn't thrilled by what he found. His eyes narrowed at the sight of Donny, wearing a white T-shirt and strategically ripped jeans, sprawled easily across the grey sofa looking as if he was having the time of his life.

They narrowed further still when he realized what was going on beneath Pandora's bright blue shirt. How could she sit there, feeding that damn baby, as if it were the most natural thing in the world? Didn't she know how she looked? Sean's lip curled in disgust. For God's sake, didn't she realize what Donny Mulligan was *like*?

'What is this, feeding time at the zoo?'

He glanced meaningfully across at Pandora, signalling her to stop it at once and make herself decent. Why she couldn't feed Rose from a bottle was beyond him. Why she was looking so clear-eyed and bloody pleased with herself was more of a mystery still.

Rose had finished anyway. As Pandora did up the two

unfastened buttons on her shirt the baby looked across at Sean. For a moment she seemed as if she was about to smile then she let out an ear-splitting burp.

Donny started to laugh.

'Hey, man, all I did was ask her what she thought of your act last night.'

'Ha ha,' said Sean coldly, because last night's act hadn't gone down that well. To further irritate him, the baby was now gazing with rapt attention at Donny. This time her toothless smile was genuine.

'So how long have you been here?' said Sean. 'You should have phoned first.'

'Couple of hours.' Donny shrugged. 'No worries. I didn't particularly come to see you anyway.'

Sean looked at him. 'I see.'

'I decided it was time I introduced myself to your daughter.' Again, the big flashing white-and-gold grin. 'She's a beauty. Takes after her mother.'

'Mm.' Sean was becoming less and less amused. What was Donny's game? Checking that Pandora was decent he drawled, 'Well, the floor show's over.'

'And it's time I was off.' Rising slowly to his feet, Donny waggled his fingers at Rose. 'Bye, sweetheart. I think I'm in love.'

'Nice to see you,' said Pandora. 'And thanks. For everything.'

Donny winked. 'Any time.'

'Thanks for everything,' Sean mimicked furiously the moment Donny had left. 'Any time. What does he think he's playing at?'

'He was just being nice.'

Too buoyed up to care what Sean thought, Pandora showered Rose's face with noisy kisses.

'And I can guess why,' spat Sean. 'He didn't really come all this way to pick up a sweater.'

The sweater, borrowed by Sean a week earlier, had provided Donny with the excuse he needed to smuggle the diary out of the house.

Pandora shrugged. 'No?'

'He's making a play for you.'

'Really?' She raised her eyebrows, unable to resist the dig. 'No wonder I didn't twig. It's been so long since *anyone* showed any interest . . .'

Sean was getting madder by the minute. 'So what the fuck *does* "Thanks for everything" mean?'

'It means thanks for an afternoon of wild and thrilling sex.' Pandora lifted the baby onto her hip. She turned to face Sean. 'Which was something else I'd almost forgotten about. Now if you've quite finished, it's time for Rose's bath.'

Having been too weary over the past few months to retaliate, Pandora realized she was making up for it now. Startled, Sean backed off.

'Look, you know what I mean. How many times have I told you about Donny Mulligan? He's a screwing machine, the biggest lech in the club.'

'Second biggest,' said Pandora.

Chapter 44

Jack pulled up outside the house at exactly eight thirty. He had on a new dark-grey suit, the cut more modern than he was accustomed to wearing. Cass wondered if Imogen had taken to dragging him round the shops, persuading him into younger, trendier styles. The pink tie, in particular, was something he would never have had anything to do with before.

'Well,' she said, as they set off back down the drive, 'this feels strange.'

'Like a first date, you mean?' Out of the corner of his eye, Jack could see her smoothing her black satin skirt over her thighs, a gesture with which he was so familiar that it seemed odd when Imogen didn't do it.

'Hardly.' Leaning forward, Cass turned down the volume of the music coming from the new state-of-the-art stereo. 'On our first date I rode on the crossbar of your pushbike.'

'And I spent the whole evening wondering how I was going to handle the good-night kiss.' Jack grinned. 'I nearly tossed a coin, you know. Heads, mouth open. Tails, mouth closed.'

Cass felt herself being drawn helplessly back to that night, one she would never forget. Even now, just thinking of it, the butterflies in her stomach were starting up.

'Where are we going to eat?'

It was an abrupt change of subject, but necessary. If they were going to spend the evening playing 'do you remember?'

she needed a couple of drinks inside her first.

Jack had booked a table at The Phoenix, a quiet restaurant in Streatham which they had visited on and off over the years. The food was sublime, the atmosphere welcoming and the doorstep mercifully free of paparazzi.

'Not San Lorenzo then,' Cass said lightly, when the waiter had handed them their menus and moved away.

Jack carried on studying the wine list. 'I didn't think you'd enjoy the attention.'

'Me?' She glanced at him. 'Or Imogen?'

'I felt it was something we could all do without.' He sat back in his chair and drummed his fingers on the table. 'Don't look at me like that, Cass. And no bitchy remarks please. Let's just have a nice evening.'

'A nice, *civilized* evening.' She remembered the term he had used on the phone, pronouncing it with due solemnity. 'To celebrate the end of a nice . . . civilized marriage. I think I'll have the smoked trout then the guinea fowl. Speaking of trout, how is Imogen these days?'

Jack shot her a warning look. This wasn't what he'd had in mind when he had invited Cass out to dinner.

'Stop it.'

'Sorry, sorry.' Cass was beginning to enjoy herself. 'OK, I've stopped now. I'll be serious. How's Imogen?'

Stiffly, Jack said, 'Fine.'

'Most of the time it's fine,' Jack amended two hours later. The fingers of his left hand pleated and unpleated a corner of the linen tablecloth. 'But she wants a family.'

'If she marries you', Cass marvelled at how composed she

was able to sound, 'she'll get one. Three gorgeous step-children,' she said innocently. 'Goodness, even a step-grand-child thrown in for luck! What could be nicer?'

'Come on,' said Jack. 'You know what I mean. She wants a family of her own.' He heaved a sigh. 'In fact, she's obsessed with the idea.'

'Ah.' Cass nodded. 'And you aren't.'

Jack's expression was bleak. 'Can you seriously imagine going through all that again? I mean, actually *wanting* to, at our age?'

Our age, thought Cass. But Imogen wasn't their age. She was only in her twenties.

'Hang on.' She frowned. 'Isn't this a bit serious? Imogen's desperate to have children, you're horrified at the thought. What are you going to do if she gets pregnant?'

'What can I do? It's not what I want.' Jack paused while the waiter removed the last of the plates from their table. 'But I dare say I'd survive. I wouldn't run a mile, if that's what you're thinking.' He gave Cass a brief smile. 'I'm not that much of a shit. I know I would grow to love a new baby just as much as I loved the old ones. It's a bit of a daunting prospect, that's all.'

'One you'd better get used to, all the same. Imagine,' said Cass, 'in less than a year there could be baby-sick on the shoulders of that new designer suit. Look how fertile I was – I only had to think about babies and I got pregnant.'

'Hmm.' Jack sighed. 'The thing is, she's *been* trying. Since Christmas. Seven months now and nothing's happened. It's really getting to her.'

Cass wondered if she was expected to feel sorry for Imogen. The temptation to remark that maybe this was her punishment for being such a marriage-wrecking cow in the first place was tempting in the extreme . . .

Heroically, Cass resisted the temptation. Instead, downing her Sambuca, she said, 'Well, isn't that quite useful? As far as you're concerned, surely it's good news?'

'That's what I thought.' For a moment Jack wondered if he should really be confiding all this to his ex-wife, but what the hell. 'The thing is, she's fixing up all these infertility tests.'

'For her, you mean?' said Cass.

If she laughed, Jack thought, he would kill her.

'That's the trouble.' He gave her a gloomy look. 'For me, too.'

It was almost midnight when they left the restaurant.

'Imogen will be wondering where you are,' Cass remarked as he drove through the darkened streets, taking the familiar route back to Hampstead. 'Is she jealous? What'll happen when you get home? Will she bombard you with questions about tonight?'

'No.' Jack smiled, as if the idea were an amusing one.

'Why not?' Offended, Cass twisted round in her seat to face him. 'Aren't I enough of a threat? Just because I'm your ex-wife does that mean I'm not worth getting jealous about?'

The black satin skirt, unbeknown to Cass, was riding up her thighs. One dark-stockinged leg was half tucked under the other. With her piled-up blond hair escaping from its combs and her eyes bright in the reflected glow of the street lamps, Jack wondered if she had any idea how havoc-making she looked.

His conscience began to prick him. It just went to show, he

thought, how deep an effect poor self-esteem could have. Cass's lack of confidence in her own appeal was so unfounded it would be laughable if it weren't so sad. What she needed, Jack thought, was a man in her life. Some highly satisfactory sex. He wondered, as they approached the house, if she would invite him in.

'Of course you're worth getting jealous about.' He braked and turned left through the gates and up the gravelled drive. Relenting, he went on, 'And yes, OK, I dare say Imogen will give me the third degree. She'll want to know what you were wearing and how you – Oh! Whose car is that?'

The denim-blue Mercedes was carelessly parked across the top of the drive.

It was empty.

'How sweet,' exclaimed Cass. 'Rory had a meeting up in Newcastle. He said he'd try and get back but I didn't think he'd be able to make it. Gosh, I hope he hasn't been waiting here all evening—'

'Rory? Rory Cameron?' Weeks ago Sophie had mentioned in passing that Cass had gone to some wedding with Rory Cameron but there had been no word of him since. Jack stared at the car with indignation. The fact that it was unoccupied meant Rory must have let himself into the house. 'You can't be serious. You aren't seeing him?'

'Yes I am,' said Cass.

'But not actually ... *seeing* him ... ?' Jack floundered, struggling to find the appropriate words.

'If you mean sex,' Cass supplied with a trace of impatience, 'then yes, having sex too. Why so shocked, Jack? Did you think you were the only one allowed to do that kind of thing?'

'But—'

'And don't you dare say I'm too old for him.' Having unfastened her seat belt Cass was out of the passenger door in a flash. Almost as if, Jack thought darkly, she could hardly wait to leap into bed with her new and deeply unsuitable lover.

'You might not be too old for Rory Cameron, but you're definitely too good for him.' The man was a smooth-talking rogue. Just the thought of the pair of them together filled Jack with a kind of helpless rage. So much for thinking Cass might have invited *him* in for coffee.

'Don't be so stuffy. Rory's fun, he's kind and he makes me laugh,' said Cass. Blithely she added, 'And he's divine in bed.'

'Well?' Imogen demanded when Jack finally rolled in at twenty to one. Oh dear, it was all very well being determined not to sound like a shrew but when it came down to it how else could you find out what you needed to know? She smiled to soften the effect. 'How did it go?'

Jack shrugged. 'OK.'

Imogen's suspicions were instantly aroused. She thought it bloody odd, anyway, that he should feel the need to take his ex-wife out to dinner to celebrate their divorce. If anything, surely it would have been more appropriate for Jack to have taken *her* out to dinner to celebrate the fact that he was now free to remarry.

'You can't just say OK.' She followed him upstairs and sat on the edge of the bed watching him undress. Jack was an extremely tidy undresser. 'What was it like? Was she upset? Did she cry?'

Did you kiss her, comfort her, sleep with her, were the questions Imogen was dying to ask.

'No.' Jack had his back to her. She watched him hang up his suit, ensuring the trouser creases were straight. His white shirt went into the laundry basket. Imogen knew she would have to check it tomorrow morning for lipstick.

'I thought that was the whole point of taking her out,' she persisted, oh-so-casually. 'To cheer her up. She must have been a *bit* upset.'

Jack knew he wasn't helping matters. He knew exactly what was going through Imogen's mind. The trouble was, all he could think about was Cass in bed with Rory Cameron. Having fun, Jack thought savagely. Being made to laugh, laugh, laugh and enjoying endless *divine* sex . . .

'You could at least tell me what she was wearing.' A petulant note had crept into Imogen's voice. 'Unless, of course, she wasn't.'

'Look.' Wearily Jack turned to face her. It wasn't Imogen's fault. He mustn't take it out on her. 'Cass is involved with someone else. It's come as a bit of a shock, that's all. I know him and I'm not sure she's doing the right thing.'

'Oh!' Taken aback but hugely relieved, Imogen said, 'Is she happy?'

Jack's mouth twisted in an unamused half-smile. 'Oh yes, *she's* happy . . .'

What was he looking at now? Following the line of his gaze Imogen saw that it was her thermometer and ovulation chart, lying on the floor next to her side of the bed.

'That's all we need,' she said with helpless bitterness. 'Cass to get pregnant before me.'

Chapter 45

The royal film première was to be one of those glittering affairs so beloved by the media. The paparazzi were working on overdrive as limousine after rented limousine slid to a halt, disgorging yet more done-up celebrities. Half a dozen different TV crews jostled for position. Microphones were being shoved under perfect remodelled noses. Leicester Square was bursting at the seams with fans.

'All this and jet lag too,' murmured Cleo as she stepped out of the hired limo to face a barrage of flashbulbs. Wincing at their brightness she said, 'Got any aspirin?'

'Don't worry.' Dino, right behind her, put his arm around her waist and whispered into her ear. 'The film's crap. You can sleep right through it.'

Cleo pulled a face. 'Great. I fly back on the red-eye from New York. You invite me out to the movies. I'm wearing a dress that costs as much as a three-bed semi in Swindon . . . and now you tell me the film's crap.'

'Miserable old bag.' Dino gave her non-existent spare tyre an affectionate squeeze. 'I thought you'd enjoy a night out. I wish I'd invited someone else now. Cher,' he added in mocking tones, 'would have been here like a shot.'

The fans were cheering, waving autograph books and screaming out the names of their favourite stars. The photographers, more concerned with the money they would make selling their pictures to magazines and newspapers worldwide, yelled out: 'Here, Cleo!' 'Over here!' 'Give us a smile . . . let's get a good look at the dress.' 'Hey, Dino, this way! Give the girl a kiss . . .'

'Cleo Mandeville and Dino Carlisle!' A gushing female interviewer, swooping down on them, was closely followed by her TV crew. 'On a truly star-studded night, may I say how fabulous it is to see the two of you together. Now, the film you're about to see is a romance.' The interviewer's eyelashes fluttered. Avid for details she turned coquettishly to Dino. 'So! Is this a hint? Are you and Cleo seeing a lot of each other? Could this be . . .' quick turn, exaggerated smirk to camera '. . . luuurve?'

Cleo's dress, as Dino had cheerfully informed her earlier, consisted of two slivers of material smaller than ironing-board covers. These slivers, one at the front and one at the back, one black, one white, were held together with narrow strips of transparent perspex. It wasn't the kind of outfit that lent itself to underwear.

Dino grinned at the interviewer, who had orange lipstick on her teeth.

'Well, I think we're all seeing a fair amount of Cleo at the moment.'

'Ah, but are you two an item?' Persistence was this interviewer's stock in trade. 'I must say, you certainly make a striking couple. Cleo – *amazing* dress, by the way – perhaps you have something to add?'

The crew, Cleo realized, were from a popular London-based early-evening news and entertainment programme. It was what Joel generally watched if he was home from work in time. For a split second she imagined him lounging across the sofa with his feet up, starting in surprise at the sight of her on the TV screen, racked with envy and remorse . . .

'Dino's everything I've ever looked for in a man,' she told the astonished interviewer. Dino looked momentarily astonished too. 'He's gorgeous. We're very happy,' Cleo went on. 'Of course, he has to be back in the States soon, work commitments you know, but I'm not worried. We have absolute trust in each other, don't we, darling?'

Dino, whose wrist was being pinched, said good-naturedly, 'Sure we do. Absolute trust. Darling.'

'Well, that is splendid news,' gasped the interviewer, all the more startled because no one ever gave her the kind of exclusives really worth having. 'So, is marriage on the cards?'

The arrival of the royal entourage was imminent. Men with walkie-talkies were rushing around gabbling into them.

'Sorry,' Cleo said sweetly, 'looks like we're being herded inside.'

'Well?' said Dino when they had been ushered upstairs to the plushly carpeted foyer. 'Is marriage on the cards?'

'Ha ha.' The flexible strips of perspex were beginning to dig into Cleo's hips. Surreptitiously easing the pressure with her fingers, realizing that two and a half hours in a cinema seat were going to be sheer hell, she heaved a noisy sigh.

'*Now* what's the matter?'

'My dress hurts. Look, there's the royal party.' Cleo pulled a face. 'I must say the prince looks thrilled to be here. I know how he feels.'

'This bad mood of yours.' A note of exasperation crept into Dino's voice. 'Planning on staying in it for long?'

She glanced at him. 'I might.'

'Yeah? So when exactly did it start?'

Cleo stuck out her lower lip. 'Ages ago.'

'You mean when you got dumped?'

'Oh, hang on—'

'When that guy dumped you,' Dino mused, slowly nodding his head. 'That was *months* ago. Ah, now I get it. The thing for the TV cameras. That was for his benefit, right?'

Cleo looked more mutinous than ever. 'Maybe. But it wasn't my fault I got dumped. He *tricked* me.'

'Pull yourself together,' said Dino. Having never been in love for more than thirty minutes himself, he had no sympathy at all for Cleo's plight. 'And for Chrissake cheer up. I've never seen such a miserable bloody face. Come on, they're opening the doors.' He took Cleo's hand. 'We've got a film to watch.'

'You mean a crappy film,' said Cleo. The stupid perspex strips were still digging into her flesh. 'And if you think I'm miserable,' she added, scowling as she followed Dino into the darkened auditorium, 'you should meet my friend Linda.'

'This is crazy,' Dino sighed, four hours later. The film, as crappy as he had predicted, had had the effect of sending him to sleep. Waking up, he had found his pockets being rifled. The hopelessly contrived ending had reduced Cleo to tears and she – who never cried – was desperate for a handkerchief.

The post-première party at The Ivy had improved matters not at all. Normally bursting with energy and game for anything, Cleo was unnaturally subdued. Not even bothering to table-hop, she sat, apparently lost in thought, endlessly stirring the bubbles out of her untouched glass of champagne.

'Come on,' said Dino as they headed in the limousine back to Hampstead. 'The guy's history. You can't keep letting him get to you like this.'

'I know, I know.' It was what Cleo had spent the evening telling herself. It was just a shame, she thought, that it should be so easy to organize other people's love lives and so bloody hard to sort out your own.

'What you need is something to take your mind off him,' Dino went on, then corrected himself. 'Or rather, someone.'

Cleo had been telling herself that too. It certainly seemed to have worked for her mother, who had cheered up no end since the arrival of Rory Cameron in her life. Cleo wondered if it was possible to *make* yourself fancy someone, even if the sexual attraction wasn't immediately apparent. It must be, she realized. Look at all the arranged marriages in the world. They seemed to work well enough.

'What are you doing?' Dino looked startled as she slid along the back seat towards him.

'It's an experiment. Relax,' said Cleo. 'It's just something I want to try out.'

Before she could lose her nerve she took his face between her hands and drew him to her. She had, of course, kissed Dino loads of times before, but they had been kisses on the cheek, affectionate pecks, mere gestures of friendship.

This time it was different, the works, the full Monty. This time she meant business.

The chauffeur, a consummate professional, recognized that now was not the time to stop the car. Instead he drove smoothly past the gates of the Mandeville residence and carried on down the road. He would drive round in circles and await further

311

instructions. In his opinion the odds were on a trip back to Mayfair and Dino Carlisle's five-star hotel. Lucky sod.

Whilst the chauffeur cast discreet glances in his rear-view mirror Cleo concentrated all her attention on Dino. Kissing him was surprisingly easy, and it was nice that – having overcome his initial surprise – he was joining in. His mouth was soft and he tasted faintly of champagne. She liked, too, the way his fingers lightly stroked the back of her neck. That was something Joel had often done.

'Sorry.' Cleo pulled away with regret. 'It isn't going to work.'

Dino raised an eyebrow. 'I see. You tried me out and I failed the audition. Now you're going to toss me aside.' He paused. 'Like a used condom.'

'I did say it was an experiment.' But that was the great thing about Dino and their friendship; Cleo knew he wasn't really offended. She tucked an arm through his and gave it a conciliatory squeeze. 'Pretty bizarre though. Most women shut their eyes when they're with their awful husbands and fantasize that they're being made love to by some gorgeous Hollywood movie star. And here am I . . .'

'Charming.' Dino gave her a pained look. 'You mean there I was, giving it my all, and all the time *you* were pretending I was your hopeless case of a used-car salesman.'

'I can't help it.' Cleo started to laugh. 'He's not a hopeless case. And I did say I was sorry.'

'So I should bloody well hope,' Dino drawled. 'You took shameless advantage of me. I'm crushed. Who knows, I may never recover . . .'

'That bad, huh?' Cleo half smiled. 'In that case you should definitely meet my friend Linda.'

He grew serious. 'I'm still worried about you.'

'Oh, I'll be OK. I'll meet someone else.'

'What, another used-car salesman?'

Cleo was beginning to feel better. 'Definitely not.'

'Hmm,' said Dino. 'The way you're going you'll end up with an estate agent.'

'Left here, sir?'

They were back outside the house. The chauffeur momentarily met Dino's eyes in the mirror.

'Left here, Edward.' Dino briefly nodded. 'Tell me, Edward, between us men, what were you betting on? A quick U-turn back to the hotel?'

'Beg pardon, sir?'

'Yeah, yeah.' Dino's grin was unrepentant. 'Me too.'

Chapter 46

Pandora, lying in bed, heard the rattle of the letter box downstairs. The papers, all eight of them, landed with a series of thuds on the doormat. She hoped the noise wouldn't wake Rose. She wondered if Sean, next to her, was really as asleep as he looked.

It was hard to believe a whole year had passed since Donny had discovered and hijacked her diary. Harder still to believe that, the idea having been sold to a highly regarded production company who had in turn – eventually – persuaded ITV they had a ratings winner on their hands, the series was about to be made.

It was a dream come true. At last Pandora could admit to Sean what she had done. All she had to do was take a deep breath and say it.

Any day now, she promised herself. But not quite yet.

Sean's own series for Channel 4, due to be screened months ago, had twice been shelved, apparently as a result of scheduling difficulties. Rumours had begun to circulate, hinting that maybe it wasn't as great as the producers had first hoped. Sean, desperate to scotch that particular item of malicious gossip, had taken time off from the club, planning to write a whole load of dazzling new material. He had promptly gone down with comic's block. The funniness wouldn't come. Nothing he wrote was even remotely amusing. Yet more rumours began to do the rounds: he was burned out, washed up, finished.

Unused to failure and far too proud to admit his feelings to anyone, least of all Pandora, Sean had reacted by spending less and less time at home. Pandora, who knew exactly how he felt but was powerless in the face of such determined stonewalling even to begin to help, had kept her own exciting news to herself. It was all Sean needed to hear, she decided, when his own career was going through such a dodgy patch. When Channel 4 decided to screen Sean's series and he had a few encouraging reviews to boost his self-confidence, *then* she would tell him . . .

Meanwhile it was something of a novelty having Sean here next to her in the bed. Even when he did come home these days he was more likely to crash out on the sofa than make it upstairs. Gazing down at him, Pandora felt the familiar involuntary leap in her chest as her heart turned over. Too damn handsome for his own good, that was how a female columnist had described him in one of the tabloids the other week. She had followed it up with the scathing question: but is this the comic's equivalent of premature ejaculation? Has Sean Mandeville run too soon out of steam?

Sean had reacted with predictable fury to the article. It didn't make him easy to live with.

Life, Pandora thought wearily, would be a whole lot easier if only she didn't love him so much.

'I'm not asleep,' said Sean. He opened his eyes and rolled over onto his side. 'You may as well go down and get them.'

The first episode of *Sean Mandeville On Show* had been screened last night. Now all they had to do was find out how it had been reviewed. The fact that it had gone out against unfairly stiff opposition – ITV had premiered a big-budget Mel Gibson movie – was not, Pandora felt, a promising start.

Rose, sixteen months old now and as light a sleeper as ever, heard the stairs creak as Pandora tiptoed downstairs. Ears-on-elastic, Donny had taken to calling her. In his view Rose would make a terrific concierge when she grew up.

By the time Pandora had made tea, heated a bottle and collected up the great heap of papers on the hall floor, Rose's yells had worn Sean down. Back upstairs, Pandora found the two of them sitting up together in bed. Climbing in next to them, she winced. Rose's nappy was sopping wet. It would never occur to Sean to do the honours and put her into a dry one.

The next ten minutes ranked amongst the worst of Pandora's life. As Sean scanned each review in turn his face grew progressively stonier. A muscle twitched in his clamped jaw. The only sounds in the room came from Rose, happily slurping from her bottle with one hand and shredding the torso of a *Sun* page-three girl with the other.

Finally shoving the whole pile of papers across to Pandora, Sean pulled back the dark-blue duvet, levered himself out of bed and disappeared without a word into the bathroom.

'Oh dear, a dud from Mandeville!' sneered the first review Pandora came to. 'Sean's Yawn,' declared the second before going on to catalogue his apparently endless failings. 'Sean Mandeville has the looks of a film star,' the third critic had written, 'and the wit of one too. Sadly, that film star is Lassie. Lassie, go home. Please.'

The rest were just as scathing. The reviewers seemed to be falling over themselves to outdo each other in the insult stakes.

Only one had suggested the fault might lie with the programme's actual format which intercut the live stand-up with documentary-style behind-the-scenes footage. This had resulted in the loss of any sense of continuity. It was an idea that hadn't worked out. You couldn't sit back and enjoy the comedy because it was never on for long enough. You couldn't enjoy the documentary because it kept being interrupted by the stand-up.

Pandora felt sick. Reviews this bad were going to have the viewers turning off in droves. This was terrible news for Sean. What he must be going through right now didn't bear thinking about.

'What?' Sean said irritably when she pressed the handle of the bathroom door and found it unlocked. For a terrible second Pandora wondered if he had been crying. But when he turned to look at her she saw only blazing anger in the coal-black eyes.

'I'm sorry.' She felt so helpless. All she could do was let him know she was on his side.

'What for? Did you write the reviews?'

'No, but—'

'Well then. Don't apologize.' The last thing Sean wanted was Pandora feeling sorry for him. At that moment, just to twist the knife a stage further, Rose appeared in the doorway. Sodden nappy dangling, she waddled across the bathroom and flung her arms around Sean's legs.

'Danny. Danny.'

'Daddy,' Pandora hurriedly corrected. Rose had taken to muddling up Daddy and Donny, which didn't amuse Sean in the least.

'Everyone who's anyone has had rotten reviews in their

time,' she went on, even though Sean plainly wasn't interested. Making it up, Pandora said, 'Morecambe and Wise, Tommy Cooper, Paul Merton—'

'Don't patronize me.' Sean prised Rose's loving arms off his knees, picked her up and handed her to Pandora. 'Do something useful instead. Take her downstairs. I'm going to have a shower. And if the phone rings, for Christ's sake don't speak to any journalists.'

Sean was out of the house before nine. He didn't say where he was going and Pandora hadn't the heart to ask. She was not very successfully spooning cornflakes into Rose's mouth when the phone rang. Only when Pandora heard who was on the other end did she switch off the answering machine and pick up the call.

'Well? Did you tell him?'

'Oh, please.' Men, thought Pandora. They could be so *male* sometimes. 'Of course I didn't tell him. Have you seen the reviews for last night?'

'Only the *Sun* and the *Express*. They were enough to be going on with.'

Donny was in a good mood. There was, after all, something satisfying about Sean Mandeville getting his come-uppance at last. Realizing belatedly that it wasn't so easy for Pandora he said, 'Come on, he'll survive. Everyone gets knocked back at some stage.'

'I know.' Pandora spoke with feeling. 'Just don't try telling Sean that, OK.'

'You still have to break the news to him about your series,' Donny chided. 'They're about to go into production. It's hardly the kind of thing you can keep quiet.'

'I know that too.' Pandora sighed. 'But have a heart. Not just yet.'

On the other end of the line, Donny gazed at the clearly defined white bikini strap mark across the smooth brown back of the girl lying asleep next to him. He had picked her up at Comedy Inc. last night and he was almost sure her name was Sarah. Pandora disapproved of his one-night stands, which Donny felt was pretty rich when you considered how she had come to get so hopelessly involved with Sean.

Donny had a heart all right. Sadly it belonged to Pandora.

'How about lunch?' he said. Theirs really was the daftest of relationships, in some ways not unlike a furtive affair. With all of the subterfuge, thought Donny, and none of the sex.

'Lunch?' Pandora sounded doubtful. She watched her daughter plunge both hands into the blue bowl of cornflakes.

'You said he'd gone out. I'll come and pick you up.'

'What about Rose?'

'She'll be all right. We'll find somewhere child-friendly.' Next to him the girl whose name was probably Sarah began to stir. Donny's heart sank as he saw the mascara stains imprinted on his pale green pillowcase. Didn't these women realize what hell mascara was to get out?

'Not Le Gavroche then,' Pandora said gravely. 'Ugh, are you sure you can put up with her? She's just stuffed cornflakes into her ears.'

Donny grinned. He adored Rose.

'How is my girl, anyway?'

'Fine thanks.' Sarah – it was definitely Sarah – opened her eyes. 'I wouldn't say no to a coffee, though.' She looked at Donny. 'Who's that you're talking to?'

'My wife.'

'OK, come round at twelve,' said Pandora. 'I should have finished shampooing breakfast out of her hair by then.' She paused. 'Are you talking to someone else?'

Donny wondered why nobody had thought of manufacturing disposable pillowcases for one-night stands.

'No one,' he said blithely. 'Twelve o'clock it is.'

As he replaced the receiver, Sarah propped herself up on her elbows. Unaware of the mascara streaking her cheeks she said, 'Did I hear someone say Le Gavroche? Can I come too?'

Chapter 47

Sean had known better days. A meeting with his blandly reassuring agent did nothing to reassure him. Every cab he took was driven by some loud-mouthed git who had, naturally, watched last night's show and was full of opinions as to precisely where he had gone wrong.

Having decided the person with whom he wanted to drown his sorrows was Donny, Sean had been unable to get in touch with him. Not in the mood to face the rest of the crowd at Comedy Inc. he ended up instead in an almost deserted pub in Camden Town where if the barman recognized him, at least he had the decency not to say so. There, silently brooding and making commendable progress through a bottle of Glenmorangie, he might have stayed all afternoon.

Instead, another customer came into the bar.

'Ah, it's you.'

Looking up, Sean found himself being addressed by a complete stranger, a middle-aged man with a neatly trimmed moustache and highly polished shoes.

When Sean didn't reply the stranger said, 'Well, well, hardly surprising you've fallen flat on your face. You know where you went wrong, don't you, lad?'

Fan-fucking-tastic. This is all I need, thought Sean: to be collared by yet another know-it-all, a Mr Fixit with a surefire cure for failure. What was he, an off-duty cabbie?

'No.' He had to say something. The man was standing right over him, less than two feet away. Wearily Sean glanced up. 'Why don't you tell me? Where did I go wrong?'

'Didn't stick with your own kind, did you?' The look in the stranger's pale eyes was one of triumph. 'Had to mess with one of those black bitches. *And* put her in the club. You should be ashamed of yourself, my lad. Oh yes you should. And that's why your TV show's crap. Don't you get it? This is your punishment. Serves you right, see, for betraying your own kind.'

Sean may have been drinking but he was still fast. Less than a second later the man lay flat on his back, groaning.

'Sorry about the blood,' Sean told the barman. He slid a couple of tenners out of his wallet. Glancing down, he noticed splashes of blood on the front of his own white shirt. Well, a split lip had a tendency to gush. At least the man on the floor wasn't spitting out teeth.

'Do you know him?' asked Sean, when the stranger had finally dragged himself to his feet and with a malevolent glance over his shoulder left the pub.

'No.' The young barman shook his head and gave Sean a sympathetic look in return. 'But he knows you.'

He arrived back at two thirty to find the house deserted. Wanting to tell Pandora what had happened – for some reason laying out that nutter in the pub had cheered him up – Sean did a bit of detective work.

The kettle was stone cold, so she hadn't just gone out. He could detect a faint whiff of her perfume in the air, so she was unlikely to have taken Rose to the park. But the pushchair was still here. So was Pandora's car, minus its child-seat. This meant they had been taken out by someone else. Giving up, Sean helped himself to a can of lager from the fridge. On his way through to the sitting room he almost broke his foot on a dopey-looking Duplo giraffe.

The phone rang within minutes. Sean, convinced it was Pandora, didn't wait for the machine to pick up the call. He lay back on the sofa, balancing his lager can on his stomach, and reduced the volume of music blaring from the stereo.

'Yes?'

'Is that Sean?'

Damn. Not Pandora at all. But the voice was both sexy and female. It also belonged to someone Sean felt he dimly recalled. He didn't put the phone down. Instead, with extreme caution, he said, 'Mm.'

'Sean, how *are* you? Gemma Hogan,' exclaimed the voice. 'You probably don't remember me, but I did a piece on you last year for the *Clarion*.'

Sean remembered. Gemma in the flesh had been something of a disappointment, one of those girls whose physical attributes didn't match up to her voice. But the article she had written had been a charming one and as a journalist she was less awful than most. Nor, he realized, could he spend the rest of his life refusing to speak to the press.

'Go on.' He pinged the side of his can, watching it sway like one of those bottom-heavy punchball dolls. Not unlike Gemma herself, in fact. 'Go ahead, say it. The series stinks, I'm past it and what are my plans for the future?' Barely pausing for breath, Sean went on, 'Well, I thought I'd probably do the decent thing and stick my head in the oven. It's called going for the sympathy vote. At least it might stop the ratings sliding into minus figures—'

'Actually,' Gemma Hogan sounded almost apologetic, 'I was going to ask how you felt about the competition from your girlfriend. Is there any rivalry between the two of you, now that her own TV series is about to go into production?'

A long silence followed.

Finally Sean said, 'Which girlfriend?'

It was Gemma Hogan's turn to be taken aback.

'*Your* girlfriend. Pandora, of course.'

'Somebody's made a mistake here.' Sean paused to take a mouthful of lager. 'Pandora doesn't have a TV series.'

Another hesitation. Then Gemma said, 'Um . . . yes she does.'

Pandora was wearing make-up and a pink dress Sean had never seen before. She came into the sitting room carrying Rose's car seat.

'Oh.' She stopped when she saw Sean lying with his feet up on the sofa and was promptly cannoned into from behind by Donny, carrying Rose. Rose, in turn, waved a silver-and-white helium balloon in one hand and half a rapidly melting Cornetto in the other.

'What's this,' Sean drawled into the ensuing frozen silence, 'been playing happy families without me?'

'Donny took us out to lunch.' The look in Pandora's brown eyes was defiant. As she sat down Sean caught another waft of the perfume he had bought for her. She was wearing high heels too. Pale pink ones, to match the dress. He hadn't seen her this done up in years.

'Lunch. Great. Don't tell me; it's your birthday.'

'You know it isn't.' Evenly Pandora said, 'Look, I'm sorry you came home and didn't know where I was, but I thought you were out for the day.'

'So *you* thought you may as well make the most of it.' Through narrowed eyes, Sean observed the trusting way Rose's chubby brown fingers curled around Donny's neck. She seemed entirely comfortable being held by him. The happy families jibe hadn't been so wide of the mark. They looked, thought Sean with a lurch of anger, like a happy bloody family.

'Nothing's been going on, man.'

Donny felt it was his duty to say as much, since that was clearly what was on Sean's mind.

'You mean apart from the fact that my best friend has been seeing my girlfriend behind my back.' Sean's smile was icy, unamused. 'Not to mention playing surrogate daddy to my child. What the fuck else *hasn't* been going on, may I ask?' His gaze flickered in Pandora's direction. 'Next you'll be telling me you haven't written your own TV series.'

'Ah.' Pandora looked defensive. 'I was *going* to tell you about that.'

'Do it now,' said Sean. 'Tell me everything. Just blurt the whole sodding lot out . . . TV shows . . . affairs . . . everything. Believe it or not, I'm interested.'

'You hypocritical bastard.' Donny passed Rose, who was beginning to whimper, across to Pandora. 'It's OK for you to do whatever the hell you want, isn't it? You just don't like it when it's done back to you. Except Pandora hasn't even *done* it back to you—'

325

'Oh well, maybe she should,' Sean hissed. If he was being irrational he no longer cared. As Rose's whimpering escalated to a full-blown wail he raised his own voice to be heard above it. 'Do you know what I did today? Decked some lunatic for telling me I should have stuck with my own kind. I'll probably get done for GBH.'

Pandora, horrified, said, 'What?'

'I know. Ironic, isn't it?' Sean shot her a look of disgust. 'There I was defending you, and now it seems he was right all along. Because while I was punching the guy's lights out, what were you doing? *Sticking with your own kind*.'

Pandora eventually persuaded Donny to leave.

'It's OK, I'll be fine,' she assured him. 'He's had two shocks in one day. We just need to talk things through.'

'Phone if you need me.' Donny was reluctant to go but Pandora was standing firm. Not for the first time he wished he could have chosen someone easier to fall in love with.

'Go home.' Pandora smiled. 'You never know, that girl you left in your bed this morning might still be there.'

With his luck, Donny thought gloomily, she bloody would.

Chapter 48

'I didn't want to tell you about the TV thing until I knew for sure it was going ahead,' said Pandora. 'And you weren't exactly thrilled the last time I wrote something. I wasn't trying to cash in on your fame either. We sent the script in under the name P. J. Grant. The producers assumed I was a man.'

Dusk had fallen outside. Rose was upstairs asleep in her cot. They were, Sean realized, having their most in-depth conversation in almost two years. He found himself by turns both enlightened and confused. Particularly noticeable was the change in Pandora.

Sean didn't know if it was due to Donny's interest in her – because even if they weren't sleeping with each other it was pretty obvious the lecherous bastard wished they were – or to the fact that she had, according to Gemma Hogan, evidently written the sitcom of the year. Either way, the difference was there. He couldn't think how he hadn't noticed it before. It was as if the old Pandora, the one he had met and fallen for with such dizzying intensity, was back.

'Well?' she prompted when he didn't react. 'Aren't you going to say anything?'

Slowly Sean nodded. 'Well done.'

Pandora looked wary. It was hard to tell, sometimes, if he was being sarcastic.

'I mean it,' Sean said. 'I felt pretty stupid, I can tell you, getting caught out on the phone earlier. I wish I *had* known about it, but I can understand why you put off telling me.' He paused, then patted the space on the sofa next to him. 'By all accounts you've written a terrific script. You deserve to be congratulated. And I am proud of you. I like your dress too. Why don't you come and sit over here?'

'I'm not having an affair with Donny.' Pandora needed to make sure he understood. It felt strange, sitting next to Sean. When he put his arm around her the gesture was oddly intimate, more so than being in bed together. It was these small, affectionate gestures she had missed so much.

'I know you aren't.' A smile flickered at the corners of Sean's mouth. 'You had me worried though. Is it true what they say about black men?'

'On the grounds that it might incriminate me, no comment.' Unable to resist it Pandora added, 'Better ask Donny.'

Sean raised his eyebrows to heaven. 'Donny's the one who keeps telling me it's true.'

It was inevitable that they would end up making love. What amazed them both was the renewed intensity of their feelings for each other, the absolute rightness of it all. At midnight, perspiring and sated, they lay happily in bed guzzling chilled nectarines, Kraft cheese slices and wafer-thin prosciutto, the only picnic-type food Sean had been able to find in the fridge.

'You still haven't told me properly what happened in that pub at lunchtime.' Pandora's head rested against his bare chest. She found it hard to believe Sean had actually punched someone. 'Did this bloke really just come up to you and start ranting or had you said something to him first?'

Two's Company

'For once I'm blameless.' Sean lobbed the last nectarine stone out through the open window and licked the juice from his fingers. He ran through the brief exchange, word for word. 'More great publicity,' he concluded with heavy irony, 'if I get done as a result.'

'Well, I'm proud of you. People like that deserve all they get. I never know how to—' Pandora abruptly stopped and bit her lip.

'You never know how to what?' But Sean guessed at once. Outraged, he sat bolt upright in bed. 'React, was that what you were going to say? When people shout racist abuse in public? Nobody's ever said anything like that to me before!'

'Maybe I'm an easier target than you are.' They were being so honest with each other Pandora thought she may as well tell him. 'I've had the occasional awful phone call too. And leaflets shoved through the door. Some people just can't bear the idea of us being together, I suppose.'

'Jesus.' Sean's eyes blazed with anger. It had never occurred to him that Pandora had been forced to suffer as a result of her relationship with him. 'Ignorant fucking bastards.' He was shaking, ready to go out and take on the world. 'Why didn't you tell me any of this before?'

'I suppose I thought it wasn't your problem,' Pandora lied.

Sean saw through that too. He had behaved like a pig towards her. His arms tightened around her.

'You mean you thought I wouldn't care.'

The police station was situated less than five hundred yards from the pub. Sean walked into it the next morning and spoke to the duty sergeant on the front desk.

329

'I hit someone yesterday. I wondered if they'd reported the incident. My name's Sean Mandeville.'

'Oh yes, sir. That incident certainly has been reported.' The policeman nodded several times. Overweight and fiftyish, he had pendulous jowls that swung as he spoke. 'I dealt with the gentleman in question myself, yesterday afternoon.'

Sean's heart sank, though it was no more than he had expected.

'He did provoke me.' He looked resigned. 'So, what happens next? What do I do now? Find myself a lawyer, I suppose.'

'If I were you, sir, I'd go home and forget all about it.'

Sean shook his head. 'I don't want this thing hanging over me. I'd rather get it out of the way.'

'Look, sir, the incident was reported but it wasn't written down.' Was the sergeant, Sean wondered, trying not to smile? 'The gentleman concerned is, shall we say . . . well known to us here at the station. Pops in most days, as a matter of fact, to report some incident or other. You hit him, you say?'

All Sean could do was nod.

'Yes, well. No sign of any injuries, sir, by the time he reached us. So we'll just leave it at that, shall we? Off you go.'

'Right.' Hugely relieved, Sean nodded again. He smiled. 'Thanks. Thanks a lot.'

'Pleasure, sir.' This time the jowls were definitely quivering. 'One more thing . . .'

Sean was on his way out of the station door. He turned. 'Yes?'

The sergeant, who had watched the first disastrous episode whilst taping it for his teenage daughter, gave him a kindly wink.

'Liked the joke about the penguin, sir. Shame about the rest of the show.'

Chapter 49

It came to something, thought Sophie, when your mother was more delighted with the results of your GCSEs than you were.

Since discovering over breakfast that her brilliant daughter had scored the darts equivalent of 180 – ten flawless grade As – Cass had barely come down to earth. Sophie hadn't even been able to get to the phone to compare grades with her friends from school because her mother had spent the whole morning hogging the thing, broadcasting the news to everyone *she* knew.

'And don't you dare mention it on air,' Sophie warned when Cass finally had to give in and leave for work. 'I'll be mortified. It'll look as if you're bragging.'

'I *will* be bragging.' Cass beamed. 'I'm entitled to brag. What's more, we're going to have a party to celebrate. I've just decided. Then I'll be able to brag some more.'

'Who are you going to invite?' Sophie looked suspicious. 'Your friends or mine?'

'Don't glare at me like that, sweetheart. *Everyone.*'

'Saturday night,' Jack mused when Cass phoned him that evening. 'Damn, we've already been asked to something then. I'll need to cancel it.'

'Sophie would want you to be here.' Cass held her breath. Sophie wasn't the only one.

'And I wouldn't miss her party for the world.' Jack sounded

deeply offended. 'Sophie's my daughter, Cass. We'll definitely be there.'

We? She squirmed at the sound of the dreaded W-word.

'Um, it's kind of a family celebration.' Cass spoke rapidly. The last thing she wanted was Imogen spoiling the whole night. 'I meant just you.'

'Oh dear, come on now.' She heard Jack assume his let's-be-sensible tone of voice. An involuntary shudder went down her spine. 'Be fair, Cass. How long is it now since we separated? We're mature adults. You have your own life to lead and I have mine . . . and it's certainly time we put an end to this silly feud.'

'Silly feud?' Cass stared at the phone in disbelief.

'Well, you know what I mean. Be reasonable,' Jack urged. 'You can't spend the rest of your life inviting me to family events and leaving Imogen out. It doesn't make sense.'

It made perfect sense to Cass, but she realized this was one argument she was destined not to win. If she stuck to her guns Jack might refuse to come to the party at all.

'You were friends once,' he went on, when she didn't speak.

'That makes it worse,' Cass coldly informed him, 'not better.'

'Oh well, in that case—'

'OK, OK,' she sighed, before he had a chance to start making his excuses. 'Imogen can come too. I'll be polite. Just don't expect me to fling my arms around her and give her a big kiss, that's all.'

'Right,' said Cleo, marching unannounced into Sophie's bedroom on Saturday afternoon and expertly plucking the August edition of *National Geographic* from her sister's grasp. 'Time for a spring clean.' *National Geographic* hit the wall and slid down behind the bed. 'And I'm the one who's going to do it.'

'A, it isn't spring,' Sophie pointed out. 'B, Mrs Bedford deals with all that. And C, never mind a whole bedroom, you have enough trouble cleaning sweet wrappers out of your car.'

'I'm not talking bedrooms. You're the one in need of the spring clean.'

'Ugh.' Like an eel Sophie slithered out of reach just as Cleo made a grab for her. 'Don't, you aren't allowed! This is my day and everyone has to be nice to me. Even you.'

'I'm sorry.' Employing a change of tactics Cleo collapsed onto the narrow, book-strewn bed. 'I'm trying to be nice. That's why I want to do you up for tonight, make you look wonderful. Pleeease,' she wheedled, 'don't you think you owe it to your guests to make some kind of effort? Sweetheart, you can't just roll downstairs in a horrid T-shirt and yukky old jeans.'

Sophie scowled. It wasn't a horrid T-shirt, it was a perfectly decent turquoise-and-white Save the Whale one. She had even given it a once-over with the iron.

But Cleo wasn't nearly ready to give up.

'Pleeeease,' she said again, jumping to her feet and frog-marching Sophie across the room. Flinging open the wardrobe door she pointed Sophie in the direction of the mirror. 'Now, isn't there heaps of room for improvement? If only for Mum and Dad's sake . . .'

Sophie seldom bothered to examine her reflection but Cleo had her shoulders in a vice-like grip. Finally, with a weary shrug, she said, 'OK, so maybe it wouldn't kill me. Just for one night.' Her eyes bored into her sister's. 'But it had better not be anything drastic.'

* * *

Cleo was in heaven. This was Richard-and-Judy makeover time, the kind of magical transformation that made you rub your eyes in disbelief. Even she, with all her experience, had never suspected Sophie could come up so well. It really was gob-smacking . . .

The figure had been there all along, of course, just hidden beneath disgusting clothes. Now, helped by the fact that in the past year Sophie had shot up, it was virtually faultless.

She had all the necessary bone structure too, Cleo realized. The face was heart-shaped, the cheekbones high. And as for those eyes . . . well, they might not look much on their own, naked and hidden behind spectacles, but plenty of charcoal shadow, black pencil and mascara had brought them out like nobody's business.

Humming happily, in her element now, Cleo kept going. Lip pencil, raspberry-pink lipstick and highlighting gloss for the mouth. More blusher. A smidgeon more work on those eyebrows. And maybe another coat of mascara, to really show off the length of those lashes—

'Haven't you finished yet?' Sophie groaned.

'Shut up. Your hair's a disaster.'

Cleo wasn't joking. It really was. All she could do was slick it back with tons of gel and hope it hid the fact that Sophie still hacked away at it herself.

'About bloody time too,' Sophie grumbled when she was at last allowed to stand up and take a look at herself in the mirror. Without her glasses, which Cleo had confiscated, this was easier said than done.

'It helps', Cleo observed, 'if you try and look as if you aren't having your toenails yanked out.'

'It'd help even more if I could see.'

'Oh, for heaven's sake.'

Cleo gave the spectacles back. They didn't remotely go with the midnight-blue Hervé Leger dress she had shoe-horned Sophie into, nor with the delicate high heels. It was a miracle she had managed to squeeze Sophie into these anyway; more used to thumping great Doc Martens she had the broadest feet imaginable.

'Bleeurrghh,' Sophie wailed, seeing herself at last and going quite pale beneath the layers of bronzing powder. 'Is this a joke?'

'Come on,' protested Cleo. Standing behind Sophie, she admired her own handiwork. 'You look amazing. Like a young Audrey Hepburn. Sweetheart, this is seriously *Vogue*! I know models who would kill for your figure.'

'I look like a tart,' said Sophie flatly.

'Trust me. No self-respecting tart would be seen dead in those specs. *Don't*—' Cleo let out a screech of alarm as Sophie, still scrutinizing her reflection, ran an exploratory fingernail down her cheek. Foundation, bronzer, blusher and translucent powder came away like magic, leaving a thin white line in its wake.

'This is ridiculous.' Sophie, examining the gunge under her fingernail, began to laugh. 'Edna Everage would look *au naturel* compared with this. What gets it off, Swarfega?'

It was heartbreaking. All Cleo could do was throw herself onto Sophie's bed, gaze up at the ceiling and listen to the shower going full pelt next door. When Sophie emerged fifteen minutes later every last speck of make-up had been scrubbed off. Her face was pink and shiny, her body wrapped in a white towel.

Scrunched up in one hand was thousands of pounds' worth of midnight-blue Hervé Leger.

'Here.' She held it out to Cleo. 'Thanks, but it's not really me.' She smiled briefly. 'I think I'll stick to jeans.'

It was more than heartbreaking. Cleo now understood how people felt when they claimed to have seen a spaceship or been kidnapped by aliens. *She* knew it had happened – she had seen the transformation of Sophie with her own eyes – but she had no photographs, no witnesses, no *proof*.

Chapter 50

The taxi dropped Jack and Imogen at the bottom of the drive. As they made their way on foot up to the house they were overtaken by a blue BMW with a child-seat in the back. Glimpsing Sean at the wheel, Imogen's mind slipped back to the night of their first meeting two years earlier. Cass had impulsively invited her to that party, being held to celebrate Jack's fortieth birthday. This time Jack had been the one who had insisted she come along. Imogen's grip on his hand tightened. How things had changed since then.

The house was teeming with people. Imogen, more nervous than she cared to admit, stood by in the hall while Jack made a grandfatherly fuss of Rose.

'I keep hearing about this sitcom of yours.' For something to say, Imogen turned to Pandora who was less likely to rebuff her than Sean. 'Evidently the producers are thrilled with the way it's going. Great things are being predicted . . . Baftas, the works.' She smiled, noting how much better Pandora was looking these days. 'How would you feel about doing an interview for us? If we get a move on, we could feature it in the November issue of *Hi!* to tie in with the screening schedule.'

Pandora opened her mouth to speak.

'No thanks,' said Sean, who had been listening. He looked at Imogen. 'Better safe than sorry. You might have an affair with Pandora.'

338

The drawing room was even more crowded with guests than the hall. Sophie's school friends mingled excitedly with the kind of glamorous showbusiness types they normally only saw on TV. Even Imogen, famous by association rather than in her own right, found herself being accosted by a twittering teenager who introduced herself as Jennifer Smith-Elliott.

'I'm in the same class as Sophie,' she babbled on. 'I stood behind you once in a chemist's shop in Islington.'

'Really.' Imogen, bored already, looked round for a means of escape.

'You bought a Max Factor lipstick and a tube of Colgate.' For some reason the girl was eyeing her stomach.

'Goodness me.'

'And a pregnancy testing kit,' said Jennifer, tilting her head to one side. 'But you can't have been pregnant because you haven't had a baby. Are you still trying, or did you not really want one in the first place?'

Sophie hadn't only invited friends from school.

'Mum, I'd like you to meet Julian and Natasha.'

Cass had been deep in conversation with Jenny Duran. Turning, she realized the preconceptions that exist where names are concerned. Julian and Natasha sounded infinitely glitzy. Cass smiled and shook hands with each of them in turn. Julian had wispy beige hair, an even wispier beard and holes in the elbows of his hand-knitted grey jersey. Natasha was wearing a hippyish patchwork skirt, no make-up and a yellow tank top. They were both drinking orange juice.

'Julian and Natasha are just back from Uganda. They're

with VSO,' Sophie beamed. 'You remember, they sent me a couple of postcards.'

'Of course.' Cass vaguely remembered. Sophie's passion for all things African remained undimmed. 'Voluntary Service Overseas, isn't it?'

Vigorously and in unison Julian and Natasha nodded.

'We can't wait to go back,' Natasha enthused. 'The orphanage needs us. You have no idea, Mrs Mandeville, how much of an effect the AIDS epidemic has had on that country.'

'And the more volunteers we can persuade to come out with us, the better,' Julian chimed in. 'It's such a *worthwhile* cause. I'm sure you must be proud of—'

Sophie kicked him.

'Ouch.' Julian looked at her, surprised.

'She hasn't told them yet.' Natasha spoke in soothing tones. 'Have you, Sophie?'

'Told us what?' said Cass.

'Oh help.'

Cleo, sitting out on the terrace with Pandora and Rose, felt the hairs at the back of her neck go up. She stopped talking and stared through the open French windows.

'Ah.' Pandora followed her gaze. 'You mean Joel.'

'I didn't know he'd been invited.'

Pandora looked guilty.

'When Sophie rang us, she said to ask Joel along too. Sorry, was that the wrong thing to do?'

'Um . . .'

Peering at her more closely, Pandora began to look worried. 'You've gone pale. Are you feeling all right?'

Cleo wasn't sure how she felt. Seeing Joel again for the first time in so long – and without any warning whatsoever – had knocked her for six. Rose, recognizing him, let out a shriek of uncomplicated delight and squirmed to be allowed off Cleo's lap.

Cleo watched Rose charge across the terrace towards him. She saw Joel bend down and lift her triumphantly into his arms. For a shameful moment Cleo wished she could swap places with Rose and be smothered in kisses by that dear familiar mouth.

Shit, she had tried so hard to forget him. So much for willpower; it hadn't worked at all.

'I really am sorry.' Pandora hadn't dreamed Joel's arrival would have this much effect. Neither he nor Cleo had exactly opened their hearts to her about whatever had gone wrong between them last year. Pandora, assuming their brief affair had simply fizzled out, had similarly never thought to ask.

Joel, meanwhile, had hoisted a giggling Rose onto his shoulders and was making his way towards them. Cleo took the coward's way out.

'There's Sean being pestered by a couple of Sophie's friends.' She rose abruptly to her feet. 'If they're telling him how crappy his TV series is, he's likely to chuck them onto the barbecue. I'd better get over there, see if I can't calm him down.'

Only by the merest flicker of his eyes did Joel acknowledge having even noticed Cleo as she swerved swiftly past him.

But then he'd had the advantage, thought Pandora. He might have caught Cleo on the hop, but he had known full well that she'd be here.

* * *

Imogen, in need of a bit of Dutch courage, had downed three vodka tonics in quick succession. Now feeling much better, she found herself talking to an ex-neighbour of Jack's, a friendly-looking middle-aged woman called Daisy who, Imogen remembered Jack once telling her, had two adopted sons.

'It's so hard,' Imogen confided. 'Unless people have been through it themselves they haven't the least idea how it feels. Every time some earth-mother with six kids tells me to relax and stop worrying about it I just want to *slap* them.'

Behind her, Jack frowned. He tried to be sympathetic but Imogen's habit of blurting out intimate details of the latest tests she had undergone to all and sundry was unnerving.

'Jack. Sorry to interrupt . . .'

To gain his attention, Cass briefly touched his arm. As he turned to face her, so did Imogen.

'Cass,' said Imogen. So far this evening they had managed with some success to avoid each other. But Jack was right, it was silly to carry on like this. It was high time diplomatic relations were restored.

'Hello.' Cass nodded stiffly. She hadn't been looking forward to it either, but now at least it was done. Turning her attention once more to Jack she spoke in a low voice. 'It's Sophie. Look, can you come and have a word? She's being stubborn about something.'

Determined that it shouldn't look as if she were being snubbed by Cass, Imogen said rapidly, 'I was just telling Daisy about the problems we've been having at the infertility clinic. Getting onto a decent IVF programme is tougher than winning a scholarship to Oxford.' She forced a bright smile. 'It's ironic, isn't it? Some people seem to fall pregnant just like that, and look at us, desperate to have a child. Well, Daisy understands what we've been going through.' She glanced from Daisy, who was looking puzzled, to Cass. 'It seems so . . . unfair.'

Do I *really* have to be polite? wondered Cass.

'I think . . .' Daisy coughed delicately.

'I think you have Daisy confused with Trudy,' said Cass. 'Trudy is our other neighbour but she isn't here tonight anyway so you won't be able to bore her to tears with your sob story. As for things being unfair . . .' She stopped, her gaze sweeping coldly over the girl who had befriended her, stolen Jack and broken up a perfectly good marriage – 'Lots of things in life aren't fair.'

Jack, stunned into unaccustomed silence, could only stare at his ex-wife.

'Right.' No longer caring what he thought, Cass tapped his arm. 'Maybe now I can drag you away to have that word with your daughter.'

'I swear, you wouldn't believe how different she looked!'

Cleo, relating the story of Sophie's brief encounter with high heels and make-up to Jenny Duran, was beginning to feel more and more like the only person in the world to have seen the Loch Ness monster.

Jenny adored Sophie, who had always been the ugly duckling of the Mandeville family but more than made up for it in spirit.

'I'm sure she looked sweet,' she said to appease Cleo. Through a gap in the crowd around the barbecue she glimpsed Sophie, deep in some discussion with a group of school friends. Jenny smiled. When hacked-at hair, unflattering specs and the

343

kind of clothes only a train-spotter would wear became the height of fashion, maybe Sophie would have her chance to shine.

'I'm serious,' Cleo stubbornly insisted. 'She looked amazing.'

'Hmm. And you're looking shifty.'

At once, Cleo's dark eyes flickered. 'I am not.'

'Yes you are.' Seizing on the outrageous lie with delight, Jenny said, 'Now I get it. There was a real reason for dragging me outside. Come on, tell me everything.' Cosily she nudged Cleo's arm. 'This is what I do best. It's a man, isn't it? Damn, what am I saying? Of course it is. So what are we doing out here anyway, trying to accidentally-on-purpose bump into him? Or hide?'

There really was no stopping Jenny when she was hot on the trail of someone else's problem. Cleo, who hadn't meant to at all, found herself spilling out the whole miserable tale.

'He thinks I'm some kind of playgirl jet-setter,' she concluded mournfully some minutes later, 'with all the morals of an alley cat.'

'Well, you do jet-set.'

'Only because it's what I'm paid to do. It's my job,' said Cleo in fretful tones. 'And as far as Joel was concerned, it meant I couldn't be trusted. If I was a secretary in a tax office in Tring, I'd be all right.'

The next moment she stiffened as Joel came into view at the far end of the terrace. He was talking to Imogen Trent of all people. Cleo watched him laugh at something Imogen had just said.

'That's him, I take it.'

Cleo nodded.

'Hmm,' said Jenny, observing the way Cleo's fingernails were digging into the palms of her hands. The blond giant was good-looking enough but in all honesty he didn't compare with Dino Carlisle. Yet Dino, according to Cleo, left her cold. This thing with Joel, Jenny decided, really must be love.

Cleo glanced across at her. 'Hmm what?'

'Just thinking it doesn't suit you.'

'*What* doesn't suit me?'

'Skulking in the shadows.' She touched the long black velvet sleeve of Cleo's dress. 'Looking like a bit of rockery hell-bent on melting into the background. Hiding away . . . Cleo, it just isn't *you*.'

Cleo already knew that. She looked cross.

'So what do you think I should do? March up to him, I suppose. Grab him by the hair, fling him over my shoulder and drag him off to the nearest cave?'

Jenny grinned. 'Well, something like that.'

'It's all right for you,' grumbled Cleo. Jenny was still deliriously happy with Luke. 'What if he doesn't want to be dragged?'

'Persuade him otherwise.' As far as Jenny was concerned, it was simple. She spread her hands. 'I mean, look at you now. Be honest, what have you got to lose?'

Chapter 51

'Enough,' said Jack, because Sophie was being ridiculously stubborn and his patience was wearing thin. Determined not to lose his temper he kept his voice low. 'Look, this is neither the time nor the place. Sophie, you're in danger of spoiling your own party. Leave it for now, OK? We can talk about this properly tomorrow.'

Sophie stood her ground.

'But you'll still say no.' Behind the light-reflecting spectacles, her grey eyes bored steadily into him. 'Is that it? Don't try and fob me off, Dad. I've made up my mind. This is what I want to do more than anything else in the world. And I think you're the ones who are being unfair.' The unflinching gaze was turned on Cass. 'Everyone else around here seems to do whatever *they* want to do.'

'Sweetheart, you're too young,' Cass protested. 'You're *sixteen*.'

'Old enough to get married,' snapped Sophie.

Imogen had come in search of Jack, who had been missing for ages. She saw the determined set of Sophie's jaw. She heard the words Sophie uttered. She gazed in amazement at Jack.

Sophie? Married?

Cleo, having decided to take Jenny's up-and-at-'em advice but needing a quick nervous pee first, was on her way back from the loo. Unable to spot Joel anywhere in the garden she now found herself diverted by the realization that some kind of argument was brewing in the kitchen.

'What's going on?'

Cleo had never been over-friendly towards her but Imogen couldn't resist breaking the news.

'Sophie's getting married.'

Everyone including Sophie turned to stare at Imogen.

'Oh dear, you can tell she's a journalist,' murmured Cass.

Imogen longed to slap her.

'Don't be stupid.' Cleo's tone was dismissive. 'What is it really?'

'Your sister's being ridiculous.' Jack's eyebrows were drawn together. 'Ten GCSEs, all A grades, and what does she want to do? Bugger off to Uganda.'

'Honestly.' Sophie glared back at him. 'The way you're freaking out, anyone would think I had my heart set on a career as a King's Cross prostitute.'

'Darling—' Cass tried to calm her down.

'Or a heroin addict,' shouted Sophie, refusing to be calmed. 'I mean, what is so terrible about wanting to work in an orphanage in Uganda? And it can't have come as that much of a surprise anyway,' she rattled on. 'You know it's what I've always wanted to do. I'd be helping people who need help, doing something *useful* with my life.'

Sophie was gazing around, desperate for support. Imogen, who had never been afraid to disagree with Jack and who was still smarting from Cass's quite uncalled for put-down earlier, began to applaud.

'Hear, hear,' she told Sophie. 'Good for you.'

Nobody else joined in. Imogen realized she was on her own.

347

Even Sophie didn't seem to appreciate the gesture.

'Well, excuse me. But I'm entitled to an opinion,' Imogen mocked, 'aren't I?'

'Leave it.' Jack's voice was low. 'You aren't helping.'

Someone behind Imogen – a voice she couldn't identify – murmured, 'You can tell she doesn't have children of her own.'

'OK. This is a party.' Cass put her arm around Sophie. Determined the evening shouldn't be spoiled, she said, 'And we *are* proud of you, sweetheart. We're just saying sixteen is awfully young for such an adventure. Some of these African countries aren't safe . . . you've told us yourself AIDS is everywhere—'

'You don't catch it by talking to orphans,' Sophie shot back. With a glimmer of sarcasm she added, 'And I promise not to sleep with anyone.'

'That isn't the only danger and you know it,' said Jack. 'Civil war could break out at any time . . . Sophie, you know what we're trying to say. At least leave it another two years. Take your A levels and then go.'

'I want to go now.'

Cass frowned. What was it Julian and Natasha had said earlier?

'I thought VSO didn't accept people under the age of eighteen.'

'They don't.' Sophie remained cool. 'I'd pay my own way.'

'Oh yes?' Seizing this straw, Jack said, 'What with?'

Sophie had no money, he knew that. Every penny of her allowance was spent on books, educational trips and more books.

Realizing she'd been rumbled, the spark of battle died in Sophie's eyes.

'Don't tell me,' said Jack. 'You were going to ask us to lend you the money. Am I right?'

Sophie said nothing. Finally, and with reluctance, she nodded.

'Well,' said Jack, 'I'd be happy to do that.' He glanced at Cass, then back to Sophie. 'In two years' time. I'd be more than happy to.'

Jenny Duran, coming downstairs, bumped into Sean.

'Oh good, you're here.' She pointed over her shoulder at the first of the bedroom doors along the landing. 'I think I heard Rose crying a moment ago. Sounds as if she's waking up.'

'OK.' He nodded. 'I'll let Pandora know.'

Jenny paused on the last stair but one.

'Can't you deal with it?'

'When she's just woken up', Sean replied evenly, 'she's happier with her mother.'

'Hmm.' Jenny had encountered this type of attitude before. Her eyes narrowed. 'I'm glad you aren't my husband.'

Sean, who knew exactly what she was thinking, wondered what the hell business it was of bossy Jenny Duran's anyway.

'Not nearly as glad as I am', he drawled, 'that you aren't my wife.'

It was no good. Joel, watching from a discreet distance as Cleo chatted animatedly with a group of Sophie's friends, realized it had been a mistake to come here. Stupidly, he had imagined they would be able to put the past behind them. For the last few

349

days all he had been able to think about was how Cleo, finally seeing him again after so long, might react.

The trouble was, his imagination had got carried away. All it had managed to conjure up had been a variety of happy endings. The one reaction that had never occurred to Joel was the one he had got.

Cleo, so desperate not to speak to him that she hadn't even been able to bring herself to say a simple hello, had seen him coming and scuttled away like a panicky sand crab. It was so un-Cleo it had to be seriously bad news.

She can't bear to look at me, thought Joel. He felt sick with disappointment, and furious with himself for having been gullible enough to think things could have been different.

This was hopeless. With one last glance across at Cleo, stunning in black and more strikingly beautiful in the flesh than even he remembered, Joel reached into his back pocket for his car keys. Not having the heart to search out either Sophie or Pandora in order to say goodbye, he left.

Cleo had been battling one interruption after another. First she had been distracted by Sophie's impassioned speech about running off to save the poor starving babies of Africa. Then, before she could hunt down Joel, she was stopped in her tracks by a bunch of Sophie's friends from school. None of them was an inch above five foot three. They were all desperate to become supermodels. Only the fact that they were friends of Sophie's had prevented Cleo telling them that what they really needed if they planned a career in modelling was a damn good seeing-to with a steamroller.

Finally managing to make her excuses and escape, Cleo

resumed her search. She still hadn't formulated an exact plan, but the gist of it was there.

Find Joel.

Make him realize – in no uncertain terms – how she felt about him.

Absolutely refuse to take no for an answer.

Ten minutes later, with a sinking heart, Cleo began to acknowledge the possibility of a flaw in her three-point plan. Making Joel realize how she felt about him and refusing to take no for an answer was only going to work if she could find him first.

And Joel was nowhere to be found.

So much, thought Cleo, for thinking he might have been looking forward to seeing her again.

He hadn't been able to get away fast enough.

'I thought Rory Cameron was supposed to be here tonight.' Imogen's green eyes glittered. 'Or has he found someone nearer half his own age and given Cass the push?'

That the relationship had lasted this long had, frankly, surprised Jack too.

'They're still seeing each other,' he said. 'According to Cass, anyway.'

Imogen gave him a knowing look. 'Ah well. Cass would say that, wouldn't she? Just to look good.'

But when Rory Cameron did finally arrive at almost ten o'clock there appeared to be nothing stage-managed about the way he and Cass greeted each other. Jack looked away.

'Sorry, sorry.' Rory excused his lateness with an apologetic grin. 'Bit of a punch-up at the club between rival paparazzi. I don't know if these royals are worth the trouble they cause, I really don't.'

To show Cass and Imogen there was no need to be bitchy and ill at ease with each other, Jack made a point of being extra friendly towards Rory Cameron. It wasn't too difficult so long as he didn't imagine him in bed with Cass.

'Actually, I was wanting us to have a quiet word.' With a King Edward cigar in one hand and a tumbler of Scotch in the other, Rory led him out into the garden. He was looking well, Jack had to concede: fit and tanned and several kilos lighter than when they had last met. No doubt, Jack thought darkly, as a result of all that sex . . .

'Daft really, I suppose,' said Rory when they were out of general earshot. 'I mean, it isn't as if you're Cassie's father.' He drew carefully on his cigar and smiled. 'It just kind of feels that way.'

Since he was the best part of a decade younger than Rory Cameron, Jack felt he had a damn cheek. His own smile cooled by several degrees.

'Really.'

'OK, maybe not,' Rory conceded. Opaque smoke rings drifted up into the night sky, mingling with the expensive scent of his aftershave. 'Dear me, this isn't going to be as easy as I thought.'

Jack had by this time formed his own suspicions on the subject. A chill seemed to settle around his heart. He said briefly, 'If I were you I'd just say it.'

Imogen was half listening to a dull conversation about public schools and mentally triple-checking the dates of her next fertile period when she saw Jack emerging from the garden. Without so much as a glance in her direction he shot through the drawing room into the kitchen, where Imogen knew Cass was. No doubt he had rushed inside to discuss some new and vital family catastrophe, she thought jealously. Maybe Cleo had broken her best fingernail. Or Sean had run out of cigarettes. Imogen, who had been only too glad to leave home at sixteen and make her own way in the world, found all this constant concern for the family hard to bear.

Jack was beginning to wish he'd stayed at home.

'I've just been speaking to Rory Cameron,' he announced. Cass, the sleeves of her pale green shirt rolled up in case they melted in the heat, was taking the last tray of baked potatoes out of the oven. 'Or rather, been spoken to by him.' Jack paused, watching the way she manoeuvred the tray onto the worktop and swung the oven door shut with a practised nudge of the hip. 'You didn't tell me you were planning to marry him.'

Cass's cheeks were flushed pink, whether from the heat of the oven or as a result of his statement Jack didn't know.

'It's something we've talked about. You can't be that astonished.' She spoke with a trace of defiance. 'We've been seeing each other for over a year.'

'You still might have mentioned it.'

'Look, I'm a big girl now.' Cass turned her attention back to the potatoes, prodding them in haphazard fashion with a fork. 'I can do whatever I like. I can marry Graham Norton if I want to. It really didn't occur to me that you'd even be interested, to tell the truth. We're divorced.' The colour in her cheeks deepened. 'I wouldn't dream of interfering with your private life.'

* * *

'You were popular tonight.'

Pandora, who was driving as usual, felt her fingers tighten around the steering wheel. Things had been so much better between them recently. Still, she had been semi-prepared for this, guessing that Sean wouldn't be able to resist making some such remark. For the first time since they had met she had been paid more attention than he had.

But it was way past midnight and Pandora wasn't up to a fight. Keeping her voice low, to remind Sean that Rose was asleep in the back, she said lightly, 'I'm a novelty, that's all. It won't last.'

'Come on. I spoke to Betsy Tyler at the club last week.' Sean sounded resigned rather than angry. Betsy was one of the actresses co-starring in Pandora's sitcom, *Wide-Eyed and Topless*. 'She said your scripts were the best she'd ever read. The show hasn't even aired yet and they want a second series. You've cracked it.'

'And how does that make you feel?'

Only the fact that she had to keep her eyes fixed on the road ahead gave Pandora the courage to say it.

'Proud.' Sean hesitated for a second. 'And jealous.'

For someone like him it was a huge admission to make. Awash with love and sympathy Pandora reached tentatively across and rested her hand on his thigh.

'This new series.' It was a possibility she had already considered, a chance to maybe bolster Sean's own flagging career. 'I could write a part in it for you . . . if you think you might be interested.'

The last thing Sean needed was Pandora's charity. He gave her a long, measured look.

'Thanks for being so subtle. And no,' he said quietly, 'I fucking well would not.'

Chapter 52

'What are you doing, going into the agency?' As she skidded into the kitchen on Monday morning, Sophie collided with Cleo on her way out. Her eyes lit up. 'Brilliant, we're both heading in the same direction. You can give me a lift.'

'OK,' said Cleo when they reached Camden High Street, 'where do you want to be dropped?'

She negotiated a wobbling cyclist, pulling out and waving gratefully at the driver of the car behind.

Sophie, very casually, said, 'Jefferson's.'

Jefferson's was Cleo's modelling agency, situated off Regent Street.

Cleo frowned. 'I meant where are *you* going?'

'Jefferson's.'

'That's where I'm going.'

Sophie beamed. 'Told you we were heading in the same direction.'

Doing all but an emergency stop, Cleo earned herself a barrage of tooting car horns. The driver of the car behind, who had been quite smitten thirty seconds earlier, abruptly changed his mind. Bloody women drivers.

'What's this,' Cleo demanded, 'some kind of set-up?'

'You said I looked modellish.' Sophie remained calm. 'The other night when you slapped that disgusting gunk on my face.'

'Yes, but—'

'And modelling's a good way to earn heaps of easy money.'

'It is *not*,' Cleo howled, this time almost cannoning into the car in front. She glared at Sophie. 'It isn't easy money for a start, it's bloody hard-earned. And you don't waltz into an agency either, and get taken on just like that. Sophie, be realistic. Hundreds of thousands of girls *dream* of becoming models—'

'Come on, don't be so defeatist.' Sophie shrugged. 'I need the money for Uganda. Mum and Dad won't lend it to me but they both admit that if I can earn enough off my own bat, they won't be able to stop me spending it however I like. They're only saying that, of course, because as far as they're concerned I haven't a hope in hell of raising that much cash—'

Sophie was hopelessly deluded.

'You still can't march into Jefferson's,' Cleo wailed, 'without so much as an appointment, and expect someone to scream: "My God, it's the face of the decade, give this girl a haircut and put her on the cover of *Vogue* this *minute*." Sophie, I know what I said the other day but that simply isn't how it works!'

'Ah, but I have two things in my favour.' Sophie held up two fingers and waggled them.

'What? What?'

'I have an appointment with Janice Jefferson.' She beamed. 'I rang at nine o'clock this morning and made one.'

Startled, Cleo said, 'And?'

'I've got you as a sister.'

'Oh no, you can't use me! That's nepotism.'

'So? I need the cash.' Unperturbed, Sophie added, 'Watch where you're going. You almost hit that car.'

'I'll lend you the money,' Cleo promised wildly.

357

'I'll earn it myself. *If* we ever get there in one piece.'

'It's still nepotism.'

'So, get nepotizing,' said Sophie. 'It's in a good cause.'

Cleo sat on the edge of Maisie's desk morosely swinging her legs.

'It's all my fault for painting her stupid face in the first place. If this does come to anything, my parents are going to string me up. How can a sixteen-year-old *be* so hell-bent on going to Africa anyway? Why can't she need the money for something normal like a fortnight in Ibiza?'

'Maybe Janice will turn her down.' Unable to stand it a moment longer, Maisie reached out and grabbed Cleo's ankles, bringing the rhythmic clink of cowboy boots against wooden desk to a merciful halt. 'Sorry, you have no idea how annoying that is.'

Cleo always drummed her heels. Puzzled, she said, 'You've never told me that before.'

'I'm being assertive.' Maisie looked shamefaced. 'I've started going to classes.'

'But you're a booker; it's your job to be assertive!'

'I know, I know.' Blushing, Maisie said, 'And I can do it at work. I've just never been able to manage it in real life.'

'I wish Sophie was a bit less assertive,' Cleo said with feeling.

Maisie, who was full of admiration for Cleo, said, 'She takes after you. Look at the way you dealt with that awful Damien Maxwell-Horne.'

Cleo's thoughts flew back to the Checkamating that had ultimately proved her own undoing. Never mind the dreaded

Damien, she reminded herself gloomily, look at the way I messed up with Joel sodding Grant.

The heavy oak door leading into Janice Jefferson's office – the hallowed inner sanctum – finally reopened twenty minutes later. Cleo's heart sank into her obediently immobile boots when she realized Janice had a bony arm draped around Sophie's shoulders. Sophie was looking unbelievably smug.

'Right, we're giving her a go.'

Janice prided herself on her eye for future talent. The fact that Sophie was wearing not a scrap of make-up and still sported her Dennis the Menace haircut hadn't fazed her in the least. 'I'm sending her over to Tony this afternoon for test shots. He can make up a composite, get a portfolio under way. I've already spoken to Anna about hair and make-up. This girl *has* something. I *feel* it.' Janice's multi-braceleted arm tightened around Sophie's shoulder as she gave her a reassuring squeeze. The famous Jefferson smile, veteran of several hundred magazine covers back in the Sixties, zoomed triumphantly in on Cleo. 'And she's a Mandeville to boot, which can only be good publicity. I think we can safely say we're on to a winner.'

Sophie's expression grew smugger still, all but screaming *I told you so*.

Murmuring so only Maisie could hear, Cleo said, 'Speaking of boots, who needs a desk to kick when they have a sister?'

'Take a look at this. Who is it?'

Outside it was bucketing down. Imogen, still shaking the rain out of her hair, had barely set foot inside the front door before Jack was shoving a curly fax into her hands. Obediently

Imogen gazed at the photograph reproduced on the sheet.

'Um . . . old picture of Cleo?'

Jack was looking shell-shocked. 'New picture of Sophie.'

This time Imogen took notice.

'You are kidding!'

But upon closer examination it was definitely Sophie, complete with new ultra-short, ultra-bleached hair, no spectacles and a faceful of skilfully applied make-up. Impressed, Imogen started to laugh.

'Can you believe it? She's gone out and got herself signed up with Jefferson's, no less.' Jack shook his head. It wasn't the career he'd had in mind for his beloved younger daughter, the brightest of his three children, but he had, grudgingly, to admire her spirit. 'I mean, of *all* people. Sophie, prancing round in front of a camera for a living . . .'

'Never mind going to help out in an orphanage in Uganda,' said Imogen, marvelling at his failure to twig. 'At this rate she'll be able to afford to build her own.'

They were due to go out at eight to a party in the Barbican. Jack, who had been writing his column from home, hadn't even decided which shirt to wear. As Imogen emerged from the bathroom wrapped in a blue towel at ten to seven, she was further irritated to hear him on the phone downstairs. Having spent the last two hours attempting to get hold of Cass, he had evidently just managed to track her down.

All this fuss, Imogen thought for the hundredth time. How overprotective could you get? Rifling through her wardrobe she took out the strappy black dress she had worn to Jack's fortieth.

By the time he got off the phone it was ten to eight.

'Well, you were right.'

'Of course I was right.' Tight-lipped, Imogen chucked a clean white shirt at him. 'And we're going to be late.'

'She's *sixteen*.' Not paying a bit of attention, Jack sat on the bed. 'Why won't she listen to us? Only yesterday a piece came into the newsroom about two voluntary workers in Rwanda being shot dead.' He shook his head. 'It isn't as if we're trying to stop her going out of spite. It just isn't *safe*.'

When he was finally wearing the shirt, Imogen handed him two unmatched cuff-links. Jack didn't notice, fastening them into each sleeve without so much as a second glance.

Imogen's patience snapped.

'When I was sixteen I lived in a squat in Bayswater. A girl I shared with was raped by a tramp. One of the blokes overdosed on heroin and wasn't discovered for a week,' she shouted. 'So don't tell me how dangerous it would be for poor little Sophie in Uganda because compared with London, let *me* tell *you*, Uganda is about as dangerous as afternoon tea at the Ritz.'

The party had been an out-and-out disaster. Back at home, still barely on speaking terms, Jack and Imogen were in bed by midnight.

'Look, I'm sorry.' Imogen tried half-heartedly to make amends. The certainty that she was in the right, however, gave the words a hollow ring.

'What I don't understand,' said Jack in unforgiving mood, 'is how you can be so desperate to have children when you clearly don't want the responsibility. It isn't all bootees and

Babygros, you know. Children grow up but you don't stop loving them.'

Bastard. Imogen turned onto her side, facing away from him. If she had children of her own she *would* love them. She just didn't see why she should have to pretend to love somebody else's, particularly when they had made so little effort to like her.

Jack lay awake, gazing up at the ceiling, long after Imogen's rigid spine had relaxed and she had drifted off to sleep. Her parting shot – the sarcastic suggestion that since it was only half-past twelve at night he might like to phone Cass and spend the next couple of hours discussing Sophie's new haircut with her – wasn't so wide of the mark. They could talk about Sophie, at least. If it weren't for Rory Cameron he might have been tempted.

Jack suppressed a sigh. For over twenty years he and Cass had had some of their best discussions in bed at night. It was something he missed more than he would have imagined possible, but Imogen regarded bed as the place for sex and sleep.

Feeling very alone, Jack turned onto his side and closed his eyes. He wondered if Rory and Cass talked much in bed.

Chapter 53

The first episode of *Wide-Eyed and Topless* was screened on the second Thursday in November at 9 p.m.

Heavily hyped by the network, already well reviewed and singled out by the press as a must-watch, the tale of non-identical flat-sharing twins, one a page-three model, the other an assistant in a charity shop, was being tipped as one of the major successes of the season.

'Betsy Tyler and Allegra Ash rise splendidly to the occasion,' observed the normally dour, rip-everything-to-shreds TV reviewer for the *Mail*. 'Both script and situations are screamingly funny; we're being treated here to comedy at its finest. Set your video recorders now; if tonight's episode is anything to go by, you'll be watching this series again and again.'

And this from a man who never seemed to like anything. Pandora, who had been secretly rereading the review at fifteen-minute intervals throughout the day, was amazed the page was still in one piece.

The phone had been ringing non-stop too, with requests for interviews. Rose, realizing that something was going on but not knowing what, grew increasingly boisterous. As nine o'clock approached, Pandora felt the first flickers of apprehension. Sean had gone out at lunchtime, casually promising to be back by eight. He was late already. The series of excuses he had made for not watching Pandora's own advance tapes of *Wide-Eyed and Topless* had been feeble to say the least.

Donny phoned at a quarter to nine.

'He's been at the club all afternoon. I've just put him into a cab.'

And told him in no uncertain terms to grow up, Donny could have added but didn't.

Pandora winced. 'Is he drunk?'

'No, but I've seen sunnier smiles on traffic wardens. Congratulations on all that stuff in the papers by the way.'

'It's all thanks to you.' Pandora knew how much she owed him and was grateful.

'For wrecking everything between you and Sean?' Donny's brief laugh contained an edge of bitterness. He wished he could be there with her now. On impulse he said, 'Look, Sean's on his way home in a shitty mood. You don't have to put up with that. Why don't I come round . . . ?'

'No.' That wouldn't help at all. As brightly as she could manage, Pandora said, 'I'll be fine. It's not as if he hits me. I don't need a minder.'

But as she waited for Sean to arrive home, her stomach began to really churn. The vague, nagging ache that had been bothering her all day became a stabbing pain at the base of her abdomen.

Never mind traffic wardens, Pandora thought when Sean walked through the door at one minute to nine; she had seen sunnier smiles on bulldogs.

'There's a goulash in the oven,' she offered despite the unpromising start. 'And baked potatoes. Are you hungry?'

'No.' Sean helped himself to a brandy and sat down in front

of the TV. 'Come on, you too. You can't start dishing food out now. This is your big moment.'

Pandora felt perspiration break out all over her forehead. She hoped she wasn't about to be sick. Filling her own glass with iced water she sat cautiously next to Sean. Within seconds a plaintive wail drifted downstairs.

'Mum-mee.'

'For God's sake,' Sean sighed.

Pandora winced as she rose to her feet once more. Her legs were shaking. On the television, the blond continuity announcer said brightly, 'And now, the first episode of a brand-new series I personally can't *wait* to see . . .'

'Bet you say that to all the boys.' Sean was looking bored already, his dark eyes narrowing as if he was on the verge of falling asleep.

'Mum-meee!'

Sean wasn't proud of himself. The way he was behaving was, he knew perfectly well, nothing short of shameful. The bollocking Donny had given him earlier had been along much the same lines. The trouble was, none of it helped.

He could hardly blame Pandora, either, for staying upstairs with Rose. The funnier *Wide-Eyed and Topless* was, the more impossible it became for him to laugh. That awful familiar mixture of pride and jealousy gnawed away at his gut like battery acid. He *was* proud of what she had achieved, he just wished it didn't have to make him feel so washed-up in comparison. It was Barbra Streisand and Kris Kristofferson all over again, Sean thought bitterly, in *A Star is Born*, only this time with jokes.

And the joke was on him, he realized. From upstairs came the sound of the toilet flushing for the third time. Downstairs, as the show ended and the credits began to roll – Series created and written by Pandora J. Grant – the phone began to ring.

It was a tabloid journalist with an oily voice, scarcely able to believe his luck.

'Sean, my man! The very person I wanted to speak to. So, how does it feel to at least know someone with a successful TV show?'

Bastard.

'Feels great,' Sean replied evenly, 'thanks.'

'Oh, and do you have a contact number for Donny Mulligan?' The journalist, disappointed by the lack of response, went on, 'I need to confirm the rumour that your good lady has written a part for him into the next series—'

Sean put the phone down. Then he switched it off. Upstairs the lavatory flushed again.

When Pandora finally made it back downstairs he only had to take one look at her puffed-up eyes and drawn face to realize what had been going on.

'Been bringing our boots up, have we?' His eyes glittered. 'Oh well, if you're pregnant again at least this time you can't hang it on me.'

Luckily Rose had done no more than whimper for a couple of minutes before falling back to sleep. Pandora, who had never felt more dreadful in her life, realized she was in danger of bursting into noisy uncontrollable tears.

'You bastard, I'm not pregnant. My stomach hurts . . . I'm ill . . . owww!!'

Still wounded by the oily journalist's phone call, Sean said,

'You've written Donny fucking Mulligan into the next series. You've put him in it, haven't you? Without even *telling* me—'

'I offered it to you first.' Pandora clutched her stomach as another wave of pain seized her in its vice-like grip. Through clenched teeth she said, 'You turned it down, remember. Sean, I don't *need* this . . . I think you're going to have to call the doctor.'

She really was ill. Sean watched, with a pang of guilt, as Pandora collapsed onto the sofa.

He frowned. 'What is it? What's the matter?'

'I don't know. Please, just *phone* . . .'

Sean picked up the receiver. As he did so, the doorbell rang.

'That was quick,' said Sean.

Pandora groaned. 'Talking of quick, get a bucket—'

Cleo, woefully underdressed as usual and hopping up and down on the doorstep to keep warm, had just pressed the bell a second time when she heard footsteps coming up the path behind her.

'I don't believe it.' Staring into the darkness, she felt her heart skip several beats. 'What are you doing here?'

'I'd have thought that was pretty obvious.'

Joel glanced at the bottle clutched in her hands, then at the one in his. Cleo's, needless to say, had cost three times as much.

'I kept ringing and ringing and couldn't get through.' Cleo's teeth had begun to chatter from a combination of cold and sheer nerves. 'So I just jumped into the car and came over anyway.'

'Me too.'

'You've just watched it? Of course you have . . . how silly of me!' Damn, she was gabbling. Cleo waved the bottle at him and tried to smile, except her upper lip had somehow got itself stuck to her front teeth. 'Wasn't it brilliant? I thought we should celebrate!'

The garden was wreathed in mist, the footpath silver with frost. Cleo was wearing, of all things, a pink micro-mini and a white tank top.

Joel nodded. 'Me too.'

'Are you mad?'

Once inside the house Joel recovered himself. Removing the phone from Sean's grasp he closed the Yellow Pages with a great thud. 'Never mind ringing the doctor. Look at her, what she needs is to get to a hospital, fast. My car's right outside. I'll take her.'

'I could.' Cleo made the offer but she looked uncertain. Pandora was still throwing up like nobody's business. Cleo wasn't awfully good with sick.

'I'll take her,' said Sean. He was seriously worried now. He glanced from Cleo to Joel. 'Can someone stay here and keep an eye on Rose?'

As soon as Sean and Pandora had left, Cleo felt herself slipping into witter-mode once more. Joel had caught her off guard – yet again – and she felt like a panicky party hostess trying desperately to entertain a two-hours-too-early lone guest.

'Well, poor Pandora, what do you suppose it is? Could be food poisoning . . . you can catch food poisoning from lettuce, you know . . . Marsha Collins went down with it in the middle of a shoot for a hairspray ad which mucked up six weeks' scheduling and pissed the director off no end—'

'Should you be opening that?' Joel nodded at the bottle of Taittinger she was busily de-wiring. 'I thought it was for Pandora.'

Cleo was nervous enough as it was. The last thing she needed was criticism from the person who was responsible for making her nervous in the first place.

'I'll replace it, don't worry.'

'Good.'

The cork was on its way out. 'And if you want to make yourself useful,' said Cleo, 'you could unearth a couple of glasses.'

'Now what are you doing?' Joel demanded an hour later.

Cleo, daring him to stop her, said, 'What does it look like?' and carried on prising the cork out of the second bottle. The contents of the first had disappeared at an astonishing rate chiefly because it had given her something to occupy her hands when all she really wanted was to grab hold of Joel, swear passionate undying love and kiss the life out of him . . .

Under the circumstances it seemed safer to drink.

'You won't like it,' Joel warned as the cork flipped out. 'I called in at some off-licence on the way over and this was all they had. It's only cheap, probably as rough as sandpaper.'

'I like a bit of rough.' Cleo beamed. Joel's expression darkened and she clapped a dramatic hand over her mouth. 'Oops, wrong thing to say.'

'I think you've had enough to drink already.' Looking less

amused by the second, Joel shook his head as she attempted to refill his own glass.

'And I think you're being boring.' Cleo sloshed some over his hand for good measure. 'Come on,' she urged, 'be a sport. Time to toast Pandora and the success of *Wide-Eyed and What'sit.*'

'What's the matter with you?' Joel had never seen her like this before.

'Me? I'm fine.' Taking her first gulp of the champagne he had brought along, Cleo couldn't help but pull a face. Joel had been right: it was dog-rough. 'I'm absolutely fine,' she repeated with a shudder. 'You're the misery guts around here.'

It might have been some time ago now but Joel would never forget one of the most heart-stopping moments of his life.

'That TV interview,' he said, 'at the film première you went to. All that garbage about finding true love and being about to marry Dino Carlisle . . . had you been drinking then, too?'

'Oh, so you did see it.' Cleo was unable to hide her satisfaction. 'Good. And no, of course I hadn't been drinking. I just felt like saying it. Why?' She wagged a triumphant finger at him. 'Did it make you jealous?'

Joel hesitated, then shook his head. 'It made me realize how much better suited you were to him, than to someone like me.'

The look of resignation on his face was gut-wrenching. Cleo's dark eyes promptly filled with tears.

'But I didn't mean it, there never was anything between Dino and me.'

'So I gathered, when he went back to the States and started an affair with that new Bond girl.' In contrast with Cleo's histrionics, Joel spoke without emotion. 'But the fact remains, he's the type of man you need. At least he's in the same celebrity league . . .'

Cleo was torn now. Part of her wished she hadn't drunk so much, so fast and on such an empty stomach. On the other hand, she thought hazily as the room began to undulate around her, would I have the nerve to come out with this stuff if I was sober?

'I wish you'd have another drink.' She said it hoping it might have a similar effect on Joel.

'One of us', he pointed out, 'has to babysit.'

'And one of us has to be at Heathrow to catch the eight o'clock flight to Tunisia tomorrow morning.' Cleo groaned, belatedly remembering she had to be up at five. Ugh, now she really wished she hadn't had so much to drink.

In the meantime, however, she had something to say. Encouraged by the fact that Joel was evidently trying hard not to look at her boobs, braless beneath the white top, and wishing she had the courage to just fling herself at him – except she feared he would only fling her smartly back – Cleo took a deep breath.

'Look, I don't give a toss about celebrity leagues. I don't care whether or not someone's famous . . . if I loved someone I wouldn't care if they swept roads for a living.' Struggling to keep her thoughts ahead of her mouth, Cleo gazed wildly about the room for inspiration. She spotted Joel's bottle of barely touched, truly awful champagne. 'If all they could afford to buy me was Tizer, I'd drink it! And they wouldn't need to feel inferior because they wouldn't *be* inferior . . . the thing is, as long as two people love each other and are happy together nothing else in the world matters—'

'Phone,' said Joel, because Cleo hadn't even heard it ringing. Worried sick about Pandora, praying that whatever was wrong with her wasn't serious, he reached past and grabbed the receiver before Cleo had a chance to answer it.

'You could have let me speak to her,' Cleo protested when he put the phone down again. 'Poor thing, food poisoning's the pits. You can get it from lettuce you know. How is she, anyway? Feeling better yet?'

So much, Joel thought bleakly, for touching speeches about the meaning of true love. Cleo was absolutely plastered.

'That was Sean. They're taking Pandora into the operating theatre.' He was only thankful he had beaten Cleo to the phone. Sean had sounded as worried as he was. The last thing he needed was to have to listen to his sister's drink-sodden emotional ramblings.

'But that's terrible!' Appalled, Cleo struggled to sit up. 'What's wrong with her?'

'They don't know. Could be peritonitis.' With too much to think about, Joel lost patience with her. 'And I doubt if you care anyway,' he said icily. 'Why don't you just go to sleep?'

Chapter 54

The screech of an unfamiliar alarm clock jerked Cleo into consciousness at five thirty. Her recall of the events of the previous evening was, unfairly, both instantaneous and complete. Covered in shame and goosebumps, because Joel had evidently decided she didn't deserve a blanket, she crawled off the sofa and let out a low moan as the first knife-like spasm seized her brain.

This is it, Cleo thought numbly, grateful at least that she was still dressed. Made my pass, totally blew it, couldn't have got it more wrong if I'd tried.

The rest of the house was in total darkness. Padding upstairs, she looked in on Rose, who was fast asleep with one arm and one foot dangling through the wooden bars of her cot.

In the spare room, Joel slept. Cringing at the memory of his disgust with her – and who could blame him? – Cleo knew there was no point in waking him now. Instead she gazed silently down at the tousled blond hair and dear familiar profile and watched his tanned chest rise and fall in its slow, regular, reassuring rhythm. The longing to reach out and touch him was fiercer than ever. Sadly, she thought, so was Joel's reaction likely to be if she tried it.

Downstairs Cleo phoned the hospital, found out which ward Pandora had been admitted to and spoke with the nursing sister

on duty. When she had found out how Pandora was, she quietly
let herself out of the house.

Sean, watching Pandora sleep, realized how much he loved
her. It was as if he kept forgetting, only to be reminded of it, in
a great rush of emotion, all over again.

When she opened her eyes moments later her gaze fixed
directly on Sean.

'What are you thinking?'

He touched the back of her hand.

'That you gave me a hell of a scare.'

Pandora smiled briefly in return.

'Nothing exciting. Only appendicitis.'

'Thank God.'

'I'm still not feeling great.' She winced, touching the
dressing over the wound.

'You'll be better soon. You look . . .' Sean hesitated, unused
to expressing such thoughts aloud '. . . beautiful.'

'Liar.' Pandora knew how she must really look but it was
nice to hear. She had been scared too. 'It's almost seven
o'clock. You should be getting home.' She frowned. 'I don't
know who's going to be able to look after Rose while I'm in
here.'

'I will.'

Pandora looked alarmed.

'The doctor said I'd be in hospital for three or four days.'

'I know, I was here when he said it.' Sean had spent half
the night trying to think of someone who might be able to
come to the rescue. The trouble was, everyone had jobs of
their own. Short of hiring a nanny from an agency – a

complete stranger whom Rose would have no time to get used to – he hadn't been able to come up with anyone at all.

Now, offended by Pandora's obvious lack of faith in him, Sean rose to his own defence.

'No big deal.' He shrugged as he spoke. 'As you said, it's only for a few days. She's my daughter, isn't she?' Sean grinned. 'Rose and I'll have a great time.'

'You bloody little animal,' Sean howled twelve hours later as Rose emptied a pot of strawberry-and-melon yoghurt over her head. How anyone so angelic could do something so completely disgusting was beyond him. God, now it was beginning to drip down the back of her head onto the carpet.

Rose waited until he'd finished cleaning her up before gleefully – and noisily – filling her nappy.

Sean had to spray the room with half a bottle of Aqua di Gìo to hide the appalling smell. By the time he came back from dumping the nappy in the dustbin, Rose had rifled efficiently through his discarded jacket, discovering and helping herself to a packet of Rolos. She had also found a pen and was simultaneously dribbling chocolate and scrawling black felt-tip pen all over the blue-and-white Colefax and Fowler wall-paper at twenty-eight pounds a roll.

'I hate you,' Sean murmured, wrenching the pen from her hands and wondering if the neighbours had heard him yell at her earlier. Knowing his luck they'd be on to the NSPCC in a flash.

Rose's chocolate-brown eyes filled with tears. Appalled at the loss of the pen she let out a screech of rage and wailed for Pandora.

'If you're good,' Sean spoke through gritted teeth, 'I'll take you to see her.' But by the time he'd finished clearing up the chaos in the sitting room, Rose was screaming for juice. Next thing he knew, another nappy needed changing. Rose turned this into a marathon squirming contest and landed Sean a painful jab in the eye. By the time he managed to lever her against her better judgement into clean dungarees and two shoes that actually matched, visiting time was over.

'There, that's your fault.' Sean glared at her. Rose, on the sofa, glared back. Her lower lip wobbled. Then, without any warning at all, she fell asleep.

'How has she been?' asked Pandora anxiously the next day when Sean arrived with Rose at the hospital. Rose, wearing odd socks and the remnants of that morning's Weetabix, flung herself at her mother in delight.

'Terrible.' Was it really only eleven o'clock? He was exhausted. 'A complete toad. I'm considering adoption.'

'What a gorgeous baby,' exclaimed one of the nurses. 'And doesn't she look like you!'

'Who, me?' Sean was taken aback; the nurse was definitely addressing him.

He glanced across at Rose. Though he had barely been able to admit as much, even to himself, he had found it hard to recognize Rose as his daughter simply because she seemed to have inherited so many more of Pandora's genes than his own. She had caramel-coloured skin, candy-floss black hair and enormous dark brown eyes. He knew she was beautiful but it had never occurred to Sean that there might be any discernible resemblance to him.

'Of course you.' The nurse tickled Rose's dimpled knees,

making her squeal with delight. 'Look at her eyes, the way she laughs. And what about those cheekbones . . .'

'Look,' said Pandora when the nurse had gone, 'I spoke to one of Donny's sisters on the phone this morning. She's happy to look after Rose. Why don't you ring her?'

Sean grabbed Rose, who was about to nose-dive off the bed. He had no intention of admitting defeat. Nor did he need one of bloody Donny's sisters to show him how it should be done.

'No need,' he said. 'We can manage. We'll be fine.'

It was Cleo, ironically, who prompted the real turning point.

'She's a baby, for Christ's sake.' Calling from Tunisia that evening to find out how Pandora was, she was treated instead to a litany of everything Rose had done wrong since lunchtime. 'She doesn't understand. She isn't being naughty on purpose.'

For once in her life Cleo was right. He had, Sean realized, imagined that Rose was doing everything deliberately to punish him for not loving her enough.

From that moment on their relationship improved out of all recognition. Sean discovered that the less he shouted, the less Rose misbehaved. On the fourth morning, instead of hearing the usual call for Pandora, he went into the nursery to find Rose with her arms outstretched, beaming and yelling, 'Daddy.'

Chapter 55

Steve the photographer was taking for ever to set up each shot. It was all right for him; he was wearing three sweaters and a sheepskin jacket. Hmm, thought Sophie, blowing on her knuckles to try to defrost them, so much for modelling being glamorous.

Not that she cared. It might be bitingly cold but she was earning a bizarre amount of money for this shoot. And by the time today's photographs appeared in *Top-Teen* magazine – eight pages of Sophie Mandeville floating in ethereal fashion across mist-shrouded Cotswold landscapes in cobweb-fine dresses and lacy scarves – she would be well away, in Uganda.

Doing something useful with her life.

When they finally broke for lunch the rest of the crew wasted no time piling into the picturesque pub they had already made their base. Situated on the brow of a steep hill above the tiny, haphazardly constructed village of Cinderley, the Salutation Inn was a charming, ivy-strewn old coaching inn run by a husband-and-wife team more than happy to accommodate a photographer and his entourage from London.

The home-cooked chicken casserole smelled terrific but Sophie stuck to cheese rolls and a can of 7-Up. There was a programme about missionaries on Radio 4 she didn't want to miss.

'Missionaries, eh?' Steve, the photographer, gave Sophie a

great nudge. 'If you want to know about positions, my darlin', all you have to do is ask.'

'Ha ha,' said Sophie dutifully, because Steve might be a dickhead but he was also a good photographer. 'I just wondered if I could have the keys to the BMW, then I can listen to it on the car radio.'

'Funny little thing.' As he made his way back up to the bar for the third time half an hour later, Steve glanced out of the mullioned windows and across the car park. 'Still sitting there listening to her precious programme. I didn't know we could even get Radio 4 in that car.' He winked at Titia, the fashion editor of *Top-Teen*. 'That Sophie. She doesn't drink, you know. Or smoke. It isn't normal, if you ask me.'

'Just get another bottle of red in,' Titia drawled, 'and stop having a go. I think she's cute. If anyone's abnormal around here, my sweet, it's you.'

Sophie had polished off three cheese-and-tomato rolls, two packets of smoky-bacon crisps and her can of 7-Up. The radio programme was jolly interesting and she was enjoying being able to listen to it in peace. The view from where she was sitting was spectacular too: a deep valley dotted with honey-coloured houses, semi-naked trees and the remains of the morning's mist.

In the weak November sunlight a narrow stream glittered. Sophie, heaving a sigh of contentment, wriggled and rested her knees more comfortably against the steering wheel. From the pocket of her denim jacket she took a packet of fruit pastilles. The first two were pineapple-flavoured, her favourite, and there was still twenty minutes of the radio programme left to go. What more, thought Sophie, could a girl want?

When the passenger door was pulled open she thought it was Steve, come to regale her with more missionary jokes, pinch her last pastille and chivvy her back to work. Instead, a complete stranger slid into the car.

'Right, get moving,' ordered a boy in his early twenties with spiky blond hair and piercing pale blue eyes. He was wearing a combat jacket and grubby mud-stained jeans.

'I beg your pardon?' Sophie turned and stared at him. 'Do I *look* stupid?'

She glimpsed a flash of sunlight against metal. The next moment a knife blade was jabbed into her ribs.

'Move it,' the boy hissed. 'Just drive the car. Do as I say.'

'Look, I would if I could.' Sophie felt the coldness of the blade as it pressed against her. She shook her head. Everything seemed to be happening in slow motion. 'Really I would. But I can't drive.'

'Fuck it . . .'

Any faint hope that Sophie might have had that this could be some kind of elaborate set-up, a joke at her expense, crumbled as the knife dug into her side. She felt the skin resist. Then it gave way. Staring down, she saw a dark trickle of blood seep through the gauzy rose-pink crêpe de Chine of her Twenties-style dress.

'You can have the car,' Sophie said rapidly. 'Here,' she pointed to the keys in the ignition, 'help yourself. Just let me out and you can go wherever you want. There's plenty of petrol—'

'I didn't mean to do that.' The boy was gazing at the bloodstain on her dress. Before Sophie could reach the door handle his free hand closed roughly around her wrist. 'No chance. We need to swap places. Come on, climb over me. I'll drive, but you're coming too.'

'What the—'

Spluttering in indignation, Steve moved across to the window to get a better look. 'Jesus, I don't believe it! Sophie's got someone in the friggin' car with her and that's not the missionary position she's in either. Well, well, reckon it's true what they say about the quiet ones being the worst.'

'She must have arranged to meet a boyfriend down here.' Peering over his shoulder, Titia sounded amused. 'The girl has some nerve, I'll say that for her. Doing it in your car, in broad daylight.'

'Now what's happening?' Steve's expression changed to one of alarm as the car started up. 'Bloody hell, he's *driving* it. Is this a wind-up?'

'No wind-up.' Titia cringed as the BMW, tyres screaming, shot out of the car park. 'I swear.'

'*You* fucking swear.' Steve spoke through gritted teeth. His 5-Series, his pride and joy, was being driven off by a teenage lunatic. 'What's she doing, fucking eloping? I tell you, I'll kill that stupid little bitch when she gets back.'

Her kidnapper's name was Jez, Sophie discovered, and he was on the run from Taywood open prison where he had – until this morning – been serving eighteen months for burglary.

'I got a letter yesterday,' said Jez, 'from my wife, saying she was leaving me. She's gone and got herself another bloke. That's why I had to escape. To see her, make her change her mind.'

Sophie nodded. 'What happened?'

His blue eyes flickered. 'She wouldn't change her mind. I hit her. I suppose she's gone running off to the coppers by now. But I'm not going back to that nick.' He glanced across at Sophie. 'See, that's why I needed you. Someone to bargain with. If they try coming for me, I'll threaten to do something drastic. If they want you badly enough they'll have to let me go free.'

He was driving horribly fast. Sophie wondered where he planned to take her. She knew she should remain calm and try to strike up some rapport with Jez. For some reason the fact that he was only twenty-three lessened the scariness of the ordeal. She couldn't believe he would really harm her.

Except, of course, he already had.

'What's your wife's name?'

'Brenda. Silly cow.' His tone was dismissive. 'You should've seen the look on her face when I turned up this morning. She looked like a tart. All that make-up. Why do women have to wear that stuff?' His gaze slid coldly over Sophie's face. 'You too. You look like a tart. What d'you have to put in on for?'

'I don't normally. I hate it,' said Sophie. 'It's for a modelling job. That's why I'm wearing this stupid dress too.' She touched the leather seat. 'And this is the photographer's car we're in. We drove down from London at six o'clock this morning.'

Jez was looking interested. Maybe, Sophie thought, if he thinks I'm famous he won't hurt me. Leaning forward slowly she said, 'This sounds boring, doesn't it?' and pressed a couple of buttons on the car's state-of-the-art radio.

'You're a model?' He sounded impressed. 'I've never been to London. What's it like?'

'Big and dirty. Round here's much nicer. You can disappear in London.' Sophie, suddenly inspired, said, '*You* could disappear. Look, never mind keeping me as a hostage and bargaining your way out of this. Just drop me off here, zip up the motorway, dump the car and lose yourself.' She felt in her jacket pocket. 'I can even give you money for petrol—'

'Jesus,' Jez sneered, 'you're thick.'

Sophie's shoulders drooped. 'Sorry. I thought it was a good idea.'

'Well you would, wouldn't you?' Abruptly his mood had changed. 'You're thick. A dumb tart.'

Elton John had been playing on the radio. Now, as the final poignant bars of the song died away, Sophie heard her mother's voice.

'Lovely, lovely,' Cass sighed. 'Goodness, isn't that enough to cheer up the most miserable old day? And now, speaking of miserable old days, here's Tom Archer with the weather.'

Sophie couldn't help it. Her eyes filled with hot tears.

'What are you listening to that crap for?' Jez said rudely.

'It's not crap,' whispered Sophie. 'It's my mum.'

Keeping the knife pressed against the small of her back beneath her denim jacket, Jez marched Sophie into the house.

'It's nice.' Over her tears now, though black mascara still marked her cheeks, Sophie gazed round the small but well-maintained cottage.

Jez and Brenda had moved in here as newly-weds three years ago. Yellow-and-white Laura Ashley curtains hung at the windows. A blue-and-yellow kitchen opened out onto a small sitting room. On the floor in front of the television lay a

383

smashed glass, a buckled brass photo frame and a crumpled photograph of the happy couple on their wedding day.

'My dad went off with another woman,' said Sophie. 'Mum ripped up a few photos too. She said it made her feel better. Oh please, there's no need to tie me up.' Stifling terror, she shook her head. 'I won't run away, promise. Look, at least let me sweep up this glass. Then maybe I could cook us something to eat. You must be starving by now.'

'OK.' Jez, seeing the sense in this, chucked the rope back into the cupboard under the stairs. Then he shot her a warning look. 'But don't try and escape. I've got a gun as well as a knife.'

'And locks on every window,' Sophie reminded him. 'So how could I get out anyway?'

'True.' He almost smiled. 'Thanks to Brenda, the slag.'

'Why?'

'Double-glazing salesman. The bloke who came here and persuaded her to have the whole house done, he's the bastard she's been seeing for the past year.'

'You poor thing,' Sophie said in soothing tones. 'No wonder you lost your temper with her.' She glimpsed her reflection in the mirror hanging above the polished mantelpiece. 'And look at me, what a sight. OK if I go upstairs and have a wash?'

He looked irritated. 'Can't you do it in the kitchen sink?'

'I want to clean this up too.' Gingerly she touched the torn, bloodstained crêpe de Chine. 'Think about it; I'm not going to be much use to you as a hostage if I'm dead.'

'It's stopped bleeding,' Jez snapped. 'You aren't going to die.'

'It could become infected,' argued Sophie. 'Haven't you heard of septicaemia? Tetanus?' Her grey eyes narrowed. 'Look, I've given you my word. I won't try and escape. I'll be your hostage. But you have to treat me like a human being, that's only fair.'

To her amazement he nodded.

'OK. But no nosing around upstairs, right? You can't get out.'

'Thanks.'

'And when you've done that,' Jez said softly, 'we'll phone your mum.'

Chapter 56

Just my luck, thought Sophie, to be kidnapped by a star-struck, wife-bashing burglar.

She dialled the radio station, spoke to her mother's producer and handed the phone across to Jez.

The transistor radio balanced on the coffee-table sounded tinny – the batteries were on their way out – but at least Sophie could hear what was going on.

'And now,' said Cass, 'we have a mystery caller on the line. All I know is he's something to do with Sophie, my youngest. Personally I suspect a set-up. So, hello mystery caller from Gloucestershire, you're on the air. Now, why don't you tell us what this is all about?'

'That was great.' Jez replaced the receiver a minute or so later, running his fingers through his spiky blond hair and looking ridiculously pleased with himself. 'I've never been on the radio before.' He looked across at Sophie. 'Bloody hell. What's the matter with you now?'

How stupid she had been to think that because Jez was only twenty-three he wouldn't harm her. Panic welled up in Sophie's chest.

'You've frightened my mother to death.' She felt sick. 'How *could* you?'

'Easy,' said Jez. Bending forward, he picked up the torn

386

photograph of Brenda and himself and crushed it with his fist. 'I'm really glad I chose you now,' he told Sophie with a smile. 'This is ace. I'm going to be famous.'

'What the hell do you think you're doing?' The manager of the restaurant stared in astonishment as Terry Brannigan threw down his washing-up sponge, stripped off his apron and reached for his coat. 'Where are you going? You can't just walk out.'

'Didn't you hear that?' Terry pointed briefly in the direction of the radio he only ever paid any attention to when Cass was on. 'Cass Mandeville's a friend of mine and she's in trouble. She needs me.'

'Blimey, it's Superman,' jeered one of the waiters above a chorus of whistles and much muffled laughter. 'Don't forget to put your pants on over your tights.'

There was a mountain of washing-up still to be done.

'If you leave now,' the manager said icily, 'you're sacked.'

'Hooray,' said Terry. 'About bloody time too.'

The restaurant was less than half a mile from the Kingdom Radio studios. Luckily Terry had dropped Cass off there often enough in the past to persuade the security guard on the gate to let him through now.

'I know, I *know*,' the producer was shouting into a phone when Terry reached the studio from which Cass's show was broadcast, 'she's in no state to do anything but we don't *have* a stand-in. Bob's gone down with flu, Serena's in France and Jenny's buggered off to Egypt. There *is* nobody else to take over—'

'I'll do it,' said Terry. Through the glass, he saw the petrified face of the weatherman valiantly attempting to hold the fort and failing abysmally.

The producer glared at Terry.

'Who the fuck are you?'

A door behind him swung open. Cass, white-faced, threw herself into Terry's arms.

'It's a nightmare.' She shook her head, choking back tears. 'Jack's on his way over. We're flying straight down there now.' Her body began to sag. 'Oh God . . . and to think when Sophie phoned I thought it was some kind of silly joke.'

Terry held her. The producer was still glaring at him. 'I had to come. I want to help. I was going to offer to drive you, but—'

'There's no one to do the show,' Cass said shakily. 'The stand-in's off with flu. You could do it.'

'I can do it,' Terry assured the producer.

'Yes, yes.' The producer, who was too hyped-up to be grateful, ground his expensively capped teeth. 'So you keep bloody saying. But just who the fuck *are* you?'

The siege moved into its second day and Cass began to wonder if she had the strength to stay sane. The cottage was surrounded by police marksmen. A trained negotiator was attempting to build a rapport between himself and Jez Potter. He had also spoken to Sophie, who appeared to be bearing up well.

This was partly due to the fact that she didn't know all there was to know. Jez Potter, the police had carefully explained to Cass and Jack, was in fact serving seven years for the manslaughter of a nightclub bouncer who had dared to wink at his wife. There were possible psychopathic tendencies. And nobody had seen or heard from Brenda Potter since the morning of Jez's escape.

'I can't bear it,' Cass sobbed, clinging to Jack and trying to blot from her mind the terrible sight of Jez Potter using their daughter as a shield whilst he gesticulated wildly with his gun. 'Why did he have to pick Sophie? It's so *unfair*.'

The cruel irony of the situation hadn't escaped Jack. Having deemed the Uganda trip too dangerous he had driven Sophie to this instead, a modelling shoot in deepest Gloucestershire . . . and more danger than he could ever have imagined.

They were staying at the Salutation Inn, the picturesque pub on the outskirts of Cinderley from whose car park Sophie had been taken hostage. The place was crawling with press despite the fact that a news blackout had been imposed. The police had no intention of pandering to Jez Potter's lust for fame.

Susie Wheeler, the landlady of the Salutation, felt desperately sorry for Cass and Jack Mandeville. She had also, two years ago, avidly followed the public breakdown of their marriage and had felt every sympathy for Cass.

That they should now be sharing a room – along with their grief – was only right and perfectly natural as far as Susie was concerned. Which was why, when Imogen Trent rang from London for the third time that day sounding rather more suspicious about Jack than worried about how Sophie might be, Susie decided she was bored with being discreet.

'The thing is, he said he'd phone me and he hasn't.' Imogen paused then added furtively, 'I know you've left a message in his room. But I wonder if I could trouble you to leave one in Mrs Mandeville's too.'

'No need, my dear.' Susie Wheeler smiled; she couldn't help it. This was too good a chance to miss. 'You see, they've only got the one room. And the note's right there waiting for him, slap-bang in the middle of the bed.'

'Are you going to kill me?' asked Sophie.

'Course not.' Jez was sitting on the floor playing with the revolver, twirling it between his fingers like Billy the Kid. 'Well, probably not.'

'I think you should give yourself up.'

It was three o'clock in the morning. Arc lights beamed outside. Sleep was out of the question. Sophie was cold, too, but Jez's offer of one of Brenda's sweaters for some reason gave her the creeps.

'Never.' He shook his head. 'I told them to send a helicopter, didn't I? It'll be here in the morning.'

'Where's it going to land, in the vegetable patch?'

'Shut up.'

'No need to get cross. I'm just trying to be realistic.'

Jez looked as if he were about to cry. 'I can't give myself up.'

'Why not?' Sophie shivered.

'Just shut up.'

'How much longer?' whispered Cass, clinging to Jack and wondering if she would ever feel warm again. 'Something has to happen soon.'

Imogen had no need to worry. They might be sharing a bed but sex was the last thing on either of their minds.

'The police will sort everything out,' said Jack.

'But what if they don't?'

'Stop it.' His arms tightened around her, his mouth brushed her forehead. 'They will.'

Sophie had finally drifted off into a fitful sleep but the dreams racing through her brain were as hard to bear as reality. Almost glad to be rid of them she woke with a start. Terrible sobbing noises were coming from the hallway.

'Jez?' Stumbling to her feet, she crossed the sitting room. He was on his knees by the front door, peering through the letter box, his wet face contorted with grief.

'I didn't hurt you.' He turned and stared up at her, his eyes pink-rimmed. 'Did I? I didn't hurt you?'

Sophie felt numb. She shook her head.

'Tell them I didn't.'

'What, now?' Did he want her to shout through the letter box?

'Just tell them.' Wearily, Jez shook his head. 'I couldn't help it. She made me do it. Just so long as they know I didn't hurt you.'

The next moment, to Sophie's bewilderment, he rose slowly to his feet and unlocked the front door. Pushing her outside, he disappeared back into the house. Like a rabbit caught in car headlights, Sophie stood there blinking. A voice through a loud-hailer said evenly, 'Sophie, walk down the path. It's OK, keep moving towards us. We're here. You're doing fine . . . just keep walking . . .'

Sophie did as she was told.

Behind her, upstairs in the cottage, a single shot was fired.

Chapter 57

Jez Potter had shot and killed himself. The body of Brenda Potter, as the police had suspected, was discovered lying in the spare bedroom. Considering what she had been through, the police told Cass and Jack, Sophie had come through her ordeal remarkably well.

'I can't believe she's safe.' Cass hung on to Jack's arm, giddily euphoric and teetering on the brink of tears. Their reunion with Sophie in the early hours of the morning had been indescribable. Now, having been thoroughly checked over by the police surgeon – the knife wound in her side was only superficial – she was catching up on some much-needed sleep.

By eight o'clock they were back in their room at the Salutation. Dawn was breaking; the spectacular view of the valley beneath them was shrouded in veils of mist. Everything looked just the same as it had yesterday, but everything was different. Sophie was safe. Cass, so happy she didn't know what to do with herself, kept gazing out of the window thinking guiltily of all the people they should be ringing with the news.

'You should phone Imogen.' As far as Cass was aware, Jack hadn't even responded to her calls yesterday.

'I know.' He came to stand beside her. Instinctively Cass found herself leaning into his shoulder.

'Go on then.'

'I don't want to.'

Cass hardly dared look at him. She tried to sound reproachful.

'Oh, Jack.'

'This is our time together. Why spoil it now?'

He took her into his arms and Cass felt her insides dissolve. She knew exactly what he meant.

'We shouldn't,' she gasped minutes later. 'We really shouldn't be doing this.'

'Wrong.' Jack stifled her half-hearted protests with a kiss. 'We really really should.'

Their lovemaking only proved to him beyond all doubt what he had suspected for months.

'I love you.'

As he spoke, Jack rolled onto his back, suddenly unable to look at Cass. He had to say the words first and gauge her reaction afterwards. 'You know that, don't you? I think I love you more now than I ever have. If you knew how much I wish I'd never met Imogen . . . it's tearing me apart. And as for Rory Cameron . . . Christ, when he told me the two of you were planning to marry I just wanted to *kill* him.'

He stopped and turned his head, his heart pumping wildly in his chest.

Cass, lying next to him, was fast asleep.

Imogen was still in her dressing gown, huddled up on the sofa watching the six o'clock news. The TV cameras had been out in force to catch Sophie's triumphant return to Hampstead. She was being hailed as a heroine. The driveway leading up to the house was clogged with reporters. Cleo Mandeville and

Pandora Grant were both there in floods of tears. When the cars finally drew up outside all hell broke loose. Imogen bit her nails as Sophie, her natural pallor accentuated by her new ash-blond hair, waved briefly for the cameras before hugging Sean and disappearing into the house.

Cass and Jack, emerging from the car moments later, had their arms around each other. Imogen winced as she peeled one of her nails down to the tender quick.

'All I can say is that we're very tired and very happy,' Jack told the ITN reporter. 'It's been a harrowing couple of days. Thank God it's all over.'

'Yes, Sophie's in brilliant shape.' Cass's smile, when the reporter turned his attention to her, was positively radiant. 'She's fine, but we think she'll give modelling a miss from now on. Maybe stick to something less risky, like lion-taming.'

Imogen's stomach churned. Cass and Jack vanished into the house. The newsreader, putting on his 'and-now-for-the-bad-news' voice, moved on to the latest unemployment figures. Imogen wondered when Jack would remember she even existed.

Jack, preparing to leave the house at close to midnight, braced himself. He had to know.

'There's something I need to say,' he told Cass, who was looking stunning with her blond hair up. She had changed into a dark-blue velvet dress and was wearing Shalimar. Behind them, in the sitting room, Sophie's welcome-home party roared on. Terry Brannigan was launching into song, to howls of derision from Cleo and Rory Cameron. For the moment, in the panelled hallway, they were alone.

'Yes?' prompted Cass.

Jack swallowed. 'This isn't easy.'

'No?'

'Um . . .'

Cass's blue eyes searched his face. 'It wouldn't by any chance have something to do with this morning's little speech?'

'I thought you were asleep.'

'I thought I should appear to be asleep,' said Cass, 'just in case you changed your mind. It was a bit of an emotional moment, after all.' She paused. 'You might not have meant it.'

Jack leaned against the front door.

'I'm not going to change my mind.' He had never meant something more in his life. 'The question is, could you ever change yours about me?'

The door to the sitting room flew open.

'Oops.' Spotting them, Cleo promptly closed it again.

'Change my mind?'

He wondered if Cass was being deliberately unhelpful.

'I suppose what I mean is, could you ever trust me again?'

Rory Cameron was in the next room. It was, Jack realized, hardly the time or the place to be making possibly the most vital speech of his life. Still, he'd come this far. 'Could you ever forgive me?' His voice was low. 'Could you ever love me? Is there even the faintest chance of you being willing to try again?'

'Excuse me,' said Cass, 'but how does Imogen feel about this?'

Jack shook his head. 'Imogen doesn't know.'

'Ah well, I know how *that* feels.' She pulled open the front door. Infuriatingly, giving nothing away, Cass said, 'Maybe she should.'

* * *

'You don't mean it, you can't mean it, you can't . . . !'

Imogen, on her knees, clutched blindly at Jack's trousered leg. She knew she was howling like a dog. The humiliation was unbearable. But still she clung on, screaming in disbelief, refusing to accept that what he was saying could be true.

'I'm sorry, but this hasn't worked out. You know it hasn't.'

Jack wasn't finding it much easier. Imogen's torment was a painful thing to have to witness. He was also uncomfortably aware that he could be doing all this, making the break, for nothing. Cass hadn't exactly thrown herself into his arms. She hadn't yelled, 'Yes! Yes! You're all I've ever wanted.' There was every chance she might turn round, laugh in his face and tell him it served him damn well right.

But that was a risk Jack was prepared to take. Cass was the one he wanted. His relationship with Imogen was over. All he wanted was his old life back.

'I know you slept with her,' Imogen wailed. Her eyes, red-rimmed and piggy, begged him not to go. 'I know you shared a room at that place. Look, it's OK; I forgive you. But Sophie's back now, that's all in the past and we can just carry on as before, Cass and Rory Cameron, you and me—'

'No.' Jack shook his head. 'We can't. I'm sorry, but we can't.'

He winced as Imogen's fingernails dug into his leg. Any minute now she'd have his kneecap off.

'You bastard, I know what this is about! It's because I can't get pregnant, isn't it?' She was desperate now, clutching at straws. 'I can't make babies so you're dumping me—'

'You were the one who wanted children,' Jack pointed out. 'I didn't.'

'No, because you already had your family.' Imogen spat out the words. 'Your precious fucking family! And now you're going back to them like the good old family man everyone always used to think you were. Won't the tabloids just love that!'

'I said I wanted to go back,' Jack replied wearily. 'It may not happen. Cass hasn't said she'll have me yet.'

'Good grief.' Sophie opened the front door and took a step backwards. 'Whatever's happened to you?' Her eyes narrowed. 'If you're looking for Dad he isn't here.'

Imogen shook her head. She knew that. It was seven in the evening. She had deliberately waited until now, when Jack was at the TV studios, to come round to the house.

'It's your mother I'm here to see.' She glanced at Cass's car standing in the drive. 'She is in, I take it?'

'Hang on, I'll go and get her.'

Cass, evidently just out of the bath, appeared in the doorway a minute or so later. Her wet blond hair had been combed back from her face. She was wearing the same pink-and-yellow satin robe she'd had on almost two and a half years ago, when Imogen had turned up to interview her for the magazine.

A gust of icy wind plastered Imogen's black skirt against the backs of her legs. She had made the effort to dress up and look halfway decent but the look on Cass's face – not to mention Sophie's startled expression earlier – told her it hadn't worked. No amount of make-up, she thought bitterly, could conceal this much grief.

'Hello. Can I come in?'

'I think you'd better.'

Cass stepped to one side, guessing at once what had happened. She hadn't spoken to Jack today. Jack, however, had clearly spoken to Imogen.

Cass wondered if this was the happiest, most gratifying moment of her life. The next second that habitual sense of guilt kicked in. She knew how Imogen felt. It would be so easy to start feeling sorry for her.

I mustn't let it happen, Cass told herself, hardening her resolve. Why shouldn't Imogen suffer? Why shouldn't she discover how she made me feel?

Imogen, she reminded herself, deserved everything she got.

'I was just about to make myself a sandwich.' Cass led the way into the kitchen. Picking a baguette out of the bread basket as casually as if Imogen were a next-door neighbour popping in for coffee and a chat, she said, 'Would you like one?'

Imogen imagined them duelling with French sticks across the kitchen table. She shook her head. Behind Cass, the kettle was coming to the boil. She didn't want a bloody cup of tea either.

'I'd prefer a vodka and tonic.'

'You look in a bad way.' Cass handed her one but stuck to tea herself. The last time Imogen had arrived unannounced at the house, she had been the one effortlessly in charge. And I was the stupid one, Cass reminded herself, reduced to sorting out my kitchen cupboards because if I didn't do something to keep busy I knew I'd go mad.

'Of course I'm in a bad way.' Helplessly, Imogen began to spurt tears. It was no good, she couldn't even begin to hold back. 'And you know why. Look, I had to come and see you. You know how much I love Jack . . . he's my whole life. And I know he thinks he wants to come back to you, but—'

'But you don't think he does really?' Cass's tone was cool. It was so much easier, being the one in control. She wished she'd tried it years ago. 'Excuse me, but isn't Jack old enough to know who or what he wants?'

'It's this Sophie thing.' Imogen slumped in her chair. 'It scared him – of *course* it scared him – and now it's made him think he needs to be with his family.' Rubbing her eyes in despair she added, 'That wasn't what I was going to say, anyway. *You* have to be honest with yourself too. For your own sake.'

'What?'

'Come on, Cass. You must be loving this. I'm getting my come-uppance, aren't I? It's what you must have prayed for.'

The corners of Cass's mouth twitched. 'Well . . .'

'But do you really want him back,' Imogen blurted out passionately, 'or do you just *think* you do? Because cutting your nose off to spite your face isn't going to make you feel better in the long run. And you're happy with Rory Cameron, aren't you? I'm just saying don't risk your own chance of happiness.' Imogen swallowed; her throat ached with the effort of holding back yet more tears. 'Please. Don't take Jack back simply because you can.'

Imogen knew she was begging. But it was no good, she could no longer afford the luxury of pride. When desperate measures were called for, she would beg.

And she had never been more desperate in her life.

Maybe, thought Cass, this is the best moment of my life after all.

She thought for a moment before replying.

'I hated Jack for what he did to me,' she said finally, amazed by the steadiness of her own voice. 'But I never stopped loving him. Not for one minute. And don't imagine you're going through what I went through two years ago either.' Cass's china-blue eyes bored into Imogen's bloodshot ones. 'Because what I went through was worse.'

Imogen knew she was losing. Having pinned all her hopes on Cass living up to her reputation for being kind, under-standing and damn near all-round perfect, the sense of disappointment was crushing.

'If you two get back together,' Imogen hissed, 'how do you know he won't do the same thing again?'

'Maybe he's learned his lesson,' Cass replied stonily, 'with you.'

Chapter 58

'Jesus!'

Sean rammed on his brakes as Imogen, like a bolting horse, loomed abruptly out of the darkness. He winced as she ricocheted off the bonnet of his car.

Luckily – and for once in his life – he hadn't been driving like a maniac. Luckier still, Imogen didn't appear to be hurt.

Sean, who was in a good mood, climbed out of the car to make sure. With a grin, he picked up her handbag and returned it.

'Last time this happened you were walking up the drive. We must stop meeting like this.'

Then he realized Imogen was crying. Holding her in front of the headlights, he saw the swollen blubbering mess that was her face.

Sean frowned. 'Did I hurt you or is this something else?'

'You d-didn't hurt me.' Imogen twisted away so he couldn't see how hideous she looked. But it was no good; the grip he had on her arms was vice-like.

'So what is it?'

Imogen had arrived at the house by taxi. The prospect of flagging down another one and having to endure the fascinated attention of some nosy cab driver was unbearable.

'Look, I know you don't l-like me,' she gasped out between sobs, 'but w-will you drive me h-h-home?'

'Why?' Sean was getting fed up with this. It was like playing twenty bloody questions.

'Just get me away from here.' Taking matters into her own hands, Imogen wrenched herself free and stumbled round to the passenger door. '*Please.*'

By the time Sean pulled up outside the Wimbledon house Imogen shared with his father, she had stopped crying.

She had also changed her mind about going home.

'God, look at it.' In desperation Imogen gestured up at the unlit, unwelcoming windows. Jack wouldn't be back from the TV studios before midnight. The prospect of spending the entire evening alone was too depressing for words. She turned to Sean. 'You said you were going to the club. Take me with you.'

Sean sighed. If the object of the exercise was to scupper his own plans she was making a good start. The visit to his mother's house hadn't been vital – he had only driven over to see if he had left a leather jacket there the other week – but Imogen had effectively put a stop to that. And he could definitely do without her weeping and moping her way around Comedy Inc., like the spectre at the feast.

'Wouldn't you be better off here?' Sean tried to sound as if he knew best. 'I'm only going to be at the club for an hour or so myself. I'm meeting Pandora as soon as I've finished my set.'

Like a dog threatened with a bath, Imogen dug herself deeper into the passenger seat.

'It's OK. You can pretend you don't know me.' She shot him a petulant sidelong glance. 'But I'm still going, whether you like it or not.'

'Look—'

'It's a comedy club, isn't it?' snapped Imogen. 'Maybe it'll cheer me up.'

Sean had to park around the corner from Comedy Inc. As he and Imogen turned into Jelahay Street he saw Donny ahead of them. They caught up with him at the crowded entrance to the club.

'Imogen's come out for some fun,' Sean explained, because he could hardly announce in front of everyone that she'd just been dumped by his old man. Wondering if Donny might be interested in taking Imogen off his hands he winked and added, 'She needs looking after.'

Once inside, Imogen promptly disappeared to the loo to repair her face. Donny got the first round in at the bar and watched Sean sign autographs for a group of girls up from Epping Forest for the night. His act was beginning to come together again. People's memories of the disastrous TV series had begun to fade. He had even regained enough confidence to start ad-libbing on stage once more.

Not to mention knocking off his old man's mistress, thought Donny sourly an hour later. He sat next to Imogen up at the bar while Sean performed his set. Imogen, who had been knocking back vodka like a demented Russian ever since they arrived, had applauded wildly when he walked out onto the stage. Now, unable to take her eyes off Sean, she kept nudging Donny in the ribs and saying stupid things like, 'Isn't he gorgeous?' and, 'You know, I've fancied him rotten since the first night we met.'

The pair of them made Donny sick. Watching Sean

Mandeville screw his way through life had been entertaining enough when he had been doing much the same himself, and when the girls they'd bedded had been nothing more than casual pick-ups. But that was when they had both been young, free and single, thought Donny. Standing by while Sean treated Pandora like dirt had been an altogether different matter. It had bothered Donny more and more. Then, some months ago, Sean had seemed to come to his senses and the womanizing had abruptly stopped.

Until now, it seemed. He was back to his old ways with a vengeance.

'You were *brilliant*!' Imogen threw her arms around Sean when he came off stage.

Sean grinned at Donny. 'Don't you just love it when women say that?'

'Brilliant, brilliant, brilliant,' Imogen chanted, sliding off her bar stool in order to plant an enthusiastic kiss on his cheek. At the last moment she lunged forward and caught him full on the mouth instead.

'Such command of the English language.' Looking amused, Sean wiped the lipstick from his face. 'You can tell she's a journalist.'

Realizing she didn't have a hope in hell of getting back onto her bar stool, Imogen giggled and clung to Sean instead.

'I'm a terrific journalist,' she proclaimed with pride. 'I'm nearly as terrific a journalist as I am in bed.'

Donny looked away in disgust.

Sean, who hadn't yet had a chance to tell Donny what was going on, turned to Imogen.

'Why don't you run along to the loo and powder your nose while I get the next round in?'

Imogen had by this time had a great deal to drink. She was also intent on paying Jack back. She smiled lasciviously up at Sean.

'Why don't I stay here instead and mentally undress you while you're getting the next round in? Wouldn't that be more fun?'

It was time for Donny to head backstage. Having heard more than enough anyway, he was glad to get away. If Sean wanted to rot up his own life, fine. But this time he didn't want anything to do with it.

The more Imogen had to drink, the more her imagination got carried away.

'I know,' she murmured, breathing vodka fumes into Sean's ear, 'why don't we get out of here and find an hotel?'

'For you?' Sean's patience was by this time wearing extremely thin. He was trying to listen to Donny up on the stage and Imogen kept interrupting. All this stupid suggestive stuff was starting to get on his nerves too. The trouble was, he felt responsible for her. She was out of her tree and he didn't feel he could just up and leave. At this rate, Sean thought, he was going to be late for Pandora.

'For us, silly.' Imogen gave him a knowing look. 'Come on, you know you want to.'

'Sleep with you, you mean?' Sean raised an eyebrow. 'I don't.'

'Oh yes you do. You've always wanted to.'

He looked at Imogen, with her red hair tumbling around her face and her pink tongue darting wetly between her teeth. New make-up on top of old gave her a dishevelled, morning-after look but she was still undeniably attractive. If he was honest, the idea of sleeping with her had crossed his mind more than once before now.

'I may have wanted to', he said, 'in the beginning. Before you got yourself involved with my father. But not now.'

Imogen pouted. 'You wouldn't regret it.'

'I would.' Sean glanced at his watch. If he didn't leave this minute he was definitely going to be late. 'Haven't you heard? I'm a reformed character. Family man and all that. I've got Rose. And Pandora.'

'Oh yes, and everyone knows how faithful you've been to Pandora.'

'I'm going to be, from now on.'

'Bor-ing,' Imogen mocked.

'And I'm supposed to be meeting her for dinner.' He picked his car keys off the bar. 'Look, do you want to stay here or shall I drop you home? I'm sorry, but I do have to go.'

'What, stay here and be glared at by your friend Donny?' Imogen shuddered at the prospect. 'No thanks, I'll come with you.'

Donny, up on the stage nearing the end of his set, saw them leave. Imogen was still clinging to Sean's arm. Her black skirt was rucked up at the back to reveal black stocking tops and suspenders. She was a tart, he thought coldly.

And Sean was cheating on Pandora.

Chapter 59

'For Christ's sake,' Sean howled twenty minutes later, 'will you make up your mind? Who d'you think I am, Mother sodding Teresa?'

Having been driven back to Wimbledon, Imogen was now flatly refusing to get out of the car. This was the last straw. She was really pissing him off.

'I don't want to be on my own.' She said it in a wobbly little-girl voice. 'You don't know how miserable I feel. I want a drink. Look, there's a pub round the corner. Please come and have a drink with me, Sean. Just one, I promise . . .'

Short of turfing her head-first out onto the pavement there wasn't any other way of getting Imogen out of the car. Sean heaved a sigh and drove round the corner to The Queen's Head. Pandora would be wondering where he'd got to. If only he'd known the number of The Blue Goose he could have phoned the restaurant and explained that he was going to be late.

Never mind. Pandora was used to his haphazard time-keeping. At least he knew she would wait for him to turn up.

One quick drink here, thought Sean, and I'm off. If Imogen tried to kick up another fuss he would have no qualms, this time, about leaving her here less than two hundred yards from her own home.

* * *

The Blue Goose was bursting at the seams. Pandora, sitting alone at a table for two, was feeling more and more conspicuous. Sean was three-quarters of an hour late now. So much, she thought with a sickening sense of *déjà vu*, for a romantic evening together at the restaurant he had brought her to on the night they'd first met. So much, thought Pandora bitterly, for turning over a new leaf. And stupid me, for actually believing he could change.

She felt doubly humiliated because the temperature in the restaurant was tropical and she had just been approached for the fourth time by a waiter enquiring if she might not feel more comfortable without her coat. She looked ridiculous. And she was being stared at. Maybe if she were Cleo she might have the guts to stand up and announce: 'OK everyone, stop smirking. The reason I can't take it off is because I'm starkers underneath.'

It was just the kind of thing Cleo would say, probably earning herself a round of applause into the bargain. Pandora only wished she could be brave enough to do the same.

'Madam, eet ees so warm in 'ere.' Shit, this time it was the *maître d'* himself, exuding professional Gallic concern but clearly worried that other diners might think her dangerously eccentric. 'Your coat . . . do you not sink you might be more 'appy wizzout eet?'

It had seemed like such a good idea at the time, Pandora thought with weary resignation. Bloody Sean.

'No thanks.' She rose to her feet, trying to look as if the fact that she had been stood up couldn't matter less. 'Sorry. I'm afraid I have to leave.'

* * *

The Queen's Head had contained the answer to Sean's prayers. No sooner had he ordered their drinks – vodka for Imogen, tonic for himself – than a smoothly dressed thirty-something with heavily highlighted hair and a spray-on tan detached himself from the group he was with and joined them at the bar.

'Sean Mandeville.' He clicked his fingers in delighted recognition. 'Well well, fancy meeting you here! I'm a great fan of yours, a *great* fan.'

'You aren't the only one,' Imogen chimed in, almost knocking her drink over as she beamed up at Sean.

'Actually, we have someone in common.' The stranger carried on addressing Sean in chummy fashion. 'Your sister, Cleo. We . . . knocked around together for a while, a couple of years back. What a girl, eh?' He shook his head, remembering the terrific times they had shared with obvious affection. His hair, heavily sprayed, didn't budge. 'What a girl.'

'If you ask me,' Imogen mumbled under her breath, 'Cleo's a cow.'

'Look, I really do have to leave,' said Sean. He drained his glass, stood up and shook hands with Cleo's ex. 'Good to have met you, er . . .'

'Damien.' The man beamed. 'Damien Maxwell-Horne. I'm in the property business, in case you're ever in need . . . here, let me give you one of my cards . . .'

'That's really kind of you,' lied Sean. He glanced from Damien to Imogen. The guy had dodgy hair but he looked safe enough. And he knew Cleo. 'OK if I leave Imogen with you? She only lives round the corner. If you could just make sure she gets home in one piece, I'd be grateful.'

'Say no more, say no more.' Damien's eyes, which were

extremely blue, lit up at the prospect of doing Sean Mandeville a favour. Digging into his jacket pocket for his wallet, he gave Imogen a reassuring wink. 'We'll be fine, won't we, sweetheart? Come on, finish that. Let me buy you another drink.'

By the time he reached The Blue Goose, Pandora had left. Sean, eventually arriving home at eleven thirty, found the babysitter gone, Rose sucking her thumb in her cot and Pandora determinedly asleep. She wasn't going to be thrilled with him but since it hadn't been his fault Sean didn't feel too guilty. If he woke her up now, she would only shout at him. Instead he went back downstairs, watched an old Jack Dee video and fell asleep on the sofa, finally crawling into bed next to Pandora at dawn.

Pandora left him to it, sliding noiselessly out of the bed an hour later and taking a long hot bath before Rose woke up. During the bath she thought a great deal about her life with Sean and wondered if she was making too much of the fact that he hadn't bothered to turn up at the restaurant last night.

She was downstairs making breakfast when the front door bell rang.

'Morning, angel.' Donny bent to give her a decorous kiss on the cheek. At least Sean's car was in the drive. 'Is he up?'

Pandora shook her head, suddenly unable to speak. Donny was so sweet and Sean could be such a pig.

'Mm, bacon.' Sniffing appreciatively, Donny headed for the kitchen. 'How was your meal last night?'

'It probably would have been great.' Pandora found she wasn't as hungry as she'd thought. She pushed her plate across the table towards him and shrugged. 'If Sean had bothered to put in an appearance. I didn't feel like eating alone,' she said bitterly, 'so I left.'

'Shit.' At once Donny dropped all pretence of cheerfulness. Leaning back in his chair he heaved a sigh and ran his hands over his face. This time, he realized, he had to tell Pandora. She had a right to know.

'What?' said Pandora.

'OK, maybe I shouldn't be saying this but I've had just about enough of standing by and doing nothing.' He lowered his voice. 'Sean was at the club last night with Imogen Trent. She was all over him. They disappeared together at around ten o'clock. Sorry, sweetheart.' Donny shook his head. 'I thought he'd got all that stuff out of his system. It's unfair on you. You deserve better than this.'

Sean woke abruptly, wincing with pain as an empty suitcase landed across his legs.

'What the—'

Pandora was standing on a chair heaving cases down from the top of the wardrobe. She glanced over her shoulder and said, 'Sorry,' as if they were strangers on a crowded train. The next moment another suitcase came flying through the air. This one narrowly missed Sean's head.

He sat up. 'What the hell's going on?'

'Hmm?' Pandora turned round to look at him. Despite her deceptively casual tone there was a dangerous glitter in her eyes. 'Oh, not a lot. Rose and I are going to do you a favour and get out of your life, that's all. Then you'll have more room for your other tarts. No more mix-ups, no more double bookings. Think about it, Sean, it'll be great! And *so* much easier—'

'Come on, this is crazy.' He fell back against the pillows, groaning. Pandora was down from her chair now, pulling open drawers and flinging knickers and T-shirts willy-nilly into the first case. This was all he needed at the crack of dawn. She must be getting her period.

'Not crazy. I just came to my senses at last.'

Sean had by this time figured it out.

'All this,' he protested, 'just because I was late turning up at the restaurant last night? Sweetheart, listen to me. You don't know what *I* had to put up with. I was hijacked by bloody Imogen Trent. I mean, good news in one way – my old man's dumped her and it looks like my parents are getting back together – but she was *desperate* last night. Clung to me like a leech! What could I do?'

'What could you do?' Pandora drawled the words in disbelief. 'Screw her senseless, I imagine. Isn't that what you normally do with girls who wrap themselves round you like clingfilm? Like she was wrapped round you last night?'

'But I didn't.' Sean spoke through gritted teeth, willing her to believe him. 'OK, she wanted to, but I *didn't*. I said I wasn't interested. I told her I'd given up on all that.' His voice rose. 'For God's sake, I told her you were the only woman in my life.'

'Goodness me, totally believable,' murmured Pandora.

'It's *true*.'

'Save your breath.'

The first case was now full to overflowing. She moved on to the next, wrenching open the doors to the wardrobe and dragging coats and dresses off their hangers.

This was unfair. Things between them had seemed so much better lately. And now, Sean thought with annoyance, I'm being punished for something I didn't even do.

'OK,' he said tightly, 'if you don't believe me, ask Imogen.'

Pandora threw him a shrivelling look. 'Haven't I already been humiliated enough?'

'Just *ask* her.'

'No thanks.'

He shook his head. 'I've never seen you like this before.'

'It's called the last straw,' said Pandora. 'I've put up and up with your bullshit for the last two years and now I've had enough. Donny's right,' she continued evenly, 'I do deserve better.'

Sean howled, '*Fuck* Donny!'

'Well, you never know,' Pandora replied, 'I just might.'

'You bitch, you wouldn't dare.'

'Wouldn't I?'

It was all going horribly wrong. Sean heard the vengeful, bitter words spilling out of his mouth and was sickened by them. He loved Pandora. Last night, over dinner at The Blue Goose, he had planned to ask her to marry him. Dammit, he thought despairingly, it had even crossed his mind to ask her to turn up wearing the infamous beige trench coat with nothing underneath . . .

Instead, evidently hell-bent on revenge, all she was interested in was jumping into bed with Donny Mulligan.

'Where are you going?'

'I don't know.' Pandora averted her gaze. Of course she knew. She had already phoned her friends Wendy and Bill and invited herself and Rose down to their home in Bath.

'You can't disappear.' Sean began to panic. 'You can't take Rose away just like that.'

'You can't stop me.'

'I *love* Rose.' He wanted to add, I love you, but the words wouldn't come out.

Pandora gave him a weary look.

'Yes, maybe you do. But it never lasts, does it? Cheer up,' she added bitterly as she lugged the two bulging suitcases towards the door. 'By this time next week you can be madly in love with Imogen Trent instead.'

Chapter 60

Imogen knew something was wrong when she opened her eyes and saw black.

Black satin sheets.

'If you knew how beautiful you look . . .' said a soothing male voice. 'Baby, you are gorgeous.'

Black satin sheets with gold piping. Pillowcases to match. And a black-and-gold striped satin duvet.

Oh dear.

Imogen smelled coffee and Aramis. She groaned and turned over. Damien Maxwell-Horne was standing by the bed carrying a loaded tray. His dressing gown, which matched the duvet, had his initials embroidered across the breast pocket.

To remind you, presumably, who you'd just spent the night in bed with. Imogen's heart sank as the events of the previous evening came rushing back.

Yes, you did it, her memory smugly confirmed. And not just once either, but twice. The first time in Damien's chrome-and-glass sitting room, the second here in bed.

Brilliant. Imogen squinted at her watch. Good God, it was ten thirty.

'Come on, upsadaisy.' Damien, disgustingly bright-eyed, was beaming down at her. 'I've made you one of my specials, smoked salmon and scrambled eggs. There, that's it, let me help you with those pillows. And you can take this as a compliment.' Placing the tray across Imogen's lap he planted an Aramis-loaded kiss on her clamped-together mouth. 'I only make my specials for those very special ladies in my life.'

Was it the coffee or the strength of the aftershave? Imogen wasn't sure but she knew she felt sick.

'I don't think I can manage this.' She pointed feebly at the tray. 'Um . . . maybe a cup of tea?'

'Anything you like.' Damien winked and ruffled her hair before she had a chance to dodge away. 'Coffee, tea,' he went on with a suggestive leer, 'or me?'

It was over two years since Cass had last set foot in the newspaper offices where Jack worked. Stepping out of the lift on the fourth floor, she noticed the interesting variety of expressions on the faces of his fellow workers. Unannounced visits from ex-wives weren't, as a rule, good news. The last time it had happened, Cass recalled Jack telling her, the deputy editor had ended up with a belt round the ear from a Manolo Blahnik stiletto.

Glenda, Jack's secretary, had never liked Imogen Trent. She greeted Cass with delight.

'You've missed him by ten minutes. And he won't be back until midday.'

'He's gone out?' Damn, thought Cass, I should have phoned first.

'Not out-out.' Glenda pointed her index finger at the ceiling. 'Big meeting in the boardroom.' She pulled a fearful face. 'It's a do-not-disturb job. I daren't interrupt.'

'Oh well,' Cass said cheerfully, 'in for a penny.'

'What are you doing?' squeaked Glenda as Cass turned back towards the lift.

'Calling on him.'

'Heavens!' Deeply intrigued, Glenda said, 'Can I come too?'

'Mrs Mandeville,' protested Tom the old security guard, panting after them both as they headed for the boardroom's double doors. 'Mrs Mandeville, you can't go in there.'

Cass had so geared herself up to seeing Jack, there was absolutely no stopping her now. Pushing open the heavy oak doors she said, 'Don't be silly, Tom. Of course I can.'

Everyone seated at the polished table looked up simultaneously when Cass walked in. The deputy editor turned quite pale. The scar from his ex-wife's high heel may have faded but the fear that she might one day turn up and do the same again had never quite left him.

'Cass.' Jack, in shirtsleeves and with his dark hair flopping over his forehead, was on his feet in an instant. His look of horror told her at once that he thought something awful must have happened. To burst unannounced into a meeting this important somebody had to be dead at least.

'It's OK. Nothing's wrong.' Cass was aware of Glenda cringing behind her at the prospect of their famously tetchy proprietor's impending wrath. 'I wanted to see you, that's all.'

'What a coincidence,' the proprietor of the *Herald* said heavily. 'I wanted to see him too. Call me old-fashioned, but that's why I organized this meeting—'

'What is it?' Ignoring him, Jack came towards Cass.

'I've made up my mind. I want to know when you're coming home. No hurry,' Cass said lightly, though her knees were wobbling, 'any time within the next couple of hours will be fine.'

'Young lady,' the proprietor's voice dropped to an ominous rumble, 'this man is here for a purpose. I do not appreciate having my meetings interrupted. Will you *please* leave?'

'Will you please leave Imogen?' Cass murmured in Jack's ear as his arms closed blissfully around her.

'I already have.' Unable to face going back to the house in Wimbledon last night – tellingly it had always been a house rather than a home – he had booked into an hotel instead. Now, kissing Cass full on the mouth, Jack knew he had never been happier in his life.

'Ugh,' declared the proprietor, by this time purple with indignation. Three times he'd been divorced and nothing like this had ever happened to him. But then none of his miserable wives had ever looked like Cass Mandeville either. '*Now* where d'you think you're going?' he roared at Jack's departing back, even though the answer was pretty damn obvious. Christ, this was worse than that *Officer and a sodding Gentleman* . . .

'Home,' said Jack.

'And about time too,' said Glenda, following at his heels.

Such a reconciliation might be inconvenient but it was still news. Wearily turning his attention to his misty-eyed deputy editor the proprietor drawled, 'I realize we're only a newspaper, Wilkins, but I don't suppose there's a chance anyone here has a camera?'

Chapter 61

It was the second week in December, an icy Saturday night, and Cleo was having a crisis.

'I can't believe I'm doing this,' she wailed as they made their way up the steps to the hotel's main entrance. 'I can't believe I let you talk me into it. Am I gullible or what?'

Even her white-blond hair, shorter than usual so it stood up in spikes, looked panicky. As they approached the sliding doors Cass saw the four of them reflected in the smoked glass. Cleo was wearing an embroidered dress split to reveal one brown thigh and it didn't matter how much of a flap she was in, she still looked ravishing.

Next to Cleo was Terry Brannigan who looks-wise might not be in quite the same league but was determined to enjoy himself tonight all the same. Without resorting to drink, either. Cass was so proud of Terry she could burst. Pulling himself together and joining AA had taken guts but it had paid off in spades. Not only was he trimmer, fitter and far more fun to be with nowadays, but following his impressive step into the breach that terrible week when Sophie had been taken, Kingdom Radio had repaid the favour and offered him the about-to-be-vacated mid-evening show. It might not be prime time, as Terry himself was the first to admit, but it beat the hell out of washing dishes in a back-street restaurant.

Cass's fingers tightened around Jack's as the smoked-glass

doors slid open and the first volley of flashbulbs went off. Being seen together again in public was still enough of a novelty to guarantee attention. Thankfully, as Jack had drily observed, good news was never as enthralling as bad. Give it another fortnight, was his view, and the fact that the Mandevilles were a couple once more would interest the general public about as much as the single European currency.

Cass didn't care about that. It mattered to her, it was what interested her and above all it was what she wanted. She hadn't even needed to feel guilty about dropping Rory Cameron. Imogen might not have taken the split with Jack well, but Rory had more than compensated. Ever the gentleman, he had understood perfectly, kissing Cass goodbye and giving them both his blessing. Within a week he had become embroiled in an affair with a fiery twenty-four-year-old Italian singer. As Sophie remarked, he'd fallen back into his young ways.

Cleo, meanwhile, was feeling sorrier for herself by the second at the prospect of the evening ahead. This was all Cass's fault.

It had been her mother's bright idea, when invited to donate a personal item to the charity auction, to offer Cleo.

'Darling, it's a fund-raiser,' she protested when Cleo reacted with alarm. 'It's only a bit of fun, anyway! A night out with the highest bidder. And', Cass added soothingly, 'it is for charity.'

'Think of Imogen. The last time you did something for charity you ended up minus a husband,' Cleo grumbled.

Even that hadn't worked. Cass, who was being very flippant these days, had beamed. 'You'll be OK then. You don't have one to lose.'

This evening's ball, held at the Park Lane Lyndhurst Hotel

overlooking Hyde Park, was already under way by the time they reached the vast ballroom. Dino Carlisle spotted them at once and made his way over to their table.

'So you're really going to do it.' He had discovered Cleo's name in the programme amongst the list of items to be auctioned off.

'You mean kill my mother? Certainly.' Cleo gave him a gloomy look. 'I don't know why she couldn't just donate a handbag like everyone else. I'm either going to be snapped up by a white-slave trader or not bid for at all. I don't know which is worse.'

Dino grinned down at her. 'I won't let you be publicly humiliated. I'll go up as far as six pounds fifty.'

'You're all heart.'

'Good news about your parents anyway.' He nodded at Cass and Jack, evidently so happy together. 'Seeing them like that's enough to restore the faith of even a hardened old cynic like me.'

'I thought you were supposed to be having a fling with that co-star of yours.' He had just finished making a film called, appropriately enough, *All the Way*.

Dino pulled a face. 'Studio publicity. I'd rather have a fling with Cruella de Vil.' He looked at Cleo. 'Anyway, how about you? No joy with that guy you were once so crazy about?'

Cleo's throat tightened. Had she ever stopped being crazy about Joel, and had it done her the slightest bit of good? If only she could stop, she might not be so damn miserable now.

She shook her head, recalling what an idiot she had made of herself the last time their paths had crossed.

'No joy.'

'You should have snapped me up,' Dino said modestly, 'while you had the chance. Oh wow—'

'What?' demanded Cleo, realizing he was peering over her shoulder. 'Wow what?'

'Sorry. Thought I just saw someone.' He sounded miles away. 'There's a TV ad running in the States, a commercial for some new shampoo. This is going to sound stupid, but I've really had the weirdest kind of feeling for the girl in this ad . . . it almost seems as if I know her. I don't, of course.' The look he gave Cleo was unusually self-deprecating. 'But I sure would like to.'

'And?'

'I don't know for certain, but I think I just saw her. She's thin, with long dark hair,' Dino elaborated. 'Amazing eyes. Black dress.'

'Sounds like Cruella de Vil.' Turning, Cleo searched the crowds. The next moment Dino's hand tightened convulsively around her wrist. Glancing back, startled, she saw him blushing like a teenager, muttering, 'My God, it is—'

'Hi,' said a shy voice behind her. Cleo grinned as in an instant everything fell into place.

'I don't know if you'll remember this,' she told Dino, 'but I once said to you, if you really wanted to meet someone miserable I'd introduce you to my friend Linda.'

Linda, who was beaming like an idiot and evidently incapable of tearing her eyes away from Dino, said, 'I'm not miserable any more.'

Several miles away, alone in the Islington mews flat to which she had returned following the break-up with Jack, Imogen was taking a long slow bath. She listened to both sides of the latest Coldplay CD and let the tears roll helplessly down her face. Not that any of the tracks had been 'their' song – the album had only come out last week – but the lyrics, always so horribly easy to relate to, got to Imogen every time.

After her bath she microwaved a Marks & Spencer tagliatelle and poured herself a glass of white wine. Switching on the television, she flicked through the channels and tried to find something remotely watchable. Then she put Coldplay on again and spent a good ten minutes curled up on the sofa gazing at the blank wall, realizing that either way she had to face up to the truth. She couldn't put it off any longer. The deed had to be done.

It was weird, going through the exact motions she had gone through so many times before, only this time experiencing such mixed feelings about the possible end result. Sitting on the edge of the bath with her yellow towelling robe pulled around her like a security blanket, Imogen hugged her knees and counted slowly to sixty. Then she counted to sixty again, twice.

And this time when she looked, it was there. The unmistakable pink line she had so often in the past willed to appear had appeared. Plain as day. Not light pink but bright pink. She wasn't just pregnant, it seemed. She was very pregnant indeed.

As Imogen wandered trance-like back through to the sitting room, Jack's face reappeared in close-up on the television. She had taken to recording and endlessly replaying his programmes in order to feel closer to him. Not that it was working now.

She closed her eyes in despair. There wasn't a way in the world it could be Jack's baby. During their last few weeks together, as his interest in her had dwindled, so too had their sex life. It was partly why she had made such a desperate play for Sean, except he had rejected her too.

Imogen stood up and studied her ghostly reflection in the mirror. She supposed she should be glad she wasn't infertile, having agonized for so long that she might be.

Oh, but dammit, she would have been so much gladder if only she hadn't been fertile with Damien Maxwell-Horne.

Chapter 62

Cleo had never seen anything like it before in her life. The chemistry between Dino and Linda was so powerful it was almost embarrassing. She appeared to be witnessing love at first sight.

It really was extraordinary; Linda had lit up like Blackpool illuminations and couldn't take her eyes off Dino. Dino, in turn barely able to keep his hands off Linda, looked as if he wanted nothing more than to bundle her out of the ballroom, back to his hotel suite and – without further ado – into bed.

Cleo wished she didn't feel quite so jealous. She tried hard to be pleased for them both. It wasn't even as if she harboured a secret hankering for Dino herself, because she'd already tried that and it simply hadn't . . . well, happened.

But it was certainly happening to Linda and Dino right now. There was nothing secretive about it either. Cleo wondered if there was any danger they might spontaneously combust and if such overwhelming mutual lust could ever happen to her like that. Above all she wished she didn't have to feel, by extremely poor comparison, so dried-up and spinsterish and alone.

'I should be getting back to my table.' The least Cleo felt she could do was put on a brave front. Gaily prodding Dino's chest, she added, 'And you'd better get that wallet out. Don't forget, you promised to bid.'

'Six pounds fifty.' Dino grinned. 'See, I haven't forgotten.'

Linda clapped her hand over her mouth. 'Goodness, I've just remembered.' She turned to Cleo. 'I did a Paris show for Anton Visa last week. He was asking questions about you.'

'He still hates me for rotting up last year's Venice shoot.' Cleo pulled a face. 'And I hate him back. He gives me the creeps. Has he had those chins fixed yet or does he still look like a bullfrog?'

'Well, he's still pretty slimy.' Linda nodded, biting her lip. 'And he mentioned the fact that you were up for auction tonight. He said if he could get over he might even put in a bid for you himself. Then he laughed.' With a shudder Linda added, 'I know he's a genius but he certainly has a weird sense of humour.'

'Terrific.' Cleo began scanning the ballroom once more. 'At least I can't see him anywhere. If you spot a bullfrog in a dinner jacket, give me a shout.'

'OK, OK,' Dino said wearily. 'I get the big hint. I'll go up to a tenner.'

Back at their table Cleo found Cass and Jack being interviewed by one of the Dempster team.

'So you are remarrying.' The journalist, delighted with her scoop, was busy scribbling down notes. 'That's great.'

'I finally managed to talk her round.' Jack wasn't joking. Cass had been worryingly keen for them to try living in sin. 'No firm date yet, but it'll be some time in January,' he added with feeling. Having won Cass back after so nearly losing her for good, he wasn't about to take any chances. 'The sooner the better, for me.'

'Bridesmaids?' Glancing across at the expression on Cleo's face the journalist said hastily, 'Sophie, maybe . . .'

Cass grinned. 'Sophie, in a frilly bridesmaid's dress?'

'You might be brave enough to ask her,' said Jack. 'We wouldn't dare.'

The auction began straight after dinner in order to catch people at their most replete and generous. Cleo, so nervous she had barely been able to eat anything at all, watched the auctioneer – a famously charming politician – heckle his audience into a frenzy of generosity.

An ITV chat-show host outbid his BBC rival for a trip on the Orient Express. One of Shirley Bassey's dripping-with-sequins evening gowns was knocked down to a raucous transvestite who would never squeeze into it. The third item up for auction, a cameo appearance in one of the nation's most popular soaps, finally went after much fierce bidding to the charming politician's bimboesque wife.

'Now, lot number four.' As the politician announced it, he extended his hand to Cleo who had to join him up on the stage. 'An evening in the company of Cleo Mandeville. What a prize. If my wife hadn't just cleaned us out financially I'd be going for this one myself. Here she is, ladies and gentlemen . . . take a good look at what could be yours for an entire evening and dig deep into your pockets,' he added with a wink, 'because I can assure you she's worth it. Now, who'll start the bidding? Do I hear five hundred pounds . . . ?'

Cleo felt sick. There was much good-natured laughter but nobody was making a bid. Now that she was up there on the stage it was hard to make out faces in the crowd. As the seconds ticked by, each one stretching longer than the last, Cleo felt perspiration break out on the nape of her neck. Not helped by the heat of the stage lights, it began trickling down her spine. Bloody mothers, she thought, frantically trying to keep her smile intact. Bloody charity balls and their stupid embarrassing fund-raising schemes. Bloody *bloody* Dino Carlisle, evidently too enthralled with Linda to remember that it was his job to save her from exactly this kind of shame.

Except shame wasn't the word for it. This was truly mortifying.

'Come along now, gentlemen,' the politician chided with a sorrowful shake of his perfectly groomed head. 'We're talking about the opportunity of a lifetime here! OK, just to get the ball rolling . . . do I have three hundred pounds?'

'Six pounds fifty,' drawled Dino, from his table close to the back of the room. More laughter erupted. Cleo, who could have punched him, forced herself to keep smiling and remain on the stage.

'Sixty-five pounds,' came a voice from a different direction. Terry Brannigan, Cleo realized. Oh well, she supposed she ought to be grateful for small mercies.

Dino, at the back of the ballroom, squeezed Linda's hand and whispered, 'She'll kill me if I don't.' Aloud he said: 'Six hundred pounds. And fifty pence.'

Cleo stopped wanting to punch him. She blew a kiss in Dino's direction. That was it; surely now the torture was over.

'Ah, and a telephone bidder enters the fray.' The politician turned his attention to one of the young waiters hovering beside the stage with a phone pressed to his ear. Cleo turned and stared at the waiter who was murmuring into the phone. Then he nodded at the politician and mouthed, 'One thousand pounds.'

'We have a bid of one thousand pounds.' The politician, milking the situation for all it was worth, gave Cleo an encouraging wink before returning his attention to Dino's table. 'Come along now, gentleman at the back ... do I hear two thousand?'

Dino nodded.

After briefly consulting the bidder on the other end of the line, so did the waiter at the side of the stage.

'Three thousand pounds. I have three thousand pounds,' the politician declared.

'Who is it?' hissed Cleo, her eyebrows disappearing into her spiky blond fringe. 'If it's Anton Visa,' she went on agitatedly, 'refuse the bid. Because I won't go, I *won't*—'

At the back of the room, grinning broadly, Dino raised four fingers.

'Four thousand,' gabbled the politician, beginning to sound like a cattle trader. 'We have four thousand at the back, do I hear five, five, five . . . ?'

The waiter nodded. Cleo's stomach lurched.

Dino called out, 'Six.'

'Seven,' said the waiter, nodding at the politician to confirm the bid. Cleo considered leaping down from the stage and wrenching the phone off him. She wondered wildly how much further Dino, in the name of friendship, would be prepared to go to rescue her. She hoped he wouldn't expect her to go halves.

But ... horrors ... the undivided attention of everyone in the room was now back on Dino and he was shaking his head. Cleo's flesh began to prickle with alarm.

'No, that's my lot,' Dino declared. Still grinning broadly he kissed Linda's hand, and pulled her closer to him. 'I've already found the girl for me, anyway. Let Mr Bullfrog or whatever his name is have Cleo.'

At least no one else in the room knew who he was talking about. Not that anyone cared, thought Cleo numbly. They were all too busy whistling and applauding the successful mystery bidder.

As the politician led Cleo off the stage, directing her towards the young waiter with the phone still pressed to his ear, she experienced a gut-wrenching spasm of sheer panic.

'If it's bloody Anton Visa', she repeated, 'I'm not going.'

It occurred to her that if it was, she would now have to come up with the seven grand herself.

'Come on, this is unfair.' She pleaded with the waiter to put her out of her misery but he was busy filling in the necessary amount on a blank cheque. Only when he had handed it over to the politician, who in turn bounced back up onto the stage in order to continue with the auction, did Cleo have any attention paid to her at all.

'Sorry.' The waiter had a disarming grin. 'Payment in advance, you understand how it is. Now if you'd be kind enough to follow me, my client is waiting for you outside.'

'Outside?' Cleo wondered if the mystery bidder was actually anyone she'd ever met before in her life. Or was it some crank lying in wait for her out there, his imagination fired up by all the press coverage of Sophie's kidnap?

As the waiter led her through the lobby towards the smoked-glass sliding doors, Cleo said, 'Look, this isn't funny. I'm certainly not going anywhere *now*. I still don't even know who's behind this whole thing. What's more, if you think for one moment I'm going to waltz out of this hotel and climb of my own free will into a blacked-out limo—'

As she dug in her heels the waiter moved forward and pulled open the door of the limousine.

'For God's sake, woman,' came an exasperated male voice from inside, 'I could hear you whingeing all the way down the lobby. Will you shut up, do as you're told for once in your bossy life and just get in the damn car?'

Chapter 63

Sean had driven out of London in icy drizzle. As he made his way down the M4 the rain had given way to sleet. By the time he reached the Bath turn-off a flimsy covering of snow dusted the hills around him. Misreading the map which lay open across the passenger seat, he promptly got lost.

Perseverance drove Sean on. It was weeks now since he had seen Pandora and Rose. There had been no word from them, no hint of when they might be coming back. Desperate to see them again – *both* of them – he had finally managed to prise the address out of Joel.

And now, at last, he was nearly there. As he reached the outskirts of Bath, took a steep downhill turn to the right and saw the signpost he'd been looking for, Sean breathed a sigh of relief. A sharp left-hand turn a couple of hundred yards further along brought him to a narrow bumpy track with a farmhouse at the end of it.

The house was lit up and there were cars parked ahead of him, which was good news. At least someone was at home. Stepping out of his own car, shivering as a gust of wind sent a flurry of half-melted snowflakes into his face, Sean followed the rough path around the side of the house. He'd forgotten to bring a coat but that didn't matter. Any minute now he would be seeing Pandora and Rose again, holding them in his arms and beginning to make up for far too much lost time.

'I love you, I want to marry you, please come home with me tonight.' These were the words he was going to say to her, the very first words he would utter. He had been practising them all the way down the motorway.

Sean knew he needed to make Pandora understand how much she meant to him, *really* meant to him. Being accused of having slept with Imogen Trent when he hadn't had cut him to the quick. It had also made him realize how helpless and hurt Pandora must have felt all those times in the past when he *had* let her down.

Reaching the back of the house Sean discovered a party in progress in the sitting room. Full-length French windows, boldly uncurtained, gave him an uninterrupted view of the proceedings. There were thirty or forty people in the room. Bill, the Richard Whiteley lookalike, was pouring out drinks. Wendy his wife, in a yellow Laura Ashley frock, stood in front of an open fire laughing at something one of her friends had just told her. There was no dress code to speak of. A motley crew of children, from toddlers up to teenagers, were in evidence. The atmosphere was overwhelmingly informal.

And there, amongst them, was Rose, sprawled across the arm of a faded green velvet sofa, playing happily with a frayed knitted rabbit. Sean felt his heart contract with love and the need to hold her again. She was wearing a crimson sleepsuit he hadn't seen before. She was growing up, becoming a person. He *ached* with love for her. Any minute now, thought Sean, she'll spot me through the window and yell, Dad-dee . . .

'Don't tell me you've been out here all night,' said Pandora behind him.

Sean jumped. He hadn't heard a sound, the snowfall had deadened her footsteps.

'I-I was watching Rose.' Feeling stupid, like a Peeping Tom, he forgot that his first words were supposed to have been, 'I love you, I want to marry you.' When Pandora continued to gaze unswervingly at him, her expression giving nothing away, he said instead, 'How did you know I was here?'

'I came to put some food out for the badgers. I saw your footsteps in the snow.'

'You mean you recognized them?' Sean tested her with a brief smile. Pandora's denim dress clung to every slender curve. He had forgotten how beautiful she was, even in muddy green wellies. How could he ever have wanted anyone else?

But the test wasn't working. Pandora didn't smile back.

Coolly she said, 'What are you doing here?'

Sean's teeth began to chatter. It was bitterly cold and all he was wearing was a dark-blue sweater and ancient jeans. He took a step towards Pandora, who wasn't shivering at all.

'I've come to take you home. You and Rose. I love you—'

'Stop it. You don't.'

'I do.'

'You only say these things,' Pandora told him, 'because they're what you think you feel. It never lasts, Sean. That's what really hurts.'

He saw the look of resignation in her dark eyes.

'This time it's going to last,' said Sean. He knew he meant it. 'You and Rose are all I want. It's why I've come down here. And no,' he said again for good measure, 'I *didn't* sleep with Imogen Trent.'

'It doesn't matter to me whether you did or not,' Pandora replied wearily. 'I'm still not coming back.'

It was no good. He couldn't make her change her mind. Bringing Rose out into the hallway of the farmhouse so that Sean could have fifteen minutes with her without disturbing the ongoing party was as far as Pandora would go.

For the first time in more years than he could remember, Sean realized he was dangerously close to tears. When Rose ran into his arms, a lump the size of a table tennis ball rose up in his throat. He couldn't believe Pandora was doing this to him, punishing him like this, even as Rose cooed with delight, stroking his cold face and singing over and over again, 'Dad-dee.'

There was nothing else for it when his fifteen minutes were up but to turn round and drive back to London. Suggesting that he might book into an hotel in Bath did no good at all.

'I can't stop you,' Pandora said with an unconcerned shrug, 'but it won't help.' Making clear the difference between them she had added calmly, 'Sorry, but I'm not going to change my mind.'

As he made his way back down the bumpy drive, Sean decided he would never forgive Imogen Trent for this. The icy wind swirled through the open car window making his eyes sting. He had to slow down to wipe his face with the back of his sleeve.

Less than a minute later he reached the end of the dirt track. Another car, coming towards him through the darkness, flashed its headlights and braked, allowing Sean to pull out of the side-turning back onto the road.

Only when he had done so and the other vehicle had turned

left up the dirt track did Sean think twice about the number plate. Twisting round in his seat he saw the car slow to a halt at the top of the drive.

He watched Donny Mulligan jump out. It was dark, but some profiles were unmistakable. Particularly when they involved dreadlocks.

Realizing there was nothing in the world he could do about it, Sean drove on.

Cleo, in the back of the limousine, wondered if she was going to faint.

'I thought you were Anton Visa.'

'Thanks a lot.'

'I'm sorry, I'm confused.' She shook her head, struggling to come to grips with the situation. 'You've just bid seven thousand pounds for an evening out with me. I don't understand this at all. You don't even *like* me—'

'Don't be stupid,' said Joel. 'Of course I like you. For your information, you don't bid seven thousand pounds for an evening out with someone you don't like.' He took a deep breath. 'In fact, you generally have to be completely crazy about them . . . madly in love with them . . . totally *desperate* even . . .'

Cleo burst into tears. She couldn't believe she was hearing this.

'But you can't afford seven thousand pounds. And you didn't *need* to bid for me,' she wailed messily, 'because I would have gone out with you for nothing! All you had to do was ask, dammit, and I would have paid *you*!'

Deeply relieved – it had, after all, been a nerve-racking

gamble that might not have paid off – Joel handed her a clean handkerchief.

'You don't get it, do you?' he told Cleo affectionately. 'Don't you see? It was *my* turn to spend more money than anyone else. I needed to do it, just this once, to prove I could compete.'

Cleo was now crying and laughing at the same time. 'B-but seven thousand *pounds*?'

'Yes, well.' Joel put his arms around her, his smile dry. The amount had come as a bit of a shock to him too. 'Maybe I didn't allow for your mate Dino getting quite so carried away.'

'Dino's an impulsive fool,' Cleo confided. She looked indulgent. Who knew, this time it might even last. 'He's in love.'

'In love? Couldn't be like it myself.' Joel kissed her. Then he kissed her again, because Cleo might be bossy, impulsive and an incurable meddler in other people's lives but she was also totally, hopelessly addictive.

'You'd better be.' To prove just how bossy, Cleo punched him lightly on the arm. 'Enough to marry me, at least.'

Joel raised his eyebrows in despair. 'You had to be the one to ask! Isn't that supposed to be *my* line?'

'You might have forgotten to say it.' Cleo wasn't joking. More than anything else in the world she wanted to marry Joel Grant. She'd had enough of checking out other people's relationships. It was high time she concentrated on her own.

'Are you sure', Joel said carefully, 'you want to settle down with a used-car salesman?'

'Oh, but an honest one! And honourable. Wonderfully handsome, too . . . Yes yes, of *course* I'm sure!'

Cleo, way ahead of him, was already thinking of names for their children. She'd always adored Declan. Then again, she decided hastily, perhaps not.

'Right. That's it then.' Joel leaned back against the seat, marvelling that his spur-of-the-moment decision – his impulse buy – had actually worked. 'We'll get married.'

Outside, someone knocked on the car's blacked-out window. Joel pressed the switch and the glass slid noiselessly down.

'Ah, there you are,' said Jack. 'Everything OK? Just thought I'd better check you were all right.'

'I'm fine.' Cleo's megawatt smile beamed out of the darkness. 'Never better.'

'Not you, stupid.' Her father gave her a long-suffering look. 'You're always all right. I meant Joel.'

If you enjoyed

TWO'S COMPANY

look out for the new *Jill Mansell* novel

THREE AMAZING THINGS
ABOUT YOU

Out in January 2015

You can order
THREE AMAZING THINGS ABOUT YOU
now

headline
review

www.headline.co.uk
www.jillmansell.co.uk

@JillMansell
/OfficialJillMansell

Jill Mansell

THE UNPREDICTABLE CONSEQUENCES OF LOVE

In the idyllic seaside town of St Carys, Sophie is putting the past firmly behind her.

When Josh arrives in St Carys to run the family hotel, he can't understand why Sophie has zero interest in letting *any* man into her life. He also can't understand how he's been duped into employing Sophie's impulsive friend Tula, whose crush on him is decidedly unrequited.

St Carys has more than its fair share of characters, including the charming but utterly feckless surfer Riley Bryant, who has a massive crush on Tula. Riley's aunt is superstar author Marguerite Marshall. And Marguerite has designs on Josh's grandfather . . . who in turn still adores his glamorous ex-wife, Dot . . .

Just how many secrets can one seaside town keep?

Just *Heavenly*. Just *Jill*.

Acclaim for Jill Mansell's fabulous bestsellers:

'Bursting with humour, brimming with intrigue and full of characters you'll adore' ***** *Heat*

'You'll fall in love with the characters in this lovely tale' *Sun*

'A warm, witty and romantic read' *Daily Mail*

978 0 7553 5593 8

headline
review

You can buy any of these other bestselling books by
Jill Mansell from your bookshop
or *direct from her publisher*.

FREE P&P AND UK DELIVERY
(Overseas and Ireland £3.50 per book)

The Unpredictable Consequences of Love	£7.99
Don't Want To Miss A Thing	£7.99
A Walk In The Park	£7.99
To The Moon And Back	£8.99
Take A Chance On Me	£8.99
Rumour Has It	£8.99
An Offer You Can't Refuse	£8.99
Thinking Of You	£8.99
Making Your Mind Up	£8.99
The One You Really Want	£8.99
Falling For You	£8.99
Nadia Knows Best	£8.99
Staying At Daisy's	£8.99
Millie's Fling	£8.99
Good At Games	£8.99
Miranda's Big Mistake	£8.99
Head Over Heels	£7.99
Mixed Doubles	£8.99
Perfect Timing	£8.99
Fast Friends	£8.99
Solo	£7.99
Kiss	£8.99
Sheer Mischief	£8.99
Open House	£7.99
Two's Company	£8.99

TO ORDER SIMPLY CALL THIS NUMBER

01235 400 414

or visit our website: www.headline.co.uk

Prices and availability subject to change without notice.